Lady—Here's Your Wreath

...

Miss Callaghan Comes to Grief

by James Hadley Chase

Introduction by Gregory Shepard

STARK HOUSE

Stark House Press • Eureka California

LADY—HERE'S YOUR WREATH /
MISS CALLAGHAN COMES TO GRIEF

Published by Stark House Press
1315 H Street
Eureka, CA 95503, USA
griffinskye3@sbcglobal.net
www.starkhousepress.com

ISBN-13: 978-1-944520-08-3

Book design by Mark Shepard, SHEPGRAPHICS.COM

First Stark House Press Edition: September 2016

LADY—HERE'S YOUR WREATH

As Vessi is heading toward the gas chamber, a mysterious phone voice offers newspaperman Nick Mason $10,000 to find the real killer. Vessi's dying words are "Lu Spencer pulled it," but Spencer's organization is not a group you want to tangle with—shareholders include most of the men who run the city. When Mason decides to check it out anyway, he meets Mardi, Spencer's secretary, a sweet dish with the largest brown eyes. But Mason's also got a gunman on his tail. And the cold-hearted Blondie, who has a knack for turning up when she's least expected. Not to mention the mysterious person who keeps insisting he investigate Spencer. One of them is bound to be wearing a wreath before this game is over…

MISS CALLAGHAN COMES TO GRIEF

St. Louis is ripe for a change. Gang boss Mendetta is getting old and careless, so it's a cinch for Raven to step in and take over. The first thing he changes is the prostitution racket. Raven feels that too much of the profit is going to the girls. So he rounds them up, takes them off the street, puts them in new houses and rakes off all the profit for himself. And when fresh girls are needed, he simply has them kidnapped. Newspaperman Jay Ellinger senses something is amiss when he hears about a husband whose wife has gone missing. But Sadie is missing for a different reason—she saw Raven leave Mendetta's apartment, and can put the finger on him. Sadie is now a valuable pawn, able to bring the whole racket down. If only Jay can find her…

"The king of all
thriller writers."
Cape Times

The Great Americanized British Thriller

I discovered James Hadley Chase back in the early 1970s when Ace Books reprinted *Dead Ringer* in paperback. They had originally published the book in 1955 as an Ace Double paired with *Maid for Murder* by Milton K. Ozaki. I was too young in 1955 to appreciate the effort. The 1969 edition had a bright blue bikinied woman lying lengthwise across the cover in a pose that was both cool and alluring. It caught my eye. I've been hooked on Chase ever since.

I don't remember the plot, or any of the details, but if I know one thing about James Hadley Chase, it had a lot of surprises. Because Chase is a master at the art of deception, the sudden turn, the I-didn't-see-that-coming plot twist. But back in the late 1930s and early 1940s, he was just getting started.

The surprises were a little more obvious. Like killing off a major character, or pinning the crimes on someone you wouldn't suspect. Chase started by writing gangster novels. Inspired by the works of the two Cains—James M. and Paul—plus Dashiell Hammett, Raymond Chandler (who he famously ripped off in one of his early novels), Horace McCoy, Jonathan Latimer and even William Faulkner (who he also did a little borrowing from), Chase created the perfect amalgam of the American hardboiled novel.

What did it matter that he did it all from England with U.S. city maps and a dictionary of slang. Should we fault him for occasionally letting a "shan't" drop from the lips of a New York hoodlum? Nobody's perfect. He captured the *feel* of the American gangster, the total ruthlessness, the greed, the got-nothing-to-lose attitude. Chase had done his homework well, and his first novel, *No Orchids for Miss Blandish*, was a British bestseller, read by the working man on the streets and in the trenches of World War II.

His publisher, Jarrolds, wasn't generally known as a crime fiction publisher, but they knew how to promote a winner. Chase's first few British editions are filled with promos for upcoming titles. *No Orchids* had been extremely violent, the more so because of the casualness of the deeds. Chase and Jarrolds kept pushing it, but sooner or later, Chase had to take it too far. By the time of his seventh book, *Miss Callaghan Comes to Grief*, they finally pushed the sensibilities of the British government too far with a tale of white slavery. In St. Louis, no less.

Jarrolds had promoted the book with this delicate bit of understatement:

> "This is the story of Miss Callaghan. Not of any particular Miss Callaghan but of the hundreds of Miss Callaghans who disappear from their homes suddenly and mysteriously and are seen no more by those who knew and loved them. This is also the story of Raven, who played with clockwork trains, the leader of the White Slave Ring in East St. Louis, who was responsible for keeping to full strength the army of women for the service of men. James Hadley Chase needs no introduction now. He has established a reputation for unmitigated toughness and plain writing. Under his blunt treatment the traffic of women in America is shown to be what it is—a loathsome corrupt stain on the pages of American history."

The British authorities were not amused, and they hauled Jarrolds and Chase into court with a cease and desist. As it is written in Wikipedia, "the author and publishers Jarrolds were found guilty of causing the publication of an obscene book. Each was fined £100." The book was banned in 1942, and hasn't been in print in England since.

And make no mistake, it came by its reputation honestly. From the moment when the newspaper reporter sneaks a couple guys into the morgue one excruciatingly hot day and they start to check out the naked corpses, to the climactic knife scenes when the prostitutes turn the tide on their keepers, this one pulls no punches. It's as if Chase and Jarrolds really want to see what they can get away with here.

Lady—Here's Your Wreath (the first book written under the Raymond Marshall pseudonym which Chase used during the 40s and 50s) for all its hardboiled narrator, seems almost poignant compared to *Miss Callaghan*. The hero is a newspaperman—as many of Chase's heroes were at the time—who cracks wise and uses his tough exterior to cover a sentimental heart. There's a woman in peril, and another who is as tough a cookie as you're likely to find in hardboiled fiction. Between the two of them—the good girl and the bad girl—Chase plays with the reader's expectations in a way that shows a creeping subtlety to his method.

The book starts with the dying words of Vessi, a condemned gangster: "Lu Spencer pulled it. You gotta get him…" Someone—a voice on a telephone—has offered Nick Mason $10,000 if he can expose Vessi's frame-up. Trouble is, everyone's in on the take and pretty soon Mason's life is being threatened by some pretty tough hoods. Life is cheap in a James Hadley Chase novel.

Both *Lady—Here's Your Wreath* and *Miss Callaghan Comes to Grief* were published within the same period—1940 and 1941—but *Lady* is the first "Chase" book that doesn't try to blast its way to the ending. In fact, it's more of a mystery, in the vein of *Twelve Chinamen and a Woman*, than a straight-up gat-blasting gangster novel. This is James Hadley Chase—or Raymond Marshall or James L. Docherty or Ambrose Grant, whatever he called himself—finding himself, trying on various outfits to see what fits best. In the end, he perfected an Americanized (British) thriller and did a damn good job at it.

James Hadley Chase—born René ("Rennie") Lodge Brabazon Raymond—created his own persona on the printed page, that of the brusque writer of hardboiled mayhem. And 90 or so books later, he was still delighting readers across the British Commonwealth. Oh, they tried to pitch him to the American market. His early books were all published here by outfits like Avon, Eton, Harlequin (yes, the Canadian romance publisher!), and then later by publishers like Ace, Signet and Pocket Books. For some reason, the Chase thrillers seem to remain more or less a particularly British pleasure, never quite in direct competition with Chase's American literary heroes. You never hear "Hammett, Chandler and Chase" mentioned in the same breath. But you should. Not because he out-hardboiled Hammett, or out-cynic-ed Chandler, but because when it came to plotting criminal thrillers, he was one of the best.

To quote the elusive but incisive Mr. Joseph Taggart: "James Hadley Chase is a thriller writer of masterly ingenuity. Several times you think you know what will happen. Well, you don't."

—Greg Shepard, publisher
Stark House Press
June 2016

Lady—Here's Your Wreath

by James Hadley Chase

For SYLVIA, who corrected the proofs,
suffers neglect in silence, and has none of the glory

CHAPTER ONE

The boys, who had come to see Vessi die, were lined up before the bar. They were putting up a good front, but they were all scared sick.

I came into the bar just when the liquor was hitting them. When they saw me, they let out a groan.

"For Gawd's sake, look who's here," Barry shouted. "The nine days' sensation himself."

Barry Hughson was a good guy, but he'd got plenty of gristle mixed up with his brains. I just called for a rye and gave them a grin. "H'yah, boys," I said, waving my hand. "I bet some of you're goin' to change your tune mighty soon."

They didn't like that crack, and gathered round looking tough. Hughson poked me in the chest with his forefinger. That's a thing I love. Some guy poking me in the chest. Barry was tight, so I let it slide.

"Listen, Bud," he said, screwing up his eyes to get my face in focus, "this little business is by invitation only. You don't stand a chance. Be a nice lad an' scram."

I belted the rye and showed him my card. "You boys ain't the only guys," I said. "I'm with you all the way."

Hackenschmidt of the *Globe* pushed his hat to the back of his head. "How d'you pull these quick ones?" he asked, his fat face looking like a startled Dutch cheese. "You ain't got any standin' around here, but you're always in on the right things."

I nodded. "I know," I said, "it's tough, but there it is… better to be early than late, as the airline hostess said to the passenger."

Hughson filled his glass. He looked at the clock. "Deadline 12:10," he said.

Hackenschmidt grabbed a handful of drinking-straws and broke them in two; discarded one lot and carefully counted the rest. I watched him thoughtfully. "You've left me out," I said, after he was through.

The guy lifted his thick lip. It was his idea of a sneer. "Yeah?" he said. "I guess you ain't in this."

I leant forward and picked up a straw. "Put it in the bundle and don't be a punk," I said, offering it to him.

He looked at me, and I looked at him. Then he took the straw. Some of these flabby guys think they're tough. Hackenschmidt was just punk, right through.

One of the straws was a lot shorter than the others. The guy who drew the short one got Vessi's last words. I wanted the job bad.

Hughson pulled the first straw, but he didn't get the short one. I let three more have a go, then I shoved a little, and the other guys gave way. I knew the short one, so I got it.

The others stood around, glaring at me.

"You gotta play ball," Hughson said. "Don't start anythin' that ain't on the level."

I tossed the straw away. "You'll get it all," I said. "Don't you worry."

The time was 11:20. Just time for a couple more drinks. Those guys belted their rye like they expected to die themselves.

Outside, we crowded into three cars that were waiting to take us to the prison. Hughson, Hackenschmidt and I, with two other guys, got in the first car. Hughson drove and I sat beside him.

When he'd got the car moving, he said: "Why the interest, Nick?"

I grinned in the darkness. Hughson was a cagey bird, but he wasn't getting anything from me. "Why not?" I asked him. "Vessi made a big noise, didn't he? I thought I'd see him go. Anyway, this gas stunt's a new one on me."

Hughson swung the car past an overloaded truck.

"Not much you miss, is there?"

I shrugged. "I get by."

"Think Vessi did it?"

I grinned again. "Don't you?"

Hughson swore softly: "Listen, you bum, if there's anything behind this, let me have it. I've done things for you, an' I guess—"

"Skip it," I said shortly. "How the hell do I know whether he did it or not? The jury pinned it on him, didn't they?"

"I ain't interested in what the jury thought. I'm askin' what you think."

"I never think, brother," I said hastily. "I just wait until somethin' happens."

Hughson snorted. "Okay, smart guy," he said. "Wait until you want somethin'."

We reached the prison at 11:40. There were some other witnesses waiting outside the gates as we drove up. They all looked uneasy in the dim light, and moved a little way away as we came tumbling out of the cars. We stood there in a bunch, pretending we didn't know what we were there for, until the gates were opened at 11:45.

A couple of bulls inspected our cards and gave us a quick frisk. Since the Snyder execution the authorities were scared sick that another guy would smuggle in a camera. The boys knew it was pretty useless to try, and the cops knew they knew it, so the frisk was really just a matter of form. When they got through, we started through a maze of gates, each of which was locked behind us before we could pass through the next.

We marched single file, and I guess we looked a fine bunch of professional mourners. We went past the big cell buildings, our footsteps resounding on the walk. It was dark and silent in the cells. The death house was over in the far corner of the immense prison yard.

We walked round the hearse, parked in front of the death house, and a number of us just took one quick look at that wagon and tucked in our tails.

The death house had two entrances. One led to a narrow passage between the death chamber and wall of the death house. The other led to the little cell where Vessi was—a few feet from the entrance.

There was no other building near the death house. It stood alone in a corner of the yard, where the convicts played their ball games. As we shuffled across the yard the dust got on to our shoes and we took it into the death house with us.

The guard stopped at the entrance. "Who's the guy for the last words?"

I stepped out of the file and jerked my thumb.

"Okay," he said. "You wait here."

The rest of the guys trooped down the passage and grouped themselves before the glass windows of the gas chamber. Hughson was the last one to take up a position. He said to me, as he passed: "Watch yourself, Bud."

I was surprised that a grin didn't come easy. This business was getting me a little nervy.

The gas chamber was octagonal in shape and made of steel, with windows on all sides. The narrow passage where the other boys had gone was built to allow four feet of space between the wall of the death house and the chamber. There was a very high steel chimney from the chamber up through the death house, to carry off the fumes once the execution was over.

I had a little more space on my side. I looked into the chamber. It was about five feet wide, and empty except for a steel chair, equipped with straps, standing in the centre. The cyanide 'eggs' were suspended from the bottom of the chair. I didn't like the look of this spot. It gave me the heebies just to imagine myself sitting in there.

From where I stood, I could look through the window of the chamber and see the boys on the opposite side, looking through their window at me. They waved at me and I gave them the two-digit high sign. Those guys certainly looked a bunch of monkeys massed up behind the glass.

I had come to see Vessi, so I thought I might as well have a look at him.

He was sitting in his cell, smoking a cigarette. He was naked but for a pair of underwear shorts.

I looked at the guard. "What's the idea—him like that?" The guard glanced in at the cell. "We always strip 'em down as far as we can. The gas sticks to clothes and it makes it difficult for us to get 'em out."

"There's goin' to be a mighty rush for tickets when they put a dame in there," I said.

The guard made a grimace. I guess he wasn't feeling too good. "Yeah," he said, "but they'll keep you bums outta here."

Vessi was a big guy, with a sullen, heavy face. Considering what was coming to him, I thought he was taking it pretty well. There was a glassy look in his eyes, and he was looking glum, but he wasn't in a panic.

The chaplain, a short, fat, worried-looking guy, sat on a chair, his head lowered, intoning a prayer. Vessi looked at him every now and then and licked his lips. I could see he wished the chaplain would stop the intoning.

I felt a sudden shiver run through me, as if it had turned cold. But it hadn't. I was sweating. The warden came down the passage quickly. There was a greenish pallor on his face, and he didn't look at me.

He just said "Okay" to the guard.

They unlocked the door to the little cell. Vessi's skin tightened, and he looked behind the guards at me. I didn't like meeting that guy's eye, but I thought maybe I'd better give him a little encouragement. I winked at him. It was a hell of a thing to do, but I just had to tell him I was feeling for him.

The guard tapped him on the shoulder, and he stood up. He was steadier on his feet than I was.

The chaplain droned on. I could guess how Vessi felt about it. I had to hold myself in. Those prayers didn't seem to be getting us anywhere.

Vessi came out of the cell. He was handcuffed, and he kept twisting his wrists, fidgeting with the bracelets.

The warden read the death-warrant in a sombre, get-it-over sort of voice. I could see a trickle of sweat running down behind his ear. When he was through he said: "Any last words?"

This was what I'd been waiting for. I moved forward so that I was close to Vessi. Out of the corner of my eye I could see the other guys pressed against the glass window, taking it all in, and watching me closely. Vessi looked right at me. "You got the wrong guy," he said, his voice not quite steady. "I didn't do it."

The guards closed round him, but Vessi suddenly stiffened. He continued to look at me. "Break it open, Mason," he said in a low mumble. "Lu Spencer pulled it. You gotta get him—it was Lu—do you hear—?"

The guards bustled him and he was shoved into the chamber. I made a note to please the boys, but I left the last angle out.

They put Vessi in the steel chair with the pellets under it. The straps were tightened. While this was going on—it took under forty-five seconds—he kept his eyes on my face. I nodded to him, trying to tell him I was going to do something about it. He saw he'd got my attention and relaxed in the chair.

A guard brought a crock of sulphuric acid and put it under the chair—directly under the pellets. Then he took it on the lam quick. The warden inspected the straps—one around Vessi's chest, two on each arm, and one on each leg. He put his hand on Vessi's shoulder. "You'll go quick, boy," he said. "Take a deep breath—you won't know anythin' about it." Then he walked out of the chamber.

Vessi was in there alone.

The guard swung the heavy steel door shut, and shoved home the bolts. I and the warden stood looking into the chamber through the little window by the door. Ten seconds to wait, and those ten seconds seemed like ten years. I felt my heart bumping.

Vessi turned his head slowly, looking at the faces watching him. He was beginning to realise what was coming to him.

The warden had his eye on his watch. He reached out and put his hand on the lever which dropped the pellets into the acid. I could see him screwing up his will to pull that lever, and I was glad he had to do it and not me. I couldn't look at Vessi any more. I found my eyes on the warden's hand. I could see his muscles gradually tightening. Then with a little sigh, that came through his clenched teeth in a hiss, he jerked the lever down. The pellets dropped into the crock with a distinct flop. Vessi heard it and stiffened in his chair. A white gas began to drift from the acid. I could see the muscles of his arms suddenly bulge as he strained on the straps.

The gas rose rapidly. I thought I could taste bitter almonds —but I knew that was cock-eyed. My imagination was getting the better of me.

Vessi smelt the gas. He tossed his head back, twisting to escape the fumes. The steel chair held him. I could see him holding his breath. This guy was making it bad for himself. Finally he couldn't hold it any longer, and he gasped. He got a big dose of the gas that time. He screamed suddenly. The sound of his yell rattled round the chamber. It came to us muffled and eerie.

I found myself gripping on to the steel bolt of the door. This was getting me in the guts.

Vessi choked, gasped and writhed against his bonds.

The doctor at my elbow kept one eye on a stop-watch. Thirty seconds—thirty-five—Vessi still choked. Forty-five seconds and his head dropped back. The doctor scribbled the time opposite a blank on the sheet before him. Vessi seemed unconscious.

His head was back, and he had stopped coughing. The fumes filled the chamber. Slowly, very slowly, his head came forward. Gradually it dropped between his shoulders, his long, black hair fell across his eyes. I could see his stomach muscles were still contracting. Three minutes had gone past. With a little shake his head came up a bit.

The doctor said, in a low, bored voice: "He's dead."

I stepped away from the window. Hughson came rushing round from the other side of the chamber, followed by the mob. They all looked pop-eyed and slightly sick. I felt that way myself. It took Vessi four minutes and a bit to die.

"What did he say?" Hughson demanded.

I shrugged. "He said, 'You got the wrong guy, I didn't do it.'"

"Yeah?" Hackenschmidt sneered. "That's been his yap right through the trial."

Hughson was looking at me suspiciously. "Did he say anythin' else?"

I shook my head. "No… just that."

They made a dive to get out. There was an immediate scramble for 'phones and the telegraph office. I let the rush get on ahead, then I turned to follow.

The warden touched my arm. He was trying to look casual. "I shouldn't pin too much to the Spencer angle," he said.

I paused and looked at him, but he was wearing a dead pan.

"You don't think so?" I said hopefully.

He shook his head. "I should forget all about it."

I pushed my hat a little over my eyes. "Did you hear the one about the guy with a wooden leg, playin' ping-pong…?"

The warden nodded his head. "Yeah," he said, "it's got round to me."

I edged towards the exit. "I guessed maybe it had," I said, and left him.

CHAPTER TWO

I went over to the Press room at Police Headquarters. There was one guy I wanted to talk to, and I was hoping he'd be there. He was.

I pushed open the door and looked around the smoke-laden room. Four of the usual mob were playing cards round a small table in the centre of the room. I just gave them a quick glance and looked further. Over in the corner, on a battered couch, Ackie was sleeping.

Ackie was the ugliest guy I'd ever seen. He was a little runt, with coarse hair growing out of his ears, his nose and out of his collar. His face must have given the midwife a series of nightmares when he was born, but I knew he was about the smartest Press man on the beat.

I wandered over to him and pulled up a chair. Then I shook him awake.

When he saw me, he sat up and glared. "You're a sweet pal," he said. "Can't you let me snatch some sleep?"

"Aw, forget it, Mo," I said. "Sit down. I want to talk to you."

Ackie rubbed his face hard with his hand, pushing his rubbery nose to the most extraordinary angles.

I took out a packet of Camels, gave him one and lit up myself. "What is it, you bum?" he demanded. "I bet you want to pick my brains again."

I shook my head. "You ain't got brains," I said. "You just think you have."

Ackie shut his eyes. "They fixed Vessi tonight," he said.

"Yeah," I said, surprised.

"What made you turn up?" he asked, without opening his eyes.

"How the hell did you know I turned up?" I demanded.

When Ackie smiled he looked horrible. I shifted my eyes. "Not much I don't hear," he said. "What made you turn up?"

"Listen, Mo," I said patiently; "I came here to ask you somethin', not you to ask me."

He lifted one hooded lid and squinted at me. "Why the interest, brother? Somethin' hangin' to it?"

These news-hawks were all the same. I dragged down some smoke and held it for a second, then let it drift down my nostrils. "I don't think Vessi did it," I said, keeping my voice low.

Ackie groaned and shut his eye. "He's dead now, ain't he? Forget it."

"This guy Richmond," I said, selecting my words, "I guess he had more enemies than Vessi?"

"Yeah, he'd more enemies than most guys. Richmond was a heel. He had it comin' to him."

"There was a woman hangin' to the killin', wasn't there? They never turned her up."

Ackie lifted his shoulders. "There were hundreds of women," he said indifferently. "That guy had women in his hair all day long."

"Who was she?" I asked softly.

Ackie raised his head. "Nothin' doin'," he said. "Richmond's dead an' Vessi's dead; both those guys were rats. It's washed up… forget it."

"Why the hell should everyone want to play this business down?"

Ackie grinned a little. "Do they?" he said.

"Now listen, Mo," I said. "There's somethin' you know an' somethin' I know. Suppose we go round to my place an' talk about it?"

Ackie shook his head. "Just as soon as you get out of here I'm goin' to sleep," he said firmly.

I shrugged. "There's a whole bottle of rye waiting," I told him.

Ackie got to his feet hastily. "Why not say so before?" he demanded. "Where the hell's my hat?"

On the way down to my apartment Ackie talked ball games. He didn't know much about the game, but he liked to air his views. I let him talk. I'd got things to think about.

Once I got him in an armchair with a big rye and ginger in his hand, I got down to things.

"This ain't to go further, Mo," I began, putting my feet on the table, "but it looks to me like I've gotta put the cards down before you'll give me a hand. I want help, Mo, and I want it from you."

Ackie grunted, but he didn't say anything.

"I stand to pick up ten grand if I start a row about Vessi's execution," I said.

Ackie looked up sharply. "Who's slippin' you the dough?"

I shook my head. "That's under my lid," I said. "Ten grand's nice money, and from what I've picked up already there's something mighty phoney about Vessi's case. It begins to look as if it was a frame-up from the very start."

Ackie looked worried. "You'd better lay off this, Nick," he said seriously. "You might run into a lotta grief."

"Come on," I said shortly, "let's have it. What's it all about?"

I could see him making up his mind. In a minute or so I could see I was going to get it all right.

"Larry Richmond was the President of the Mackenzie Fabric Corporation," he said slowly, fixing his eyes on a spot just above my head. "A great many guys are stockholders in this business. These guys are the big shots of commerce and industry. People who hold public office."

I leant forward and took the glass out of his hand and refilled it. He took it from me with a little grimace. "Shouldn't touch the stuff," he said. "It rusts my guts or somethin'."

"Keep going," I said.

"Maybe you think there ain't anythin' odd about this, but there is. Richmond privately negotiated all the stock to these people. It was never thrown on to the open market. You know how Richmond stood in society. He'd only have to go around and drop a hint or two, and the lot was over-subscribed." He paused to take a long pull at his glass. "If anything turns up now to reopen an investigation into Richmond's death there's goin' to be a lot of trouble for those stockholders."

I didn't hurry him. This was news to me, and I wasn't sure where it was getting me. "How come?" I said.

Ackie turned his eyes on me. "Even my boss has got stock in the business," he said. "He's told us boys to lay off. We don't know, but we've got a good idea that the Mackenzie Fabric Corporation is a blind, and another racket is goin' on behind the scenes that pays the big divs. The guys who've got their dough in there don't want to know anythin'— they're scared sick that some smart monkey like you'll come along an' blow the lid off."

I got to my feet. "What's the racket?"

Ackie shrugged. "Gawd knows. Could be anythin'. The point is that so many of the big shots have got their dough in the business that it's mighty dangerous to start anything."

"Vessi was the mug?"

Ackie nodded, "Sure Vessi was the mug. Some guy didn't like his rake-off, so he plugs Richmond. This guy was connected with the firm. They couldn't prosecute him without blowin' the gaff, so they find a fall-guy. Vessi gets the killin' pushed on to him. That's the story, Bud—now forget it, will you?"

I said: "Who's Lu Spencer?"

Ackie shot me a quick look. "Spencer was Richmond's right hand. He's the guy who's taken over now Richmond's dead."

"Lu Spencer was the guy who killed Richmond, huh?"

Ackie's face went blank. "I wouldn't know that," he said, a sudden caution in his voice.

"Okay, Mo," I said, "you've given me the dope. Thanks a lot."

Ackie got to his feet. "You ain't goin' to start any trouble?" he asked. There was a glint in his eye that told me he was hoping I would.

"Suppose we don't go into that?" I returned. "Whatever happens, I'll play this carefully. Didn't they say that Richmond was playing around with Vessi's girl, and that's why Vessi knocked him off?"

Ackie nodded, "Yeah," he said, "that was the angle."

"Who was she, Mo?"

Ackie frowned. "She was a French moll," he said slowly. "They kept her covered up at the trial. Andrée somethin' or other… they call her Blondie on her beat."

I scratched my head. "She a professional dame?" I asked, surprised.

Ackie nodded, "Sure… Vessie liked them to keep themselves, you know."

"I guess I want to meet this dame," I said, "I might get an angle—"

"I don't know where she hangs out, but she goes into the Hotcha Bar most nights."

I patted him on the back. "Here, Bud, take the rye," I said, turning back to the table. "I guess you've earned it."

Ackie sneered, "Come to, bum," he said, "I got that already. An' say, who's the guy that's putting up ten grand for this story to be blown up?"

I pushed him to the door. "It's my big Aunty Belle," I said, shoving him into the dark corridor.

"Yeah?" he said. "You mean your big Aunt Fanny, don'tcher?"

I shut the door behind him.

When I was sure that he had gone, I went to the cupboard and took out another bottle of rye, stripped off the tissue paper and pulled the cork. I took the bottle into the other room and sat on the bed. I undressed slowly, giving my mind some exercise. When I was ready, I fetched a glass and some ginger seltzer and got into bed.

This all wanted thinking about. It seemed to me that I'd got a job on. That didn't worry me, but I liked to see where I was heading.

Right now, I wasn't doing too badly. I was selling articles where and when I liked. Editors liked my stuff and paid fancy rates for it. I'd got a nice little apartment, and enough booze to keep me oiled for twenty-four hours a day.

I leant forward and took a poke at the rye.

Suppose I did start something, and there was an investigation? If the Mackenzie-whatever-they-called-it turned out a ramp, then there was going to be a bad smell around, and I would be the cause of it. Maybe the newspapers would warn me off… maybe I'd lose everything I'd got… just for ten grand. Looked at from that angle, it wasn't even interesting.

I put the glass back on the little table by my bed and lit a cigarette. When I got into bed with a load of grief like this, I always thought it would be swell to have some hot-looking dame right beside me to listen to my beef and give me an angle to work on.

A woman can be a lot of comfort, and the more I thought about it, the lower I got. I was just getting in a pretty bad shape when the telephone snapped me out of my pipe-dream.

As I reached for the 'phone, I looked over at the clock. It was just after two.

"Yeah?" I said, wondering who the hell it was.

"Is that Nick Mason?"

As soon as I heard that hard, metallic voice I sat up. My arm jogged the glass of rye, which went over with a crash. Even the spilling of good liquor didn't take my mind off that voice.

Four days ago she had rung me up. Without saying who she was, she told me that I'd get a pass to attend Vessi's execution and I was to try and get a word with him. If I thought I could expose a frame-up, she'd pay me ten thousand dollars. She had hung up before I could say a word.

Boy! Was I intrigued! I could handle that sort of mystery stuff from dawn to dawn. Not only was the incentive there in the way of cash, but the story angle got me excited.

And here she was again. The voice was unmistakable. It was clear, bell-like and hard.

I sank back on my pillow, holding the 'phone tight. "You got it right, sister," I said.

"Did you go?"

"Yeah."

"What happened?"

"He's dead. I got word with him. He said Lu Spencer had pulled it."

I heard her catch her breath. "He said that?" she asked eagerly.

"Yeah… now listen, what's the big idea? What's all this to you?"

"I'm goin' to send you five thousand dollars so that you can go on with this. When you've found out the truth and have written it all up you'll get the other five."

I was scared that she was going to cut off. I said quickly, "I ain't interested… I've looked into this an' there's too much to it."

There was a long silence on the line.

I said anxiously, "You there?"

She said, "Yes… I thought you'd be glad to do it. I see I've made a mistake."

"Suppose we get together an' talk this over?" I said. "This is a big set-up, baby. All the big shots are in on this… it wants talkin' over."

She said, "I think you'll do it all right," and before I could shout she had hung up.

I lay there, calling her some fancy names. It didn't get me anywhere. She was right about me doing it. I liked to push my nose into something that might scorch it. This business had a lot of angles that might prove interesting. I put the 'phone down and turned off the light. I could think a lot better in the dark.

I went through the business carefully. I'd got a few leads to follow up. First, I'd look into the stockholders of the Mackenzie Fabric Corporation. Then I might take a look at the firm and have a sniff round there. Lu Spencer wanted hunting up. Ackie was an all-right guy, and I guessed he was willing to help me if I didn't pull him into it. Then there was Blondie. Maybe I'd get a little fun with Blondie. I had a weakness for blondes, anyway. It looked on the face of it an attractive programme.

I let it go at that and went to sleep.

CHAPTER THREE

Someone woke me up by punching the front-door bell. I love that. Some guy always wakes me up just when I'm getting friendly with my dream blonde. That dame certainly is a nice little twitchet.

I dragged myself out of bed and padded across the two rooms to the front door.

A special messenger was leaning up against the door, humming Cole Porter. He looked at me, then at the envelope he was holding.

"Nick Mason?" he asked.

"Yeah," I said. "Let's have it, you mother's nightmare."

He gave me the envelope and I signed. Then he stood there waiting to pick up something. He'd got a hope. If he thought I was giving him anything he was crazy. I only hoped he'd fall downstairs on his way out and break his neck. I started to shut the door.

"You won't get any place in that sleepin'-suit," he said, and made a dash down the corridor. Maybe he thought I'd give him a poke in his puss.

I went back to the bedroom and took a look in the long glass. The kid was right. That sleeping-suit was terrible. I sat on the bed and ripped open the envelope. Five crisp thousand-dollar bills spilt on my knees. No letter—just the dough. I sat and looked at them for a few minutes. That's one thing I can always do—sit around, looking at money. Then I put the money back in the envelope and put the envelope on the table.

There was a catch in this, of course. I'd got to start right now and earn that dough. I wandered into the bathroom and took off the sleeping-suit.

The cold prickle of the shower made me feel good. Once I got through with the wet part of getting up, I always tried my hand at singing. Maybe I wasn't so good, but I'd got a lot of power. I wrapped the towel round my waist and shaved, then I wandered back into the bedroom with the idea of having a drink to help me on the final task of dressing.

Two things struck me as soon as I entered the bedroom. There was a heavy smell of scent hanging around that certainly hadn't been there when I left the room, and the envelope had gone.

I moved quickly. Dropping the towel, I grabbed my dressing-gown and struggled into it, running into the sitting-room as I did so. The front door was ajar. I raced to the window and threw it up. The street was deserted. I thought I caught a glimpse of a yellow taxi flashing round the corner, but I wasn't sure. If it was a taxi, it was moving like hell.

I went back to the bedroom and stood sniffing. I'm not one of those guys who can classify a smell quickly, but I knew this stuff all right. It was the kind of scent hot mammas used to get the boys running in circles.

Right then, I was running in circles. I was as mad as a blind man at a strip tease. I went over to the telephone with the idea of getting the cops, then a thought struck me and I sat down to think about it.

Those dollar notes had looked mighty nice, and now some dame had nicked them. I was feeling mighty sore.

After a few quick drags from the rye I felt better, and I got myself dressed. All the time I wondered what the devil I was going to do. The sooner I started in on this the better. I locked up the apartment and went downstairs for my breakfast.

I ordered two lightly boiled eggs, toast and coffee. I was just getting down to serious eating when the guy who rented the apartment opposite walked in. This guy gave me a pain. There are some guys who just can't help giving anyone a pain. You don't know why… they try like hell to put themselves across, but they stick.

I tried to hide behind my newspaper, but I was too late. He came across with an odd expression on his face and sat down.

He said, trying to look shocked, "You didn't ought to have girls in your place, Mason; it gives the building a bad name."

I said, "You're kiddin' yourself. The place had a bad name long before I moved in. Besides, I don't know what you're talking about. What's all this about dames?"

The waitress came up just then and took his order for tomato-juice and toast. When she had gone, he spread himself over the table. "I saw her when I was getting the paper," he said. "She came out fast, just like she had been chased out."

I thought: if I'd seen her, she'd come out faster than that.

"You're nuts," I said. "Soon as I saw you, I thought your liver had been shot to hell."

A look of doubt crossed his face, then he came back again. "You can't kid me," he said, with an attempt to leer. "She was some baby… a real hot mamma."

I finished my coffee and lit a cigarette. "Do you often get like this?" I said anxiously. "I bet you'll even be able to describe her to me."

"Sure I can," he said. "She was tall, blonde, with a make-up that just knocked me. She wore black, and had a large black felt hat, and a gold something or other round her neck. She was moving fast, but I'd know her any time."

I got to my feet, pushing the chair away with the back of my legs. I looked down at him in concern. "You gotta do something about this," I said. "You go an' see a croaker… you've been seeing things."

I walked out of the restaurant, leaving him snorting. Once I was on the street I walked slowly, picking my way through the crowds milling to work.

So she was blonde, tall and dressed in black. A sweet job to look for a dame with that description. Still, she'd got my five grand, and I was going to find her or bust.

Maybe Ackie would know where she fitted in. I turned into a drug-store and rang the Press room, but he wasn't there. They thought he was over at Hank's pool-room having a game, but they weren't sure.

I took a taxi down to Hank's but he wasn't there either. They thought he'd show up, so I spent a little time practising shots on one of the tables.

I never managed to get the knack of the game, but it interested me, and whenever I got near a table I just had to push the balls around. I got so interested in a cannon-shot that seemed to be going just right that I lost count of the time. After I had broken my combination up, I thought I'd better give Ackie a miss and get on to the street again. As I was moving, a long, thin dope, dressed like a mock member of the upper crust, wandered in and stood watching me.

He said suddenly, "What about a little game with a dollar or so on for interest?"

I've met these dopes before. They look so damn' dumb, you think it's a shame to take their dough, but once they've raised the ante to twenty-five bucks they make the ball do everything but eat a four-course lunch.

I put the cue on the table and shook my head. "I'm through," I said.

"You go an' get some practice."

He picked up the cue and began potting the red. I expected him to make a hell of a mess of it, but he just went ahead and gave one of the finest exhibitions of shooting I'd ever seen. He slammed the balls into the pockets from every angle, and I just dug them out and rolled them back to him. He got a spin working that made the ball float round the table, and then he finished up with a real snorter that sunk the three balls with one shot.

"I see you've been a beginner some time," I said, thinking I was lucky not to have played this guy.

He leant over the table to dig out a ball, and his coat shifted up over his hip. I saw the handle of a gun sticking out of his hip-pocket. "Me? I'm punk," he said. "I just like pushin' the balls around."

I took a close look at this guy. He still looked a dope, but when you examined him closely, his eyes gave him away. This guy was tough. He'd got a hanging lip that gave him the soft look, but his eyes were suspicious and hard.

He was quick to see my interest, and he leant against the table and began to clean his nails with a pocket-knife. "Ain't seen you around before?" he said, his voice rising a little, making it a question.

I shook my head. "Just looked in for a pal," I told him. I wondered who he was, so I thought a little harmless talk wouldn't waste my time.

"I guess I've seen your face before," he said, without looking up.

"Yeah? Maybe you have."

"You wouldn't be Mason, the news writer?" He overdid it. He knew who I was.

"Sure," I said. "Maybe you've seen my photo somewhere."

"Yeah." He folded the knife and put it in his vest-pocket. "Yeah, maybe I have." He gave me a long, hard look, then, tossing the cue on to the table, he walked out.

I watched him go thoughtfully. I couldn't quite get the angle. I went over to the bar. Hank was polishing glasses. He was a big guy with red, curly hair and tremendous hands and arms.

"Who's the dope?" I said, jerking my head towards the door.

Hank shrugged. "Search me," he said. "What'll you have?"

"Ain't you seen him before?"

"I don't remember."

Just then Ackie came in. When he saw me he grinned. "What the hell are you doin' here?" he said, crowding up to the bar. "Two ryes and ginger," he said to Hank.

"I wanted to see you," I said, "so I looked in on the off-chance."

Hank put the rye in front of us. He beamed at Ackie. "You all right, mister?" he asked.

Ackie leant forward and patted Hank's arm. "Me? I feel fine, couldn't be better."

It looked like these two knew each other, so I tried again. "That guy who was playin' on the table over there… who was he?"

Hank stopped laughing. His little eyes shifted like quicksilver. "I tell you I don't know him," he said.

Ackie looked at me, then he looked at Hank. Ackie was a smart guy. He saw the set-up without being told. "Spill it, Hank… this guy's a pal of mine," he said.

"I tell you I don't know." Hank was getting angry. "I can't waste all my time with you gents… I gotta get on with my work." He walked to the far end of the bar and began polishing glasses down there.

Ackie looked after him thoughtfully and poured himself another rye. "What's it all about?" he asked.

I shrugged. "Maybe it's nothing. I was pushing some balls around an' some guy offers to play me. I turned him down, an' while he was showin' off I spotted a gun in his pocket. Then he asked if my name was Mason, took a hard gander at me and beat it. I was just wondering who he was. This bar bozo knows who he was, but won't say."

Ackie frowned. "What's this fella like?"

"A tall, thin bird, with a hanging lip and cold, hard eyes. He looked a dope, but I guess he was tough all right."

Ackie's eyes narrowed. "This guy know how to handle a cue?"

"Sure, he's the hottest thing I've seen."

"That's Earl Katz," Ackie said. "Well! Well!"

I shook my head. "That's a new one on me."

"Yeah, you wouldn't know him. He's a bad guy all right. One of Lu Spencer's gunmen."

I put my glass on the bar with a sharp little click. "Lu Spencer?" I said.

Ackie nodded. "Yeah… looks to me like they're watchin' you already."

"What makes Hank get the jitters about a dope like that?" I asked.

"Katz a dope?" Ackie wagged his bullet head. "You're crazy. That guy's as deadly as a rattlesnake. Don't go gettin' ideas about him. Why, Hank and the rest of us are scared sick of him."

I took another poke at the rye. "Well, I don't mind telling you," I said quietly, "that guy ain't goin' to make me nervous."

Ackie shrugged. "You wait till you know him," he said.

I glanced round the room, but the place was still empty except for Hank, who was keeping away from us. I lowered my voice. "I had a little adventure last night. A dame dropped in and pinched some dough off me."

Ackie looked interested. "You mean she came in and took your roll or somethin'?"

"I was havin' a shower and she got in, knocked off a nice slice of my rent and skipped without me seein' her. A guy who lives opposite me saw her go. I'm tyin' her up to this business, an' I wondered if you might know who she was."

Ackie looked incredulous. "Why the hell should I know?"

"Can you fit in a dame that's blonde and dresses in black? Wears a big felt hat and looks like a real hot mamma?"

Ackie shook his head. "Why should you tie her up to the Vessi business?" he asked.

I wasn't going to tell him that, but just as I was getting set to air off my imagination he got it. Ackie had a lot of brain under his hat. "Jeeze! That's a howl," he said, smacking his thigh and giving one of his grunting laughs. "You got paid, huh? They slipped you the ten grand already an' someone pinches it." He leant against the counter and hooted.

When he'd got through with his fun, he mopped his eyes with his sleeve and grinned at me maliciously. "Gee! That's tough," he said. "So a blonde hotcha got away with your dough."

I said "Yeah," and gave myself another drink. "Suppose you cut out the sympathy and bend your brains on this. Can't you give me a lead on the blonde?"

Ackie shook his head. "What do you take me for? Think I know all the blondes in town?"

I said slowly, "It wouldn't be Vessi's moll, would it?"

Ackie looked suddenly uncomfortable. "Listen, Nick," he said, "I like you, but I've got to keep out of this… do you understand? You go ahead if you want a funeral on your hands, but you've gotta keep me out of it."

"All right, all right," I said, "Forget it. I'll look into this on my own."

Ackie nodded. "You're the sorta guy who might crack this without gettin' hurt."

A nice line in comfort this guy had got, I thought. I looked at my watch. It was getting on for lunch-time. "Okay, Mo," I said, "I'll be seeing you." I left him giving himself another rye.

I stood on the curb thinking. It was a theory of mine to take the fight always to the other guy. I was not quite sure if I was going to be right this time. Maybe I'd start something that I couldn't finish. I didn't know. Then I thought I might as well go ahead and see what happened, so I signalled a taxi and told the driver to take me to the Hoffman Building quick.

CHAPTER FOUR

The taxi turned me loose outside the Hoffman Building, and I took the elevator to the tenth floor.

The Mackenzie Fabric Corporation was some joint. The entrance was the finest exhibition for chromium wear I'd seen all in one spot, and, once inside, I nearly sank up to my knees in the pile of the carpet. The big reception lobby was as busy as a main-line railway station. At the far end I could make out the reception-desk, that was pretty near swamped by a crowd of shouting men, yelling to see Mr. Someone or other.

I stood inside the door, taking a look round. Every now and then a dame would come out of a room and flounce across the lobby. They were all hand-picked, and I began to think I wouldn't mind having a job of work here myself.

I wandered over to the desk. The mob was still struggling for attention. I stood watching them for a moment, then I took a match, struck it on the sole of my shoe and set fire to a newspaper one of the kikes had under his arm. I stood back and waited.

There was almost a riot when the paper flared up. While they were all trying to put the fire out, I got in front and asked the girl to put me through to Spencer's secretary.

She was also a smart jape. "Have you an appointment?" she asked, watching with half an eye the commotion going on amongst the kikes.

I was getting sick of this. "Listen, sister," I said; "ring and tell whoever looks after Mr. Spencer's business that Nick Mason's outside, an' if I'm kept waiting much longer I'm going to get annoyed."

She looked at me thoughtfully, making up her mind whether or not I was bluffing, then she decided I wasn't and rang through. I stood over her while she gave the message. She pulled the plug out. "Room 26, on your right," she said briefly.

"Thank you, baby… I hope your dreams include me tonight."

I went over to Room 26, knocked on the door and went in. It was a small room, obviously an outer office. A flat-top desk took up most of the space. The carpet was like grass, and there was one good painting of a nude on the wall. The nude held my attention for a second. It was the first thing you saw when you came into the room. I thought, after I'd taken a quick look, that if they were built that way these days the cushion trade would be shot to hell.

I got my eyes down to the desk. Sitting there was a dizzy-looking brunette. Now don't get me wrong about this girl. She wasn't Ritzy—she was the kind of girl you'd take home to your ma and not be nervous of starting a riot. She'd got a lot of soft brown hair and her eyes were large and brown. Her mouth was large and generous and her nose was small and cute.

"You'll pardon me," I said. "That dame up there got me startled. I didn't see you."

She smiled. "Mr. Mason?"

I put my hat on the desk and sat down. "Yeah," I said, "Nick Mason. I want to see Lu Spencer."

Her eyes opened a little. "Mr. Spencer's engaged. You can't see him without an appointment."

I sat back and looked at her. I couldn't understand what this girl had got that interested me. She didn't make up much, she wasn't over- or under-dressed, and yet I thought she was swell.

She broke in on my thoughts. "If you'll let me know what you want to see him about, I might arrange it."

I said, "It's a little involved, Miss… er… Miss…."

She didn't help, but just sat there, looking at me a little old-fashioned, and waited.

I got an inspiration. "Suppose you an' I go out and eat somewhere, an' talk it over." I glanced at my watch. "It's just after one, so the time's right. I got a lot to say, and maybe you can tell me if Mr. Spencer's the right guy to see."

I could see she was all set to say 'no.' At the same time, her eyes told me that I wasn't something out of cheese. She almost looked like she could be persuaded.

"Now don't be high-hat," I pleaded. "Give me a chance to tell you all about it."

She got to her feet. "Very well, Mr. Mason, let us go to lunch."

Believe it or not, I was getting a kick out of this girl. Me, getting a kick out of a girl. I could hear forty thousand floozies turning over in their graves.

We went down in the elevator. I said, "Suppose we go to Sloppy Joe's?"

She laughed. "I'd love to… where is it?"

I jerked my head at a taxi. "It's a dollar ride downtown," I said.

The yellow taxi drew up and the driver swung the door open. He took one look at the girl and gave me a wink. "I'll drive nice an' slow, Capt.," he said.

These taxi guys were a big help sometimes. I helped her in. "Sloppy Joe's, Buddy," I said, "an' just shut your window, will you?"

"Sure, Capt.," he said with a leer, "an' I won't look round. You go ahead an' enjoy yourself."

I got into the bus just a trifle flustered. I saw from a mischievous smile that she'd heard all right.

"These guys've got low minds," I said, settling down in the far corner. "Maybe we ought to know each other. I'm Nick Mason… I believe I've said that before."

She said, "I'm Mardi Jackson."

I said, "I'm glad to meet you," and we laughed. I thought she'd got a swell name. I liked that. It suited her.

"Well, Miss Jackson," I said, offering her a cigarette, "you're Spencer's secretary… right?"

She took the cigarette. "That's right," she said. "Don't you write articles?"

I lit her cigarette and mine. "That's how I keep the wolf from the door," I said. "It's a grand way to earn a livin'. I could tell you stories that would do things to you."

"Well, perhaps one day you'll tell me."

That's the way it went. Tossing flowers at each other all the way. For the first time since I reached the age I sat in a taxi and didn't make a pass. Most dames are so dumb you had to get going or you'd die of boredom. Others think they've wasted their time if you don't, but this baby was just worth looking at and saving it for a big occasion.

Sloppy Joe's was pretty full when we got there, but the Greek head waiter saw me and waved from the far end of the room. We went down the aisle between the tables. I got a big kick out of the way the men stopped eating to get a gander at Mardi. Even those guys with their own molls had a quick side look.

The Greek was all over me. I'd given his eating-joint a good write-up every so often, and I fed on the house whenever I liked.

He had a table all right. Mardi gave him an amused smile as he bowed himself in half. I could see she was making a big hit with the old guy, and somehow that pleased me, too.

I saw him shoot me a quick look and I gave him a grin. "You're lookin' pretty good," I said.

When we were seated, the Greek produced the bill of fare, that was as long as my arm. I looked at Mardi. "How hungry are you?" I asked.

She nodded. "Plenty."

"How about a mushroom canape, and a Swiss steak with what goes with it to follow?"

"That sounds lovely."

"Okay, make that twice, Nic," I said, "and make it fast."

She began stripping off her gloves. I kept my eyes on her fingers. No rings. I was surprised at my relief.

"Now, Mr. Mason, suppose you tell me all about it."

I shook my head, "Don't rush it," I said, "I gotta get used to you."

Again her eyebrows went up. "Don't you think," she said quietly, "we'd better talk business? I'm due back in an hour."

Back came the Greek with the canape.

After he had fussed around a bit and made sure we had nothing to beef about, he took himself off. It gave me a little time to use my brain. "I guess I'll put my cards on the table," I said. I seemed to be wearing that phrase out. "Have you ever heard of a guy called Vessi?"

I saw her give a little start. She looked up quickly. Her eyes were full of questions.

"I see you have," I cut in before she could say anything. "The guy who was executed the other night. Well, I'm interested in him and the story that is hanging to him. I was wondering if you could give me a line on him yourself?"

"I?" She was surprised. I told myself I'd drawn blank here. "But why should I give you any information? What information?"

I shook my head. "No, I guess I was wrong. Okay, forget it, will you?"

Her chin tilted. "No, I will not forget it," she said. "What makes you think I could have told you anything?"

I saw she was getting a little fussed. I didn't want to fall out with this baby… I liked her too much. I'd got to be careful, for all that. After all, she was Spencer's secretary. I shook my head. "I'm sorry to have brought it up," I said, "I was just bein' too smart. You're right. A girl like you wouldn't know anything about Vessi…. I guess I owe you an apology."

She smiled. A little, determined smile. "That still doesn't answer my question, does it?" she said.

I grinned back at her. "Don't put me in a spot, sister," I said. "I thought maybe I was going to get somewhere if I jumped it on you, but I see I was backin' the wrong gee. I'd tell you all about it if I could, but for the moment I've got to keep this under my hat. Suppose you tell me how I can get in to see Spencer?"

The Swiss steak did a lot to break up the hostile atmosphere, but she wasn't going to let me get away with it as easily as that.

She looked at me pretty straight. "You know, Mr. Mason, I don't like this at all. You said you wanted to talk business. My business is to do with Fabrics. Then you start some story about a wretched gunman instead. Is this a cheap joke?"

I found I was getting flustered. This certainly was something new to me.

I said feebly, "This ain't a joke. I'm dead serious, but I'm in a spot...."

She pushed back her chair. "In that case, Mr. Mason," she said coldly, "I don't think we need waste any more time." Another dame would have got herself smacked, but this baby had me jumping through hoops. I said urgently, "Don't go, don't walk out on me... I'll come clean on this."

She shook her head. "No... I think I'd better go." But she made no move. Maybe she was the cutest of them all, but she was woman enough to be curious. I took a look over my shoulder to see how close the next table was, satisfied myself that no one could hear me, and dived right into the story. I gave it to her from the first gong to the last.

She sat with her hands in her lap, her eyes wide, her lips parted. I gave her the story with everything I had, and I held her to the last word. Sitting there, I thought she looked swell.

"Apart from the ten grand," I concluded, "this frame-up interests me. It would make a swell story, and I always like to think the right guy gets the right punishment."

She said, in barely a whisper. "But... but... Mr. Spencer... no, I can't believe that...."

I shrugged. "I've never met the guy. At the same time, why the hell does he have a gunman? Why should a guy in Fabrics be mixed up with a thug like Katz?"

I saw her suddenly give a little shiver. "You know a little more about this than you're lettin' me think. Ain't that right?"

She hesitated. Then she shook her head. "I can't help you.... I'm his personal secretary.... You see that, don't you?"

I scratched my jaw. "Yeah, I guess so," I said doubtfully. "At the same time, baby, you gotta remember that this is a murder rap, and accessories don't get much pity."

She went a little white when I said this, but she again shook her head. "No, not now," she said firmly.

"Okay," I said. "Maybe later."

The Greek brought the coffee and I gave her a cigarette. We sat there in silence, smoking. I wasn't sure where I was going from here. I had hoped that something would have broken, but it seemed as tight shut as before.

"I guess I'd better look this Spencer guy over," I said at last. "Maybe I'll get something out of him."

Mardi fiddled with her coffee-spoon. "I wish you wouldn't," she said, without looking at me. "Don't you think that it would be better to leave this business alone?"

I raised my eyebrows. I must say I was getting a hell of a lot of encouragement on this job. "I've gotta get into this," I said. "Can't you understand with a thing like this there's a big angle as a story hanging to it? If I bust this thing, it'll start a riot. I shall be the guy responsible. It'll mean something then."

"I don't want to sound a crab," she said, putting her hand suddenly on my sleeve, "but isn't it a bit big? I mean… I don't want you to think…." She stopped in confusion.

"Meanin' I'm a small-town hick an' might get a swell bellyache if I bit this off an' couldn't chew it?" I grinned at her to show her I wasn't mad.

She looked at me then, and her eyes were troubled. "No, I didn't mean that quite," she said. "But if what you have told me is true… isn't it rather one-sided? Don't you think you ought to have someone to back you, if you're determined to go ahead?"

I tapped the ash off my cigarette. This was the kind of girl I'd thought about for a long time. A girl who talked things over and put out ideas. "Suppose you were handlin' this, what would you do?"

She didn't hesitate. "I wouldn't make a move until I found out who the woman was who telephoned you. Why she was giving you all that money. What were her interests in starting the investigation."

I nodded. "Yeah," I said, "that's a swell idea, but not easy. Just a voice on the telephone… wants some finding."

She glanced at her watch and gave a little exclamation. "I must go," she said, stubbing out the cigarette and gathering her gloves and bag. "Thank you for the lunch."

I pushed back the chair and followed her. "You haven't paid the check," she said softly.

I grinned. "Not in this burg," I said, waving to the Greek. He beat me to the door and held it open.

"I hope," he said, bowing in half, "you will bring the beautiful lady again."

Mardi flushed, but I could see she was mighty pleased. I nodded. "You'll be seein' her again," I promised.

I called a taxi. She turned to me. "I hope you won't come back to the office," she said quickly. "I hope you won't do anything silly until you've thought about things. Find out who that woman is first."

With a quick smile she climbed into the taxi, and I stood there and let her go.

From across the street, Earl Katz suddenly stepped from a doorway. He looked across at me, tossed a cigarette butt in my direction, and then walked slowly in the same direction as Mardi's taxi had gone.

CHAPTER FIVE

I didn't get off to the Hotcha Club until late. After Mardi had left me, and Katz had made his unexpected appearance, I had a wander round and had a little brain exercise. It didn't get me anywhere, but I did think maybe I'd wait a little while before exposing my hand to Spencer. Having a living to earn, I attended a ball game, went home and wrote it up, mailed it to a sports paper that took my stuff, and went out to dinner.

By the time I got through it was getting on for ten o'clock. It was a hot night, with stars and a big moon. I thought I'd go along and see if I could have a look at Vessi's moll.

The Hotcha Club was one of those swell dives that look good but are pretty rank when you examine them close. I got a table in a corner, ordered a big rye high-ball, and passed the time with a newspaper.

The place was pretty crowded, and the dames were not all they should be. I sat around for a half an hour, but as I didn't see anyone who really got me interested. I began to wonder what the hell I was doing there.

Finally, I gave the waiter the high sign that brought him over. He was a tall, miserable-looking guy with big, watery eyes and a blue chin.

I took a fin from my vest-pocket and began to play with it. His eyes fixed on it with interest.

"Listen, Buddy," I said, "I'm looking for a dame who comes in here pretty often. Maybe you can tell me where I can find her."

With his eyes still fixed on the note, he said, "Sure… who is she?"

"She's called Blondie," I said, "an' she works a beat somewhere around."

An oily smile settled on his face. I could see this was a pushover for him. "Sure," he said, "I know her all right. She's been in. I guess she's workin' right now."

I pushed the fin over to him and he gathered it up mighty quick. "Where do I find her?" I asked.

"Corner of 10th."

I got to my feet. "Thanks, pal," I said.

He shrugged. "She's a great dame," he said, collecting my glass.

I paused. "So I've heard," I said. "This is my first trip. Shall I find her easily?"

"Sure," he said, "you'll find her. A tall dame in black." He grinned a little. "Blondie's tough when she likes to be."

I went out into the street. A tall dame in black. A feeling of excitement surged through me. I wouldn't let my mind think for the moment. I'd wait and see this dame for myself.

The corner of 10th was deserted when I arrived. The whole street was in semi-gloom. The street lights were widely spaced and none of the shops carried lights. I thought it was a pretty poor place to find trade, but maybe she knew her job better than I did.

I stood on the corner and lit a cigarette. I stood there for five minutes. I knew it was five minutes because I was so fidgety that I kept my eyes constantly on my watch.

Then, just when I was losing patience, she came out of the gloom. I heard the slow click of wooden heels some time before I saw her and I stiffened, throwing my cigarette into the gutter. Dimly I could see her, moving deliberately towards me, a tall, shadowy figure in black.

I half-turned towards her, so that she could have no mistake as to my intentions. I watched the white blur that was her face eagerly for the first glimpse of her features.

She saw me waiting there, and her step slowed. One hand went to her hip, and she put on a slight sway as she dawdled towards me.

When she was close, I smelt her. The same heady scent that I had smelt in my bedroom. I felt grimly elated; so this was the dame who'd lifted five grand off me.

"Hello," she said, stopping at my elbow. She was nearly as tall as I was, and her big black hat screened her face. I could just make out her rather pointed chin and the sparkle in her eyes.

I said, "Hello, good-lookin', how's tricks?"

She gave that throaty, purring laugh that Mae West had made popular. "Are you coming home with me, darlin'?" she said, putting one gloved hand on my sleeve.

I grinned to myself. You bet I was going home with this floozie, and she was going to get a hell of a surprise when we got there.

"Sure," I said, "I've been lookin' for a baby like you all the evenin'."

"Have you, darlin'?" She laughed again. I wish she'd lay off the 'darlin'' for a bit. I told myself she'd be calling me something different mighty soon.

I said, "Let's go...."

"It's just here," she said, waving her hand towards the end of the street.

We walked down the street, and she was the first dame I'd walked out with who kept in step. I said, for something to say, "That perfume you wear sure knocks me."

"You like it, darlin'?"

There she went again. "Yeah," I said. "It sortta hangs around, doesn't it? I bet you leave quite a trail wherever you go."

She missed a step and her right foot went with my left. I changed, to get it right. "What a funny boy you are, darlin'," she said, looking at me quickly from under her hat.

"Yeah," I said, "crazy as a bug."

She stopped outside a door next to a small all-night eating-house. Dimly I could see a little brass plate screwed on to the door. I struck a match and read, 'Andrée Kersh'.

"My, my," I said, "so you put your name on the door."

"Of course, darlin'." She fumbled with her bag and found a key. "When you come again, I want you to find me easily."

I thought this dame was mighty good at kidding herself. The next time I called on her, she'd greet me with a flat-iron.

I followed her up a short flight of stairs, past the lobby of the eating-house, up some more stairs, past two doors, also with brass plates, and up some more stairs still.

She came to a small landing and again opened a door. "Here we are, darlin'," she said.

I stepped into the room. One of those small joints. You open the front door and step into a double bed. The room was all bed.

I wedged myself round her and got to the far end of the room. The bed divided us. I had to admit she'd taken a lot of trouble in fixing the room. It had a lot of neat little gadgets, and some of the pictures she'd got hanging on the wall even made me take a look.

I said, "You've got a swell apartment here, ain't you?"

She pulled off her hat and fluffed up her blonde hair. We took a look at each other. I'll give her this. She hadn't the usual hard, gimme face of the streetwalker. She would have been quite a looker if her chin wasn't so pointed. That rather hardened her face, but for the rough work she was all right. If I hadn't been sitting with Mardi for an hour, I guess this floozie would have interested me more than somewhat.

I tossed my hat on a peg and grinned at her. She had given me one long, searching glance, summed me up, and her smile back was full of things to come.

"You like it, huh?" she said.

That's another thing I love. When a dame says 'huh.'

At the head of the bed, and on each side, were two doors. She said, "I won't be a minute," and before I could stop her she went through one of the doors.

I sat on the bed and lit a cigarette. Somewhere in this joint was my five grand, unless she'd pushed it into a safe deposit. If she'd done that I was sunk, but, knowing how these floozies like to keep their dough right by their hand, I reckoned that I wasn't going to be disappointed.

She came in again wearing a come-hither smile.

I wish I'd started my tricks before she got going, but it was too late now.

She came over and sat on the bed. "May I have my present, darlin'?" she said.

This is where it was going to be tricky. I shook my head. "You got it all wrong, baby," I said, "I'm charging you for this outing."

I said she hadn't the usual hard, gimme face of the streetwalker. Well, I was wrong. I was crazy to have thought otherwise. Away went the bright smile and the flashing eye, just like they were blotted out with a sponge. Her face suddenly became set, "What you mean?" she said, her voice suddenly taking on a harsh note. This dame was looking tough.

I flicked the ash off my cigarette. "Just that," I said, slowly, putting myself in a position so that I could get up quick if she started anything. Something told me that she was likely to start something. "Maybe we better get introduced, baby," I went on. "I'm Nick Mason."

Just for a second she gave herself away, but then she came back again. "You aren't tight, darlin'?" she asked. She had pulled a pillow from the bed and was holding it against her.

I said, "Suppose we come down to earth. We might start by leaving out the darlings… they give me a pain."

She got to her feet and walked over to the door.

"You crazy or something?" she said. "You get out of here."

"Don't get tough," I said, still sitting on the bed. "This morning you came to my apartment and took five grand off me. You hand that back an' we'll call it quits."

She put on a good act. Her eyes opened wide and she actually managed a laugh. "You're crazy!" she said. "I've never seen you and I don't know where you live."

I got slowly to my feet. "Listen, baby," I said gently, "you ain't goin' to get anywhere with bluff. I've got you where I want you, an' I'm having that dough if I have to take this joint to pieces to get it. You ain't goin' to get tough, because I could twist your neck for you with one hand. Now come on an' be nice."

She stood hesitating, then she shrugged. "If that's the way you feel about it," she said, "maybe I'd better let you have it."

I almost laughed. I let her get to the small chest of drawers and pull open one of the drawers, before I shot over the bed and smothered her. My arms went round her, pinning her arms to her side, and I jerked her away from the chest. I was glad I'd taken the precaution. I had just time to see a gun lying in the top drawer before she came at me.

I'd been in some nasty corners during my career as a journalist, and I'd been in plenty of rough houses as well, but this was the first time I'd mixed it with a woman, and I should just like to place it on record that I sincerely hope it will be the last.

I can look after myself when it comes to an all-in scrap with a man. I know most of the dodges they get up to and I know most of the answers, but when a blonde fury comes at you I was up-creek without a paddle.

I see now that I could have saved myself a hell of a lot of trouble if I'd socked her on the button and finished it there and then, but I was crazy enough to treat her light.

She came at me with her arms whirring around like the blade of a propeller and her eyes blazing. I tried to grab her arms, but got nowhere. The weight of her body struck me like a small shell, and I went over with her.

Hands clawing at my throat, she must have weighed around a hundred and forty pounds, and that's no joke to have dropped on you from above.

I managed to grab her wrists, and, by exerting a lot of beef, held her. Get the picture if you can. There I was, lying flat on my back, wedged between the wall and the bed, with Blondie, her wrists held, looking down as if she'd start murder any minute.

I said with a gasp, "Relax, sister, this ain't the way for a lady to behave."

For an answer the hell-cat butted me in the face with her head. Maybe she did have blonde curls, but her head was as hard as concrete. She must have knocked herself a bit silly, but it was nothing to what she did to my mug. I felt the blood start from my nose and I thought my front teeth were coming through my top lip.

I got as mad as a coon, and, shifting my grip on one of her wrists, I socked her as hard as I could. If you've ever tried to hit anyone, lying on your back, and wedged tight, you will know how difficult it is, but I managed to get a little steam through, sufficiently hard to send her backwards.

That just gave me time to struggle into a sitting position and sock her again as she came at me. This time I gave her a good one, but I hit her on the shoulder, so although it got rid of her it didn't stop her.

I was on my feet by the time she had got over that thump, and we stood there glaring at each other.

"Don't start anything, Mason," a voice said by the door. I looked quickly over my shoulder.

Earl Katz was standing in the doorway. He was holding a blue-nose automatic in his hand, and the barrel was pointing right at me.

CHAPTER SIX

Surprised? I'll say I was surprised! You could have knocked me down with a mangle. What the hell was Katz doing here? What connection had he with Vessi's moll?

I wasn't going to show him that he had pulled a quick one on me. I gave him a smile. "Still pushin' them into pockets, Bud?" I said. "An' talkin' about pool, did you hear the one about...."

"Skip it, Mason," Katz said out of the side of his mouth. That's another thing I love. These guys who've been to so many tough movies that they just have to talk out of the side of their mouths, because they think it's the thing to do.

I sat on the bed. I said: "Suppose you put the gun away and take it easy. This is a private matter between Blondie and me... it don't call for any outside interference."

Katz said: "You talk too much. Keep your trap shut. I'll do the talking an' you just answer... get it?"

I shrugged.

"What are you doin' here?" he asked.

I grinned. "That's an easy one," I said. "What the hell would any man be doin' here?"

Katz pushed his hat at the back of his head and leant against the wall. He put a finger and thumb in his vest-pocket and took out a toothpick. He put the toothpick in his mouth and chewed it thoughtfully.

"If you don't like to talk straight," he said, "it's goin' to be tough for you."

I said: "Be your age, Katz. You can't get that way with me. I could make this town so hot for you that you'd have to take a powder quick."

Katz shifted the toothpick. "You're all washed up," he said. "You ain't nothin'. Suppose you get wise an' talk? What are you doin' here?"

I shrugged. "I guess I'll be on my way," I said, getting to my feet.

Katz said: "Sit down." There was a threat in his voice.

"We won't get anywhere," I said. "I'm goin'."

Katz shifted a little, so that his back was against the door. "Don't start anythin'," he said. "I ain't ready to plug you yet, but don't rush me."

I said: "You better get out of the way." I was getting mad with this gunman. I guessed he'd think twice about letting the gun off. After all, we were on a main street, and guns can make a noise.

Maybe Katz gave Blondie a signal, or maybe she acted on her own initiative. I had been keeping my eyes on the gun, making up my mind whether I could jump Katz or not, and for a moment she was out of the picture. Well, I deserved what came to me, because I had had a taste of her before.

Something hard and heavy hit me on the side of my head, and I went down on my knees. The room tilted and the lights began to spin.

Dimly I heard Katz say: "Don't hit him again… I wantta talk to this bird."

Someone grabbed my arms and twisted them behind me and a hard, cold strap bit into my wrists. I felt myself tossed on the bed. My head cleared and I struggled to sit up, but a hand, out of the mists, closed over my face and slammed me back on the pillow. I lay still until I could focus the lights properly, then I raised my head cautiously and looked at them. They stood at the end of the bed, watching me.

Blondie had her arms crossed over her breasts. Her face was indifferent, but her eyes smouldered. Katz chewed the toothpick and held the automatic loosely.

Without taking his eyes off me, he said to Blondie: "What's it all about?"

"He's crazy. He came up here an' said I'd taken five grand off him."

Katz shrugged. "Well, didn't you?" he said. He moved round the bed and sat down close to me. "Listen, punk," he went on, "I'm goin' to tell you somethin'… then you're goin' to tell me somethin'. We've got your jack all right. Blondie lifted it, like you thought she did…."

Blondie made a move forward. "What the hell…." she began.

Katz turned his head, "Shut up," he said. "I'm handlin' this. I want this guy to know where he gets off."

He turned his head back to me. "We've been watchin' you for some time. You went to Vessi's bump-off, didn't you?"

I said: "What of it?" It struck me that if this guy talked enough, I might learn something.

"We're interested to find who sent you… get this right, we don't care about you… we just want to find who's paying you; get it?"

I looked at Blondie. I was getting a little of the angle. "I thought you were Vessi's side-kick," I said. "I see I'm wrong. Vessi was framed, an' you know it. This guy's no pal of Vessi's… what the hell are you playin' ball with him for?"

Blondie said viciously: "You lay off that. Who sent you that five grand… that's what you gotta tell us."

I shook my head. "I can't tell you that… I don't know myself. I just got a note offerin' me five grand to bust the frame-up open, an' I was interested. I went along to see Vessi die…. I didn't learn anythin', and the five grand turned up to encourage me, an' you knocked it off. That's the history as far as I'm concerned."

I was careful not to tell them I had my instructions by 'phone, because I didn't want to give them a lead that it was a woman. I reckoned I'd given them just enough information without telling them more than they knew.

Katz scratched his jaw with his thumbnail. "That all?" he said.

I nodded.

Blondie said suddenly: "What the hell's the matter with you, Earl? Why don't you rough this guy around. You won't get anywhere talkin' soft to him."

Do you get the idea now? This dame was real poison ivy. I said quickly: "What more do you want me to say? I can't tell you somethin' I don't know."

Katz still sat there scratching his chin with his thumbnail. He kept his eyes fixed on my face, and I don't mind telling you that I didn't like the look in his eye. This guy was as tough as Blondie, only in a different way. He wasn't all wind. When he started something, you'd know about it all right.

He said at last: "Okay, I guess you can beat it. You better keep clear of this place. You won't find that five grand, an' you'd better not go to the cops about it… get it?"

Blondie pushed forward. "You're crazy," she said. "Look what this heel's done to me. You ain't lettin' him get away with that?"

A sudden flash jumped into Katz's eyes. He looked mean. "Listen, Roundheels," he said, "You lay off. I'm handlin' this… so shut your trap."

Blondie stepped away, shrugged, and walked into the bathroom. Katz watched her go and then turned back to me. "She's mad with you," he said, chasing holes in his teeth with the pick. "I'd watch my step with her. Once she gets mad with a guy, she stays mad."

Katz leant against the chest of drawers. He still held the automatic limply at his side. "Take my tip, bozo," he said, looking at me from under his hat, "you lay off this Vessi business… it ain't healthy. We don't want to get a guy like you into trouble. We know all about you. You ain't bad. The boys think you're an all-right guy. Okay, that suits me, but stay an all-right guy."

I raised my head and shot him a look. "Meanin'?"

"Just forget about Vessi, an' go on with your pen-pushin'. Forget about everythin' an' forget you ever seen me or Blondie."

"Suppose I don't; what happens then?"

"Well, things happen, you know. The guys who run this show are big guys. They could make a smear of you if they wanted to. They could run you outta town. They could turn on the heat. Yeah, I guess plenty would happen."

I scratched my head. "You sure got this thing worked out," I said. "I guess I'd better think it over." I got to my feet and hunted around for my hat. I found it lying by the door. Someone had trodden on it. I stood there working it into shape. "You better kiss Blondie good night for me… I don't think I could trust myself to do it."

Katz compressed his lips. He didn't seem to think much of my humour. "Sure," he said, "I'll tell her you've gone."

I opened the door and took a step on to the landing. "I guess I'll see you some time," I said, and pulled the door to.

I wanted a drink badly. My nose was feeling like hell, and my right eye was beginning to close. I thought a stiff drink might set me up.

When I got into the street I walked rapidly to the end of the block, hailed a taxi and directed him to a bar near my apartment.

I was glad the bar was empty. The barman gave me a long look, but he didn't say anything. After the second bourbon I began to feel better. I had a third and took that one more slowly.

My mouth was feeling sore, but I lit a cigarette and held it in my lips without much trouble. Fighting dames was going to be struck off my list of hobbies.

Although I hadn't got my five grand, I had learnt a lot. It looked to me that Vessi had been properly double-crossed. If his girl friend had joined the other side, he'd had a raw deal all round. It was over Blondie that the shooting was supposed to have happened. Maybe they had given her enough dough to fix the trial. I would have a look into this angle. Then I paused. Or should I? This guy Katz was dangerous, and I was bucking a big outfit. Was it worth going on? What had I got out of it up to now? I felt my nose and eye thoughtfully.

Unless I found out something good that would blow the lid off this business quickly, I was going to run into trouble. I ordered a fourth bourbon. Suppose I left it alone? Okay, I'd still be right where I was, and maybe I'd be a lot better off.

With the bourbon inside me, I decided definitely to go home and forget all about it. Then I suddenly thought of Mardi. When I thought of her, I felt good. Now that was my idea of a swell girl. She'd got everything. I told myself that to-morrow I'd take her out to lunch. I could do with a lot of her company.

I didn't take long to get to my apartment. As I let myself in the telephone began to whirr. I hesitated before answering it. The bourbon had made me feel fine, and I didn't want any more trouble for tonight. Anyway, I answered it.

"Nick Mason?"

It was that dame again. I sat on the edge of the table. "Yeah," I said.

"I sent you—"

"I know," I broke in. "I've had a swell time since you sent me that five grand. You don't know what you've been leadin' me into, baby. First Vessi's old moll steals the five grand. Then I go round and see her an' we have a hell of a scrap, that's nearly ruined me. Then Katz, Spencer's gunman, turns up and points a rod at me, and tells me to lay off or else...."

I grinned a little at the sudden silence at the end of the 'phone. I guessed that had certainly given her something to hold.

"An' what is more, baby, I'm through... I ain't interested any more, so forget all about it, will you?"

"So you are not interested any more?" Her voice was very cold.

"You've got it right the very first time," I said.

There was a short pause, then she said: "But you will be, Mr. Mason... believe me, you will be very interested before long," and she hung up.

Just like that.

CHAPTER SEVEN

The first thing I did when I woke was to inspect the damage Blondie had done to me. I looked like hell. My nose was about twice its usual size and my right eye was closed. I looked like I'd been pushing Joe Louis around.

I went back to bed, plenty mad. With a wrecked pan like this I had to wash out taking Mardi to lunch. I couldn't expect to put my stuff across, looking the ruin I was.

I lit a cigarette and thought over my troubles. If Mardi and me were married it wouldn't matter a hoot how many black eyes I had. In fact, she would be running around fixing me up and fussing me. As soon as that thought filtered through my brain I sat up with a jerk. I was crazy. Me, getting married. That was a laugh. Me, the guy who ribbed the boys who got hooked. Taking one dame on for the rest of my days was one mistake I'd promised myself never to make. And here I was, lying in bed, pondering how nice it would be.

I got out of bed and grabbed myself a drink. I told myself I'd better take some exercise or something; I was losing my grip.

I'd just finished my shower and rinsed off the shaving-soap when the front-door bell whirred violently. Slipping on my dressing-gown, I opened up.

Ackie was standing there, his eyes glittering with suppressed excitement. "H'yah," he said, pushing his way in. His eye spotted the half-pint standing on the mantelpiece and he went straight across and sunk half of it.

"Finish it up," I said dryly from the door, "don't mind me."

Ackie shook his head and put the bottle back. "Never drink in the mornin'," he said. "Pity… that ain't bad liquor."

I said: "Come into the bedroom while I finish dressing."

He followed me in and sat on the edge of the bed.

"What's the excitement?" I asked, pulling on my shirt.

"I gotta job—" He broke off and gaped at me. "Hi!" he exclaimed, his eyes popping, "what the hell's matter with your face?"

I shrugged. "Got into a little scrap last night," I said carelessly. Tell Ackie that a dame had done this? Not a chance! The boys would rib me to death.

Ackie still stared. "Huh," he said, "gettin' tough, eh?"

"You should have seen the other guys," I said, knotting my tie carefully in the mirror. "Three great hoodlums set on me—"

"I know… I know…." Ackie grinned. "And you beat hell out of 'em all. Yeah! You don't have to tell me."

"I ain't goin' to waste time tellin' you anythin' if you ain't goin' to believe it," I said.

"Okay, then don't, 'cos I won't."

I shoved my legs into my trousers. "Gettin' back to the point. What's the excitement?"

Ackie stiffened up, as if he suddenly remembered an urgent job. "Yeah," he said, "I got somethin' for you. How'd you like to pick up a hundred bucks?"

I put on my coat and fixed my hair. Ackie giving away a hundred bucks was someone I didn't know. "Doin' what?"

"You know Colonel Kennedy?"

I turned my head and looked hard at Ackie, but his face was blank. "You don't have to ask that; you know I do."

"Pretty thick with him, ain't you?"

"Come on, come on." I stood over him. "What is this? What's Kennedy got to do with it?"

"Listen, Nick, we're in a jam. We gotta see this guy, an' we gotta talk to him."

This sounded screwy to me. I sat on the table. "Why come an' see me?"

Ackie fidgeted. "Well, this guy's being difficult, see? He won't see anyone. We reckoned you could talk to him."

My instinct told me that there was a story hanging to this. A story that might be big. Colonel Kennedy was one of those rich playboys with so much dough that he never found time to finish counting it. The kind of guy who gives away a couple of million and doesn't have his bank manager running round in circles.

Some time ago I helped this guy out of a jam. He was running in a yachting race with a nickel cup hanging to it. He could have bought up the whole cup factory if he'd wanted to, but no, he had to go out in a rough sea and try and win it. Just before the gun went, his crew broke his arm. There was Kennedy hopping mad because he thought the cup was escaping him. Well, I was around and I offered to help him out. Somehow or other we got home first, and that guy was tickled to death.

Doing Kennedy a favour meant something. For the first month I was nearly smothered with the things he used to send me. After four weeks of it I couldn't stand any more, so I changed my apartment and got under cover. Now here was Ackie asking me to go through it all over again.

"You'd better tell me the whole story," I said. "I ain't movin' without it."

Ackie groaned. "Listen, Bud," he said earnestly, "this has gotta be done quick. Suppose you come with me an' let me tell you as we go."

"Go? Where?"

"The Colonel's up at his fishing-place. You know where that is."

I knew Kennedy had a retreat in the hills where he used to go when he wanted to get away from people. It was sixty or seventy miles out of town. I'd never been there, but I'd heard a lot about it. I was too much the newspaper man to waste time talking, so I grabbed my hat and what was left of the half-pint and went downstairs with Ackie. He'd got a big Packard outside, with two of the boys sitting in front. One of them nursed a camera complete with flashlight on his lap. They grinned at me as I got into the back with Ackie.

The way that Packard shot away from the curb was nobody's business.

I lit a cigarette and settled down in the corner. There was plenty of room in the car and the springs were swell. "You do yourself well," I said, bouncing a little to test the springs.

"Official car," Ackie said. "This is somethin' big, Nick. The old man himself told me to get you."

"Suppose you let me have it," I said.

Ackie looked worried. "I don't know what the hell it's about," he said. "As far as we know, a servant at the lodge 'phoned the police around twelve o'clock this morning and reported hearing a shot fired downstairs in the front room. She was too scared to go down an' investigate. Well, the cops went out there and spent a little while inside. I guess we'd never have heard of the business only one of our boys was at the desk when the call came through. He tipped the night editor, who thought it big enough to send someone up.

"Well, they sent Hackenschmidt and he gets nowhere. He 'phones for help and a wagon-load of boys go up. I guess they know Kennedy and hoped for free drinks all round, but Kennedy doesn't show up. We ring him up and he answers the telephone, but as soon as we start askin' questions he hangs up quick. The old man gets mad because Kennedy's news, an' he sends for me. I waste an hour tryin' to get in, but don't get to the first base. The old man then says for me to get you… quick."

I rubbed my nose thoughtfully. "What do the cops say?"

Ackie shrugged. "Kennedy's slipped 'em plenty. They say the maid was screwy an' nothin' has happened."

I laughed. "You'd look mighty sick if it were true," I said.

Ackie shook his head. "There's somethin' phoney goin' on, an' whatever it is is news. So you're bein' paid a hundred bucks to get in an' find out just what."

A hundred bucks! That was a laugh! If I got in there and there was something hanging to this, it was going to cost the *Globe* a lot more than a hundred bucks.

I said: "Maybe I shan't get in."

Ackie's eyes opened wide. "You gotta get in," he said, "the old man's ravin' mad now. You just gotta get in."

I love a situation like that. A big newspaper begging you to do something. That always means dough, and lots of it.

"Okay," I said, taking the Scotch out of my pocket. Ackie fixed his eyes on it. I didn't leave him much.

We did that trip under a hundred and fifty minutes. I was glad when they pulled the car to a standstill. Driving like that without any breakfast didn't do me any good.

Kennedy had got a swell place, make no mistake about that. The lodge was hidden from the main road by a big belt of giant trees. The surrounding country was wild and woody. Not far from the lodge a swift river about a hundred yards wide flowed strongly, twisting through the woods like a snake.

It was the sort of place I would have bought myself if I had the dough. The sort of place Mardi and me would be happy in. Even with a big story breaking I kept linking myself with that girl.

We piled out of the car and began to walk up the narrow, wooded path that led to the lodge. We hadn't gone far before we heard voices.

Ackie grinned a little. "The boys've camped out here," he said.

He was right. We turned the sharp bend in the path and suddenly came upon the lodge and the boys. There must have been eight or nine of them hanging round the lodge, watching the windows, smoking and talking.

When they saw us they came towards us hurriedly.

Barry Hughson greeted me with an ironic cheer. "Jeeze," he said, "you here again!"

Ackie scowled at him. "The old man sent out an S.O.S. You watch your step… this guy's a big shot."

Hughson started to say something, but stopped. Maybe he thought it would be wise to quit ribbing me.

"We ain't seen a sign of anyone," he said. "We got the place surrounded, and we've tried getting in, but short of smashin' a window we don't stand a chance."

"You nuts?" I demanded. "This is goin' to make the Colonel as sore as hell. What do you think you're playin' at?"

Hughson shrugged. "We got to get the dope," he said. "The cops won't spill it… there's somethin' goin' on inside there, an' our public want to know."

We all had a laugh at that.

"Listen, Nick," Ackie said quickly. "Suppose you have a shot at it. You get in there an' find out what it's all about… then, if you can, persuade the Colonel to let the boys in… tell him he's news. We gotta see him!"

If I could get in I should certainly line up with Kennedy. I had no sympathy with headline hunters. I was always on the look-out for a good story, but this way of getting it didn't appeal to me.

"Call your dogs off," I said to Hughson. "I shan't get in unless you boys are out of sight."

They were so eager to get that story they'd've jumped into the river if I'd told them to.

When they had all got under cover, away from the lodge, I walked up to the front door. I took a slip of paper out of my notebook and scribbled on it: *"Maybe I can help you out of this. Nick Mason."* I rang the bell and shoved the letter through the box.

I stood there waiting. I waited so long that I thought I wasn't going to pull it off. Then I thought maybe Kennedy was thinking it was phoney, so I stood away from the lodge so he could see me.

That worked it. He came to the door himself. I expected to find him plenty mad. I knew he'd got a hell of a temper once he got going.

"Come in, quick," he said, holding the door ajar.

I stepped into the hall and he shut and bolted the door behind me.

"Am I glad to see you," he said, wringing my hand. "Where the blazes have you been all this time?"

I grinned at him. "Suppose we skip that for a moment, Colonel," I said. "Seems like you've got yourself in a bit of a jam."

"Jam?" He certainly looked worried sick. "I'm sitting on dynamite. Listen, Mason, are you going to help me out again?"

"Sure," I said. "That's why I've come out here."

"Come in and have a drink," he said, leading the way into a long, low room, with a big, empty fireplace at one end. I looked round admiringly.

"You certainly've got a swell joint here," I said.

He was busy fixing the Scotch. "How did you hear about this?" he asked.

"The *Globe* knew that we had been sort of friendly, and they thought maybe I could get in and find out what the trouble was about," I said, taking the glass from his hand. "They figured that you would talk to me."

Just for a second he stared at me, then he grinned. "So you came out to fool them?"

I nodded. "Sure, I came out to fool them."

The Scotch went down very well indeed.

He sat down in a big armchair and ran his hand through his hair. He was a distinguished-looking guy, with a big, fleshy face and good eyes. I should think he was getting on for fifty, but he was tough and as hard as teak. He pointed to another chair. "Sit down, Mason, and tell me how you're going to get me out of this."

I sat on the table so I could look down on him. "I guess you gotta start talkin' first," I said. "I gotta find out just how things are. All I know is a shot was reported and the cops came up. After a little while they came out, told the boys there was nothing to it, and beat it. If the cops were satisfied, I guess there ain't anythin' to get worried about. You ain't just bein' cussed, are you, Colonel?"

Kennedy took a long pull at his glass. "It's worse than anything like that," he said. "It's a woman."

I hid a little grin. The Colonel was a good guy, but he'd got a way of making dames fall for him. He didn't do much to encourage them. He just sat around and smiled, and along they'd come.

"Huh, huh," I said. I wasn't going to commit myself.

He finished up the Scotch, fidgeted with the glass, and scowled out of the window at the boys sitting on the grass about two hundred yards away. I didn't hurry him.

"You know how it is," he began, still looking out of the window.

"Sure," I said to encourage him.

"I was crazy to have anything to do with this woman," he said. "She's got big connections. There'll be a devil of a scandal if anything leaks out, and she can't afford that, nor can I."

I took his glass and mine and filled them up. The vices of the upper crust always interested me. I'd got enough inferior complexes for rich folk to think they always did their vices so much better than I did mine. I guess it was just a complex, because I've thought about it a great deal, and I never really could think how they did it better than I, but that was maybe because I hadn't enough imagination.

"I've got to get her out of this place, and I don't know how the blazes I'm going to do it."

I nearly spilt the liquor. "You mean she's still here?" I said.

He twisted his head and looked at me. "Of course she is," he said, showing a little of his old temper. "Why do you think I'm sitting here, letting those fellows make a monkey out of me?"

"Okay, Colonel," I said. I didn't get it. "The jam is getting the lady away without the boys seein' her; that it?"

Kennedy nodded. "Do you think you could do it?" he asked.

I thought about it, then I said: "Yeah, I guess it would work out all right. The boys want to see you. At the moment they don't think there's a dame in here. Right, what you gotta do is to see them, and while you're holding them with talk I'll get the dame out through the back door."

Kennedy sat there thinking. I could see he didn't quite like the idea. I could guess why. "You ain't got to worry about me, Colonel," I went on. "I don't make capital out of friends of mine."

He looked up hastily. "No—I wasn't thinking of that. I… well, I guess, even you can't know who she is… she wouldn't stand for it."

I said: "Between you an' me I guess this dame's a little difficult, eh?"

Kennedy nodded. "She's crazy," he said. "Damn it, she pulled a gun on me last night."

I stared at him. "Then there was some shootin' goin' on?" I said.

He hesitated. "Yes," he said at last. "There was a misunderstanding.

She's got a quick temper and the gun went off."

I couldn't help it. I laughed. It struck me as mighty funny. "Wouldn't she fall for your stuff, Colonel?" I said.

For a moment I thought he was going to get mad, then he grinned ruefully. "For Pete's sake keep this quiet," he implored me. "But I guess that's about it."

I slid off the table. "Suppose you go an' explain things to her. I reckon we gotta hurry, the boys out there are getting restless."

He got to his feet, looking worried. "I hope she'll listen to reason," he said. He stood there like a schoolboy screwing up his courage to go inside for a belting. Then he walked out of the room.

I let him go, and when I was sure he had gone upstairs I gumshoed to the foot of the stairs and flapped my ears.

I heard his voice. He was putting the problem forward in a low voice. I could just catch a word here and there, but nothing more. There was a moment's silence, then a woman spoke. She just said: "Very well, if you think it is safe," but it was not what she said that made me stiffen. It was the voice. I'd know that voice anywhere. The cold, hard, metallic ring in it.

Colonel Kennedy's girl friend was the woman who had called me up twice on the telephone. The woman who had sent me five thousand bucks.

I said, "Well, well," to myself and walked slowly back to the big room.

CHAPTER EIGHT

Kennedy came down again after five minutes or so. He went to the window and looked out, then he turned round to me. "I've talked to her," he said uneasily. "She wants you to get the car ready and have it drawn up outside. Then she's going to make her getaway by herself."

This didn't suit me. I was looking forward to a long drive with this dame. "What happens to the car?"

A little frown settled on Kennedy's face. "You don't have to worry about that," he said. "I just want you to do that… nothing more. Will you do it?" There was a touch of the soldier in his voice.

I said: "Sure… anything you say."

He looked relieved. "You go and call these fellows in. Once they're in, you go round to the back and get the car out. Then come back here."

I told myself I was at least going to have a peep at this dame. "Okay. Shall I start now?"

"Just wait a minute." He went out into the hall. I heard him call up the stairs. "Come down now."

It wasn't possible for me to go to the door and watch because he would have seen me, and I certainly was burnt up to stand there and let that dame get away with it.

I heard someone run down the stairs quickly and walk with clicking heels down the passage. Then Kennedy came back. He nodded to me. "Fetch 'em in," he said.

I walked to the front door and flung it open.

The boys came running. They looked like the Klondyke gold rush.

"The Colonel will see you now," I said. "Take your hats off, wipe your feet, an' for Gawd's sake behave like gentlemen."

They crowded past me and barged into the big room. I certainly handed it to Kennedy. He stood at the end of the room, looking at them coldly, not a muscle of his face moving. As soon as the last one had piled himself into the room I quietly shut the door.

I ran down the passage, keeping my eyes open, but I didn't see a sign of her. There were a couple of doors on each side, and she might have been behind either of them, but I couldn't very well look and see.

At the far end of the corridor was a door leading to the back of the grounds. I opened it and looked out cautiously. There was no one about. I hadn't put it past Ackie to leave one of the boys snooping outside. Maybe they didn't think I'd pull it off, and the surprise put it out of their heads.

I ran over to the garage and pulled open the doors. There were two cars. I chose the small one. It didn't take me a moment to run it out facing the exit. Then, leaving the motor running, I hurried back to the lodge.

As I came down the passage, Ackie stepped out of the big room. He was looking suspicious.

"What the hell are you doin'?" he asked.

I kept on coming at him. If that guy could read my thoughts he'd have curled up and busted right away.

"I just had a look outside to see if any of the boys were left out of the prayer meetin'," I said.

Ackie said, "Oh yeah?" and made to step past me.

I put out an arm and collared him. "Come on, Mo," I said. "I wantta hear what the Colonel's sayin'."

Ackie stiffened, but he couldn't break my hold.

He said furiously: "You're double-crossin' me!"

I grinned down at him and walked him away from the back door towards the big room. "I got you into here to see the Colonel," I said.

"Well, you're goin' to see the Colonel… that's all."

I heard a door shut behind me. If Ackie hadn't barged in I'd have seen her. I loved Ackie a lot right them. He tried to turn but I still held him tight. I shifted my grip a little and suddenly put on some pressure. He gave a squawk.

"You're breakin' my arm," he howled.

I said evenly: "I'd like to break your neck."

Faintly I heard the door of the car slam and the sudden sound of a car accelerating. Ackie opened his mouth to yell, but I clapped my hand over it.

"Shut up!" I said sharply. "You start anythin' an' I'll smash you."

I waited out in the hall until I was sure she'd got away, then I released him.

He stood glaring at me furiously. "What a pal," he spluttered. "Think you're gettin' that hundred? What a laugh."

"Now listen, Mo," I said quietly, "there is more in this than meets the eye… you're right. But it ain't the sort of news you can print. If I'd let you go ahead just now your rag would be up to its ears in a libel suit. A libel suit with Kennedy on the wrong side would put your crowd out of business. If you're a good boy and keep your trap shut, I'll give you the inside dope…. It ain't to be printed, though."

Ackie could never stay mad for long. He scowled at me, then his face cleared. "I might have known it," he grumbled. "Of all the double-crossin' punks, you are the biggest. All right, I'll keep it quiet. Now what's it all about?"

I lowered my voice. "Seems like the Colonel got too ambitious. You know what he is with dames. Well, this one wasn't playin', an' what's more she outs with an equalizer an' starts poppin'. This dame is one of the upper crust. Even I don't know who she is. I agreed with Kennedy to smuggle her out while you boys were talkin'."

Ackie brooded. "No one got hurt?" he asked bitterly.

I shook my head.

"Hell! There ain't a story at all. Everyone knows about Kennedy an' his women. That ain't news. Pity she didn't drill him. Boy! That would have been a front-page splash!"

I looked at him with distaste. "Ain't you a nice guy?" I said. "But now you know. You can see it wasn't worth the fuss."

Ackie glanced at his watch. "I guess I'm beatin' it," he said. "Maybe I was a little hasty about the hundred bucks. I'll see you get it."

I grinned. "Suppose we split it?" I said. "Send me fifty an' I'll receipt the hundred."

Ackie nodded. He looked quite happy again. "You ain't such a bad punk," he said. "Maybe you'll play straight one of these days, an' then I'll quite like you."

The other boys began to crowd out of the room. They looked at us curiously, but Ackie didn't let on. He took them off to the waiting cars.

"You wantta come?" he asked over his shoulder.

I said, "Sure… I ain't got any reason to walk."

Kennedy appeared at the doorway. "No," he said. "You stay. I want to talk to you."

I was glad. I liked this guy, and I was getting mighty hungry. As soon as the last car had driven off, Kennedy came back from the porch and shut the front door. He grinned at me. "Well, that was a nice bit of work," he said approvingly. "You sure pulled me out of a jam. It seems that I'm continually getting into your debt."

I said hastily, "Forget it, will you? That sort of talk gives me the itch."

He laughed. "I haven't seen you for so long, I guess we got plenty to catch up on. You're going to stay with me for a few days. What do you say?"

I hesitated, but he shook his head. "You're staying, Mason, so make up your mind."

I grinned. "It's okay with me," I said.

He glanced at the clock. "Suppose we have some lunch and then I can telephone for my man to pick up some of your things and bring them out here. He's got to bring some of mine, so he may as well make himself useful."

Lunch was ready by the time we had had a wash and a drink. It was laid out in the suntrap outside: a small verandah, screened by glass, overlooking the river. We sat down to a swell meal.

"You got a grand spot here," I said, helping myself to lobster salad.

Kennedy nodded. "It is very convenient," he said, with a faint smile. "I don't see people for weeks here. Just the place for relaxation."

I looked at him quickly. "I've got another name for it," I said with a grin.

He laughed. "You don't look as if you've had much relaxation," he said. "What have you been doing with your face?"

That put me in a fix. I wasn't sure how far he might be involved in this business. I said carelessly, "Oh, I got into a scrap last night."

We finished our meal and sat there in the sun with a nice cigar and some old brandy, and talked. I said casually, after we had been talking some time, "I'm thinkin' of buyin' some stock. Can you advise me?"

He began to go through a list of names that didn't mean much to me.

"What about Mackenzie Fabrics?" I shot out.

He looked startled. "That's funny," he said, "I've just been getting rid of some of those myself."

"What's so funny about it?" I asked, keeping my voice casual.

He shook his head. "Oh, nothing," he said shortly, and changed the subject.

I wondered if the dame who'd just gone had anything to do with this. I didn't like to risk asking him outright who she was. These guys, once they've been through the army, have got ideas about mentioning names of women who they've compromised. He might have turned tough, so I shelved it for the moment.

After we had settled our lunch, we went out and had a look at the grounds. The more I saw of the place the more I liked it.

He'd got everything. Even a bathing-pool, cut in the rocks in the thickest part of the wood, and fed by the rushing water of the river.

We spent the next four days fishing, swimming, and lazing about. He and I hit it off together pretty well. The food was good and there was plenty to drink and I'll say this, it was one of the nicest holidays I've spent. There was nothing that guy didn't know about fishing, and with his help I found I wasn't doing too badly myself. We'd go out after breakfast with rods and long waders, and walk slowly into the shallow, fast-moving river and fish. It was a grand way of spending the day.

One evening we were sitting on the verandah in the moonlight, finishing a cigar before turning in. The night was still and hot and we were both pleasantly tired. I was thinking that it was time I got back and did some work, when he looked up suddenly. "You know, Mason, a guy like you ought to marry and settle down. You'd make more money that way."

Six months ago a crack like that would have made me laugh, but now I pondered before answering him. "Yeah," I said at last, "I guess there's somethin' in that."

He was silent for a little while, then he went on, "When you find the girl, I'm going to give you this place."

Didn't I tell you this guy smothered me? I sat up sharply. "You be careful what you're saying," I said, "I might take you seriously."

He smiled a little. "I reckon it would be a bit heavy for you to carry, anyway," he said. "There's a hell of a lot of upkeep that goes with it. But this I will promise you. When you get married, you can use this place as often as you like. I'm getting out pretty soon. I want to go to China. Maybe I'll be away a number of years. So when you're fixed up, let me know."

I said it was mighty white of him and we let the matter drop. All the same, I kept thinking of Mardi, and I kept thinking what a surprise it would be for her to come here for our honeymoon. I kept thinking about it until I got restless. I told myself that I'd been there too long. My eye and nose were back to normal and I was anxious to get away.

The following morning I broke the news to him. He just grinned. "I believe you've got a girl, after all," he said.

I nodded. "You're right. It's just a matter of fixing things up." Although I spoke like that, I was wondering how long it would take to get Mardi on the dotted line. Maybe I would come unstuck. Anyway, it was worth a try.

I got back to town the next afternoon. And I rang up the Mackenzie Fabrics right away. "I want to speak to Miss Mardi Jackson," I said to the operator.

"Hold on a minute," she snapped. I heard a faint flopping as she jerked out the plug and connected it somewhere else. Then she came back over the line again. "Miss Jackson no longer works here," she said, and cut off.

I put the telephone down very thoughtfully. So Mardi wasn't working any more for the Mackenzie Fabrics. Why? Had she walked out on them, or had they given her the bird? How long had she been gone? I suddenly felt annoyed with myself for staying with Kennedy so long. If I'd phoned her on the day Ackie took me out, I might have caught her.

Now where was I going to find her? I hopefully checked the telephone-book, but she wasn't in that. Maybe she stayed with her people or in a boarding-house. There were about a thousand Jacksons to choose from.

I suddenly remembered that on the day we had first met, Katz had seen us together. Did that mean anything? Had Katz scrammed back to Spencer and told him that I had contacted her? Was that why she no longer worked there? I remembered Ackie saying that Katz was as dangerous as a rattlesnake, and I began to get a little hot and bothered. Did Mardi know anything? Had they got her out of the way? It was no use sitting around asking myself dumb questions. I'd got to find out.

I grabbed my hat and left my apartment at a run. A taxi took me to the Hoffman Building quickly. I paid him off and checked the time. It would be one o'clock in ten minutes or so. I went into the nearby drug-store and bought myself a drink. The guy behind the counter looked like he might have some brains. After I had finished the Scotch I ordered another.

"I'm lookin' for a dame," I said confidentially to this guy, as he put the glass on the counter.

"Ain't we all?" he said, putting his elbows on handles of the soda jerker and resting himself.

I said, "You're right. Maybe you can help me."

He looked interested. "Sure," he said. "Anythin' I can do."

"I'm looking for a dame who works at the Mackenzie Fabrics. I've just heard that she's been fired out an' I want to know where she's gone."

He looked sort of dreamy. "They've got some swell dames workin' in that joint," he said wistfully. "They're high steppers. I can't get to the first base with any of 'em."

"Do they come in here to eat?" I asked.

"Sure. The rush starts right now."

I took a five-dollar bill from my vest-pocket and pushed it across to him. "Suppose you let me know when one of them comes in. If I could get her talkin' maybe I could learn where this dame's gone to."

He grabbed the fin. "I'll do that okay," he said. "You just sit around."

A little after one o'clock the place began to fill up. Almost immediately he jerked his head at me. A tall, blonde doll was just settling herself on a stool, preparing to put on the nosebag. She'd got a friendly look about her, and I thought I'd get places with her if I handled her in the right way.

I let her settle down, then I left my place and took the stool next to hers. She was against the wall, so we were more or less isolated from the others.

She glanced at me and then went on packing a club sandwich away. The guy behind the counter came over and gave me one, too. He winked at me, and then took himself off to deal with a rush at the far end of his beat.

I said cautiously, "You'll pardon me, but I guess you could tell me something about Miss Jackson."

She jerked round like a virgin at bay. Her eyes popped a little and I thought she was going to get tough. "What did you say?" she asked.

"I'm looking for Miss Mardi Jackson," I explained, putting on my best manners. "I was told you work for the Mackenzie Fabrics, and I thought maybe you could tell me."

The startled expression died out of her eyes, and she swung herself round on the stool so that she faced me. "Are you a friend of hers?" she asked.

I took a chance. "I'm her boy friend," I said.

"Really? Now isn't that a scream?" she exclaimed. "You know, I always knew Mardi was deep… I told the other girls…. Not that they didn't think so themselves… you know how it is, don't you? A girl like Mardi ought to have a boy friend… it's only natural, isn't it? She never said anything about having one… she kept to herself a lot… don't think we didn't like her… we did. We were all struck in a heap when she left.

I blinked. "Listen, lady," I broke in. "Maybe you can tell me what happened? I've been away for a few days, an' I've got some news to catch up on."

"Why, surely." She was ready to give me the whole set-up. I could see that. The trouble was that when a dame like this once got started, it was difficult to stop her. Anyway, I told myself, I'd got the whole day, so I should worry.

"You go right ahead an' tell me all about it," I said, lighting a cigarette and giving her one.

Her eyes grew big again. "Well, I don't know if I ought… but you being her boy friend… well, it's different, isn't it? I mean to say… I wouldn't tell anyone… what I mean is I don't go talking about people to anyone…. Well, I guess you can read character… you can tell that, can't you?"

I said, "Sure. Don't you worry about that."

"Well, Mardi came back from lunch about a week ago… she seemed all up in the air… sort of dreamy… and the girls thought she'd been out with her beau or something… then Lu calls her in… Lu is Mr. Spencer, the big shot of our firm… but I expect you'd know that… well, Mardi goes in and she stays inside for some time then I heard Lu getting mad… he gets awful mad sometimes… he shouts and bangs around no end… well, I thought Mardi was getting into trouble, so I listened outside the door…. I don't do that ever, really… you see, Mardi was a friend of mine… I just thought I'd be there in case Lu got really mad… but he shouted so much I couldn't hear what he said. Mardi said, 'I'm sorry, Mr. Spencer, but it's really my own business who I lunch with,' and that made Lu crazy as a bug… by that time some of the other girls had come and were listening… Lu says it's okay with him… but Mardi could pack up and get out… so she comes out quietly… you know how like a lady she behaves… and away she goes. Lu comes out and stands in the doorway and watches her go… we don't have a chance to say good-bye… that's all I can tell you."

I said, "Haven't you heard from her since?"

She shook her head. "No… I just can't make it out. We've all been waiting to hear from her… but not a word."

"Do you know where she lives?" I asked.

She wasn't as dumb as I thought she was. Her eyes suddenly hardened. "Hey!" she said. "You her boy friend, and you don't know where she lives?"

I saw I'd got to tread carefully here. I took her over the ground gently. "That may sound phoney to you," I said, "but I've only been running around with her for a day or so. You see, I'm crazy about her, but I don't know how she feels about me. I want to go on with this, but I've got to find her first."

"Isn't that too marvellous?" She looked almost coy. "Well, I'll help… I think a girl needs a man… don't you? Look, I'll write down her address."

I gave her a pencil and my notebook. She scribbled down an address on the west side of the town, and I put the notebook carefully back in my pocket.

I slid off the stool. "I'm goin' right away," I said. "You've been a swell help. I'll ask you to the wedding."

I left her at the run, with her mouth open to start all over again. I guess that dame enjoyed her lunch-hour. It certainly had given her something to talk about. And could she talk?

CHAPTER NINE

All this didn't get me anywhere. When I got to the address the blonde had given me, Mardi wasn't there. She had left about two days ago, the landlady told me, taken her bags and left no address. Was I pleased?

I returned to my apartment, feeling sore. The only thing I did know was that Mardi had left her job because of me. That told me that Spencer thought she knew something and wasn't risking anything. If what she knew was important, maybe he'd hidden her away. Against that, the landlady had told me that she had come by herself to pack her bags and didn't seem very worried. She did say that she had to go out of town on business, and didn't know when she would return. This was probably an excuse to satisfy the landlady, or was it?

I sat on the table and brooded about it. I wondered if I should find her again by proceeding in the investigation of the Vessi frame-up. While I was thinking about it the telephone rang.

The hard, clear metallic voice floated over the wire. "Nick Mason?"

I didn't beat about the bush with this baby. "Yeah," I said. "Been shootin' any more colonels?"

I couldn't help grinning a little. I seemed to be always slipping a nasty one in with this dame.

She said, "You know about that?"

"Sure," I said. "I was the guy that got you out of the jam. I recognized your voice."

There was a moment's silence, then she said, "You are looking for Mardi Jackson. I told you last time that you would be interested before long. You see, I am not wrong. Mardi Jackson knows too much. I don't think you will see her again. All the same, you might have a look at the Wensdy Wharf tonight at nine o'clock. You might see something there that will interest you further."

"Why the hell must you be so mysterious...." I began, but the line went dead. If I ever caught up with this dame, I thought savagely, slamming the telephone back on the table, I'd give her something to be mysterious about.

All the same, I was alarmed. She had confirmed my suspicions. Mardi did know something. I didn't like that crack about not seeing her again. I wandered round the room restlessly. Who was this woman? Why was she so anxious to get me started on this business? Kennedy knew who she was. I guessed that my next step would be to go along and have a straight talk with him. If I put my cards on the table, maybe he would open up.

In the meantime, I decided to check the morgue, just in case Mardi was there, unidentified.

I was mighty glad to get the job over. I didn't find Mardi. There were a good number of young girls lying on the slabs waiting for someone to claim them, and by the time I got through I was feeling low.

I had a chat with the morgue attendant before going. Casually I asked him if he knew anything about Wensdy Wharf. To my surprise he knew quite a lot about it. His brother used to work close by the place.

"A real tough spot," he told me. "No one uses it now. They go farther up river to Hudson's Wharf. You will find all the river rats around Wensdy. Mike... that's my brother... used to say that Wensdy Wharf was used for smuggling. I guess it's cleaned up a bit since then. All the same, it's a tough spot."

I got directions from him how to get there, gave him a couple of bucks, and beat it.

The rest of the day I spent sorting out my correspondence and seeing some of the boys. Things were quiet, and there were no big news stories coming in.

Around about eight o'clock I took my battered Ford and drove over to the *Globe* buildings. I went in and found Hughson just preparing to leave.

"H'yah," he said. "I never really thanked you for fixing Kennedy for us. It was grand work."

I waved aside his thanks. "Know anythin' about Lu Spencer?" I asked.

Hughson shrugged. "I should forget it," he said. "That Vessi business is buried. You won't get anywhere digging around that mud-heap."

I shook my head. "No… I wasn't lookin' at that angle," I told him. "I just wanted to find out the type of guy he was. A girl friend of mine used to work for him and she's disappeared. I wondered if he'd got anything to do with it."

Hughson shook his head. "Spencer ain't that sort of a guy. He's got a wife an' he's crazy about her. He wouldn't go two-timin' with one of his workers. Of course, I may be wrong, but I don't think so."

I offered him a Camel. "Spencer's a pretty tough bird, ain't he?" I asked.

Hughson shrugged. "Yeah, I suppose he is. He's smart and he makes dough. Don't you worry your brains about Spencer."

We went downstairs together and I drove him part-way home. I left him at a convenient subway and drove on towards Wensdy Wharf.

So Spencer was married. I told myself that I'd got to meet this guy soon. I must find Mardi first and hear her story. Then I could go along and talk to Spencer. It seemed I was getting involved in this business, whether I wanted to or not.

Wensdy Wharf was at the far end of the east side of the town. There were some pretty tough quarters to go through to get there. I had to drive carefully, as the roads were narrow and people walked carelessly.

I parked the car at a small garage when I got close to the wharf.

The morgue attendant was right. This place was mighty tough. The streets were narrow and the dark houses seemed to lean forward so that the roofs blotted out the sky above. The pavements were wet and slippery, covered with all sorts of smelly refuse.

The garage hand had told me where I should find Wensdy Wharf. He looked at me as if he thought I was crazy. Maybe I was, but that wasn't going to stop me.

I walked fast. The river mist was coming up slowly, and I could hear the deep note of a distant siren. Soon I left the shops behind and I seemed to be quite close to the river. Turning a corner, I came on Wensdy Wharf. At the far end, I could see the oily water reflecting the light of a solitary street lamp.

On each side of the wharf tall, straggling houses loomed out of the darkness. Yellow chinks of light gleamed from the windows, coming round the ill-fitting blinds. I suddenly felt cold. The mist was damp, and there was a chilly wind coming off the river.

"Well," I thought, "here I am." Wensdy Wharf didn't appeal to me a lot.

I wandered to the edge of the water and looked out across the dark river. But for an occasional tug, with its storm lantern, I could see nothing. I glanced at my watch. It was just after eight-forty-five.

She had said Wensdy Wharf, but that was all. The place was built in a three-sided square with the river for the fourth side. It was easy to watch. I selected a pile of old rope in a dark corner and sat down.

From this point I could keep an eye on the whole of the wharf, and at the same time I was out of sight and in comparative shelter from the wind.

This was not altogether a grand way of spending the evening, but if I was going to find Mardi I wasn't complaining. I was afraid to smoke, and I wanted a drink bad. After ten minutes of this I began to get sore. I thought up a few fancy names to call that dame on the telephone. I'd just like to meet her once. It would only have to be once.

When my watch had told me I'd been there for over thirty minutes, I began to get restless. I got up and paced up and down in the deepest shadows, getting the stiffness out of my bones. Nine-fifteen and nothing had happened. Maybe this dame was taking me for a ride.

Then suddenly things started. I saw the flickering light from a car coming slowly round the corner. Quickly I ducked back behind the coil of rope and knelt down, peering, like they do in the movies, over the top. A big, closed car was nosing itself into the square. The headlights lit up the darkness and blinded me. I kept down until the light swung away from me, then when my corner was once more in darkness I quietly stood up.

The car came to a halt outside one of the houses. This house was in complete darkness. Unlike the others, it showed no lighted windows whatsoever.

I moved cautiously towards it. As I did so two of its doors swung open. A short, thickset man, well muffled up, got out from under the steering-wheel and went to the other door. He leant forward, his head and shoulders disappearing into the car. Then he withdrew himself.

I stiffened. He was holding something. His back was turned, and for the moment I couldn't see what was going on. Then he stepped back and someone else clambered out. They lurched across the pavement. They were carrying someone wrapped up in a coat. Instinctively I knew it was a woman, and it didn't take me a second to surmise that it was Mardi. I was just going to jump forward when two other guys bundled out of the car. This pulled me up quick. It was no use me running into trouble I couldn't handle. Maybe I'd get tossed into the river, and that wasn't going to help Mardi.

They all disappeared into the house, and I heard the door slam to. I stood there waiting. After a few minutes the thickset guy came out, got into the car, and drove away as silently as he had come. Well, anyway, I told myself, that only left three.

I walked softly to the house and glanced up. A light was now shining from a window on the second floor. Even as I saw it a blind was hastily drawn down, blotting the light out.

I knew which room they had put her in, which was something. I suddenly wished I'd got a gun. The almost eerie feeling from the wharf and the nearness of the river were giving me the heebies. I put out my hand and gently tried the front door. It was locked all right.

I decided to go round the back and see what that looked like. There was a narrow passage running by the side of the house and I went down there cautiously. I had brought a pencil torch with me, and I switched it on as soon as I was hidden from the street. The bright little spot-light lit up the evil-smelling passage. At the end was a rotten wooden fence. I stretched up and looked over. It gave me quite a shock. The back of the house looked on to the river.

It didn't take long for a guy with my brains to figure that one out. If they wanted to get rid of Mardi, all they had to do was to kill her and toss her out of the window.

What I had to do was to get into that house quick. If it did mean a little trouble and maybe a little damage, right at this moment Mardi was in a worse fix than anything that could happen to me.

I found a window on the ground floor, and by shining my torch through the glass I could just make out a small, unfurnished room. This would do to get into the house. With the aid of my knife, I jacked up the window. It was stiff, but it went up without any noise. I swung my leg over the sill and stepped into the room. Then I shut the window. You try busting into a dark house with three toughs upstairs, in a vicinity like this, and see how you like it. I didn't. My nerves were jumpy, and my throat was dry as hell.

I gumshoed over to the door and turned the handle. The door came to me as I pulled on it gently. It creaked a little, but not badly. Outside was dark, and I stood listening. I couldn't hear a thing. Cautiously I edged out into a passage, flicked on my torch to get my bearings, and shut the door behind me. On my right was a narrow staircase.

I started up, testing each step before putting my whole weight on it. It was as well I did. Some of those stairs were mighty rotten and they creaked like hell.

I was half-way up when I heard a door open on the next landing, and a sudden flood of light lit up the staircase. Someone came out and shut the door. Once more the staircase went black. Footsteps began to shuffle to the head of the stairs. I stood against the wall. If this guy put on a light, I was sunk. Down he came. I could hear his hand sliding on the banister rail. I squeezed myself farther into the wall. He went past me. I felt the tail of his coat brush past my knees. I let him get one stair down, then I swivelled round quick and kicked out hard with my right foot.

It was a nice kick. At that range it would have staggered an elephant. I felt my toecap sink into something hard, heard a strangled gasp and then a fearful crash. I didn't wait a second, but flashing on my torch I tore up the stairs, three at a time.

As soon as I reached the next landing I turned off the lamp and stood against the wall. Before I did so I caught a glimpse of a door near the head of the staircase. Just as I got away from it, the door jerked open. A thin guy with a black hat crushed on his head stepped on to the landing.

"Hey, Joe," he called, peering down over the banisters. "What the hell you playin' at?"

When a guy leans over a rail like that, there is only one thing to do. I did it. Moving fast, I hooked my fingers under his trouser legs and heaved. Although he was thin he was heavy, but I'd put enough steam into my heave to launch him okay. Away he went with a startled howl.

After that I didn't get anywhere. A hoarse voice said behind me, "Hold the pose… exactly like that."

I had visions of a gun covering my back, but for all that I turned my head. The gun was there all right. The guy who was holding it looked mean. He was short and fat with close-cropped white hair. By the way he held the gun, I could see he knew how to use it.

"Okay," I said quickly, "I'll be good."

"Come away from there, lug," he said. He'd got a very hoarse voice, as if his larynx had gone back on him. "Keep your hands up an' don't start any funny business."

While this was going on a lot of noise was coming from downstairs. I've heard bad words in my time, but what came floating up from the darkness was enough to set the river on fire.

The fat guy said, "Stand with your mug against the wall. I'll drill you if you make a wrong move. Don't let me tell you twice."

I did as I was told. It struck me that maybe I was in for a bad time. My only hope was that I'd put those other two out of action.

"You hurt, Gus?" the fat guy croaked, not taking his eyes off me.

"Come on up… I've got the punk here."

The only reply to this was another flow of blasphemy. That guy down there certainly knew all the bad words. The fat guy was in a spot. He didn't like to detach himself from me, but at the same time I guess he was itching to get down there and find out if the other two were badly hurt. There was only one obvious thing for him to do, and it didn't take him long to work it out for himself.

Although I was expecting it, I didn't expect a guy of his size to move so quickly. I managed to get my head rolling, but I didn't get started fast enough. The butt of his gun bounced on my head, and I slipped off the rim of the world.

CHAPTER TEN

Faintly, in some bottomless pit, I could hear a woman screaming. I didn't care much, until the screams got louder, then I wished she would stop.

I opened my eyes and looked round. The flickering light of a candle that seemed to be floating above my head worried me, and I shut my eyes again. The woman who had been screaming had stopped. I thought that was a good thing. I tried to move my hands, but I found I was unable to do so. I began to take an interest in myself.

I opened my eyes again. Then I remembered. It was like having a pail of water tossed in my face. I tried to sit up, but they'd tied me. My head ached, but every second it was getting clearer. I always did say my skull was tough.

I was lying on the floor with my hands knotted behind my back with some thin twine that cut into my wrists. It hurt like hell.

Above me a solitary candle burnt. It was stuck on the mantel-shelf, and its light sent dancing shadows round the room.

Cautiously I pulled myself up into a sitting position. The blood drummed in my head and I had to shut my eyes and take it easy for a bit. Then I got on to my knees and climbed to my feet. They hadn't tied my legs. I took a few steps up and down the room, to get my circulation working. In a minute or two, but for a headache, I was feeling fine.

Just then the door opened and the tall, thin guy walked in. He came in with a little limp, and he stood just inside the door and looked at me.

"H'yah, Gus," I said, "I thought you'd broken your neck."

In the flickering light Gus would scare most people. He'd got a completely flat face with small eyes and a little screwed-up mouth. The bones of his face seemed to be doing their best to burst through his lead-coloured skin. The bridge of his nose had been surgically removed.

He came into the room and shut the door. He shut the door very slowly and deliberately. I had a feeling that he and I were not going to hit it off.

He said, "I've got a way with wise guys." His voice had the whine of a run-down gramophone. "You won't be so snotty when I've been through you."

I moved slowly away from him. "Now don't do anythin' your ma wouldn't like to hear about," I said. "Suppose you an' I talk things over."

I was putting a lot of pressure on that twine, but it was so thin that it threatened to cut right through my wrists.

He followed me right across the room, until my back came against the wall with a little jar. I could just make out a little grin on his face as he swung at me.

I timed the blow and shifted my head. His fist sailed past, scraping my ear. His left followed that, but I twisted and took it on my shoulder. For a thin, miserable-looking guy, he'd got plenty of steam in his punches. I knew I wasn't going to keep this up for long.

Along came his right again, moving like a steam pile for the centre of my face. I bent my knee and dropped my head on to my chest. His fist parted my hair. Then I came up quickly, and dug my knee in his stomach. Can you tie that? This punk let me give him one like that.

He made a row like a deflated tyre and went over backwards. I wasn't going to sit around and nurse him. Stepping back, I took careful aim and kicked him on the side of his head as hard as I could. Over he went, his arms flung wide. That kick was a good one. He stayed right where he was.

I stood over him to hand him some more, but he was past caring about me. When I was sure he was out for keeps, I pulled my hands under me and stepped through my wrists, bringing my hands in front of me, instead of at the back. I examined the twine carefully. I looked at the candle and decided to have a try. I burnt myself once or twice, but I got free. The twine snapped after the third application to the flame. I rubbed the life back into my wrists and scratched the back of my head.

On the face of it, it looked like I'd only got the fat guy to worry about. I knelt beside Gus and went through his pockets. I should have felt a lot easier if I could have turned up a gun. But I didn't find one.

Having made sure, I stood up and walked softly to the door. I reckoned that I could take the fat guy on if I surprised him. I found I still had my torch. Moving softly, I slid out into the passage. I stood there listening. If I'd got my bearings right, Mardi should be behind the door on the far end of the passage. I walked quietly down and listened.

Just as I had my head almost touching the door, a sudden wild scream made me jerk back.

I almost burst in, but stopped myself in time. The idea was to get the fat guy to come out to me. I raised my hand and rapped on the door sharply. Then I stepped away to the head of the stairs and flattened myself against the wall. The passage had a sharp bend, so I was fairly under cover.

There was a moment's silence, then a light appeared. I crouched down to afford as small a target as possible, and prepared for trouble.

Nothing happened. I went lower still and moved a little to the bend. I wasn't risking anything, so I just stretched my ears. I could hear the fat guy wheezing. He, too, must have been listening, and wondering what it was all about. "Gus?" he croaked. "That you, Gus?" He sounded like he was scared.

I let the silence worry him. He came out into the passage and stood just outside the door. The light was behind him. By keeping close to the wall and peering round the bend, I could just see him; at the same time I was out of his sight.

He raised his voice. "Gus," he shouted, "I want you."

I very softly tapped on the ground with the butt of my torch. I made just enough noise for him to think he'd heard something, but not enough for him to be sure. I could see him cock his head, then with a grunt he moved towards me. I waited for him patiently, my muscles tense. Just when I was sure I'd get him, he stopped and stepped back. Maybe his good angel had tapped him on his shoulder. He went back into the room quick and shut the door.

Was I pleased! I couldn't afford to wait any longer. I told myself I had to go on in there and chance getting into trouble.

Just as I was getting set, I heard the sound of a bell ringing somewhere in the house. That stopped me. I beat it down the passage quick to the room where I had left Gus. He was still lying on his back, dreaming sweet dreams.

The bell rang again impatiently. This was serious. If more of the boys were arriving, it looked like I was in for a siege. I stood by the door, listening. The fat guy finally made up his mind to make the trip. I heard him open his door and step into the passage. I could see the flicker of a torch coming slowly along.

Would he look in and see if all was well here? If he did, I should have to start something. If he didn't and went downstairs, it might give me enough time to get in that front room and see what was going on in there.

While I was thinking this out, he decided things for me. I saw the handle of the door suddenly move, and I knew he was going to have a look. I had no time to clear Gus out of the way. He lay in full view in the light of the candle. I stepped hastily behind the door and waited. The door opened softly and the fat guy put his head round. It would have been funny if I hadn't been in such a jam. He just stuck his head round the door and his eyes lighted on Gus.

I didn't give him a chance to get set. I flung my weight on the panel of the door, crushing his head. He looked like a side-show. His eyes popped and they rolled round until they lit on me.

"Relax, brother," I said, and hit him on his chin with a nice round-house swing that had everything I'd got packed into it. The punch connected on his button with a crisp click. The jar of the blow ran right up my arm and I lost most of the skin off my knuckles. His eyes went blank and I slackened my weight on the door; down he went like a stricken elephant.

I jerked the door open and stepped over him. The bell rang again furiously, and someone began to drum on the door. I ran my hands over him and found his gun. It was a .45 Smith & Wesson. A nice argument in any rough-house.

Boy! Did that gun feel good in my hand!

The hammering and ringing off stage packed up suddenly. That meant they were nervous of waking up the neighbourhood and were going to get in through a window. I didn't kid myself that they would go home.

I dived out into the passage and burst into the other room. Now I was expecting to find Mardi there. I already had visions of being quite the hero in her eyes. I went so far as to imagine that she would sink into my arms, so it set me back a long way when I saw Blondie sitting there.

Blondie? Can you tie that? There she was, tied hand and foot to a chair. Her eyes were brooding sudden death and her general expression like a tigress about to start something. I stopped in my tracks. "Well, for the love of Mike!" I said.

She was as startled as I was. "Get me out of here," she said hoarsely.

It was when she spoke that I saw she had been having a bad time.

I went behind her and sawed through the twine with my knife. "This gets me," I told her as I worked. "I've been knocking guys all over the house an' riskin' my skin because I thought I was helping a girl friend of mine… now I find it's you."

She didn't say anything, but the way her breath whistled through her nose told me she was plenty mad.

I had to move quickly. I just didn't know how long those guys downstairs would be before they walked in on us. As soon as I had got rid of the twine, I jumped to the door.

"Get a little life into your limbs," I said to her as I went. "We gotta get out of here quick."

I gumshoed to the head of the stairs and looked over. There were two guys coming up. They must have heard me, because they snapped out their light quickly. I swung the .45 and fired one shot, making sure that I didn't hit them.

The way those two fell downstairs to get out of the way made me laugh. I shouted down to them, "Don't come up. I want to be alone."

Then I beetled back to Blondie very quietly. She was standing up rubbing her wrists. Her mouth was set in a thin line. That dame didn't look scared, she was just mad.

"Next floor," I said briefly. "As quiet as you like."

She took a few hobbling steps forward and then she stopped. She began to curse. I hastily grabbed her arm. "Pipe down," I said. "What's up? Are you hurt?"

She tried to move forward again, but stopped once more. Her big white teeth chewed her lip. "I can't make it," she said jerkily.

I didn't bother to argue, time was pressing. I gave her the fireman's hoist and started up the other flight of stairs. Carrying a dame of Blondie's build up thirty stairs is hard labour. Along with the feeling that some guy is going to open up with a popgun and perforate your pants it's plain hell. By the time I got on to the next landing, I was sweating hard.

Once I got up there, I used my lamp. The landing was similar to the downstairs one. The same number of doors. I entered the back room and dumped Blondie down on the floor. "Try an' snap out of it," I said. "We ain't home yet."

I went out on to the landing again, leaving her the lamp. Then I leant over the rail and fired a shot down into the darkness. I thought maybe those guys down there wanted a little scare. I got one myself. A gun exploded out of the darkness and I felt the wind of the bullet close to my face. I jerked back, then shifting my position I fired once more, this time straight down the stairs.

Two guns replied, and if I hadn't been lying flat on my face I should have stopped something. These guys knew too much about shooting to please me. I crawled into the room and shut the door softly.

Maybe they wouldn't try to rush the place for a little while. I wasn't sure how many slugs I'd got left, and I thought I'd better save what I'd got.

Picking up the torch, I examined the room. The first thing the spot-light fell on was a heavy cupboard. I went across and pulled it from the wall.

Blondie climbed to her feet and moved over to me. Although her face was twisted, I'll say she was game.

"Take it easy," I said to her. "I can manage this… you nurse yourself."

Her reply was unprintable. That's the advantage of meeting up with a dame like Blondie. You don't have to worry about your manners. She and I got the cupboard across the room and against the door. It would hold it for a little while.

I went to the window and looked out. Below was the black river. I could just make out the oily reflection from the overcast moon. It looked a hell of a way down.

I turned back. "Can you swim, sister?" I asked.

"Yeah," she said, "but I ain't swimming in these clothes."

That's a woman!

I lit a cigarette. "Unless the cops move in… it looks like you'll have to," I said. "These guys outside mean business."

She came over to the window and, brushing past me, she looked out. I could smell her scent. She turned round and looked at me. "It's a long way down," she said. There was just a faint quaver in her voice.

I told myself that whatever else she was, she'd got plenty of guts. "Don't you worry about that," I said. "You just push yourself off… it ain't any-thin'. I'll be right behind you. I guess you don't want to face up to the slugs instead, do you?"

She pulled a zip on her dress and stepped out of it. Then she kicked off her shoes. Blondie was the sort of dame that always wears black undies. I could just make out the faint white of her shoulders and that was all.

Three violent reports sounded outside the door and I heard the bullets smack against the wall opposite. Then someone began to heave against the panels. It was time we got going.

"Come on, baby, it's cooler outside," I said. "Sit on the sill and hang your legs outside."

She climbed up and I held her until she was steady, then she sat down, her legs in space. With my hands on each side of her hips, I felt a little shiver run through her. "Keep your nut," I said softly in her ear. "I'll be right after you. Just take a deep breath… off you go."

I shoved her off the sill and leant out to watch her go. Down she went into the darkness and I heard a loud splash. Then I vaulted after her.

Was that water cold? I seemed to go down for hours. Then just when I thought maybe I'd go on for ever, my head broke the surface. I shook the water out of my eyes and looked around for Blondie. I couldn't see her for several seconds, but then at last I made out a bobbing head several yards to my right.

I turned on my side and swam over to her fast.

"H'yah, baby," I said. "You all right?"

"Some guy's goin' to pay for this," she said furiously, "you see if he don't."

I had a little grin to myself in the darkness. This dame's temper couldn't be put out even with water.

"Suppose we go home?" I said, swimming along at her side. "I guess we've done enough for one night."

Together we swam quietly to the lights on the waterfront.

CHAPTER ELEVEN

It was tricky work smuggling Blondie into my apartment. If she didn't mind getting herself talked about, I did.

We certainly had all the luck. After swimming around for a little while, we made the waterfront. A docker nearly had a fit when we climbed up the side of the wharf right at his feet. Once he'd got over the shock of seeing Blondie in her wet undies, he extended a helping hand. He took us along to his place and fitted us out with a couple of worn-out suits. We both looked tramps, but we didn't give a damn.

The docker seemed quite content to accept a phoney story I'd made up for his consumption, and when I promised him twenty dollars if he got us a taxi, he couldn't do enough for us. That was how we got home.

Right now, Blondie was lying in the bath soaking her bruises, and I was crouched over the fire with a glass of Scotch in my hand.

I wasn't too keen having Blondie here. She just wouldn't go back to her apartment. There was nothing else to do but to bring her here. I wanted to get her story, and although she didn't say more than three or four words in the taxi… and they were bad ones, I had hopes of getting something out of her.

"When you've finished," I bawled out to her, "you might remember I'm waiting."

"All right," she called back. "Come and give me a towel and I'll come out."

I said, "You can get it yourself. Remember I'm modest, if you ain't."

She didn't say anything to that, but I heard her climb out of the bath, and after some time she came out wrapped in my woollen dressing-gown. Her eyes were still stormy and her mouth was set in a sullen line. She jerked her head towards the bathroom, and poured herself out three fingers of Scotch.

I went into the bathroom and had a quick one. The hot water did a lot to restore me, and when I came out again I was feeling fine.

Blondie was crouched over the fire. A cigarette dangled from her lips and the Scotch was way down in the bottle.

I sat down close to her and lit a cigarette. We remained like that for several moments. Then I said, "Maybe you'd like to tell me what happened."

She twisted round so that she faced me. This dame was tough all right. I guess the street knocks hell out of these women. They've learnt to have no feelings, and to be on the look-out for a double-cross at every step. It is the one weapon they have to protect themselves.

Looking down at her hard face, I could see no redeeming expression. She was a swell looker, but that didn't get a dame far. If you'd got eyes like granite and a mouth like a trap, I guess the rest of your looks can't even that lot up.

"Listen," she said evenly. "You pulled me out of a jam, but you did it because of someone else and not because of me. You an' me have had a little trouble before. I guess we don't mean anythin' to each other. Well, if you're extending sympathy, you can stick it on the wall. I can manage okay without you handing out any grease; get all that?"

Talking with a dame like her was like playing 'handies' with a rattlesnake. There was only one way to talk to a dame who gets like that, so I handed out some of her own stuff.

"I'm not handing you any grease, sister," I said, "I haven't any grease to pass on to your type. I save it for those who can appreciate it. I want to know your story. I've got myself mixed up in this business, and I guess, as I pulled you out of a jam, I'm entitled to know something about it. So come off your high horse, cut out the dramatics, and shoot."

She turned back to the fire. "I ain't talkin'," she said.

I got up.

"Okay," I said. "Beat it… go on… get the hell out of here… blow!"

She stood up. Her face startled and her eyes wide.

"If you ain't outside quick, I'll call the cops an' hand you over. You can guess what the charge'll be… an' I'll make it stick."

She saw she hadn't a leg to stand on. Her sullen face cleared and she laughed. She could look mighty nice when she laughed. "Okay, darlin'," she said, "I'll be good."

"You see how it is," I said, moving back to the fire, "I've got you where it's crisp."

She poured herself out another Scotch. This dame certainly liked her liquor. "Yes, darlin'," she said, all honey. "You're the boss."

"While we're on the subject," I went on, "I reckon I've told you before. That 'darlin'' of yours gives me a pain. You ain't on business now."

She came over and put her arms round my neck. "I could be," she said, digging down into her box of tricks and putting on a swell act.

It only made me nervous. I got rid of her arms none too gently and pushed her into the chair. "Relax," I said. "I wantta catch up some sleep some time. It's gettin' late."

For a moment she looked as if she was goin' to get mad again, then she thought better of it.

"Now what's the story behind all this?" I asked.

She shrugged. "I guess Earl's a little tired of having me around. This is the sort of hint that guy hands out when he wants you to take a powder."

Not quite right. One of those difficult answers, half-truth and half-lie. If I was going to get anywhere with this dame, I'd got to lead her along carefully.

"Those three thugs work for Katz?"

She nodded. "That's right."

"What did they want to know?"

She glanced at me quickly. Once again her lips smiled, but her eyes were suspicious. "They didn't want to know anythin', darlin'," she said.

"Yeah? Then why did they beat you up?"

The memory of that made her face darken, "I've told you… that's the way he gives out he's tired of you."

I shrugged. I certainly wasn't getting anywhere on these lines. "What do you know about Spencer?"

She looked blank. "Never heard of him."

If she and Ananias got swopping stories, I'd know who I'd have my money on.

"Ever heard of a girl called Mardi Jackson?"

Again she shook her head. I gave up. She was too tough to get wild with. She would only laugh at me.

"Okay, sister," I said, getting to my feet. "I can see you an' I ain't goin' places. Maybe one day you'll think better of it an' give it me straight. I'm hoping it won't be too late for you. Suppose you tell me your plans. I can't keep you here, you know."

She said, "I'm leaving this town to-morrow. I want you to go along to my apartment, put some things together for me, and bring them back here. Then I'm off."

For nerve, this dame was the tops. I was too tired to argue.

"Anythin' you say," I grunted. "You'll be comfortable either in here on the couch or in my bed… I don't care which you have, just make up your mind. I'll take the other."

The following morning was dull and overcast. I got up around eight. It didn't take me long to get to her apartment. A spare key was under the mat. I'd taken the fat guy's .45 along with me. It didn't seem to have suffered from the water, and I had taken care to have cleaned it well. I wasn't going to be surprised by Katz, and I don't mind telling you that I was a bit nervous going into the place.

She had given me a list of the things she wanted. It was not a long list and I was soon through. I then went carefully through the apartment and searched it pretty thoroughly, but I didn't find anything.

After all the excitement, I was no further to finding Mardi. That was getting me steamed up. I had one taste of the type of thug that Spencer employed, and if they were capable of getting tough with Blondie the same methods could be handed out to Mardi.

I was certain that Blondie knew something and they were trying to find out what it was. The fact that she had made up her mind to leave town showed that she was scared. To leave a nice little apartment like this in a hurry, as well as to lose her connections, pointed that she knew that she was on the spot.

I'd never get anything out of her unless she wanted to tell me. She was far too shrewd to be jumped. Now that Mardi was missing, I had to bust this thing open. There was no other way round it.

When I got back to my apartment I found Ackie there. He was sitting on the foot of my bed, talking to Blondie.

I stood in the doorway and glared at him. He looked over his shoulder. "H'yah, pal," he said. "I'm mighty glad I looked in."

I dumped the suit-case down and glanced over at Blondie. She seemed to be enjoying herself.

"Well, for God's sake," I said, "can't you keep out of my place when I'm busy."

Ackie shook his head. "You may have to thank me," he said. "Don't bother to introduce us, we've already done that."

"So I see," I said sourly. "You might keep your trap shut about this… I don't want the whole town talkin'."

Ackie grinned. "Hear that?" he said to Blondie. "You'd think he was a saint, wouldn't you?"

Blondie liked to see me getting fussed. "He ain't no saint," she said, bringing her arms and shoulders into view.

"Come on, Buddy," I said, "you an' me will have a little talk outside.

The lady wants to get up."

He was obviously reluctant to go, but I got him outside at last.

"Well, well," he said with a leer, "I shouldn't have thought it of you."

I was pardonably annoyed. "I can't explain just now," I said heatedly. "But for Gawd's sake keep your trap shut about this. You recognize that dame?"

Ackie screwed up his face thoughtfully. "Yeah," he said, "I know her all right. I suppose you're still chasing up the Vessi affair. Well, I guess you're having a swell time doin' it."

"Suppose you tell me what you want bustin' in like this?"

He thought for a moment, then his face brightened. "You know, I'd forgotten all about it. When I walked into your bedroom and found that dame in your bed, I certainly had a shock. Yeah, now about tonight. The boys are throwing a little party down at Hughson's place. I thought maybe you'd like to come with me. It's as well to meet the boys every now and then, what do you say?"

To get rid of him, I'd've agreed to anything. "Sure," I said, "that's grand. Suppose you pick me up, and we'll go along together."

I took him by the arm and led him to the door. He got it all right. "Now mind you be careful," he said.

I shoved him out the door and slammed it behind him. Then I went back to Blondie. She was doing her hair with my hair-brushes. Everyone seemed to be using my place like it was a hotel. I sat on the bed.

"A real funny guy," I said.

"Oh, I like him, darlin'," she said, glancing back over her shoulder. "I think he's cute."

She would. They were a pair.

"Well, baby," I said, anxious to get her off my hands, "I got your stuff so I guess you'll be moving out."

She finished her hair and opened up the suit-case. I saw her make a little grimace at the way I had packed her things, but that didn't worry me. She'd got a hell of a crust asking me to do it, so if she didn't like it she could do what the monkey did.

She sorted some things out that she wanted to wear and began to get dressed. I sat there and watched her. The thing uppermost in my mind was that she was leaving town and I might never see her again. She was an important link between Katz and Spencer, and consequently she might be able to lead me to Mardi. I risked everything and had another try.

"There was a girl working for Spencer at the Mackenzie Fabrics. She was a mighty swell dame an' I got interested in her," I began.

"Listen, hayseed," she said, without looking up. She was bending over, fixing her suspender. "I ain't interested in your love life."

I was tempted to take a sock at her, but I kept my hands in my pockets. "This dame has disappeared," I went on. "I can't find her—"

"If she was a good girl she's saved herself a lot of grief," she said, straightening up and reaching for her dress.

"I could do things to you," I said grimly.

"I know—I know. It's no use makin' a beef now."

I went over to her and put my hands on her arms. I held her tight. She looked up at me, her face hardening. "Don't start getting tough," she said. "I'll get that way too."

"You haven't thought that Katz is hanging around waiting to put a slug in you, have you?" I said. "You think you're bright enough to play a solo hand on this and get away with it. You might, but then again you might not. If one day I read that a nice-lookin' blonde has been fished out of the drink, I'll have a laugh. I am ready to take this thing over if you're ready to tell me what you know. If you wait too long, you might never be able to talk. So this is your last chance to get it off your chest."

She sneered. "What a mouthful," she said. "I can look after myself, big boy, don't let that grieve you. I've done it before, an' I'll keep on doin' it. I ain't tellin' you a thing. If you're so anxious, try and find out for yourself."

I shrugged and let her go. "Okay, wise guy," I said. "Go ahead and work on your own. Don't say I haven't warned you."

She pulled on her dress and fixed her hat. As she closed her case, she said: "The next time you see me, raise your lid. I shall be in the money."

That crack told me something. Blondie had her eye on some easy dough. That meant blackmail. It explained why she wanted to work on her own. It explained quite a lot of things.

I said: "You watch your step, Blondie. That game's dangerous."

Her face was expressionless. She picked up her bag and moved to the door. "I'll get by," she said. "If I don't see you again, keep sober."

She opened the door and stepped into the passage. I watched her walk away, her tall figure swaying a little and her head held high.

I was just going back to my room when I saw the guy opposite standing in his doorway. His eyes were popping.

"Still seein' things?" I asked pleasantly, and went inside, shutting the door quietly against his palpitating curiosity.

CHAPTER TWELVE

By the time Ackie and I got round to Hughson's place the party was well under way.

There were eight couples crammed into his small room and the air was thick with smoke. Everyone was drinking as hard as they could put it down and everyone was smoking.

There was a general shout when Ackie edged his way in. Most people got a laugh when they saw him. He got rid of his hat and coat and grabbed a bottle of Scotch.

Hughson came over to me and shook hands. "This is a bum party, Nick," he said apologetically. "But I'm glad you've come."

He led me round the room, introducing me. Most of the *Globe* guys were there and five stream-lined dames. They all looked so good I had to remark about it. Hughson explained they were from *The Moon and the Fiddle*, a musical that was running at the Plaza.

He got me settled down with a redhead and a glass of Scotch-and-soda in my hand, and then he went off to do the host with Ackie. Not that Ackie wasn't looking after himself.

The redhead was pretty tight and giggled a lot. She told me her name was Dawn Murray. When I asked her what her real name was she giggled a lot more but wouldn't tell me.

These parties always go the same way. Everyone gets plastered and talks about nothing and laughs when there's nothing to laugh about. I guess it's just an excuse to get tight.

Dawn started talking about books. This surprised me because I thought she wouldn't bother about reading. She'd just finished Steinbeck's *Grapes of Wrath*.

"Now I bet that guy knows what he's writing about," she said. "I bet he lived in those camps. That's the most marvellous book I've ever read."

A tall, lanky guy who I didn't know, and whose name I hadn't caught when I was introduced, pricked up his ears when he heard that and came over. He'd read it too, so I guessed they were soul-mates. I got up quietly and left them to it.

The certain sign that a party is going well is when the people start going into the kitchen. I thought I'd have a look and see if any one had got there yet. I drifted in and found a couple with their arms around each other and their faces glued together.

That told me the party was going all right.

"If she bites you, I'll give you the verdict," I said.

The fellow prised himself loose. "I bet your ma thinks you're a scream," he said coldly.

Not so good. I went back to the sitting-room. Dawn and the lanky guy had exhausted Steinbeck and were sitting playing handies.

Someone started the gramophone and everyone broke up into couples to dance. There was no room for much movement, but so long as they'd got their arms round a girl and could shuffle their feet a yard or two, they didn't care.

I was content to sit in an armchair and watch them. Hughson came over after a little while and sat on the arm of my chair.

"The old man's pleased at the way you handled the Colonel for us," he said. "He thinks you made a swell job of it." Hughson was the sort of guy who would never let anything rest. He kept on plugging at the thing, and how nice the Colonel was about it, until I thought I'd go haywire.

Then right in the middle of it the door opened and Mardi walked in.

I saw her at once, and I couldn't believe my eyes. Standing behind her was a tall guy with a lot of wavy hair and the sort of brown complexion that dames fall for and, of course, very bright blue eyes. This guy was handsome all right.

I stared at Mardi through the haze of tobacco smoke and thought I was seeing things. I said cautiously to Hughson: "Who's the dame?"

He got off my chair arm. "I don't know, but I'm goin' to find out… she's a peach, ain't she?"

He went over and shook hands with the tall guy. Then he had a few words with Mardi. I was suddenly aware that I was pretty high, and I was sorry about it. I was feeling a little sore about the tall guy. That didn't look so good.

Hughson had stopped them dancing and was taking the two round introducing them. I got out of my chair and put my tie straight. They got round to me at last. In the confusion of the crowd and the thickness of the atmosphere, Mardi hadn't seen me. Now she was standing right in front of me. We looked at each other and her face went white.

Hughson was saying: "You must meet Nick… you'll like this guy. He's done more for the Women's Friendly Societies than most men. The trouble is he gets too friendly so they give him the gate in the end."

I wasn't listening to what he said. Mardi was trying to tell me something without speaking. Her eyes were wide and she looked scared; then, seeing that I was still dumb, she said: "Why haven't I met you before?"

I got it all right then. For some reason or other she didn't want to let on she knew me.

I said: "You've got your chance now and I'm hoping you won't be disappointed." It was a lame comeback, but I was up-creek without a paddle.

Hughson introduced me to the tall guy. He said: "Nick, I want you to meet Lee Curtis," then turning his head he went on: "Curtis, this is—"

Mardi interrupted him. She broke in quite naturally: "Oh, Barry, who's the funny little man over there?"

Hughson grinned. "That's Mo Ackie. The smartest news-hawk on the street. Come on over and meet him."

He led them away from me and Ackie started doing his stuff right away. I was learning fast. First, Mardi didn't want me to show that I'd met her and, second, she didn't want the big guy to know my name. I added that together. I was in a spot. I wanted to go over and get friendly with the girl, but obviously she didn't want Curtis to get any inkling, so I had to stay there and water at the mouth.

Dawn came over to me. "Dance with me, hot man," she said. "Crush me up in your arms. My instincts are starving."

I could have gladly wrung her neck, but thought I'd better mix in with the crowd. Mardi and Curtis were talking in a corner with Hughson. Curtis had his back to me, but Mardi kept her eyes on me as I shuffled around the room.

Dawn said: "You might pay me a little attention. That brunette isn't going to fall for you."

I jerked my eyes away from Mardi and grinned at her. "You don't need to worry," I said. "Anyway, you could have the curly-haired guy, if she did."

She shook her head. "I don't want him," she said.

I manoeuvred her to the far end of the room. "What do you know about him?" I asked, jerking gently to the swing.

"Know about Lee Curtis?" Her eyebrows shot up. "Plenty."

I danced her round the room again and then the record finished. "Suppose we go out into the kitchen and have a drink?"

"That's what I like about you. You anticipate my thoughts."

We slipped out of the room and into the kitchen. It was in complete darkness, but I knew where Hughson had left his torch. She held the light while I fixed a Bacardi cocktail. Then we sat down on the table with the torch between us.

"I'm interested in this guy Curtis," I said. "Suppose you tell me about him."

She sipped the Bacardi thoughtfully. "There isn't anything to tell. He's got some dough, likes a good time, runs around with anything easy and changes his bedfellow once a week."

I wondered what the hell Mardi was doing with him. You can tell if a girl's a tramp more times than not, and I was prepared to swear that Mardi was on the level.

"What's he do for a living?" I said.

"Oh, he's something big in the Mackenzie Fabrics. Secretary of the company or something. Do you mind not talking about him any more… I'm getting bored."

"Sure, that's all right," I said.

My brain was busy. So this guy was tied up in the same business. That told me why Mardi wanted to keep my name out of it. I told myself that Mardi knew something and I was going to find out what just as soon as I got her to myself.

Because she expected it, I did a little necking with Dawn and then left her sitting on the table in the gloom, patiently waiting for me to come back. I'd made up my mind that I wasn't going to be alone any more with that dame that night.

I looked into the sitting-room. The party was still going on. Mardi was dancing with Hughson. Just as I was going to walk in I heard the telephone in the hall ringing. Hughson looked at me and he called: "See who it is, will you, Nick?"

I said, "Sure," and went over to the telephone. "Hullo? This is Barry Hughson's apartment."

A woman said: "Is Mr. Curtis there? Mr. Lee Curtis?"

I said, "Hold on," and put the telephone down. I went into the sitting-room. Curtis was doing his stuff with Ackie's Spanish dame. I went over. "You're wanted on the 'phone," I said.

He looked startled. "You sure?" he asked, getting to his feet.

"If your name's Curtis, I am," I said.

He gave me a quick, hard look and then went outside. I saw him shut the door carefully behind him, and I looked around for Mardi. Before I could spot her, the Spanish dame started doing her stuff. At times, women are hell.

By the time I'd got away from her Curtis had come back into the room. He was looking mad all right. He went over to Hughson. "I'm sorry," he said, "I've had an urgent telephone message. I've got to get home."

Hughson didn't worry a lot. He made sympathetic noises. "You're not taking Mardi with you?" he said anxiously. "She an' I are gettin' on well together."

I moved a little closer so that I could hear.

Curtis looked down at Mardi. "I'll take you home first," he said, "or do you want to stay? I'm damn' sorry about this...."

She shook her head. "I'll stay. You go on. Maybe you can come back."

He hesitated. I could see he didn't want to go and he was sore as hell.

Hughson put in: "I'll see her back. You don't have to worry."

"All right. I'll see you to-morrow," Curtis said to Mardi.

He went out of the door quickly, not bothering to say good-bye to any of the others. That's the sort of guy Curtis was. No one was of any interest to him unless he was sure that he was going to get something out of them.

Mardi said to Hughson: "I'd love a gin-and-lime."

"Sure, I'll fix you one. Just wait a moment. I won't be long," kidding himself that she was going into mourning until he came back.

I stepped up to her as soon as he went into the kitchen. I was hoping that Dawn would hold him for a little while. "I want to talk to you," I said quietly. "May I take you home?"

She nodded.

I got a swell feeling just standing looking at her. "Mind if we go soon?"

She shook her head. "When you like," she said.

Hughson came back with the gin-and-lime. When he saw me his face darkened. "On your way, big boy," he said. "There's a virgin in the kitchen waiting for you."

I shook my head. "You're too late. Mardi an' me are old friends. She's just having the drink and we're going home... together and alone."

Hughson turned to Mardi. "I've warned you about this guy," he said heatedly. "He spends all his time grabbing things that don't belong to him and wrecking homes."

Mardi laughed. "I feel like being wrecked right now," she said. "It's getting late, Barry, and I ought to go."

Hughson groaned. "Give me one more dance and I'll let you," he said. "You had much better let me see you home."

I nodded to her behind his back. I didn't want this to look too sudden. They danced off together and I went over to Ackie. I told him I was moving off.

He was so plastered that he didn't care if I was going to commit suicide. "Don't be hard on her," he said, screwing up his eyes. "She looks a swell girl."

I signalled to Mardi that I'd meet her downstairs. I didn't want Dawn to arrive just as we were going. I need not have worried my head about her. She had passed out under the kitchen table.

Five minutes later Mardi came running down the stairs. She wore a perky little hat and a nice fur coat. She looked good.

We didn't have to wait long before a taxi crawled by. I waved and he pulled up at the curb. "Where shall I tell him?" I asked.

She hesitated. Then she said: "I—I haven't got a home any more… do you think I could put up at a hotel or somewhere?"

I gaped at her. "Have you got any luggage?"

She nodded. "It's at the station," she said. "I could go there first and collect it, but I want to catch an early train."

I said: "If I suggest you come back to my place, I want you to know that I don't mean anything wrong. I just offer you my roof and hope you will accept it."

She stood looking into my face for several seconds, then she said: "Thank you. It's nice of you."

Hardly believing that I had heard correctly, I handed her into the taxi.

CHAPTER THIRTEEN

On the short trip from Hughson's apartment to my place we didn't say a word. It was incredible to me that she was sitting by my side, willing to share my rooms with me, and I'd only known her for such a short time.

When a girl shows such willingness, I'm usually sure that I'm on to a good thing. With Mardi it was different. There was something about her that built up a surrounding wall that protected her from any mean thoughts that might come her way. I'm not going to say that every guy wouldn't try to make a pass, but as far as I was concerned she got me like that.

She sat quietly in the corner of the taxi and looked out the window. Every now and then, when we passed a street light, I could see her clearly. With that perky little hat on her head and the fur collar tight at her throat, she looked swell.

We got to my apartment and I paid off the taxi.

Quietly we crept up the stairs. I was nervous of the guy opposite me, but as it was getting on for two o'clock I guessed he'd be asleep.

We got into my apartment without disturbing any one. I shut the door, turned on the light and tossed my hat on the settee.

"Whew!" I said. "I was sure gettin' the jitters comin' up the stairs."

She stood looking round the room. "But it's nice," she said. "What a lot of books you have… and isn't that cute?"

She went over to examine my miniature bar in the corner. We both kept our voices low like two conspirators. I wandered over and got behind the counter. "What would you like?" I said. "Suppose we have some rye and ginger... it's grand stuff to sleep on."

She again looked at me. I could see she was just a little doubtful of me: not scared, but not quite sure.

I grinned at her. "Baby," I said, "you don't have to worry about me. I know what you're thinkin' but you can forget it. With another dame, yes, but with you, no. I guess you would never have come here if you didn't want some help bad... well, I want to help, an' there won't be a cheque comin' in."

When I said that, she relaxed. She said: "Make it a very small rye and a lot of ginger."

While I was fixing the drinks, she went over and sat in the big armchair. It was one of those chairs that give to the floor. From where I was standing I could see the top of her hat and a lot of her legs. She opened the fur coat and draped it over the side of the chair.

It was chilly, so I switched on the little electric stove I used between the periods when the steam heat was off and the evenings got cold.

I came over with the drinks and gave her one of the glasses. Then, leaning against the mantelshelf, I nodded to her over the rim. "Safe landin'," I said, and we drank.

She lay back in the armchair, holding the glass in one hand, and for a minute shut her eyes. I didn't hurry her. I guessed she wanted to get her facts together, and I was happy enough to stand and watch her.

"I *do* want your help," she said at last, looking up at me.

"All right. You're goin' to have it. If you're in a jam, you don't have to get scared. We'll work it out together."

"Why, Mr. Mason, are you doing this for me?"

With an opening like that I wasn't going to act the village hick. "Because I'm crazy about you," I said. "You're the first girl I've met that I can look at and talk to without wondering if I could take you for a ride. You're the first girl I've met who's got everything and yet... and yet... oh, hell! I can't explain it... but, you've got me jumping through hoops...."

This outburst startled her all right. She tried to struggle out of the chair.

"Now wait a minute," I said hastily. "You asked me an' I've told you. That doesn't mean that you an' I aren't still on the level with each other. I don't want you to think I'm just putting on an act. I'm not. I'm being straight with you, so for the love of Mike don't start thinkin' up wrong angles to this."

She sank back into the chair. "Really, Mr. Mason—" she began.

"Listen, could you make it 'Nick'? I won't insist if you don't feel you can, but it would tickle me to death."

She laughed at me. "You're crazy," she said. "But you're nice. Thank you for saying what you have said. I want someone who will tell me what to do. I think I'm very lucky to find you."

Can you tie that? She thought she was lucky to find me! Now I ask you!

When I got over it, I said: "Okay, now suppose you tell me what it's all about?"

She handed the glass back to me. "I don't want any more." Then she got out of the chair and took off her hat and coat. She was wearing a dark-green evening thing that fitted her like a snake-skin and spread out into a full skirt. I reckoned that cost plenty of money.

"May I have a cigarette?"

She could have had the moon. I lit it for her and she sat on the arm of the chair. "This is the craziest thing that's ever happened to me," she said at last. "Perhaps I'd better start at the beginning. You remember the day when you took me out to lunch?"

I nodded. Remember the day? Why, I'd got it tattooed on my brain.

"When I got back Mr. Spencer sent for me and was furious that I had gone out with you. I couldn't just understand what he was talking about. I guess I got mad too and told him I'd go out with whom I liked in my lunch-hours. So he fired me."

She paused and looked to see what I thought of that. I didn't think it was the right time to tell her that I knew this already. Maybe she might've got a little sore if she knew I'd been around making inquiries. So I made a few tutting noises waggled my eyebrows up and down.

"I was so mad I just walked straight out of the office and went home. The next morning I got a letter asking me to come in and see Mr. Spencer. I threw the letter away and took no notice. I spent the morning looking for another job. It surprised me the number of offers I got."

"Just a moment," I put in. "You say you got a lot of offers. Why did that surprise you?"

She shrugged a little. "You know how it is to-day. Jobs don't grow on the trees. But I really got some fantastic offers. It made me think there was something wrong about them, so I didn't close with any of them. I went home to think about them."

"Did you tell them that you'd been working with Mackenzie Fabrics?"
"Of course."

"And were you trying for a job in the same trade?"
She looked at me hard. "Yes," she said at last.

I grinned at her. "Then that ain't a mystery to me. Your Mackenzie Fabrics pay the biggest dividend in the trade. They have more dough than all the rest put together. Why, naturally those guys wanted you to work for them. They were hoping they'd learn how the business was run."

She looked a little blank, then she laughed. "I didn't think of it like that," she confessed ruefully.

"I bet you thought the boss was goin' to come the heavy?"

"I'm afraid I did." She coloured a little. I had to make a strong effort not to pat her.

"All right," I said, "forget it. You know now that you can get a swell job if you want to, so let's have the rest of it."

She shook her head. "I can't, that's the trouble. When I got back to my apartment I found Lee Curtis waiting for me. He's Spencer's right-hand man. We don't like him a lot in the office, and I was none too pleased to find him there. He told me that Spencer wanted me to come back. He was sorry that he'd shouted me out and would forget it. Well, I was still sore, and I knew I could get something just as good, so I said no. Curtis started pressing me and finally persuaded me to come back and see Spencer.

"The way Spencer went on made me suspicious. I didn't know what it was all about, but I didn't like the way he almost begged me to come back. I turned him down." She shivered suddenly. "I can see him now: He sat behind his big desk, his face went white and he looked as if he could strangle me. 'You'll be sorry about this,' he said in a horrible, quiet voice. 'If I were you, I'd get out of town.'

"He really terrified me and I didn't get to sleep that night. Then from that moment to this morning I've been watched. A tall, thin man, dressed in black with a black slouched hat pulled over his face, always turns up wherever I go. Two days of that decided me. I packed my things, gave notice to my landlady and prepared to leave town."

"Where were you going?" I put in.

"I thought I'd go down to the coast. I wanted a vacation and I had got some money put by, so I thought I'd go down there until they had forgotten about me."

I didn't want to scare her, but I thought they were not likely to forget her. I just said: "So what happened?"

She twisted her hands in her lap, and a little frown settled in her eyes. "I thought I was being awfully smart," she said. "I arranged with my landlady to get my stuff to the station, and I went off on a long ramble round town, taking the thin man along behind me. I thought I could give him the slip, get to the station and leave town without anyone knowing." She smiled at me ruefully. It certainly did me a lot of good when that honey smiled at me.

"I was all set when I ran into Curtis. He wouldn't take 'no' for an answer. He stuck to me like glue for the rest of the afternoon and then insisted on bringing me to Barry Hughson's party. That's all."

I shut my eyes and let my brain sort it out.

"Why do you think he brought me to Hughson's and then walked out on me?"

"Curtis think a lot of you?" I asked.

She looked uncomfortable. "He has been rather pressing," she admitted. "But then, he's like that with most girls."

I could think of a number of reasons why Curtis had taken her to Hughson's, but I wasn't going to tell her. Suppose Spencer had planned to get rid of her and Curtis knew about it? If this guy was a little soft on her, and I'm not blaming him if he was, he'd probably hang around with her to see that nothing happened. Once she was round at Hughson's place, he might think she was safe for a while. Then this other dame rings him up and he has to get out and leave her.

It struck me Mardi wasn't any too safe running around at large. The point was to find out how much she knew.

I said quietly, "Suppose I tell you all about this business, then maybe you can see where you fit in."

"Do I fit in anywhere?"

I grinned. "Yeah, I'm afraid you do." I lit another cigarette and got down to it. "I wantta put this to you just like you knew nothing about it. Maybe if I put it to you like that, you might get a slant on it. To start at the beginning. Larry Richmond was shot to death almost a year ago. This guy was a rich playboy who called himself the President of the Mackenzie Fabrics. He was no more President than I am, but that don't matter for the moment. His chief job seemed to be peddling the stock of the company to his rich friends. Well, he succeeded, not because he was a good salesman, but because the shares were worth having. They kept climbing and everyone was happy. The Mackenzie Fabrics was a blind for some illegal racket, with a list of shareholders including the Police Commissioner and the Customs officials. Richmond was playin' a cagey hand. As everyone was gettin' a share under a strictly legal guise, no one was going to kick. Okay, that's the first set-up. The fact that Richmond never showed up at the office and just fooled around spending the dough points to Spencer being the guy who runs the racket." I got up to give myself a drink.

Mardi sat quite still. Her face was a little pale and she looked tired. It was getting on towards three o'clock, but I'd got to get this thing sorted out.

"Then Richmond gets bumped. Very unfortunate this, because Spencer did the bumping. I guess he was getting tired of doing all the work and seeing Richmond doin' all the spending. If Spencer took the rap the lid would come off Mackenzie Fabrics all right. That wouldn't please the shareholders. I don't know, but I can guess what happened. They all got around and wagged their heads about this and came to the only conclusion. Someone had to be the fall-guy.

"Now Richmond played around with the dames. As long as the dame was a looker, she was okay by him. He was fooling around with a floozie of the streets just before he was knocked off, and this bird usually ran around with a guy named Vessi, a real twelve-minute egg. What could be simpler? Vessi is the fall-guy. They frame that bohunk so fast he's dizzy in the head. The cops frame him, Spencer frames him, the lawyers frame him, and the judge frames him. So he's framed. Just like that. To make matters safe an' sound, they get his moll to frame him.

"This is where I come in. The case to me was just a sordid bit of shooting with no news angle for my particular stuff. One night a dame rings up and tells me she's sending round a ticket that'll let me in to see Vessi's execution. She tells me that Vessi will give me an angle on this business, and she will pay me ten grand to explode the frame. This dame is plenty steamed up. Before I can turn it down she rings off.

"Okay, I'm the mug. I go along and see Vessi have a noseful. Before he hands in his pail, he tells me that Spencer pulled the shootin'. I pass the news on to the mystery woman, who sends me five grand as an act of good faith. Before I can lay my hands on the dough, Blondie, that's Vessi's late moll, nips into my room and grabs it. I do a bit of Philo Vance stuff and track this moll to her lair. We have a few words and then in blows Katz. Now Katz is Spencer's bodyguard. A guy that walks around loaded up with shooting-irons and itching to use 'em. All he seems keen about is to find out who's been staking me to start trouble. This guy gets plenty tough so I tell him a story that's not quite true but which he falls for.

"I then do some thinking and decide that I'm not interested. I'm a peace-lovin' guy an' this seems too excitin'. Anyway, why the hell should I worry about Vessi? He was just a smalltime crook. So when the dame comes on the 'phone again I tell her I'm through.

"This dame interests me. I want to know who she is. I had a bad break the other day. I nearly ran into her but just missed it. I won't go into that now, but maybe I'll tell you about it later. The next excitement is you. I wanted to see a little more of you, and when I heard you were missing I got worried. I got still more worried when this dame rings up and hints that I'll find you in trouble at an old east-side wharf.

"I go along there and have an argument with three guys, and instead of finding you I run into Blondie again. She also is on her way out of town. Then I run into you, and I guess that's where I stop." I sat back with a sigh of relief.

Mardi said: "I believe I can help you. There are a lot of things I couldn't understand which now I think I could fit into the puzzle."

"Suppose we look at it from this angle—" I began.

She smiled at me. "Could it wait until to-morrow?" she asked. "I'm so tired. Look at the time. I feel as if I shall go to sleep right here in this chair."

I got up quickly. "Sure," I said. "I guess I'm over-anxious. You get some sleep. We can talk over what you're goin' to do and all about this business to-morrow."

She got out of the chair slowly and stretched. Standing there in front of the electric stove, the strong reflection of the elements outlining her legs through her dress, her grand little head back, and her arms raised a little, she looked good. I wanted to put my arms round her. It was tough going not to start anything.

I said: "Through there is the bedroom. You go ahead. You get some sleep."

She said sleepily: "Can I borrow things from you?"

I went ahead of her and fished out a pair of my pyjamas and my dressing-gown. I tossed them on the bed.

She came in and stood watching me. "It's nice of you," she said, "giving up your bed. Do you mind an awful lot?"

I didn't move. I just didn't trust myself. "No, I don't mind," I said.

The sudden unevenness in my voice made her look at me quickly. "I'm sorry I can't do what some girls would do," she said steadily. "Not because I think it's wrong, but because I think it's too soon."

I went over to her and stood very close. "You're swell," I said, "I don't want that. I just want you to know I'm crazy about you. I want to help you and do things for you."

She put her hand on my arm. "Thank you."

I gave a grin and walked out, shutting the door behind me.

The fat guy and Gus were sitting under the lamp waiting for me. The fat guy held an automatic directed at my belly. He said: "Reach up, lug, grab a handful of heaven."

CHAPTER FOURTEEN

Those two guys got me rattled for the moment. I leant against the door and put my hands up. There was a vicious look in the fat guy's eyes that I didn't like. I guessed he was feeling mighty sore with me.

Did he know Mardi was right behind me? Was he after her or was he just going to settle things up with me?

I said softly: "How's your noggin, Gus? You birds want a lot of shakin', don't you?"

The fat guy waved the gun at me. "Come away from the door, lug, we want the dame. Come on… I ain't goin' to ask twice."

I yelled: "Mardi, lock the door quick… trouble's arrived."

Gus sprang towards me with a curse. He came at me from the side so that his body didn't get in the line of the fat guy's gun. I wedged myself against the door and let him come.

The fat guy said: "Get him away… if he starts anything, I'll drill him."

Gus gripped my arm and tried to swing me from the door. I was too heavy for him and just for a second he came off balance. I jerked my arm a little, and he fell forward, right in the line of fire. I clutched him to me like he was my long-lost brother and lammed a couple of short ones to his belly. My heel thudded against the door and I yelled again: "Lock up, quick."

The two punches I had shot into Gus held him for a second and then he caught me with a swinger on the jaw. It was a nice punch and it sent me over. I took him with me and we went down in a heap on the floor.

The fat guy came forward and rammed the barrel of his rod into my neck. "Take it easy," he said softly, "this gun don't make much noise."

The cold barrel digging into me cooled me off quick. I let go of Gus, who scrambled to his feet. The fat guy said: "I don't want to rub you out, but I'll do it all right if you ask for it."

I met his eyes. This guy meant everything he said.

"I'll be good," I said.

The barrel of the gun looked like a cannon to me.

Gus said: "Watch him… he's slippery."

The fat guy shook his head. "He'll be all right now, you'll see."

I sat on the floor hoping that Mardi would start yelling out of the window. I didn't hear a sound, and my heart sank.

"Come on, get up," the fat guy said, digging the gun into me again.

I got to my feet.

"If you think you're goin' to start anything, I should forget it. This rod's got a light trigger."

I guess that guy would think nothing of touching his gun off, so I just stood.

Gus came round the back of me and jerked my arms behind me. For a moment I stiffened my muscles, but the gun kept digging into me. I thought maybe I'd be more useful to Mardi alive than dead, so I let him rope me.

I tried the dodge of expanding my arm muscles, so that I could have a little slack when the time came, but Gus knew all about roping, and when he put the pressure on I called him some fancy names.

They stood back and looked at me.

Gus said to the fat guy: "We gotta get goin'." He went over to Mardi's door and turned the handle. The door was locked. I knew that door would want some opening. They could only do that by making a hell of a noise.

I said: "Skip it, you two guys, can't you leave us alone? You ain't getting in there without callin' out the riot squad, so why not turn it in?"

The fat guy gave a little chuckle. When he laughed he certainly looked mean. "This is easy," he said. "We'll get her out quick an' quiet."

He went to the door and pushed Gus on one side. He put his bullet-head against the panels. "Come on out, sister," he said, speaking in his hoarse, croaking voice. "We want you out in ten seconds or we start on your boy friend."

I yelled: "To hell with them, Mardi! You stay where you are. Yell out of the window…!"

Gus hit me across the mouth with the back of his hand. His bony knuckle cut my lip and I staggered across the room, getting my balance.

The fat guy knocked on the door again. "Wait a minute, sister," he called. "Don't you start anythin' until I'm through. Then you can make up your mind. I know you're in there, so you don't have to be cagey. You can hear me okay?"

"I can hear you." Mardi's voice was pretty steady.

"If you don't come out right now, I'm going to get tough with your boy friend. When I say tough, I mean tough, get it? I'll give you ten seconds, an' if you ain't out by then I'm goin' to give him the works."

I dodged Gus's rush and yelled, "It's a bluff… yell out of the window… don't open

Again Gus's fist smashed into my face and this time I went over. I was quick enough to jerk my head away from the kick he aimed at me.

Mardi opened the door and came out.

The fat guy and Gus stood motionless staring at her. I saw Gus's eyes open and he pursed his mouth.

She stood framed in the doorway, one hand hanging by her side and the other holding the door handle. Her face was pale and her eyes were wide, but she held her head up and she wasn't looking scared.

"What do you want?" she said, her voice steady and cold.

I felt mighty proud of the way she faced up to these two thugs. The fat guy came forward, his face beaming, but his eyes very mean.

"Well! Well! Ain't she a peach?" he said, standing in front of her. "We're all goin' for a little ride. Get your wrap, will you? An' make it fast."

I struggled to my feet. "Listen," I said, keeping an eye on Gus, who was beginning to sidle towards me, "you won't get anywhere on a gag like this. Drop it, will you?"

The fat guy glanced at Gus. "If that punk opens his trap any more, shut it for him and shut it for good."

Gus drew a rubber truncheon from his back pocket. He balanced it thoughtfully in his hand. "Sure," he said, and grinned.

Mardi came over to me, but the fat guy stepped between us. "We don't want to get tough," he said, "but we will if you don't behave."

She looked at me and I gave her a pale grin. I was feeling bad about all this. Then she squared her shoulders and picked up her wrap.

The fat guy stepped to her side. "That's fine," he said. "Now we go downstairs. If you start anythin', Gus'll wash up the punk. Hear that, Gus?"

Gus said, "Sure." He threw my over coat cape-wise over my shoulders and jerked his head. We all went out into the corridor and went silently down into the street. There was a big closed car standing outside the house. The streets were deserted and the pale dawn was coming up over the roofs. It would be over an hour before any one would be around on the streets.

Gus shoved me in the back of the car and the fat guy got in next. Mardi followed. We three sat in a row. Gus went to the front and climbed under the wheel. He switched on the ignition and engaged the gears. The car shot away from the curb at a high speed.

The fat guy said to Mardi: "You ain't got to get scared. I'd be sortta soft with a honey like you if you were nice."

"Listen, greaseball," I put in. "Suppose you skip your stuff. It gives me a pain."

His face suddenly set. "I'm getting mighty tired of you," he said. "You're goin' to run into plenty of grief before long."

I wondered what chance I had if I jumped him. I thought I could sock him in his puss with my two hands and while he was getting his breath I might do some more damage.

He was no fool. I guess he saw I was getting ready to start something, so he dug his gun into me. "Pipe down," he said curtly.

The big car flashed through the empty streets with hardly a roll. In the faint light from the dashboard I could make out the outline of Gus's head. He kept his eyes on the road and drove hard.

"Where the hell do you think you're takin' us?" I asked for something to say.

The fat guy said, "Did you hear that, Gus? He wants to know where we're goin'."

Gus shrugged, but didn't say anything.

I wanted to keep the fat guy's mind off Mardi, so I kept talking. "What's your name?" I asked. "I get kind of embarrassed callin' you 'greaseball.'"

He turned a little. I could see he was getting mad. "You won't get anywhere with that stuff," he said evenly. "Suppose you keep your trap shut; I'm gettin' tired of hearing your yappin'."

Mardi hadn't said a word the whole time. I couldn't see much of her, and when I leant forward the fat guy gave me a hard one in the chest with his elbow.

I thought when the time came for a show-down, I was certainly going to give this punk the works.

I suddenly recognized the sound of a ship's siren. So we were going back to Wensdy Wharf again. Sure enough, in a few minutes, the car turned into the wharf and pulled up outside the same house.

Gus got out first and opened the door. "Come on out," he said to Mardi.

She stepped out and he pushed her into the house. The fat guy followed, jerking me with him. We all silently trooped upstairs into the room where Blondie had been kept prisoner.

"Home again," I said, leaning against the wall. I had been testing the ropes round my wrists and arms during the drive, but I could get nowhere with them. They were on for good.

Gus shoved me into a chair.

The fat guy went outside, and I heard him go into another room. I heard him say something, then a deep voice answered him. I saw Mardi start a little and she looked rather wildly at me. She said something with her lips, but I couldn't get it.

Then the door opened again and a tall, heavily built man came in, followed closely by the fat guy.

He stood and looked at Mardi, then he said, "I'm sorry about this, but you're rather in the way." The way he said it made me suddenly feel cold. He was so casual and calm, but there was a definite threat in his words.

He certainly scared Mardi. She took a step back. "But, Mr. Spencer…" she began and stopped.

So this was Lu Spencer. I looked at him closely. There was nothing very grand about this guy. He was running a little to fat and he was getting thick in the middle. His coal-black moustache and his white hair made odd contrasts. He looked like he had dyed his moustache. His eyes dropped a little, as if he were very tired, but the light in them belied any sign of fatigue.

He selected a cigar from a pigskin case and put it between his teeth. "Give the lady a chair," he said to Gus.

When Mardi had sat down, her hands twisting a little in her lap, he glanced over at me.

"So you're Mason," he said, moving over to get a good look at me.

"Yeah," I said. "If this is your idea of a good gag, I don't think much of it. Suppose you cut this movie stuff out right now."

He went over and sat on the edge of the table. "It's time we had a little chat," he said, tipping the ash off his cigar with his finger. "I'm cautious, Mason, always have been. When I think trouble's coming my way, I act quick. I don't wait for trouble to get going, I meet it before it starts and I stop it starting."

I shrugged. "Where do I find that little fable?"

"You've been warned off before, but it seems like you won't learn. I've decided to stop you putting your oar in."

Boy! Would I like to have my hands free so that I could have socked that guy one? "Ain't you barkin' up the wrong alley?"

"I'm going to be frank with you," he went on. "It would be very inconvenient to have a further investigation in the Richmond murder. I've got the business to think of and, as I say, it would be inconvenient. You've been offered big money to start trouble, haven't you?"

I looked at him thoughtfully. Then I said: "Maybe your pal Katz has told you my angle."

Spencer nodded. "Yes," he said, "I know about that."

"All right," I said. "Now I had decided to leave the business alone. What's one cheap crook among so many? I didn't have to grieve about Vessi. I was bein' offered ten grand. That ain't such a lot of dough. So I decided to leave it alone. Then, when you started trouble for Miss Jackson, I just had to come into it again."

Spencer glanced at Mardi and then back at me. His eyebrows went up a little, and he pursed his mouth. "So that's how it sits, huh?"

"If you mean that I ain't sitting still when you start pushing a nice girl around, you're right," I said.

"No more than that?"

I wanted to belt that guy in the puss very badly indeed. I didn't say anything.

He chewed his cigar thoughtfully. "You've got me in a spot, Mason," he said at last. "You and this young woman here could be a nuisance. Between you both you might start trouble which might upset my plans. If we can't come to terms, I'm afraid you two are in for a bad time."

His voice was very casual, but I didn't like his tone. I glanced across at Mardi and she wasn't looking too grand.

"Suppose you put your cards on the table," I invited.

He looked over at Gus. "Clear out, you two," he said. "I'll call you if I want you."

When they had gone he began to pace up and down the room. I could see he had a lot on his mind.

"Look," he said at last, "I've got to find out who's at the bottom of all this. Who's willing to pay you ten grand to make things awkward for me."

I bet he'd like to know that, but he wasn't getting any help from me. I had already made up my mind that I was going to look into that also.

I shrugged. "You can search me," I said. "I've been asking myself the same question."

He came over and stood close to me. "I've got a hunch that you know something that would give me the key to this. I'm going to ask you to come clean."

As I began to speak he held up his hand. "Don't be in a hurry," he said. "Think first. If you can't remember, I'm going to jog your memory."

I said, "I've told you I got a note which was typewritten. I've no more idea than the dead who it could be."

He said, "Would it be a man or a woman?"

I shook my head. "I tell you I can't help you."

He stood looking at me, his face slightly flushed. "That's a pity," he said. He walked over to the door and jerked it open. "Gus, come in here."

The thin dope shuffled in and stood waiting. His little eyes restlessly wandered from my face up to the ceiling and back again.

Spencer said, "I think this guy knows something. At the moment he won't talk. Suppose you start on our friend here... maybe he'll get inspiration that way."

Mardi started to her feet. Her face had gone very white. Gus stepped over to her, and as she turned to run he grabbed her and twisted her round. One of his hands held her wrists.

Spencer looked over at me. "Well," he said, "you can make your mind up. Gus has done this sort of thing before."

I said with difficulty, "Tell that swine to take his hands off her."

Spencer said coldly, "You're wasting time." He jerked his head at Gus. "Go ahead," he said.

Gus grinned at me and moved towards Mardi. She suddenly came to life and kicked him on his shin. Her shoes weren't hard enough to stop a guy like Gus.

I said quickly, "Okay, don't touch her."

Spencer said, "Hold it, Gus." Then he turned to me. "Was it a man or a woman?"

"It was a woman."

"How do you know?"

"She came through on the telephone."

Spencer said to Gus, "All right, wait outside."

Gus went out slowly.

Mardi leant against the wall. I could see her mouth was quivering, but she still kept her chin up.

Spencer looked at me keenly. "What sort of voice did she have?"

I shrugged. "I guess she disguised it. It was hard and metallic, but it wasn't a natural sort of voice."

He wandered about the room a bit, then he came and stood over me. "So it was a woman, eh? I've got to look for a woman."

I didn't say anything.

He looked at Mardi and then at me. "As for you two…" he passed his hand over his hair, "you don't know what you're bucking. Take my advice and keep clear of this business. If that woman comes over the 'phone again, let me know. I'll give you a lot more than ten grand if you can turn her up."

I said, "I'm through with this business, anyway," and meant it.

"I'm going to turn you loose, but take my tip… get out of town." He walked over to Mardi. "I'm sorry you got smart, baby," he said. "You did some good work for me."

Mardi turned her face away and he shrugged. Then he walked to the door and went out.

Mardi came over to me unsteadily.

"Get me free, honey," I said urgently. "I don't like the sound of this."

She got the knot undone after a struggle and I stood up, rubbing my wrists.

The fat guy came in, holding his gun. He jerked his head. "You can beat it," he said curtly. "Come on, get out of here."

We went down the dark stairs, and he followed us closely. Gus was standing holding the front door open. I had my muscles tense, ready to start something if those two wanted trouble, but they just saw us to the door.

We stepped into the dark, cold street and the door slammed behind us.

I turned and looked at Mardi. "Well, for Pete's sake," I said. "What do you make of that?"

Mardi put her hands to her face and I heard a little choking sob jerk in her throat. I put my arms round her and pulled her to me. She came to me with her head on my chest.

"It's all right, honey," I said. "We're out of it now. Don't worry.... It's all right now."

In the distance a siren hooted, and the wash from a passing ship suddenly slapped against the side of the wharf.

I said, "Let's get out of this. We've had enough grief for one night."

It was several minutes before she drew away from me, and I was mighty sorry to feel her go. We went down the street together, out of the dark into the lights of the main street.

CHAPTER FIFTEEN

It was noon before I woke. For several minutes I couldn't make out where the hell I was, then I remembered and sat up on my couch with a rueful grin.

The sun was shining all right, and Mardi was in my bed in the next room. I didn't have anything to beef about. I swung my legs to the floor and went into the bathroom. A cold shower did a lot to bring me to the surface, and after a shave I felt good.

I put on my silk dressing-gown and ran a comb through my hair, then I put my head round Mardi's door and took a look at her. I could just see a small lump in the bed and I guessed she was still sleeping. I got a big kick out of thinking she was right there in my bed.

I telephoned downstairs for a double breakfast, and while I was waiting I smoked a cigarette.

The service waiter looked at me curiously when he wheeled the tray in, and he took a quick gander round the room. I gave him a dollar and he grinned at me. Maybe he'd been young once, and maybe he remembered using a double breakfast in a single room. Anyway, the dollar did the trick and he took himself off without any crack.

I knocked on the bedroom door. After the second try I heard her call out. I put my head round the door. "H'yah pal," I said. "Feel like puttin' on the feed bag?"

She struggled up in bed and blinked at me. Some dames look like the wrath of God in the early morning. Mardi looked swell. Her hair was all curls and her eyes looked large and lazy.

She stretched a little. The long sleeves of my pyjamas hid her hands. "Give me two minutes," she said, "and I'll be right with you."

She jumped out of bed and slipped on the woollen dressing-gown and flopped off to the bathroom. I wheeled the tray in and parked it beside the bed. Then I pulled up one of the blinds and left the other. Strong sunshine after a night out is apt to come tough.

She came back after five minutes and smiled at me. "Did you sleep well?" she asked, climbing into bed.

"Very well," I said, feeling sappy. I guess no one had asked me that one since I'd been out in the world earning my first dollar. "How did you make out?"

She arranged the pillows and sat up; the dressing-gown spread over the sheet. "Oh, I feel grand right now," she said. "I thought I'd've died last night, I was so tired."

I brought the tray over to the bed. "I'm glad we were together on that," I said, looking at her. "I'd've hated you to run into those guys on your own."

She took the cup of coffee, but she didn't take her eyes off my face. "I'm glad, too."

"Do you want to talk about last night?" she said.

I shrugged. "What's there to talk about?"

"Will it be all right?"

Again I shrugged. "I don't know," I said, "I've been puzzling my brains. I can't see how we can worry Spencer. After all, we have no proof and we don't seem to be getting anywhere. Somehow, I reckon it would be as well to leave the thing alone. How do you feel about it?"

She frowned a little. "I'm afraid we won't get away with it as easily as all that. You see, there's a lot you don't know about it all, and I'm scared sick that you're going to get yourself involved more than you think."

I lit a cigarette. "Tell me," I said, getting up to take the tray and to give her a cigarette also.

She relaxed back on the pillows. "It all begins some time ago," she said.

"I think I know who your mysterious lady is."

I sat up. "You do?" I said.

She nodded. "Yes, I think it's Sarah Spencer, Lu's wife."

"Well, for Pete's sake."

"It fits, once you know the inside story. You see, I was Mr. Spencer's private secretary, and I used to spend a good bit of my time at his house. He worked late and he liked to have me around to straighten things out for him. Sarah Spencer was around a lot and I was always running into her. Spencer is crazy about her, but she two-times him from morning till night. How it is he hasn't got wise to her beats me. You see, I do know that Vessi was one of her boy friends."

I got to my feet and began to wander around the room. "I'd like you to expand on that," I said.

"She was very fond of Vessi," Mardi told me. "Really fond of him. Sarah is the type who likes them rough, and Vessi meant a lot to her. When he was executed she nearly went out of her mind. I had to work for two days right in the house, so I should know. She drove us all haywire. You have no idea. I think she hates Lu."

I sat on the bed. "You've opened the door," I said. "As you say, it fits. She wants to get Lu on trial. That evens things up with Vessi and it gets rid of him. She couldn't come out in the open and accuse Lu of knocking Richmond off. The Vessi angle would come out in court and it wouldn't be nice for her. So she hides behind a telephone and makes me the goat."

Mardi nodded. "Yes," she said, "I think that's what it all means."

I thought some more. "It would have been easy for her to know what was going on," I said. "All the things she knew to tell me over the 'phone came from keeping her ears open and listening in to Lu's talk with his boys. I dare say she had ample opportunity of doing that. Then again she's rich, I take it, and ten grand would have been peanut money for her to get rid of Lu."

Mardi stubbed out her cigarette. "She's crazy about the men. She's running Curtis now. He's working for Lu, as you know, and I guess he told her all she wanted to know."

I suddenly thought of Kennedy. Was he an old flame of hers? I guessed I was getting near to the truth.

"Well," I said, "this is going to get her nowhere. I'm through, so she can whistle for another goat."

Mardi fixed her big eyes on me. "You don't know Sarah Spencer," she said quietly. "I'm scared. She won't let you go as easily as that."

I grinned at her. "Don't you worry your head," I said. "No dame's goin' to rush me into somethin' I ain't keen about."

"Please don't…." She looked so scared that I got up and went over to sit on the bed.

"Now take it easy," I said, putting my hand on hers. "Just take it easy."

She said, "But you don't know her. She's dangerous. She won't stop at anything."

I liked the feel of her hand in mine. I took each finger in turn between my finger and thumb and gently pressed her nails. "Suppose we wait an' see," I said. "It's no good getting steamed up before anythin' starts. Now forget about it, honey, we got other things to think about. I've gotta make plans. What are we goin' to do with you?"

She was quite content to leave her hand in mine. We sat there looking at each other, and when she saw I wasn't worrying she relaxed and smiled at me.

"You're good to have around, Nick," she said. "I guess I'd be in a bad spot without you."

"I'd like you to be around always."

She shook her head. "Don't say that," she said, taking her hand away. "You don't have to say it."

"I know. I wouldn't say it if I didn't mean it. I've tried to get you out of my system, but you stick. I guess this sounds cock-eyed to you, but I want to go on with you." I stopped because I just couldn't get the words out.

She saw what I meant all right. She said very softly, "What about me? Do you think—"

"I'm thinking about you. I wouldn't've started this if I hadn't've been thinking about you. It's because of you that I want you and me to go on. I think you and I could go on—"

I got up. It was no use. I couldn't put it over. I guess I regretted being what I was for the first time in my life. I regretted all the other dames. I regretted almost everything.

I went over to the window and looked out. The silence in the room made me think of a church. Then she said, "Nick…." She was crying.

I went over to her and put my arms round her. I didn't say anything. I just put my arms round her and held her. She cried against my silk dressing-gown. I could feel her body trembling.

"Be kind to me," she said. "We are going to have a strange life together."

When she said that, I felt good. It was like coming through a bad storm, shutting the door on the wind and the rain and knowing that it was quiet inside.

I shifted my position so that I lay beside her, and she put her head on my shoulder. Her soft hair touched my face and I held both her hands in mine.

When she had stopped crying and was quite calm again, I said, "Suppose we go an' get married quick? Would you like that?"

She stayed so still, after I had said that, that I thought she had not heard me, but I just waited, wondering how it would all come out and if she really wanted me. She sighed then, and relaxed.

"Would you say a thing like that if you didn't really mean it?" she said at last, leaning away from me so that she could look up at my face. Her eyes were very bright and her lips were parted, and behind the brightness of her eyes I could see she was scared.

I said, "No, I wouldn't. It's how I want it to be."

She shook her head. "You're crazy, Nick. You don't want to marry me."

"I know why you say that. You think I'm just like the rest. You don't know me yet."

"No—I do know you. It's not because of you, it's because of me. What do you know of me? How can you—"

I grinned down at her. "I know you're swell an' I want you. Let's be nice to each other, honey—we'll get along."

She gripped my hands hard. "You mean you'll marry me? You'll marry me?"

"What is it, baby?" I didn't get her angle. She seemed scared that I'd change my mind. This was crazy to me, because I thought I was the one to be getting scared.

She smiled suddenly. "You haven't kissed me yet."

"I will if you'll marry me."

"Kiss me, then."

And that's how it was.

It was over an hour after, when we got down to the first stage of making plans and wondering what we were going to do, that I remembered Kennedy. Why I hadn't remembered that guy before beat me. Right there I had the solution to everything.

I said, "I've got the place. You'll be tickled to death with it."

She said, "Where?"

And I told her. She sat there, her eyes rather wide, not saying anything until I had finished. Then she shook her head. "No, Nick, we couldn't go there."

I got off the bed. "You don't know the place," I said. "You wait until you've seen it."

She put out her hand. "No, I mean that. I couldn't meet anyone just yet."

"I ain't asking you to meet anyone. No one will be there. Kennedy will be away. We'll have it to ourselves."

When I said that she relaxed. "You must make sure," she said.

After four unsuccessful 'phone-calls, I tracked the Colonel down and I told him how things were. Kennedy was an all-right guy. He was mighty pleased.

"Sure," he said, "you go ahead. I've got out of the lodge now and you can have it. Yes, you go ahead. I'll fix everything for you, an' you stay there as long as you like."

I told him what a regular fellow he was, but he just laughed it away. "Forget it," he said. "You have your honeymoon and enjoy yourselves. I'm glad you've got a girl; it's what you've been wanting."

We did a bit more back-slapping and then I put the receiver on the prong. I looked over at Mardi. She didn't have to be told, she saw it all right. "I said so, didn't I?"

She spread her hands helplessly. "Oh, I want it to be true," she said, "I want it to be true."

"You stay there until I get dressed. Then I'll go out and make it true," I told her. "We'll get this wedding fixed and then we'll go out to the lodge."

She sat up in bed. "I don't want you to leave me," she said quickly, her eyes looking scared. "Not now I know. Don't leave me, Nick."

I patted her arm. "Look, I'll fix it with Ackie. Then we can both stay right here and let him do it all."

She said, "Yes, do it that way," and her eyes lost the scared look.

I went over to the telephone and got hold of Ackie. I thought it would give him a shock. It did.

He said, "Hold everythin'. I've gotta see this jane first. Now for Gawd's sake hold everythin' until I get right over."

I hung up and grinned at Mardi. "He certainly is excited," I said. "He's coming right on up."

Mardi scrambled out of bed. "Run away, Nick," she said, "I want to get dressed."

Before I went into the next room I kissed her. Then I went off and got dressed myself. I was feeling swell. I felt like I could jump over the Empire State building.

I'd just finished dressing when Ackie blew in. He stood in the doorway, his monkey face looking worried. He said, "Where is she?"

I jerked my head to the door. "She won't be long," I told him. "She's getting dressed."

"Now listen, Nick," he said, coming over to me. "What is all this? You don't mean you're really gettin' married?"

I thumped him on his chest. "You bet I am," I said, "and you've got to fix it for us."

He lowered his voice. "She holdin' you up?"

"What do you mean… holdin' me up?"

He looked furtive. "You know… she ain't in trouble?"

"Now listen, you gutter-minded monkey, Mardi an' me are like this." I crossed my fingers. "I'm marrying her because it's the one thing I can do that I want to do. Now do you get it?"

He walked slowly away from me. "You mean you want to marry this jane?" He sounded incredulous.

"Yeah."

"And you want me to help you?"

"That's right."

"Well, by Heck! I guess you're nuts."

Just then Mardi came out. She stood in the doorway and Ackie got an eyeful. She certainly looked the cutest thing, with her big smoky eyes and her smile. Ackie just gaped. Then he looked at me. "Well," he said.

"Now do you get the idea?" I asked.

He shook his head mournfully. He went over to Mardi. "You poor little thing," he said, shaking hands. "What a break. You don't know what you're doing. You can't marry this guy… he ain't fit to marry anyone."

Mardi just laughed at him. "Are you going to help us?" she asked.

"You really want to get linked up with this heel?"

"He is rather nice. You don't know him as well as I do."

Ackie looked at me over his shoulder. "You've done a nice job grabbin' yourself this one," he said. "Why, sure, if I can help you, just count on me."

I fetched a bottle of Scotch and we two had a couple of quick ones. I said to Mardi, "Honey, while I talk with Mo, would you like to put my things together?"

I showed her where my grips were and left her sorting out my clothes. I got Ackie in a huddle. I told him the whole story, and he just sat there drinking it in along with my Scotch. When I had finished he heaved a sigh. "That's a swell story," he said. "Maybe when you've been bumped off I can print it."

A nice comforting sort of a guy to have around.

"There ain't goin' to be any bumpin'," I said sharply. "I'm goin' to get under cover and I'm goin' to stay that way for a little while. Kennedy's let me have his lodge. We plan to get married right away and then move on over there."

Ackie scratched his head. "It beats me how you do it. How you get a swell jane like that to have anythin' to do with you beats me. You certainly know how to look after yourself."

I gave him some money. "Go along an' see how quickly you can fix things. We'll go over to the Belmont Hotel until everything's fixed. I ain't too keen to be hanging around here. You get goin' and then come on over to the hotel."

I gave him another drink and he went in to say good-bye to Mardi. Ackie was an all-right guy, and I could see he was pleased that I'd got Mardi. It was just his way of putting things.

Mardi was sweet with him and he went off looking like the cat that got the cream.

I stood around watching Mardi pack. She made a swell job of it.

"How'd you like bein' a wife?" I said, sitting on my heels beside her.

"You mean doin' all this?" She paused and looked at me over her shoulder.

"That's right."

She closed the grip and sat on it so she could get the locks shut. I helped her. "I want to be good," she said seriously. "I want to do everything for you."

I laughed. "You be careful. You might be changing your mind."

We got the things together at last and I sent for the porter to take them down. Then I arranged to square up for the rent, and that was the finish of my apartment.

"I guess we can go," I said, looking round the room. "Everything's down. Put your wrap on and we'll go to the station and pick up your things."

She said, "I won't be a minute."

When she had gone into the other room someone knocked there.

I've an outer door. I thought it was the porter, so I just yelled out for him to come on in. The door opened and Blondie stood there.

I've had some shocks in my time, but this one rang the bell. I couldn't say anything.

She stood here, looking at me, her eyes cold and suspicious. "Movin' out, huh?" she said.

"What the hell do you want?"

She sidled into the room. "You don't sound so pleased to see me, darlin'," she said. "Didn't you say to come when I had somethin' to tell you?"

Keeping my voice down, and hoping Mardi wouldn't hear, I said, "I ain't interested any more. You scram quick. I've had enough of your outfit for life."

Just then Mardi came out. Blondie looked at her the same way a snake might look at its Christmas lunch. "So," she said.

I love a dame who talks like that.

Mardi went white. Not paper-white, but the blue-white of porcelain. She put one hand to her mouth and flinched away from Blondie.

I said sharply, "Leave me for a moment. There's no need for you two to meet."

Mardi turned and went back into the room.

Blondie said, "Wait...."

Mardi kept going and she shut the door.

Blondie turned on me. "So that's how it is?" she said, her eyes brooding thunder and lightning.

"Save it," I said tensely. I wasn't taking anything from this dame. "On your way, Blondie, and make it snappy."

She shook her head. "You ain't getting away with it like this," she said. "I've got to have a little talk with you."

I walked past her and threw open the door. "If you ain't outside in two seconds, I'll toss you out," I said.

At that moment the guy opposite me has to come out. He stood there, his eyes popping. I took no notice of him. I just waited for Blondie to take it on the lam.

She hesitated, but she knew she wasn't in the right place to start trouble. She walked slowly past me into the corridor. "All right, you heel," she said, "I'll make plenty of trouble for you."

"Save it," I told her. "I don't like you, and I never did. Keep away from me if you want to stay healthy, or else you'll run into a nasty shock."

I stepped inside and shut the door.

Mardi was looking out of the window. I wondered if it were going to make any difference. When she heard me come in she turned and ran over to me.

"Is it all right?" she said.

I put my arms round her. "That was Blondie. She's gone now. You see, we can't get away from this business until we get away from here. I'm sorry about it, honey, but she's gone. I guess we won't see her any more."

Mardi put her hand against my face, "I wish you had never started this," she said. "I wish—"

"Come on, honey," I said, taking her arm, "if I'd kept out of this I shouldn't have met you. We're goin' where it's good and where we can forget all about the whole business... you see."

And looking back, I guess that was about the dumbest crack I've ever made.

CHAPTER SIXTEEN

Trouble started four days after we had settled down at the lodge. They were four of the grandest days I ever spent. We had the place to ourselves and we did just what we liked. We dressed how we liked and we ate when we wanted to. We got up when we had had enough of bed, and we fooled around with fishing-lines until we had had enough of that. It was too good to last.

The first sign of trouble came with the postman. I got three articles returned. I couldn't believe my eyes. I sat there staring at them and looking at the printed rejection slips. I had had enough of them in the past to know what they were without reading the blab.

Mardi came in from the kitchen carrying a tray. She stood still when she saw my face, then she put the tray down and came over. "What is it?"

I said I didn't know. I said maybe there was a mistake or something. She said, "But what is it?"

I showed her the rejection slips. She stood reading them, her brow wrinkled. "Perhaps they weren't good enough," she said at last.

I said I thought maybe that was it. But I knew it wasn't. Something had gone wrong and I didn't like it. I had been feeding these papers with stuff for years and they had grabbed everything I had given them. Now, without a word, they turned me down.

I said, "Listen, honey, we gotta go slow for a bit. I was banking on this stuff to get us by for a couple of weeks."

She looked at me seriously. "You mean you are short of money?"

I shrugged. "Well, yes... I guess that's about right."

"Is that all? Are you sure that's all?"

It was enough, but I didn't want to worry her. "Yeah, that's all... I'll be just a little short."

She put her arm round my shoulders. "We'll get by," she said. "Don't you worry. We don't have to have a lot of money."

When we got through breakfast I went off to the study and thought things over. I checked my bank deposit and found I was shorter than I imagined. This was getting me worried. I put through a long-distance 'phone call to one of the editors. When I got him on the line at last I said,

"What's the big idea sending my stuff back?"

"What do you mean?" He sounded curt.

"Look, Johnson, this ain't the way to treat me," I said. "I've done some good work for you. If you didn't like that article, why not write and tell me what's wrong with it?"

"I'm sorry, Mason, we don't want any more of your stuff. We're looking round for new talent."

I said, "You don't have to give me this bull. I've been a good friend of yours, Buddy. Why not give it to me straight? I can take it."

He said very quietly into the 'phone, "Suppose you come up to town and we'll have lunch,"

I said, "I'll do that," and hung up.

I went out to find Mardi. She was in the suntrap, fixing some flowers.

"I gotta go up to town," I said. "It's about these articles. I gotta talk things over with the editor."

She said, "May I come with you? I mean, may I come up and look at the shops while you're busy?"

I shook my head. "Not just yet, honey. I want you to keep out of sight for a little while. I'll be right back."

She said, "I'll have a nice supper for you." I could see she didn't like being left, but she wasn't going to make things awkward. I put my arm around her. "Can I bring you anything back?" I said.

She shook her head. "We've got to save our money."

I laughed. "It ain't so bad as all that."

"Isn't… not ain't."

"You're the teacher."

She looked at me anxiously. "I don't nag you, do I?"

I grinned. "Sure you do… all day an' most of the night." I got up to town around twelve o'clock. It seemed all wrong after the silence of the fishing-lodge. I went into a bar and bought myself a drink. After I had wasted a little time I went round to the *Globe* building.

Johnson was waiting for me outside the place. I thought that was funny, but I didn't say anything. The way he shipped me into a taxi made me think he was anxious not to be seen with me.

I said, "You certainly gave me a surprise."

He fidgeted with his tie. "Yes, I'm mighty sorry about all this," he said.

"All right. Let's have a drink first and then we can talk about it. You tell me, how're things with you?"

He shrugged a little. "Oh, I'm making out all right."

"And the wife?"

"Yes, she's fine."

We rode the block in silence after that. I was beginning to get the jitters. We got out at a quiet restaurant off the main street that was unlikely to be crowded, and we made our way upstairs.

When we got settled, and after we had knocked back a few drinks, I thought it time for him to get down to things. "Now, what is all this about?"

"Well, I'm darned sorry about this, Mason, but we just can't take any more of your stuff."

"Can't or won't?"

He twiddled with his glass, and he wouldn't meet my eye. "It's nothin' to do with me," he explained hastily. "I've had instructions from the old man."

I sat back and let that one sink in. As I didn't say anything, he went on, "I guess you've got yourself in bad somehow. The old man's put the bar up."

"Did he say why?"

Johnson shook his head. "He just sent me a note. You know the type of note he sends out: 'Mr. Hawkin's compliments, and do not accept any further work from Mr. Nick Mason.'"

I shrugged. "I guess he's gone nuts," I said. "Here, have another drink."

We got through the meal somehow and then Johnson took himself off. I could see he was mighty glad to get shot of me. I stayed on after he'd gone and thought about things. Then I paid the bill and went over to a telephone-booth. I rang the press-room and asked for Ackie.

"Listen, Ackie, am I barred?"

"Yeah," he said, "you're washed up. What can I do about it for you?"

I thought a moment. "This is Spencer's idea of getting me out of town."

"Looks like it."

"I'm in a spot, Mo," I said. "I want some money."

Ackie gave a groan. "Hell! Is it as bad as that?"

"Well, I guess not as bad as all that. I can run for a couple of weeks, but I've gotta get some dough."

"You can count on me. I'll let you have some."

I grinned ruefully into the mouthpiece. "That's swell of you, but I've gotta earn a livin'. You can't keep me and Mardi all your life."

"Maybe it'll clear up by then, or maybe you'd better get moving."

I said, "I'll let you know," and I hung up.

So I was barred. This was serious. I walked out into the street thinking. Spencer looked like getting his own way. I knew I was up against a powerful mob, and I knew when to quit. It looked to me right then that I'd better pack up and move to another State.

I was feeling pretty low by the time I got back to the fishing-lodge. I didn't want to worry Mardi, but at the same time I wanted her to know just how I stood. I didn't know how far Spencer's influence carried. He was rich enough to carry weight with all the nationals. If the bosses had shares in this phoney business, they'd be glad to give him my head on a plate.

I walked up the drive, after I had parked the car in the garage. There was no sign of Mardi. I went quietly so that I should surprise her.

On my way up-town I'd got her two pairs of silk stockings. I'd felt pretty mushy buying them, but once I got clear of the shop I was glad. I guessed she would be pleased, because up to now I hadn't bought her anything.

I beetled into the hall and made for the kitchen. She wasn't there. So I went into the dining-room. The light was burning, but she wasn't there either. I was just going upstairs when I saw something that brought me up short.

I stood there feeling cold chills running through me, and a sick feeling gathering inside me. I tried to kid myself that the two dark stains at my feet were paint stains, but I knew they weren't. Slowly, I knelt down and touched one of them with my finger-tips. It was wet and sticky.

I stood up, looking at my fingers in the electric light. They were a bright red. Without knowing what I was doing I walked into the kitchen and let the water from the sink tap run over my hands. Deliberately I took a towel and wiped them dry.

I was so scared and sick that I was afraid to do anything else. I just stood there holding the towel, sweating ice. I heard myself say out loud: "Don't let them have killed her… don't let them have killed her… please, God,… don't let them have killed her."

I told myself I'd have to go and look. I had to go upstairs and see where she was, but that's as far as I could go. Nothing would get me out of the kitchen and upstairs.

I put the towel away after folding it carefully. I had to do something. I went back to the middle of the kitchen and stood there waiting. I said to myself that Mardi would come in in a moment from the garden, but I knew she wouldn't. Katz had found her, and he had killed her; that I knew was what had happened, but I wouldn't let myself believe it. I kept saying she'd be along in a moment or so, that the stuff on the floor outside was paint, it just couldn't be Mardi's blood, but I knew it was.

Then I thought of her all alone when Katz came. I could see her against the wall, her big, smoky eyes very wide, but her chin up. That would be the way she'd face up to Katz. She'd be thinking of me, and all the time she was going away from me I was talking to that bastard Johnson. I was worrying about dough when Mardi was being killed.

The sick feeling inside me began to ease a little, and the first shock gave way to a numbed feeling at the back of my brain. I went outside and stood looking at the bloodstains in the sitting-room. They were near the wall. When I looked closer I could see two bruises on the paint on the wainscoting. They looked like two heel marks. I could picture Mardi trying to press herself into the wall as Katz came at her. It made me feel so bad that I had to sit down.

Then I did a thing I'd never done since I was a kid. I didn't know I was doing it until I tasted the salt in my mouth. Going on like this wouldn't get me anywhere so I got up and gave myself a shot of Scotch. I took three-quarters of a tumbler and it went down like water. I guess it did the trick all right, because I got a grip on myself and I began to use my brain.

I went over to the telephone and dialled. I knew I couldn't handle this on my own. I had to share this with someone. I said to Ackie: "Come on out here fast."

That's the big thing about Ackie, he always knew when you wanted him bad. He didn't ask why, nor did he make excuses. I knew that he was right in the middle of going to press, but he just said: "Keep your shirt on, I'm on my way," and he hung up.

If he came fast he could make it in an hour. I knew I couldn't wait an hour before going upstairs. I went over to the sideboard and belted the Scotch again, then I decided to go on up and see.

I went into the hall and looked up the stairs. The lodge was silent. Standing there, facing the stairs, I realized how much Mardi meant to me. I began to walk forward. The stairs seemed to go on a long way. I couldn't hurry, but I kept on. When I reached the top I felt heavy in the legs, just as if I'd been walking through glue.

On the landing there were two bathrooms, two bedrooms and a dressing-room. All the five doors were shut. Mardi might be behind any one of these. I knew the most likely would be our bedroom, but I didn't try that first. I went into one of the bathrooms. She wasn't there. I left the door open and the light on and went into the dressing-room. She wasn't there either.

I went out on to the landing and stood looking at the other doors and I felt bad. It took me a little while before I could go on. This time I went to our bedroom. I turned the handle slowly and pushed the door open, then I put my hand round and turned on the light. I didn't go in at once. I just stood looking in.

I looked everywhere but at the bed, because I knew she would be there. Then I brought my eyes down to the bed. I felt the cold trickle of sweat running down my back.

There was a large stain on the white sheet, which was drawn over her face. I could see, from where I was standing, the small hills that marked her feet, her hands, her breasts, and her nose. The sheet was drawn tight and I could clearly see those small hills.

I leant against the doorpost and just looked. Then I began to hate Spencer and his wife and Katz and the fat guy and Gus and the whole hellish business as I had never hated anything before. I wanted to get close to them all and get my hands on them. I wanted to hurt and kill them all because of what they had done to me. I no longer cared what would happen to me. I just wanted to even things up, knew that I was just kidding myself, because if I did kill them all it wouldn't help me. It wouldn't bring Mardi back and it would never take the picture I had of her facing what she had faced alone.

If only I had been there with her we could have gone out together. I know she wouldn't have minded.

I didn't go into the room. I turned off the light and went downstairs again. In the sitting-room I sat down and fumbled for my cigarette-case. I noticed, as I struck a match, that my hands were very steady. I was a little surprised. I just sat there smoking with a blank mind until Ackie came.

I heard his car roaring up the drive and I went out to meet him. He had come faster than I thought. He was out of the car before I could get to the front door, and when he had a look at me he just pushed me back into the lodge and shut the front door.

"What is it, Nick?"

I opened and shut my mouth, but no sound came. I just stood looking at him.

He put his hand on my arm. His face had gone very grim. "Mardi? Somethin' happened to Mardi?"

I took a deep breath. It was worse than I thought. It made it much more real to have to say it. I had to put out a big effort to get control of myself. I could feel the muscles in my stomach fluttering. "They've killed her, Mo." Well, it was out now.

Ackie didn't believe it. He pushed me into the sitting-room. "They wouldn't do that," he said. "Get a grip on yourself, Nick. Come on an' have a drink. They wouldn't kill a kid like that."

I grabbed him by the arm and swung him round. "I tell you they've killed her, the swine. She's up there on the bed. Look… they killed her here. Look at the blood. Do you see that? That's hers. That's from her body. They killed her down here. They came on her when she was alone and the yellow curs killed her against the wall."

Ackie took a look at the bloodstains. Then he shook his head. "Take it easy," he said, "take it easy."

I seized his coat-front in my fist and shook him. "Don't say that to me!" I shouted at him. "I tell you she's up there…."

He hit me across the face with the flat of his hand very hard. I guess I wanted that. It shook me up and it hurt a lot, but it fixed me. I blinked at him and took my hand away. "I'm sorry, Mo," I said, stepping away from him. "I guess I was excited."

"Sure," he said. "Suppose we go up?"

With Ackie, I felt I could do it. We went upstairs quickly. I turned on the light in the bedroom and walked over to the bed.

I heard Ackie say: "Good God!"

I pulled the sheet down with a steady hand. The floor seemed to rise up under me and I felt Ackie grab at my arm. We both stood staring.

Even in death Blondie looked hard and suspicious. Her glazed eyes were fixed in a terrified stare and the vivid paint on her mouth glistened in the electric light. A small bullet-hole just above her left breast told me how she had died.

CHAPTER SEVENTEEN

Ackie said: "No… don't say anythin'. Let me think."

I walked away from the bed. My brain was stiff.

Ackie put his hand on Blondie's arm, then took her wrist and raised it. I just stood there and watched him. "She ain't been dead long," he said. He covered her with the sheet and came away from the bed.

He said: "We'll look in the other rooms."

I stayed right there and let him do it. He came back after a while and shook his head. "There's no one anywhere."

I sat down.

"You see, they didn't kill her… they've only taken her away," Ackie said.

He went out of the room again.

I repeated after him: "They've only taken her away." I guess I felt as bad as when I thought she was dead.

Ackie came back again with the scotch and two glasses. He put the glasses down on the table and poured the whisky out carefully. Then he came over and put one of the glasses in my hand.

"If you want to get Mardi back you gotta snap out of it," he said.

He was right.

"This is a frame-up, Nick," he went on, "the old gag again. The same stunt as they pulled on Vessi. Blondie knew too much so they knocked her off and planted her on you. The next thing you'll know is that the cops will roll up and make a pinch. They'll get away with it just like they got away with it the first time."

He was right again.

I finished up my Scotch and got to my feet. My own danger didn't worry me, but if I were behind bars there was no one to find Mardi. I had to get this angle right first.

"You better keep out of this, Mo," I said. "I can't drag you into it."

Ackie filled up his glass again. "Forget it."

"No… I mean that."

"I'm in with you from now on. We're going to bust this thing wide open. We're going to get Mardi back and we're going to get Spencer on trial. We're going to find out what's at the bottom of the Mackenzie Fabrics, and when we've done all that we're going to write the grandest news story, and we're going to get someone to print it."

I said: "Do you mean that?"

"Yeah, I'm in on it, and you can't keep me out."

I was glad to have Ackie with me. He was an all-right guy and a tough egg to have around when trouble starts. "We gotta get this dame outta here first. We gotta do that quick. That'll spoil any frame-up they're hoping to slap on you."

"How the hell are we going to do that?"

Ackie scratched his head. "We'll take her out in my car and drop her somewhere."

"It would be better to take her round to her own apartment and leave her there. In her profession she might've been knocked off by anyone."

Ackie nodded. "We'll do that."

We had a couple of drinks, but they didn't do much good. Ackie got her hat and put it on her head. He pulled it down hard, so that it hid the glassy look in her eyes. He stood looking down at her. "I guess she looks okay now," he said, scratching his head.

"I'll be glad when we've got her out of here."

Ackie nodded. "I guess we'll get goin' right away. I bet you evens she stiffens on us before we get her there."

"I've had enough grief for one night. I ain't taking bets with you."

"Well, let's go."

We sat Blondie up and adjusted the short fox-fur cape over her shoulders that we had found in the room. It hid the bloodstains all right.

Ackie said quickly: "You'll have to carry her… she's too heavy for me."

I put my arm round her waist and the other arm under her knees and lifted her off the bed. Make no mistake about it, that dame was heavy.

Ackie said: "Don't be standoffish, madam, put your arm round his neck."

I said: "If you don't cut that line right out, I ain't goin'."

Ackie rubbed his hand over his face. "Jeeze, it I don't make a joke of it, I'll go nuts."

"Well, go nuts, but cut that line out."

Going downstairs I nearly dropped her. My teeth began to rattle in my head.

Ackie was coming down behind me. He had brought the bottle of Scotch, and every step down he took a quick drag at the bottle. He was getting cock-eyed as hell. I put Blondie down on a chair and took the bottle away from him. "Listen, you punk," I said evenly, "you're supposed to be helpin' me. Will you get a grip on yourself an' help?"

"Sure," he said, "sure… you don't have to worry."

Blondie suddenly stretched out her legs and began to slide off the chair. We both stood staring at her, unable to move. Ackie said, in a quavering voice: "I don't think I'm goin' to stand a lot of this."

Blondie sat down on the floor with a little bump and then flopped on her side. Her hat came off and one of her shoes.

Ackie sat on the stairs and hid his face. "I think I'll commit suicide," he said.

When I straightened her out I found her muscles were hardening. "Quick, Mo," I said, "she's gettin' stiff."

Ackie got up and gave me her hat. "Maybe she'll be easier to handle that way," he said hopefully.

I crammed the hat on her head again. "Get hold of her knees… we'll never get her into the car."

We carried her out into the dark night. I could only hear Ackie's heavy breathing and the sound of our feet crunching on the gravel. Overhead, the sky looked stormy. Big clouds raced across the face of the moon.

The car was a big six-seater, but it took us all our time getting her in. We got her fixed at last in the corner of the seat. In the dim light of the roof-lamp she looked good. No one would have known that she was dead.

Ackie said: "That's a swell job,"

"You stay here… I've got to get her shoe."

"If you think I'm staying out with her alone you're barmy," he said with great feeling. "We'll do this together or not at all."

We turned out the light inside the car and went back inside the lodge.

"Before we go we'd better clean up this mess," I said.

We did that. When we were through we had another drink and then turned out the lights and went out to the car.

"We'll toss who drives," I said.

I won.

Ackie began to get in beside me. "You get in the back… that's why we tossed," I said. "You see she doesn't fall over."

"And I called you a pal of mine," Ackie said. He stood hesitating, then he finally made up his mind. He opened the door and got in. "Now be a good girl," he said to Blondie.

I engaged the gear and rolled the car down the drive.

Ackie said after a while: "She's sitting as quiet as quiet. I guess I could come on in the front."

"You stay right there."

"Listen, Bud, if I've gotta stay here I've got to have a drink. There's a pint just by your hand… pass it over."

I groped around in the dashboard cupboard and found a bottle. I passed it over to him.

"You ain't got much gas," I said, looking at the gauge. "That's careless of you, Mo. I shall have to stop and get some."

Ackie didn't say anything for a minute… I guessed he was giving himself a shot. Then he said: "That's your funeral, Bud, me an' the girl friend'll leave all that to you."

I said: "For Pete's sake keep as sober as you can."

"If you were right here, you'd try an' get as tight as a tick… that's what keeps me from goin' crackers. How'd you like to be sitting next to a corpse? She's looking at me all the time. I'm tellin' you, this dame just can't see enough of me. It's givin' me the heebies."

"Aw, shut up," I said, and concentrated on the dark road. After a little while Ackie began to sing. I couldn't stand that. I took my foot off the gas-pedal and stamped on the brake. I twisted round in the seat. "For suffering in silence," I said, "will you lay off it?"

"She likes it," Ackie said. "You ask her an' see."

I switched on the light inside the car. Ackie was crouched up on the far side away from Blondie, his face the colour of a fish's belly and his eyes popping. I reached out a hand and took the bottle away from him. He'd been working on it. There was only just one small drink left, and I had it. I tossed the bottle off the road.

"Take it easy," I said; "for Pete's sake take it easy."

"Sure… you just go on… we're fine here. I tell you we're fine."

I started the car rolling again. The gas was getting low and I couldn't risk running out on a well-lit road. I'd have to take some on board at the nearest hick station.

I didn't have to go far before I sighted one. I slowed down.

"I've got to pull in for some gas," I said. "Keep quiet an' don't start anything."

"Start anything? Don't make me laugh. Blondie an' me are playin' at graves."

I wished Ackie had kept away from the bottle. In this state he was likely to land us all in a jam. When I thought of Blondie sitting right behind me, I sweated some.

I swung the big car into the narrow station and killed the engine. An old guy came out with a goatee beard. So that he didn't get too close to the car I stepped out.

"Give me ten," I said briefly.

As he was adjusting the dial a motor-cycle came banging up out of the darkness. When I saw the dim outline of the stetson hat I stiffened. It was a State trooper.

I said to the old guy, "Snap into it, Buddy, I'm rushed."

The State trooper dismounted and wandered into the light. I recognized him. He was a guy named Flanaghan. I'd known him in my cub days. Although I tried to duck into the shadows he recognized me.

"Ain't you Mason?" he said, peering at me.

I gave him my hand. "Well, well," I said, pump-handling him. "Ain't it a small world?"

I'm glad that guy couldn't read my thoughts. He was a nice social fellow and he might have had a shock.

"What are you doin' around here?" he asked after we had got through with the back-slapping.

"Been staying at Colonel Kennedy's lodge," I told him. "Just taking a run into town."

He glanced over at the car. At that minute Ackie rolled the window down and stuck his head out. "Hey, Nick," he bawled, "watch this dame."

Flanaghan took a step forward. "Well, if it ain't that old son-of-a-gun from the *Globe*," he said.

Ackie gaped at him. "H'yah," he said feebly. "Who thought you'd be around?"

"Who's the dame?" Flanaghan asked. He had always been a great guy for the dames.

Ackie glanced at me. This had sobered him a little. "You don't have to worry about her," he said, keeping his voice down. "She's cock-eyed."

"How do you mean, cock-eyed? You mean she's stiff?"

Ackie jerked his head at me. "Did you tell him?" he asked in a croaking voice.

I said, "Mo means she's a little tight."

There was an awkward silence, then Flanaghan said, "I hope you boys ain't up to no dirty work."

Ackie withdrew into the car and sat down. Past his shoulder I could see Blondie's big hat. I felt the sweat trickling down my back. "You know how it is," I said. "She ain't used to our drinking and she took a little too much. We're taking her right home to sleep it off."

Ackie moved over to Blondie and put his arm round her. I guess that guy was still pretty high.

Flanaghan stepped round me and peered into the car. Ackie took a quick look at him over his shoulder and moved closer to Blondie. He effectively screened Blondie from Flanaghan.

He said in a loud voice, "Hey! Wake up, honey. There's a cop askin' after your health."

I took off my hat and wiped my forehead.

Flanaghan pushed in closer.

"You all right, baby?" Ackie bawled.

Then out of the silence that followed a horrible soprano voice floated out of the car. "Sure I'm all right. Tell the officer to go take a pill."

With horrified fascination I saw Blondie nod her head twice and move her arm a little.

Satisfied, Flanaghan stepped back. "I guess that dame's as stiff as a board," he said. "You'd better get her home."

I shoved some money into the hand of the old guy and slid under the wheel. "I'll be seeing you some time," I called, and I engaged the gears. The car shot away from the service station fast, leaving Flanaghan scratching his head, looking after us.

Ackie said in a faint voice, "You wouldn't call this dame a hot one now. I'm about frozen to death."

I said, "For the love of Mike keep quiet, you bum."

We drove the rest of the way in silence. When we reached Blondie's apartment it started to rain. Big drops the size of nickels came splashing down on the street. That was the one break we had had on the journey. Rain as hard as this would keep the streets cleared.

I swung open the car door and climbed out. "Wait until I get the door open," I said.

Ackie said, "Sure, leave me with the corpse every time."

I went over to the front door. In the faint light I could just make out the glitter of the plate. I thought she wasn't going to need that any more. I only had a vague idea of how I was going to get in, but when I tried the handle the door opened. I stood hesitating, then I stepped inside. I ran up the stairs quickly to Blondie's room. There was no one in the bedroom and the room was in darkness.

Down I went again and called to Ackie. "It's okay. We'll get her out."

Ackie said, "You get one side, I'll handle the other."

We got her under the arms and ran across the pavement with her. I had to take her up the stairs, there wasn't room for the three of us. I can tell you when I reached her bedroom I was mighty glad.

Ackie said behind me, "Put her in a chair. She'll sit more natural that way."

Then the bathroom door opened quickly and Katz slid into the room. He took just one look at me and went for his gun.

CHAPTER EIGHTEEN

If a guy pulls a rod on you in a small room and starts popping at you, there is only one thing to do, apart from saying your prayers.

I did the best I could do under the circumstances.

I dived across the room and landed on Katz. He tried to get his leg up to kick at me, but he was just too late. His rod jerked out of his hand and fell on the floor somewhere. I thought Ackie would be bright enough to collect it.

Katz got a grip round the barrel of my chest that surprised me. This guy looked like a thin dope, but he'd got plenty of what it takes. Before I could grab him, he had tossed me away so that I came down hard on Blondie. I was too rattled to care much about that, and as I scrambled to my feet Katz swung his legs round and caught me in a scissor-grip round the neck. I knew all about those sort of tricks, and I had his shoe off and was giving his big toe the works before he could start to put on any pressure.

"Sock into him," Ackie yelled from the doorway. "Give him hell, Buddy."

It broke the hold all right, but I collected a stiff kick in the face as I was getting set to jump him. I was glad that the kick came from the foot without a shoe, otherwise I should have seen a few bright lights.

Anyway, I went over backwards and it gave Katz time to get off the bed, then I went for him again. I was remembering Mardi now, so I hit that guy hard where it would hurt him. It did. He flopped on the bed, his eyes glazing. I had him by his long hair and snapped another wallop to his jaw just to make sure. He went out like a light.

I stood over him, blowing on my knuckles.

"I was just beginning to enjoy it," Ackie said. "You shouldn't've washed him up that quick."

I went round the bed and gathered Blondie up. She'd lost her hat, but she still looked as suspicious and hard as ever.

I put her in the one armchair and made sure that she wouldn't fall forward.

Ackie leant against the doorpost watching. "Gee! This looks like one of those horror plays," he said, jerking his head at Katz, lying flat on the bed, and then over to Blondie.

"I've got to get this guy round. I want him to talk," I said. "Lend a hand, Mo; we'll tie him up first in case he starts trouble."

Ackie's face brightened. "You goin' to give him the works?" he asked.

"Yeah, I'm going to give it to him until he's come as clean as Aimee's surplice."

Ackie scratched his head. "You're sure headin' for trouble. This guy's the bad man of the town. He'll start something which might come awkward."

I didn't bother to answer. I knew that things would start to hum pretty soon, and as long as I was making them hum I didn't care. I ran through Katz's pockets. The first thing I turned up was a roll of money. I didn't have to count it. I knew that it was the five grand that Blondie had lifted off me. I showed the roll to Ackie. "That's why he was up here," I said. "Just lining his pocket, the yellow punk."

"You keepin' it?"

I shook my head. "I'm not takin' any chances. I'll leave it where I found it. If the cops are looking for me, that would be a fine one to pin on me."

"You think of everything, don't you?" Ackie looked at me admiringly. He was nearly sober by now, and I guess the drink was dying on him hard.

"Go into the bathroom and get some towels. I want to fix this bird."

Ackie came back after a moment with a couple of towels. "Nice joint this, ain't it?" he said.

I grunted and took the towels from him. I tore them in two and trussed Katz. I made a good job of it. Ackie leant over the bed-rail and watched.

I knew Ackie was scared, but he wasn't saying anything. He just stood and watched. I knew he was thinking that if we didn't get away with this, we were going to get into a pretty tight jam. I thought it mighty white of him to come in with me.

I hauled off and slapped Katz across the face twice. He moved his head, muttered and then opened his eyes. As soon as he saw me he sat up. I put my hand over his face and slammed him back on the bed. Even though he was just coming to the surface he'd got enough savvy to try and bite me.

"Get a grip on yourself," I told him, "I want you to do a little talking. If you're smart, you'll start right away, but if you think you can get away with anything you're going to get the works."

Katz drew his breath in with a sharp little hiss. His eyes half closed and his mouth became a slit in his white face. "You're crazy to start this, Mason," he said. "Why, you punk, you sure must be crazy to think you can get away with this."

I was in no mood to talk turkey to this guy. As I hit him a thin trickle of blood came from his nose and ran down to the side of his mouth. He put his tongue out and carefully licked his lips. I guess that guy hated me as much as he could hate anyone.

I sat down on the edge of the bed, close to him. "I don't care if I have to rip you to bits," I said, speaking softly, "but you're going to talk. Where's my wife? Where's Mardi Jackson?"

He didn't know. I felt a cold chill of disappointment grip me when I saw the expression in his eyes. He didn't say anything, but I knew he wasn't bluffing. The question had come as a surprise, I could tell that.

"All right," I said, "I'll try again. What's behind the Mackenzie racket?"

This time he shifted his eyes. "You go to hell," he said. "You ain't makin' me talk."

I said to Ackie, "Sit on his legs."

Ackie came round the bed like I'd asked him to sit on a rattlesnake. He didn't look at Katz, but he pinned him just the same. I jerked off Katz's sock and looked at him. "When you're ready to talk, just let me know," I said, "I ain't in no hurry."

I took a cigarette from my case and lit it. When the end was glowing, I took it out of my mouth and brought it near his foot. If Ackie hadn't been sitting on him, I guess that guy would have bounced off the ceiling. I guess these tough guys are all the same. He just curled up, the sweat jumping out of his face.

"Okay… okay…" he said hoarsely. "I'll talk."

"There's your rattlesnake," I said to Ackie. "Just yellow right through."

Ackie stood up and sneered. "Why, you punk," he said, "we ain't even started on you yet."

"Leave him alone, Mo. You talk rough to this guy an' he'll take his hair down and weep."

Katz just lay on the bed glaring at us.

I threw the cigarette into the fireplace. "Come on," I said. "What's behind the Mackenzie racket?"

It took some time to drag it out of him, but I got it out of him at last. The set-up was simple once you got the key. The Mackenzie Fabric Inc. was an enormous clearing-house for stolen goods. It worked like this: with the big imports from China and England of clothes and silks, all kinds of stolen articles were smuggled in the bales. In the same way articles stolen in America could be shipped out to the various continental agencies representing Mackenzie Fabrics abroad.

Spencer was the big shot. It was his job to buy or to sell whatever came into his hands from the various gangs operating throughout the States. With most of the high officials getting a rake-off in the form of dividends, the racket was watertight.

I knew that once Katz got free he'd stop at nothing to finish us both. We knew too much now ever to be safe. There was only one way and that was to see that Katz was under cover long enough to give me the time to bust the racket.

I didn't fancy knocking him off in cold blood, but at the moment I couldn't see what else I could do. Ackie was watching me and he understood what I was thinking about.

"Leave it to me," he said, "I guess it'd be easy to frame him for twenty-four hours."

I looked at him hard. "Twenty-four hours ain't so long," I said. "It's going to take most of that to get into action."

Ackie shrugged. "That's as long as we can hold him, I guess," he said. "We just gotta make things move."

The longer we argued about it the more time we wasted, so I let Ackie go ahead with his idea.

"We get this bird down to the station house and book him under assault. I can tip the sergeant to keep him under cover for a bit. He's a pal of mine an' he'd lose a rat like that for a little while."

I stood up. "Okay... let's go."

Katz wasn't putting up a beef. He went with us down the stairs, his hands still tied behind him. Ackie went first, then Katz and then I followed. Before leaving the room I made certain that we'd left no tell-tale clues that might hook us up with Blondie's death, then with one last look at the still figure in the chair I snapped off the light and followed Katz down.

When we got to the street door I rammed his gun into his back. "Don't start anything, brother," I said. "We've got nothing to lose and I'd like the chance of putting a slug into you."

He hobbled across the pavement and got into the car. I got in beside him and Ackie got under the wheel.

"If there's any liquor left," I said, "I guess a slug apiece wouldn't come hard."

Ackie groped around and shook his head. "There ain't none," he said dispiritedly. "Ain't that hell?"

"Well, go on… the sooner we get this bird put away the better."

During the run to the station house I was busy thinking. The first thing I'd got to do was to find Mardi. Nothing else mattered as long as I found her. Then I'd got to find enough evidence to bust up Spencer. If I wanted a clear field, I'd gotta do that within twenty-four hours. Not an easy programme, but I guess I had to do it.

If Spencer hadn't kidnapped Mardi, who had? I might be wrong thinking that Spencer hadn't done it, but Katz hadn't known anything about it, and Katz was Spencer's right-hand man. Maybe the fat guy and Gus had pulled it, but even then Katz would have known about it. And that was one thing I was sure about. Katz knew nothing about it at all.

I suddenly remembered. I could see Mardi's frightened face and I remembered what she had said. "You don't know Sarah Spencer. I'm scared. She's dangerous. She won't stop at anything."

Sarah Spencer! I sat up. Was she at the bottom of all this? Was it she who had taken Mardi away from me? The more I thought about it, the more likely it seemed to be. By the time we got to the station I was itching to get after that dame.

Ackie drove round to the back entrance and got out. "You stay here," he said. "I want to see if the coast's clear."

I looked at Katz and dug him in the ribs with the gun. "You're soon going to have a nice long rest," I said, "an' I hope you'll have plenty to think about."

Without looking at me, he said, "You won't last long now, Mason. If you think you can buck this racket you're nuts. You're the nearest thing to a corpse I've ever put my eyes on."

When he'd got that little lot off his chest, he laughed. Oh yes, this guy had got his nerve back, once he knew we weren't going to knock him off. I didn't like the sound of his laugh either.

Ackie came out and jerked his head. "I'm glad I went in," he said, keeping his voice down. "Lazard was in there. The smartest mouthpiece in town. If he'd spotted this guy coming in, he'd have sprung him' so fast he'd've made you dizzy."

I looked at Katz uneasily. A lot depended on keeping this guy out of mischief.

"Where's this Lazard now?" I asked.

"He's just comin' out. We'll wait until he's scrammed, then we'll go on in."

While Ackie was saying this, I saw a figure come out through the rear exit. A short, fat figure with a large gallon hat on his head. Katz saw him the same time as I did and he let out a hell of a squawk.

I spun round and hit him as hard as I could. I guess Katz was expecting it because he ducked down and my fist crashed against the bony structure of his forehead. It felt like I had hit a brick wall and a white-hot pain shot up my arm. The force of the punch stunned Katz and he sank limply against the cushions of the car.

Ackie said softly, "He's comin' over."

Lazard had heard the squawk and he stood listening; then he moved cautiously towards us. Ackie took a step or two from the car to intercept him.

"What's goin' on here?" Lazard asked.

Ackie stood squarely in his way. "Nothin' that'd interest you," he said shortly. "Suppose you drift, brother. I don't like guys askin' questions."

Lazard peered at him. "Why, Ackie," he said, "what the hell are you doin' here?"

"Scram, brother," Ackie said patiently. "You're in the way."

This guy Lazard was smart all right. He said with a little grit in his voice: "If you're holdin' someone against their will, I guess it is something to interest me."

Katz was coming out of his trance. I said very softly to him, "One yap from you, an' I'm goin' to wrap this gun around your mug."

In the meantime Lazard was trying to edge round Ackie. They looked like they were going into a slow motion of an African dance. Ackie got mad suddenly. "If you don't scram," he said suddenly, "I'm going to do things to you."

The threat in his voice brought Lazard up short. He took two steps back quickly. "I guess you're drunk," he said. "You be careful, you can get into a lot of grief being that way."

He stood hesitating for a moment, then he turned and walked away.

We stood and watched him go in silence, then I relaxed a little. I wiped off my hands on the sides of my coat. "I don't like that, Mo," I said.

Ackie cursed a little. "We gotta watch that guy. I'll go in and fix the sergeant. You wait here."

He didn't take long and he came back again with a hard grin on his face. "It's okay," he said. "Bring him in."

We got Katz out of the car and ran him over to the station house. Not until I'd got him inside did I feel at all easy; even then, I wondered if it would be better to take him to the other station house on Riverside.

The desk sergeant came out of an adjoining room and nodded at me. He was a big, red-faced Mick, with a cold, hard eye.

Ackie said, "Get this bird under cover… Lazard may come back."

The sergeant looked at Katz. "I've always wanted to get my hands on you," he said. "Bring him in here." He kicked open another door and led the way down a long passage.

Katz suddenly bent double, swung round, and made a dash for the street door. I was expecting it, but I didn't expect him to move so quickly. He nearly got away. He got to the door and, just as he was passing through, I collared him round the knees. We went down together with a crash.

The sergeant was close behind me and together we dragged Katz back into the station house. Katz fought like a madman and yelled at the top of his voice.

I managed to step clear for a second and I hit him on the point of his jaw. He went slack. The sergeant dragged him down the passage, down some stone steps, into a large bare room.

Ackie came in a minute or two after, looking worried. "Lazard saw all that," he said. "I spotted him across the road."

The sergeant was furious. He took hold of Katz and shook him this way and that. Then he dumped him like a sack of coal on the floor.

Ackie said to him, "Lazard'll get him out, Pat, if you give him the slightest chance."

The sergeant shook his head. "This guy'll stay right here until this time to-morrow," he said. "No one comes down here. I've got the key and the rat can bawl till he busts… no one'll hear him."

I said, "I guess we'll leave you to play with him. We'll be along to-morrow night to charge him."

The sergeant didn't even hear me, he was moving slowly towards Katz, his fists held a little forward and a deep growling sound coming way down in his chest.

Ackie and I stepped outside the room, shutting the door on a sudden terrified howl that sprang from Katz's throat.

CHAPTER NINETEEN

Ackie said: "That starts it, Nick. We gotta go ahead now."

"You think Lazard'll try an' spring him?"

"I guess he'll see Spencer. A guy like that always jumps into anything with both feet."

I went over to the car. "Listen, Mo, we gotta break this business up fast, before they get him out. You go to the Federal Bureau an' tell 'em everything. Get the sergeant to turn Katz over to the Bureau tonight. Once they've got him, Lazard won't get to the first base."

Ackie pushed his hat to the back of his head. "What are you goin' to do?"

"I'm lookin' for Mardi," I said grimly.

"Yeah—but where? You just can't run around in circles. You gotta have some system."

"I ain't had time to get round to Sarah Spencer with you yet," I said. "I'm makin' a guess, but I swear I'm right. She's got Mardi hidden up."

I told Ackie the tale as far as I knew it myself. What Mardi had told me, and how we had fitted Sarah into the set-up, and why I thought she had kidnapped Mardi. "She's gettin' desperate," I concluded. "I'm bettin' she's bankin' on me startin' a lot of trouble as soon as Mardi disappeared. She's right, but she ain't goin' to sit on the fence any more. I'm goin' to push her off, and let her have some trouble for herself."

Ackie listened with his jaw slack. When I had finished, he shook his head. "No—it don't fit," he said. "Sarah Spencer ain't got it in her to pull a job like that. I've seen her, you ain't. She's just a dizzy blonde, with the brain of a cow an' the morals of an alley-cat. 'Sides, she's crazy about Spencer—I can't believe that tale."

I shrugged. "You don't know everythin', Mo," I said shortly. "Anyway, I'm goin' to have a look at this dame—I might find somethin'."

Ackie screwed up his face, but he didn't say anything. I could see he thought I was up the wrong alley, but I told myself that I had to start somewhere. If Sarah Spencer was the woman on the 'phone, she'd have to tell me a few things before I was satisfied that she hadn't had something to do with Mardi's kidnapping.

I gave him a little push. "You've got to get goin'," I said, "an' make it stick—"

Still Ackie didn't move. "Just how much am I to tell these G-men?"

"Tell 'em everythin' Katz told us. That's enough. Don't bring Blondie into it, and don't mention Mardi. Just blow up the Mackenzie Fabric racket—that's all you gotta do."

Ackie nodded. "How far do you want to be in this?"

I thought it over. "Yeah, you're right. Suppose you leave me right out of it. I might want to do a lot of running around, an' if I've gotta sit answerin' a lotta bull from the cops it might cramp me."

Ackie began to drift. "You take the car," he said, "I'll get a taxi. You'll take it easy, won't you, pal? Don't start anythin' you can't finish. That's a tough gang to play around with."

I gave him a little shove. "Don't worry about me," I said, "I'll watch out. When you're through with the cops, go back to the pressroom— I'll contact you there."

I climbed into the car and engaged the gear. Ackie stood at the corner of the street and raised his hand as I swept past him. Although I didn't know it, I wasn't going to see that guy for several weeks.

Spencer had a swell house on Parkside. It didn't take me long to get there, and I drew up on the opposite side and killed the engine. The house stood in about a couple of acres of grounds with a lot of trees and shrubs that more or less hid the house from the street.

I swung open the off door and got out. Crossing the street, I took a look at the big gates. I told myself I wasn't going to walk up the drive and ring on the bell. I was going to surprise that dame. Then something happened that surprised me. The electric horn on Ackie's car gave a strangled croak, just like someone had touched it gently. I looked over at the car quickly, my hand going to my hip pocket, where Katz's gun was. In the darkness, I could just make out someone sitting in the car.

Pulling the gun out, and holding it by my side, I crossed the street again. I moved with stiff legs, rather expecting a sudden blast of lead. Someone called softly as I got nearer. "Nick—it's all right—Nick—it's me."

It was her, too. Mardi was sitting crouched down in the car, peering at me through the open window with a white, scared face.

I stood there, holding on to the door of the car, looking at her. I just couldn't believe my eyes. I said, "Mardi—"

"Yes—please get in. We must get away from here. Nick, get in quickly." The urgency of her voice made me act. I pulled open the car door and slid under the wheel. I put my hands on her, and I could feel her trembling.

"But, honey—what happened? What are you doing here?" I said, putting my arm round her and pulling her to me.

With violence that startled me, she pulled herself away from me. "Nick—don't talk. Get me away from here…" she said. There was a high note of hysteria in her voice.

I leant forward and started the engine, then rolled the car down the street. I didn't move it fast, but kept it going. "Where do you want to go, baby?" I said. "Just take it easy, I'll take you wherever you want to go."

She said, "I'm so frightened, Nick, we must get far away. Don't talk now, but get me away—anywhere, but get me away."

I shoved the pedal down and the car picked up speed. It was no use asking her questions when she was like this. Something bad must have happened to have got her so scared. I headed the car out of town. I sat holding the wheel, looking at the two bright pools of light thrown by the headlights ahead of me, and wondering what it was all about. I could feel Mardi shivering against me, but I didn't look at her. I thought the best thing was to let her calm down before I fussed her.

It wasn't until I had left the town some miles back, and got on to the desert road, that she began to relax. I could feel the tenseness going out of her body, and her shivering gradually stopped. I put out a hand and found one of hers and squeezed it. She was cold, but she gripped my hand hard, so I knew it was all right between us.

I said, "Suppose we stop an' have a little talk, baby. We can't go on like this all night."

She said, "Don't stop, Nick—we've got to go further than this. Please go on."

She leant against me and I put my arm around her.

I said, "We'll go on, if you want to."

And on we went. After a little while, Mardi fell asleep. I could feel her breathing softly on my hand. When I was sure she was sleeping heavily, I slackened speed. I didn't know where we were heading, and I didn't want to get landed somewhere without any gas. I'd got enough for some way yet, but I wanted to have a talk with her before we went much further.

The desert road runs for about a couple of hundred miles through sand and shrub, it links up with a small town called Plattsville, and then starts all over again to the Pacific. Just a long ribbon of road, straight, flat and monotonous, linking up small hick towns, like a string of badly spaced beads.

I checked the time. It was just after two o'clock. I reckoned that in about an hour I should run into Plattsville. I made up my mind, I wouldn't go further than Plattsville without finding out what was scaring Mardi. Maybe, after a sleep, she'd get a grip on herself.

I pushed the car along at a faster rate. At this time in the morning the wind nips off the desert, and I was beginning to feel cold. I was not only wanting a drink bad, but I was beginning to feel sleepy. I told myself that I'd stop at Plattsville whatever happened.

My guess that it would be about an hour's run was near enough. The hands of the dashboard clock stood at three-fifteen when I spotted the few street lights of Plattsville. I shoved the clutch out and ran the car to a stop by the side of the road. The little jerk woke Mardi, who sat up nervously.

"It's all right, baby," I said quickly. "We're running into a town. I thought maybe you'd like to talk things over with me before we go any further."

She peered out of the window, then she turned round to me and put her hands on my arm. "Oh, Nick, it's good to have you," she said. Her voice was quite steady, and I knew she'd got her nerve back.

I lit a cigarette and gave her one. "We've come a mighty long way," I said. "So you don't have to get scared any more."

She shook her head. "No, I'm all right now. I was so frightened, Nick. I wanted to get away. I don't want to go back. Promise me you'll not go back any more."

I patted her arm. "It's all right now. We've washed them up. You don't have to worry your head any more. We've turned the whole business over to the Federal Bureau to deal with—"

She clutched my arm. "The whole business?" Once more her voice trembled. "Do you have to be in it?"

"Now take it easy," I said. "I'm out. Ackie's doin' it all. You an' me are out of this."

She drew a deep breath. "I see," she said.

I said, "I must know what happened at the lodge."

She turned her head and looked at me. "Happened? Why, what do you mean? Happened?"

I shifted a little in my seat. "Where were you? I got back to the lodge and you weren't there."

She shivered. "No—I got scared and ran away."

"What scared you, honey? Where did you go to?"

"I don't want to talk about it, Nick. Can't we drive on now?"

I took her in my arms and pulled her round so she faced me. "I'm sorry, baby, but this is serious," I said. "When I got back to the lodge I found you gone and Blondie dead."

I felt her body stiffen. "Dead? You mean someone killed her?"

I said, "Yes… someone killed her."

Mardi began to cry softly. "Oh, Nick, and she came to warn me. She came and told me that they were coming for me. I was so scared that I ran out of the place into the woods and left her there. She said that Katz had told her that Spencer wanted us out of the way. He thought we knew too much and Katz was on his way to the lodge."

I said, "But Spencer didn't know we were at the lodge."

She hid her head. "He knows everything—I tell you he knows everything."

I drew her to me. "Well, it ain't goin' to do him much good now," I said. "When the Feds get on his tail that guy's going to have a bad time. Listen, baby, suppose we put up at this town until the gang's smashed up, then we can go back and get started again."

She shook her head. "I can't think now. Tell me about the woman... what happened, Nick? Have you told the police?"

I saw she wouldn't relax until I told her the whole story. So, leaving out the messy details, I told her how I had come back to the lodge, how I had thought it was she who had been killed, how I had found Blondie and the whole set-up. She sat, hiding her face from me, crying softly.

"That's how it was, honey," I said. "You ain't got anythin' to cry about. Maybe she did come an' warn you, but she had it comin' to her. Blondie was a tough baby, you don't have to mourn for her."

Mardi put her handkerchief to her nose and looked at me with bright eyes. "What made her come like that, Nick?" she asked. "Why should she risk her life for—me?"

I leant forward and started the engine. "Search me," I said. "I never would have thought she'd done a thing like that."

As I began to roll the car, another thought struck me. "How did you know I'd be goin' to Sarah Spencer's?"

"I had to take the chance—I didn't know, but I didn't know where else to look for you. I thought if you got back to the lodge and found me gone you'd come on to her place."

"That's pretty cute of you, baby," I said admiringly. "That's pretty cute."

We drove on after that in silence. I knew Mardi was still tense. I guessed the shock of hearing about Blondie's death had shaken her pretty badly. I was glad when we ran into Plattsville and found a hick hotel that we could stop at.

The guy behind the desk seemed three-quarters dead, but the other quarter was enough to get us a bedroom and me a drink. When we got left on our own, I hit that bottle as hard as most bottles can be hit. Mardi sank on to the big, old-fashioned bed, her head dropping with fatigue.

I took one look at her and made up my mind. "You're going straight into the sheets an' sleep. I've gotta ring Ackie, then I'll be up. Come on, honey, I'll get you fixed first."

She raised her head. "It's all right, Nick, you go and 'phone. I can manage. You'll be quicker if you go now."

That was sense, so I left her and got through to Ackie on the 'phone downstairs. That guy was full of it. He just didn't give me a chance to tell him where I was, but jumped into his story with both feet.

"Boy! You ain't seen anything' like this since the San Francisco fire!" he bawled. "You gotta get into it quick. The lid's off an' hell's hoppin'. I got round to the Bureau and gave them the works; at first they thought I was tight but, knowing me, they finally decided they'd do somethin', so we all gum-shoed along to the jail and had a look at Katz. Gee! That sergeant had certainly patted him around. Katz was in no state to crack wise. He just opened his mouth and kept it open. That guy spilled the dope so fast, the G-men couldn't get it down quick enough. Then they took him outside. I guess no one thought of it except me, but I wasn't worrying my head. I stayed in the station until it was over. I wanted a story and by golly I was getting it. The G-men an' Katz no sooner got outside into the street than a couple of the boys opened up with a Thomson. Katz got a barrel of slugs and folded up an' one of the G-men caught it, then the other two started with their artillery an' there was a grand gun fight up an' down the street, with yours truly yellin' the news like a broadcast commentary down the 'phone to the press-room.

"I'm tellin' you, it was a grand five minutes. Anyway, that did it. The Federal Bureau got so mad that they raided Spencer's place, the Mackenzie Fabrics an' the Wensdy Wharf all at the same time. It was a grand clean-up. They've got 'em all. Spencer, Gus, the little fat guy, an' the whole mob of thugs. They got enough evidence that'll put that bunch away for fifty years, an' I've got the story. It'll be on the street in a couple of hours."

I said, "That's a grand bit of work. You kept me out of it?"

"Yeah, you didn't come in at all… like you said. Listen, brother, I was mighty glad that Katz got his, otherwise he'd have pinned Blondie's killin' on you. I was scared sick that he'd bring it up right away, but maybe his own troubles tied up his memory."

I stood, holding the 'phone, going a little cold. I'd forgotten that. Katz could have got me in a jam. I was glad he was dead, I never did have any use for that guy.

"Okay, Mo," I said, "I'm goin' back to bed. Listen, I've got Mardi, and we're keeping under cover for a bit. I'll watch the newspapers; when the trial's over, we'll come back. I ain't riskin' that baby gettin' drawn into it."

"You keep out of it," Ackie agreed. "Give her my love, an' look after her, you tramp—she's a grand girl."

"You're tellin' me," I said. "'Bye, pal, an' watch yourself," and I hung up.

I ran upstairs and into the bedroom. Mardie was sitting up in bed, waiting for me. I could see something was wrong by the tense expression in her eyes. I didn't say anything about it, but began to get undressed.

"I've had a talk with Ackie," I said, pulling off my shirt. "He's crazy with excitement. The whole thing's blown up an' Spencer's in jail. Everyone's in jail, an' you an' I don't have to worry any more."

She said, "Is Lee Curtis in jail?"

I stopped, holding my trousers in one hand, and stared at her. "Lee Curtis? Why worry about him? Ackie said they were all in jail."

"But did he say Lee Curtis was in jail?" Her voice was almost hard.

I came over and sat on the bed. "What makes you ask about him… more than the others?"

She looked at me in an odd way, and shook her head. "I just wanted to know."

There was something behind this, but I didn't want to press it. "He didn't mention Curtis, but he's being taken care of, all right."

"Oh," she said in a flat voice, and looked at her finger-nails carefully. I sat on the bed, in my B.V.D.'s. I was beginning to feel like hell, but I couldn't get to sleep until I got this straightened.

"Tell me, baby," I said gently.

She looked up at me, and her eyes were big and wild. "Nick, do you love me?" she said. "Do you really love me? Not just for yesterday and to-day, but for to-morrow and all the to-morrows?"

I put my hand over hers. "You're everything to me, Mardi," I said, and meant it.

She said, "Will you do something big for me? Something that'll mean you love me?"

I nodded. "Sure, what is it?"

"I want you and me to go away. Never come back to this State. To go south a long way, and start all over again—will you do that?"

"You mean never come back?" I asked.

"Yes."

"But, Mardi, we've gotta live. My connections are here. I've lived here so long. I'm known here. I'll keep away with you until the trial is over, but if I've to earn enough dough it's here that I can earn it."

She shook her head. "Money doesn't matter. I have all we want." She pulled a long envelope out of the bedclothes and put it into my hand.

"Look, it's for you."

I opened the envelope blankly and shook out a bundle of bearer bonds. There were twenty thousand dollars. I pushed the bonds away from me and sat a little stunned, looking at her.

"They're mine," she said fiercely. "They're for you and me—with that, surely we can go away and you can start again."

I said, "But, Mardi, that's a lot of money for a girl to have. How did you get it?"

She said, "At the Mackenzie Fabrics. I saved and I heard tips. Spencer invested for me—"

"I see."

She began to cry. "Say you'll take the money and come away with me, Nick—please...."

I rolled into bed beside her, shoving the envelope under her pillow. "Suppose we leave it until to-morrow? We'll be able to think clearly to-morrow," I said.

I felt her stiffen. "No," she said, "it must be now. I couldn't sleep. I must know. It's so important to me."

"Why is it, Mardi? Why should you want to hide yourself away?"

"Nick, you'll lose me if you go back," she said, suddenly sobbing violently. "I can't tell you why, but I feel that is what will happen. You must say now."

And because nothing really mattered to me except her happiness, and because I knew she loved me as much as I loved her, I gave her the promise.

She said, "You really mean that?"

"Yeah," I said. "We'll take the car on and we'll go to the coast. We'll get us a small house somewhere near the sea with a garden and we'll be just you an' I."

"And you'll be happy?"

"Sure, I'll be happy. I'll find something to do." Lying there in the dark, I suddenly felt fine about the idea. We'd got money, we were going to the sun, and we had each other.

CHAPTER TWENTY

We got a place a few miles out from Santa Monica. It was small, but it was cute—the kind of place movie-stars week-end in. As soon as we saw it, we fell for it. The garden ran down to the sea, and if you wanted a bathe you just opened a gate in the wall and stepped on to the hot yellow sands. The sea was right ahead.

The house had two bedrooms and a large sitting-room leading out to a piazza that encircled the whole building. The garden was big enough to screen the house from the road. The rent was high, but we didn't think twice about it—we took it.

Maybe I should have felt a heel taking all that money from Mardi, but I didn't. If the money had been mine, I should have wanted Mardi to share it with me. Well, the money was hers, and I wasn't going to spoil things by refusing to share with her.

We had a grand time fixing that house up. It took us a week to get straight, and we did all the work ourselves, even to fixing the carpets. When we got through, we were tickled to death with it.

Getting Mardi to the sea was a good thing. In a week or so it began to make a big difference to her. She lost the drawn, tense look that had begun to worry me, and she tanned mighty quick in the sunshine and sea air. She was happy and so was I. I reckon I never felt happier.

We got up every morning and had a bathe in the sea. It was grand swimming in that deep blue water, with no one to watch us—just the two of us, in the rolling swell of the sea. Mardi wore a white swim-suit that made her figure look better than it was, and that's saying something. She never bothered about wearing a cap, and we played around with each other without a care in the world.

Mardi said to me, a couple of weeks after we had settled down, "Nick, you must start working." I'd just come out of the sea, and was lying down on the sand, too lazy to dry myself, and letting the hot sunshine do it for me.

"That's okay with me," I said. "I'll look around and see what I can find."

Mardi knelt over me, her knees and thighs buried in the soft sand and her hands crossed in her lap.

"Nick," she said, "I've been thinking. Why don't you write a book?"

I blinked up at her. "Write a book?" I said. "Why, hell—I couldn't write a book."

She shook her head. "You've never tried," she said, which was true. "Look how some novels sell. Why don't you try, and see what happens?"

"Yeah, but look how some flop. I guess novel-writing ain't so hot."

She said, "Why don't you write a novel about a newspaper man? Don't you think you could do that?"

There was an idea there. I sat up and thought about it. Ackie had enough background to fill three books, and I had had a few experiences. Mardi could see that I was looking at the idea favourably, and she began to get excited. "Oh, Nick, wouldn't it be fun if you could. You wouldn't have to leave me then, would you? I could get your meals and sit around darning your socks, and you could be working—"

I grinned at her. "Don't sound much fun for you," I said, but she scrambled to her feet.

"You stay and think about it, Nick," she said. "I'll go back to the house and get the breakfast on. I'll call you."

Well, I thought about it, and the more I thought the more I liked the idea. Before she called me, I was itching to make a start. I went back to the house, bolted my breakfast and got down to it. It took me all the morning to work out the general idea of the book, and when I was through it seemed pretty good to me.

I took it along to Mardi, who was in the kitchen, and explained the synopsis to her. She leant against the kitchen table, her eyes wide and bright with excitement, and was as enthusiastic about it as I was.

"Okay, honey," I said, when I had finished. "The next move is to get a typewriter, and I'll make a start."

It took me two months to get the book done, and if it hadn't been for Mardi it would never have been written. I got stuck half-way through and lost patience with it, but Mardi kept at me until I just had to go on. She was so excited that I hadn't the heart to fold up. When it was finished, and I read it through, I knew I had something. It wasn't going to be a best seller or anything like that, but it was good enough.

Mardi said, "This is only the beginning; you're going to write more and more and you will very soon be famous."

I grinned at her. "Don't pin too much on this. Maybe it'll come back with the usual rejection slip."

Mardi had faith. It didn't come back, it stuck. A couple of months after sending it off, I had a letter from the publishers in New York I had mailed it to, saying that they liked it and would I come on over and meet them.

I didn't expect to hear so soon, and we were right in the middle of painting the outside of the house. Mardi insisted on my going, and she stayed behind to finish the work. I knew she'd be all right on her own. We'd been clear of the trial and things had settled down. Spencer and his gang had all caught pretty stiff raps, and although, at the time, Mardi was pretty het up, she'd forgotten about the business by now.

So I took the train west and left her. The publishers were mighty nice to me, offered me a very fair advance, and a contract for two more books. I wasn't going to waste time hanging around New York. Once I got their contract signed, I grabbed a taxi and made for Central Station.

I found I'd got a couple of hours before I could make connections to Santa Monica, so I turned into the refreshment bar for a drink, before deciding where I'd go to pass the time. Standing at the bar was Colonel Kennedy.

He said, "Well, this is a surprise."

I took his hand. "You're right," I said. "Colonel, this is a fine time to meet you. I've got a lot to thank you for." We ordered more drinks and made ourselves comfortable. "What have you been doing all this time?" he asked, once we were settled.

"I'm living at Santa Monica now with my wife," I said. "You know, I've never thanked you enough for letting me have your lodge for a honeymoon."

He grinned. "That's all right, Nick," he said. "I'm glad I had it to lend you. Why live so far away? I guess I'd like to meet that wife of yours."

"Well, what are you doing? Why not come on over for a week or so? We'd be glad to have you with us."

He shook his head regretfully. "I can't, I'm afraid. I've got commitments right now."

I smiled. "They're still falling for you, Colonel?" I said.

He nodded. "I guess I haven't much to worry about," he said.

I glanced at the clock. "I've got almost two hours before I pull out," I said. "How about having lunch with me?"

He slid off the stool. "Sure, I'd be glad to."

Now that I had met up with him again, a sudden curiosity to file off the rough ends of the Spencer business seized me. When we got seated in a quiet little restaurant not far from the station and had given our order, I got the conversation round to the angle I wanted it to go.

"Colonel," I said. "You remember the Mackenzie Fabrics trial?"

He looked at me, and nodded. I wasn't sure, but I fancied he looked a little taken aback. "Yes, I remember it—caused quite a sensation."

"Yeah," I said, "I was in that business right up to my neck."

"You were?"

"Yeah. I'd like to tell you about it, because I think you could finish the tale off for me."

He shook his head. "I don't know a thing about it," he protested.

"Wait a minute, Colonel," I said. "Maybe I can jog your memory."

I took him carefully through the whole story, and he sat there, his lunch forgotten. When I had finished with the death of Blondie, and how Mardi and I had quietly slipped away to Santa Monica, he sat back and gently blew his cheeks out. "Well, I'll be damned," he said. "That's some yarn. I can't see where I come in, for all that."

This is where it was going to be a little tricky. "You remember when the newspaper boys had you bottled up at the lodge with a girl friend, Colonel?" I said.

He frowned. "Now I don't want to go into that," he said abruptly.

"The girl friend was the woman on the telephone," I told him quietly. "I want to know who she was."

He shook his head. "You've made a mistake."

"I'm givin' you this straight. I heard her voice, and that was enough for me. I'd know that voice anywhere."

"I can't discuss this any further, Nick. I'm sorry."

I said, "Listen, Colonel. I've got a right to know. That dame might have caused me a lotta grief. The trial's over, and the whole thing's washed up. You know me well enough to know that I won't use any information you give me. It's just that it is an unsatisfactory ending—not knowing."

He sat brooding. "I guess maybe you have a right," he said with a little smile. "I wouldn't tell it to any other man, but you've done a lot for me."

He was just salving his conscience, but that didn't worry me. "Thank you, Colonel; it'll go no further."

He hummed and hawed a bit, then said, "I don't know who she was— that's the truth. She came out to see me, representing a fellow named Lee Curtis. This fellow was associated with the Mackenzie Fabrics Co. and I had just put in for a bundle of their stock. This girl was authorized by Curtis to make me an offer for them. She was a devilish pretty woman, and I asked her to stay to dinner while we discussed the matter. I was curious to know why Curtis, who was the secretary of the place, should want to get hold of such a large block."

"How much was it?" I asked.

Kennedy shrugged. "I forget now, I think it was about ten thousand dollars—something like that. Anyway, we had dinner. All the time, she refused to give me her name, but kept on selling me the idea of parting with the stock. She had some story which didn't convince me, but in the end I decided to negotiate. Curtis was offering a high percentage on the stock, and I thought it might be worth while."

"You mean, you don't know who she was?" I said, disappointed.

"No—I don't. The rest of the story doesn't reflect to my glory, but you may as well have it. Once the business part was over, and she gave me Curtis's cheque, I thought we might get a little more friendly. I did tell you that she was a remarkably pretty woman?"

I nodded a little grimly. "Yeah—you mentioned it."

"Well, she got a little scared and pulled a gun. I was never so astonished in my life. I tried to take the damn' thing away from her, and it went off. The rest of the story you know."

I sat back. "Well, that don't get me very far," I said. "I was hoping to tie that dame down."

Kennedy glanced at the clock. "You'll have to be on the move or you'll lose your train."

I beckoned the waiter for the bill. Kennedy said hastily, "I'll pay that."

I shook my head. "I've just sold a book, Colonel. I guess it's a nice experience to buy a guy, with all the dough you've got, a lunch."

Kennedy laughed. "I'm glad you've settled down, Nick. But you're not to hide yourself away. You must bring your wife up to town."

I took out my wallet and found a ten-dollar bill which I gave to the waiter. A photo of Mardi was amongst my papers, and I flipped it across to Kennedy. "That's my wife, Kennedy—you'll think she's a grand girl when you meet her."

I took the change from the waiter and gave him a buck for himself. Then I turned to see what Kennedy was making of Mardi. He was sitting staring at me, his face a little white and his eyes like granite.

I said, "What's wrong?"

He said in a hard voice, "What's the idea, Mason?"

I stared at him. "You gone screwy, Colonel?"

He tapped Mardi's photograph. "If you knew about this girl, why ask me?"

I sat for a full minute, staring at him. Then I said, "That's my wife, Colonel—I don't know what you're gettin' at."

"That's the woman Curtis sent to me to negotiate the stock I was telling you about."

I pushed back my chair. "You've made a mistake," I said unsteadily. "That's Mardi—my wife."

He picked up the photograph and looked at it carefully. All the time he was doing that, my heart was beating against my ribs like a pile-driver. Then he looked up. "Who was your wife before she married you, Nick?" he said.

With the sudden horrible feeling of things crumbling, I said, "She was Spencer's secretary."

Kennedy pushed the photograph across the table towards me. "It fits, doesn't it?" he said quietly. "There's no doubt about it, Nick."

I just sat there in a heap. Kennedy wasn't the kind of guy who made mistakes. I said unevenly, "But this is crazy."

He got to his feet. "Suppose we leave it, Nick? I've got to run along. I'll be seeing you." He put his hand on my shoulder for a moment, then walked out of the restaurant. I picked up the photograph and put it in my wallet. I couldn't think. I didn't want to think. I got up, pushing the chair away from me with the back of my legs and walked over to the hat rack. I put my hat and coat on slowly. The waiters were looking at me curiously, but I didn't care about them; then I went outside into the street.

The train to Santa Monica was already in the station and I got a seat. I settled myself and looked out of the window. My eyes didn't see anything, and although it was a hot day I felt cold.

The train began to glide out of the station, taking me back to Santa Monica—and to something I was frightened to face.

CHAPTER TWENTY-ONE

By the time I had reached Santa Monica I had got over the shock. The explanation must be simple, I told myself. Either Kennedy had made a bad mistake, or else Mardi had been forced to play some deep game by Curtis. Whatever the explanation was, it wasn't going to break up Mardi's life with me. I'd spent a lot of time playing around with girls, and I knew when I had found the right one. Mardi was my girl. I wasn't going to let anything come between us. I'd talk the whole thing over with her, and she'd tell me the truth. The truth wasn't going to be bad—it mustn't be bad.

I took a taxi from Santa Monica station. I wanted to get back there fast. It seemed a long way, and I sat on the edge of my seat urging the driver to push his cab along. I got there at last. The front door was standing open, but Mardi wasn't in the garden. I walked up the long path, feeling suddenly a little sick. I kept on telling myself that it would be all right, but somehow at the back of my brain I knew that what I had built up was already crumbling.

I stepped into the hallway. A man's hat and coat hung on the rack—they weren't mine. I put my grip carefully on the floor and stood looking. Then I got rid of my own hat and coat and walked into the sitting-room.

They were there waiting for me.

For a moment, I didn't recognize him. He was a tall guy, with a lot of wavy hair, a tanned complexion and bright blue eyes. It was Lee Curtis, all right. I stood in the doorway, with the blood roaring in my ears.

I looked at Mardi. She was sitting listlessly in an armchair. Her face was white and her eyes looked like big holes cut in a sheet. She didn't even look at me.

Curtis said, "I've been waiting for you."

I couldn't say anything.

"I've been here four days—she an' I've been living together."

I felt suddenly brittle inside, like someone had stepped in close with a half-arm jab, but still I couldn't think of anything to say.

He looked at me thoughtfully, then he put his hand up to his chin. I could hear his nails rasp on his beard. He said, "Take it easy—it's no use gettin' rattled."

I walked with stiff legs over to Mardi. I said, "I'm with you all the way—but I've got to know the truth."

She didn't look up. She just sat there as if I hadn't spoken.

Curtis turned on his heels, so that he was facing me. He said, "I've been waiting for this, for some time. Now I've got you both where I want you."

I turned my head and looked at him. I guess I must have had a flicker in my eye, because he jerked a gun out of his hip pocket. "Take it easy," he said. "I don't want to start shootin', but I'm not risking anythin' from you."

I said between my teeth, "Talk quick an' get out."

He sat on the edge of the table, still holding the gun levelled at me. "It's quite a tale," he said, with a sneer. "Sit down—you'll get tired."

I didn't move.

"A couple of years ago," he said, swinging his leg slowly to and fro, "I got a job with the Mackenzie Fabrics Corporation as their secretary. She worked for Spencer—you know that. She also lived with Spencer— maybe you didn't know that." He stopped talking and fumbled for a cigarette, but not once did he take his eyes off me. "I soon found that there was something going on behind the scenes, and finally Spencer took me into his confidence. I saw the set-up was big—very big, and I wasn't getting much out of it. Nor was she. So we got together. We thought if we could pin Richmond's murder on Spencer, and get him out of the way, I could take over, and have some of the profits. So we picked on you. We wanted a guy who would bust the Vessi frame-up wide open, and we decided you could do it. She contacted you on the 'phone—quite smart the way she can change her voice. She wasn't living with Spencer any more—she was living with me."

I said, "You can stop talkin'. I don't want to hear any more. Get out!"

He grinned. "You don't know the half of it yet, smart boy," he said.

"I'm only gettin' started. She's a romantic little thing, and I guess she fell for you—fell for you hard. Then she tried to double-cross Spencer, who fired her out. I tagged along behind her, because I wasn't sure if she'd try and double-cross me. Just when she was set, Blondie turned up. Now Blondie knew all about her. She knew she had lived with Spencer, and she knew she'd lived with me. Blondie wanted some easy dough, so she tried blackmail. You took yourself to town and left our little friend at the lodge. Blondie had been watching, and she called on her as soon as you were out of the way. Blondie didn't know what she was up against. Mardi shot her. Do you hear that, you big pushover, your girl friend shot Blondie. Now you know why she was so scared. Now you know why she wouldn't stay in town, but beat it across all these States, until she was sitting on the edge of the Pacific. She wasn't content at murder, she double-crossed me. As soon as she knew that Blondie was dead, she came to my place and took twenty thousand dollars of bonds out of my safe. I told you she had lived with me, didn't I? Well, she knew all about my safe an' how to get into it. So she knocked off all I had and beat it with you.

"The Feds nearly got me, but they didn't. I've been hunting for her for months, and I found her just after you left for New York. Well, I guess she's had to pay for her double-cross."

I said, "Mardi, don't worry—I'm still with you."

She put her hands over her eyes and shuddered.

Curtis tossed the butt on the floor. "So you're still with her—are you?" he sneered. "You still think you're goin' to live around with a chippie whose sideline's murder, huh? You can forget it! You won't want her around any more."

I said, "Now you're through—get out!"

He raised his eyebrows. "Who said I'm through? That's a laugh. Listen, punk, I want dough. I've got enough on that judy to fry her. Okay, I ain't working any more. I'm living on you. You're going to give me plenty of dough, and when I've spent that I'll come and ask for more. So you're going to be busy earning it."

I sat down quietly. I knew that this guy had got us. There wasn't going to be any more happy days. There wasn't going to be any more swims in the sea, or any more of anything. This guy would be with us until he died. My brain lurched a little. *Until he died.* I looked at him thoughtfully. One against two. One life making two lives unhappy. It didn't add up. I felt slightly sick, but there was no other way out of it—I'd gotta kill this guy.

I said in a quiet voice, "How much do you want?"

"What can you afford?" He looked over at Mardi, then back at me. I knew he was playing with us.

"Fifty bucks a week," I said, for something to say. I knew he'd got a figure, so I wanted to get to it quick.

He laughed. "I want fifteen grand now, and a hundred bucks a week until I get tired of asking for it."

So that was that.

I got to my feet slowly. "You're crazy," I said. "We ain't got fifteen grand."

He shrugged. "You had twenty grand from me. You've got half of it salted away. You can sell the house and the furniture. She's got some trinkets—you've got a few things around that'll fetch something. You'll make it up all right."

"So you're stripping us clean."

He nodded. "Sure—ain't she worth it to you?"

I wandered over to the window and looked out. "The Feds are after you, too," I said. "Suppose I turn you over to 'em?"

"Be your age. She'll go with me—and it's the hot squat for her."

I was just wasting time. Somehow I'd got to get his gun and kill him. I was surprised how calmly I was setting about this. Once I had made up my mind that he'd have to go, I felt no more misgivings than if I'd planned to tread on an ant. I'd just got to make the opportunity.

"Well, if it's like that," I said, "I'll have to go ahead. I can't give you the dough now."

He said, "Write me a cheque for ten grand. That'll do to go on with—I'll be round for the rest of the dough in a month."

I began to look dejected, but I was acting all the time. I slouched from the window, and headed for the writing-desk. He still sat on the table, watching me. I stopped at the other end of the table and rested my hands on the table-top.

"Listen, Curtis," I said, "give us a break—won't you? Take the ten grand an' call it quits."

He laughed. Just for a second his eyes were off me and I acted. I grabbed the table and heaved. It was easy. He was sitting on the far end and it flew up with a crash. I flung my weight on the table so that it toppled over on top of him, pinning him flat. His gun shot out of his hand.

Kneeling on the table, and keeping him flat, I said to Mardi, "Get the gun quick."

She reached forward and picked it up.

"Give it to me."

She turned and looked at me. She could see in my eyes what I was going to do. Instead of giving me the gun, she stepped away.

I said desperately, "Honey, give me the gun."

"No—you're not going to kill him," she said fiercely. "I won't have you kill anyone."

"For Pete's sake—can't you see? It's the only thing to do. We've gotta get out of this somehow. If this rat lives we're finished—give me the gun."

All this time, Curtis was lying on his back, with his head just appearing above the edge of the table. His eyes were bolting out of his head, and his skin was green.

Mardi said, "Nick—I wouldn't have killed her. But she wanted to smash up the only decent thing I'd ever had. Your love for me. I was mad to have done it, but I wanted you so much. I tried to forget, but it's always been with me—"

I said, "I'm going through with this—give me the gun."

"I tried to save our love by killing someone, but it didn't work out that way. You want to do it too. We could never face each other. Let him go, Nick."

She was right. I stepped off the table and stood away. Curtis got to his feet slowly, his face twitching.

Mardi said, "Wait here. I'll get you the cheque."

I turned my back on Curtis. I just couldn't bring myself to look at him. Mardi touched my hand as she went past me. "It'll work out all right, Nick—if you can still love me," she said.

I turned, but she had already run out of the room, across to her bedroom, where I knew she kept her cheque-book.

Curtis said, "By Heck! You try any more tricks—"

From Mardi's room came the sound of a revolver shot. The sharp crack of the gun made both of us start forward. Then we stopped and looked at each other.

Curtis drew his lips off his teeth. "So she's double-crossed me again," he said.

He stood hesitating, then he walked into the bedroom. I didn't move. From where I stood I could see him looking into the room. I could see a sudden shiver run through him, and he turned away and came into the hallway. He didn't look at me. He stood, thinking. Then he walked to the front door and went down the long path. I could hear him walking on the gravel, but I didn't watch him go.

When he had gone, I went out into the garden. I went down to the sea, and stood looking at the blue rollers. I didn't want to look at Mardi now. I wanted to remember her as I had known her. I wanted to see her as she had always been. I could not weep for her, because everything had dried up inside me. A big seagull suddenly flew over my head and circled round me. Then, as if startled by my stillness, it sped, like a departing spirit, swiftly out to sea.

THE END

Miss Callaghan Comes to Grief

by James Hadley Chase

PROLOGUE

It was a hot night. Oven-heat that baked the sweat out of the body and played hell with the dogs. It had been hot all day, and now the sun had gone down the streets still held the stifling heat.

Phillips of the *St. Louis Banner* sat in a remote corner of the Press Club getting good and drunk. He was a long, thin bird, with melancholy eyes and lank, unruly hair. Franklin, a visiting reporter, thought he looked like a bum poet.

Phillips dragged down his tie and undid his collar. The long highball slopped a little as he groped to put it on the table. He said, "What a night! What's the time, Franky?"

Franklin, his face white with exhaustion and his eyes heavy and red-lidded, peered at the face of his watch. "Just after twelve," he said, letting his head fall back with a thud on the leather padding of his chair.

"After twelve, huh?" Phillips shifted uneasily. "That's bad. That's dug my grave good and deep. Know what I should be doin' right now?"

Franklin had to make an effort to shake his head.

"I gotta date to meet a dame tonight," Phillips told him, blotting his face and neck with his handkerchief. "Right now that babe is waiting for me. Is she goin' to be mad?"

Franklin groaned.

"Franky, pal, I couldn't do it. It's a low trick, but not on a night like this. No, sir, I couldn't do it."

"Break it up," Franklin pleaded, scooping sweat out of his neckband. "I want to freeze myself to death in a big refrigerator."

Phillips raised himself slowly. A look of faint animation came over his thin face. Drunkenly, he patted Franklin on his back. "You've got somethin' there," he said. "Gee! The guy's got brains. I've been doin' you dirt. Boy, you've certainly got somethin' there!"

Franklin pushed him away. "Sit down," he said crossly; "you're tight."

Phillips shook his head solemnly. "Come on, bud, you've given me an idea."

"I ain't moving. I'm staying right here."

Phillips grabbed his arm and hauled him out of the chair. "I'm goin' to save your life," he said. "We'll take a cab an' spend the night in the morgue."

Franklin gaped at him. "Wait a minute," he said. "I ain't goin' to sleep with a lotta stiffs. You're crazy."

"Aw, come on. What the hell? Stiffs ain't goin' to worry you. Think how cold it'll be."

Franklin wavered. "Yeah," he said, clinging to the table, "but I don't like it. Think you can get in?"

Phillips leered. "Sure I can get in. Know the guy there. He's a good guy. He won't mind. Now come on, let's get goin'."

Franklin's face suddenly brightened. "Sure," he said; "it ain't such a bad idea. Let's go."

Out in the street they flagged a taxi. The driver looked at them suspiciously. "Where?" he demanded, not believing his ears.

Phillips shoved Franklin into the cab. "The County Morgue," he repeated patiently. "We're passin' in our pails. This is just a matter of convenience, see, buddy?"

The driver climbed off his box. "Now listen, pal," he said, "you guys don't want the morgue. You wantta go home. Just you take it easy. I'm useta handlin' drunks. You leave it to me. Where do you live? Now, come on. I'll have you in bed before you know it."

Phillips peered at him, then put his head inside the cab. "Hi, Franky, this guy wants to go to bed with me."

"Do you like him?" Franky asked.

Phillips turned his head and looked at the driver. "I don't know. He seems all right."

The driver wiped his face with his sleeve. "Now listen, you guys," he said pleadingly, "I ain't said nuttin' about gettin' into bed wid youse."

Phillips climbed into the cab. "He's changed his mind," he said mournfully. "I've got a mind to slosh him in the puss."

"Well, maybe you're lucky. I thought he'd got a foxy smell about him. I don't think you'd've liked that."

The driver came close to the window. "Where to, boss?" he asked, in what he thought was a soothing voice. "This ain't the time to fool around. It's too goddam hot."

"The County Morgue," Phillips said, leaning out of the window. "Don't you understand? That's the one cold spot in this burg, an' we're headin' for it."

The driver shook his head. "You'd never make it," he said; "they wouldn't let you in."

"Who said? They'll let me in all right. I know the guy there."

"That on the level? Could you get me in too, boss?"

"Sure. I could get anyone in there. Don't stand around usin' up air. Get to it."

Franklin was asleep when they got to the morgue. Phillips hauled him into the hot street and stood supporting him. He said to the driver, "What are you goin' to do with the heap?"

"I guess I'll leave it here. It'll be all right."

They stumbled into the morgue, making a considerable row. The attendant was reading a newspaper behind a counter that divided the room from the vaults. He looked up, startled.

Phillips said, "Hyah, Joe, meet a couple of buddies."

Joe laid down his newspaper. "What the hell's this?"

"We're spendin' the night here," Phillips said. "Just look on us as three stiffs."

Joe climbed to his feet. His big fleshy face showed just how mad he was. "You're all drunk," he said. "You better scram outta here. I ain't got time to horse around with you boys now."

The driver began to edge towards the door, but Phillips stopped him. "Listen, Joe," he said; "who was the swell dame I saw you with last night?"

Joe's eyes popped. "You didn't see me with no dame last night," he said uneasily.

Phillips smiled. "Don't talk bull. She was a dame with a chest that oughta have a muzzle on it, an' a pair of stems that cause street accidents. Gee! What a jane!" He turned to the other two. "You ain't seen nothin' like it. When I thought of that guy's poor wife, sittin' around at home doin' nothin', while this runt goes places with a hot number like that, I tell you, it got me."

Joe undid the counter-bolt and pulled back the little door. "Okay," he said wearily, "go on down. It's a goddam lie, an' you know it, but I ain't takin' chances. The old woman would just like to believe that yarn."

Phillips grinned. "Down we go, boys," he said.

They followed him down a long flight of marble steps. At the bottom there came to them a faint musty odour of decomposition. As Phillips pushed open a heavy steel door the pungent smell of formaldehyde was very strong. They all entered a large room.

The sudden icy atmosphere was almost too violent after the outside heat.

Franklin said, "Jeeze! There's hoar frost formin' on my chest hairs."

On one side of the room were four long wooden benches. Round the other three walls were rows of black metal cabinets.

Phillips said, "If you don't think about it you'd never know there were a lotta stiffs in those cabinets. I like comin' here. I jest sit around an' cool off, an' it don't worry me at all."

The driver took off his greasy cap and began twisting it in his hands. "That where they keep the corpses?" he said, his voice sinking to a whisper.

Phillips nodded. He went over to one of the benches and laid down. "That's right," he said. "You don't have to think about that. Just settle down an' go to sleep."

With his eyes on the cabinets the driver sat down gingerly. Franklin stood hesitating.

"I wonder if Joe would stand for me phonin' my girl friend to come on down," Phillips said sleepily. He shook his head. "No, I guess he wouldn't stand for it." He sighed a little and settled himself more comfortably. "Franky, put that light out, will you? It's tryin' my eyes."

Franklin said, "If you think I'm goin' to stay here in the dark, you're crazy. This place gives me the heebies. I don't mind stayin' here so long as I can see those cabinets, but in the dark—why, hell, I'd be thinkin' they might be gettin' out an' lookin' me over."

Phillips sat up. "What you mean, gettin' out? How the hell can a stiff do a thing like that?"

"I'm not sayin' that they'd do it. I'm sayin' what I think they might be doin'."

"Don't be a nut." Phillips swung his feet off the bench and got up. "Now I'll show you somethin'. Let's have a look at some of these guys."

Franklin backed away. "I don't want to see them," he said hurriedly. "This burg's spooky enough without lookin' at corpses."

Phillips went over to the cabinet and pulled out a drawer. It slid out silently on the roller-bearings. In the drawer was a big negro; his pale pink tongue lolled out of his mouth and his eyes seemed to be bursting out of his head. Phillips hastily slammed the drawer shut. "That guy was strangled," he said shakily. "Let's try another or I'll dream about him."

The driver edged close, but Franklin went over and sat on the bench. Phillips pulled another drawer open. An elderly man, his face covered with a good half-inch stubble of beard, came into view.

"You wouldn't think he was dead, would you, boss?" the driver said.

Phillips shoved the drawer to. "Naw," he said, "he looks like he was stuffed." He walked over to the other side of the room. "Let's have a look at some of the dames."

The driver's face brightened. "That's an idea, boss," he said. "Can you unwrap 'em?"

Phillips looked over at Franklin. "For Gawd's sake, did you hear that?" he said. "This gaul wants to see some Paris pictures."

The driver looked abashed. "Don't get me wrong, boss," he pleaded. "If you don't think I oughtta look, I won't."

Phillips was pulling open drawers quickly, peering inside and hastily shutting them. "Real hot numbers don't seem to die these days," he said regretfully. "All old dames here." He paused and pulled a drawer open further. "Say, this looks better. Hi, Franky, come an' look at this."

Franky got up slowly and came over, impelled by irresistible curiosity. They all stood looking down at the girl lying in the drawer. She had flame-coloured hair, that showed a darker brown at the roots. Her thin pinched face wore a tragic look of one who has missed the good things in life. Her lips were gentle in death, in spite of the almost pathetic smudge of the lipstick that smeared her chin.

Phillips pulled off the sheet that covered her.

The driver said, "Oh, boy!" and trod on Franklin's toes to get nearer.

She was slender, but firmly rounded. Her body was as perfect as the three men had ever seen.

Franklin took the sheet from Phillips and made to cover her again, but Phillips stopped him. "Let her lie," he said, "she does somethin' to me. By God! She's nice, ain't she?"

The driver said wistfully, "It'd take a heapa jack to play around a dame like that."

Phillips continued to stare at the girl. He pulled the tag of identification from its slot in the drawer and studied it. "Julie Callaghan," he read. "Age 23. Height 5 ft. 4 inches. Weight 112 lbs. Address not known. No relations." He pulled the tag out further. "Cause of death: Murder by stabbing. Profession: Prostitute."

He released the tag, which snapped back into its socket. "Well, well," he said.

The three men stood silently looking down at the figure in the drawer, then Franklin said, "You never can tell, can you? Here I was workin' up some sympathy for her, and she turns out to be a whore."

Phillips glanced at him. "What's the matter with that?" he said. "Can't you give her any sympathy?"

Franklin threw the sheet over her and closed the drawer. "You ain't one of those guys who tries to put glamour in that type, are you?"

"You've got the angle wrong. That dame's doing a job of work. Maybe it ain't a good job of work, but all the same, she's human, ain't she?"

Franklin wandered to the bench and sat down. "Come off it," he said, "that don't hold water. I'll tell you something. I hate these broads. I despise them. To me, that dame is just one more of 'em out of the way. She got what was comin' to her. She was too damn lazy and too damn brainless to do anythin' else."

Furtively the driver had opened the drawer again and was looking with fascinated eyes.

Both Phillips and Franklin took no notice of him.

Phillips said, "Some of these girls are forced into the trade, Franky. You ought to know that. Gee! You ought to be sorry for them."

"Don't talk a lotta bull. Sorry? That's a laugh. Listen, there's too much crap going around about forcin' japes into prostitution. If a woman don't want to do it, you just can't make her. They do it because they want the things in life the easy way. They've got what you want, and they make you pay for it. They give you nothing. They'll cheat you, rob you, lie to you, and they certainly hate you. They're a breed on their own. To hell with them!"

The driver said, "Maybe this was one of Raven's girls."

The two looked at him. "Why do you say that?" Phillips asked. "Are you sure?"

The driver closed the drawer regretfully. "No, I ain't sure, but he always had the best girls; and she's a honey, ain't she?"

Phillips looked at Franklin. "You're wrong, Franky. Some of these girls had a bad time. Raven's girls had a terrible time. It's hick-minded to group them all together."

"Who's this Raven you're talkin' about?" Franklin wanted to know.

Phillips exchanged glances with the driver. "So you don't know Raven?" he said. "Well, well! Where've you been all this time?"

Franklin sat down. "Okay, okay, I'll buy it, just so long as you'll stop this sissy talk about whores. Tell me."

Phillips reached for a cigarette. "Raven was quite a boy," he said, setting himself comfortably. "He came to this town about a year ago. As a matter of fact, one of our crowd, working on the old rag, first got on to him. It was odd how it started. Damned odd. If old Poison's wife hadn't gone off the rails, maybe Raven would still be operating right now. It happened this way...."

PART ONE

I

June 3rd, 11:45 p.m.

"Take me out for a little drive, Gerry darling," Mrs. Poison said as the music stopped.

Hamsley looked at the big bulk of wrinkled flesh and was appalled.

"It's such a very, very hot night, isn't it?" she went on, walking across the ballroom floor. "It'll be nice out in the car"—she gave his arm a little pat—"with you."

Hamsley wiped his face with his handkerchief. "Yes, Mrs. Poison," he said.

He knew what was coming. He'd seen it coming for the last week. He had a sick feeling inside him as he followed her steady march across the floor. He could see people looking at him and smiling to each other.

As he went past the band the conductor said something he didn't hear. He knew what it was, and it made him sicker than ever. At the door he tried to persuade her to stay. It was like pushing the sea back with his hands.

It was dark outside, cool after the heat of the ballroom. They stood on the top step, trying to pierce the darkness.

Mrs. Poison put her hand on his arm. He could feel her trembling. "Isn't it wonderful?" she said. "My, my, it makes me feel young again."

Automatically he said, "Don't talk such nonsense. You're a young woman." She and the other old women paid him to say things like that.

"You mustn't tell untruths. I'm not young, Gerry, but I'm not old. I'm in the best years of my life."

Hamsley shuddered.

Out of the darkness a two-seater slid up to them. The young mechanic got out quickly and stood holding open the door.

Hamsley felt completely trapped. She'd arranged everything.

The mechanic winked at him and made a sign with his hand. Hamsley climbed in beside Mrs. Poison, ignoring him. He could have wept with shame.

He said desperately, "It's cold out here. You sure you won't catch cold? Maybe we ought to get back."

"Oh no!" She gave a giggling little laugh. "It's cold now. But we'll be warm soon."

There, she had said it. He knew beyond any doubt now. His hand shook as he engaged the gears and let the clutch in with a jerk. "Where shall we go?" he said, driving the car slowly into the road.

"Go straight. I'll tell you." She leant against him. He could feel her soft hot body pressing into his shoulder. He drove down the road for a couple of miles, then she told him to turn off to the left. He could hear the tyres bite into the dirt road, and the trees overhead blotted out the sky.

She said suddenly in a hoarse voice, "Stop."

He pretended not to hear. His foot pressed down on the accelerator.

She said in his ear, "Gerry darling, I said stop. I want to talk to you." At the same time she reached forward and turned the ignition key. The car slid to a standstill.

Hamsley stared into the night, holding the wheel tightly in his hands. Neither of them said anything for a moment.

"Gerry darling, you're a lovely looking boy," Mrs. Poison said. Her hand touched his.

Hamsley moved away from her. "I'm glad you think so, Mrs. Poison," he said. "I guess it's pretty kind of you to think that."

He could feel her quick breath on his face. "Yes, Gerry, you're the handsomest boy I've ever seen. I don't know what Mr. Poison would say, but I could be very kind to you."

Hamsley shuddered again. "Why, Mrs. Poison, I guess you're always giving me things. I guess you couldn't do any more."

"There's one thing I haven't given you, Gerry." Out of the darkness her voice sounded horribly harsh. "Gerry, I'm crazy about you. I'm mad about you."

She put out her hands and caught his head, pulling him towards her. She began to kiss him furiously. Her wet mouth made him want to retch. He suddenly pushed her away, his hands loathing the feel of her breasts.

He said, "No. I'm taking you back. I'm—I'm not going to break up your home."

She came at him again. "Don't be a fool!" she said harshly. "Come here—don't talk!"

He pushed her back more violently so that she thudded against the side of the car. He could see her staring eyes in the dashlight. She sat there heaving and panting, looking as if she could kill him. Then her mouth opened and a thin, reedy scream came out of the slack cavity that went through his head like red-hot wires.

He fumbled with the door-handle, pushed the door open, and got out of the car. He didn't say anything. He just wanted to get away from her. So he ran into the darkness, leaving her still screaming.

2

June 4th, 5:10 p.m.

Jay Ellinger sat behind his battered desk and scribbled on his blotter. His hat rested on the back of his head and a cigarette dangled from his lips. His completed copy lay in a wire basket by his hand, and he was through for the day. He had nothing further to do, but he made no effort to leave the office. He just sat there scribbling and smoking.

The house phone buzzed and he looked at it without interest. "You're lucky, laddybuck," he said, reaching out. "Two minutes, and you'd've missed me." He scooped the receiver to his ear. A girl said, "Mr. Henry wants to see you." Jay made a face. "Tell him I've gone home," he said hastily.

"Mr. Henry said if you'd gone home I was to ring you."

"What's the trouble? Is there a big fire or somethin'?"

"You'd better come. Mr. Henry sounds awful mad." She hung up.

Jay pushed his chair back and got up. Henry was the editor of the *St. Louis Banner*. He was a good guy to work for and he didn't often get mad.

As he walked upstairs to Henry's office Jay searched his mind to find any reason why he might be called on the mat, but he couldn't think of a thing. There was that little business about the extra expenses last week, but surely Henry wasn't going to crib about that. Maybe he was getting sore about the way Jay belted Mendetta in the Rayson trial, but then he'd passed the copy himself.

He shook his head. "Well, well, let's see what's bitin' the old guy."

He pushed open the frosted-panel door and walked in. Henry, a big fat man in his shirt-sleeves, was pacing up and down his small office. His cigar hung in tatters from his teeth. He looked up and glared at Jay.

"Shut the door!" he barked. "You've been a long time coming."

Jay lounged over to an arm-chair and sat down. He hung his legs over one of the arms and shut his eyes. "I'm sorry, Chief," he said; "I came as fast as I could."

Henry continued to pace up and down, ferociously chewing his tattered cigar. "What do you know about Gerry Hamsley?" he barked suddenly.

Jay shrugged. "Oh, he's a nice kid. He dances at Grantham's joint. Gigolo—but a better type of the usual breed."

"Yeah?" Henry planted himself in front of Jay. "A better type, hey? Well, let me tell you that guy has started somethin' that will mean my job and yours as well."

Jay opened his eyes. "You don't say," he said. "What's it all about?"

"The little swine tried to rape Poison's wife last night."

"What?" Jay sat up, his face startled, then he remembered Mrs. Poison and suddenly began to laugh. He lay limply in his chair and howled with laughter. Henry stood over him, his face black with fury.

"Shut up, you coarse-minded Mick!" he yelled. "There's nothing to laugh about. Do you hear me? Shut up!"

Jay mopped his eyes. "I'm sorry, Chief, but damn it, you ain't swallowin' a yarn like that? Gee! Is it likely? She's old enough to be his mother, an' she's as fat an' as ugly as an elephant."

Henry snarled, "Want me to phone Poison and tell him that? He's been on to me. My God! You ought to have heard him. He's in a terrible way."

"Well, what's behind it? You know as well as I, all that's bull. What's he want you to do?"

Henry struck the air with his clenched fists. "He wants Hamsley on a plate. He wants Grantham's joint closed down. He's yelling murder, an' he's got blood in his eye."

Just then the phone rang. Henry looked at it doubtfully. "That's him again, I bet," he said, lifting the receiver off gingerly.

From where Jay sat he could hear a sudden bellow come over the line. Henry winced and nodded to Jay. "Yes, Mr. Poison. Sure, Mr. Poison. I quite understand, Mr. Poison."

Jay grinned. It did him good to see his chief sweat. "Why, yes, Mr. Poison. He's here now. I'll tell him to come to the phone." Henry looked at Jay with a grim little smile.

Jay waved his hands frantically, but Henry handed him the phone. "Mr. Poison wants you," he said, and stood, mopping his face.

This was the first time that Jay had ever spoken to the proprietor of the *St. Louis Banner*. "Ellinger here," he said.

Something exploded in his ear and he hurriedly removed the receiver. Holding it almost at arm's length, he could plainly hear Poison's roar. "Ellinger? You the guy I pay each week to be my crime reporter?"

"Yes, that's right."

"Say sir when you speak to me, you young cub!" Poison bawled.

Jay grinned at Henry. He pursed his mouth and made silent rude signs. "Yes, Mr. Poison," he said.

"Get after Grantham, do you hear? I want everything you can find about him. Get after that swine Hamsley. I'm going to close down the 22nd Club and I'm going to break Hamsley. I want action. Get out now and do something. Now give me Henry."

Jay handed the phone back to Henry and sat back fanning himself with his hat.

Henry listened for a few moments with an agonized look on his face, and then the line went dead. He hung up gently. "The guy's crazy," he said miserably. "He's been on to the D.A.'s office. He's been on to the police. They can't do anything. Grantham's in the clear. His joint's respectable."

Jay scratched his head. "Why doesn't he give Hamsley in charge?"

Henry came round the desk and pounded the top of Jay's chair. "For the love of God, don't say a word about Mrs. Poison. No one's to know about that. Poison only told me because I flatly refused to touch Hamsley. I'm not supposed to have told you."

Jay grinned uneasily. "Sure, if that yarn got around, Poison would be laughed out of town. Surely, he doesn't believe it?"

Henry shrugged. "Of course he doesn't. It's the old cow that's causin' the trouble. Poison's scared to death of her. She's after Hamsley's blood—and you'd better find out why."

"Listen," Jay pleaded. "I'm a crime reporter. What you want is a nice private dick, not me. Let's get Pinkerton on the job. He'll turn up the dirt quick, an' we'll all be happy."

Henry scowled at him. "You heard Poison. Go out an' get busy. Don't come back until you've got something."

Jay got to his feet. "For cryin' out loud," he said. "If this doesn't beat anything that's ever come my way. What chance have I got to hang anythin' on Hamsley? Besides, he ain't such a bad guy."

Henry sat down behind his desk. "I'm warning you," he said seriously, "you've got to find something. If we don't give the old man what he wants, we'll be out. I know him when he gets like that."

Jay stood by the door. "But what?" he said. "What am I likely to find? Grantham's all right, ain't he?"

"As far as I know. I hate to say it, Jay, but if you don't find something, we'll have to frame those two guys. I'm getting too old to look for anything else."

Jay shook his head. "Not on your life," he said. "I ain't framing anyone because Poison's wife thinks she's young again. I'll sniff around. If nothin' shows up I'm resigning. But I ain't framin' anyone."

Henry sighed. "Perhaps you're right," he said. "Anyway, for God's sake dig hard."

"I'll dig all right," Jay returned, and went out, shutting the door behind him.

3

June 4th, midnight.

There was a cop at the street corner, standing watching the traffic, swinging his night-stick aimlessly.

Raven saw him as he came out of the alley, and he stepped back hurriedly into the shadows. Obscenities crowded through his brain, and his thin wolfish face twisted with frustrated rage.

The cop wandered to the edge of the curb, hesitated, then began to pace down the street.

Raven edged further down the alley, further into the sheltering darkness. He'd let the cop go past. Across the road he could see the large block of apartments with their hundreds of brightly lit windows. On the sixth floor, Tootsie Mendetta had a six-room suite. From where he stood Raven could see Mendetta's windows.

He stood against the wall, his head thrust forward and his square shoulders hunched. He looked what he was, a bitter, screwed-up thing of destruction.

The cop wandered to the mouth of the alley. Raven could see him looking carelessly into the darkness. The cop took off his cap and blotted his face with a large white handkerchief. It was a hot night. Standing there, his mind dwelling on a long, cold drink, he was completely unaware that Raven waited so patiently for him to go away. He put his cap on again and moved on past the alley, on towards the bright lights, towards the cafe where he could bum a drink on the quiet.

Raven gave him a few seconds, and then he walked to the mouth of the alley and glanced up and down the street. He saw nothing there to alarm him, and squaring his shoulders he stepped into the light of the street lamps.

In his apartment Mendetta amused himself with a pack of cards. He held a cigar between his thick lips and a glass of whisky-and-soda stood at his elbow. He played patience.

The apartment was silent except for the faint shuffling of cards as Mendetta altered their position. He liked patience, and he played with tense concentration. He heard Jean, in the bathroom, drawing off water, and he glanced over at the clock on the mantelpiece. It was just after twelve.

The phone suddenly jangled. He half shifted his bulk, his brows coming to a heavy frown, and stared at the phone.

Jean called from the bathroom, "Shall I answer it?"

He got up and walked with heavy steps across the room. "No, no. It'll be for me," he said, raising his voice so that she could hear. He picked up the receiver. "Who is it?"

"That you, Tootsie? This is Grantham."

Mendetta frowned. "What's the trouble?" he said sharply. "This is a hell of a time to ring me."

"Yeah, but this is a hell of a spot we're in." Grantham had a cold, clipped voice. "Listen, Tootsie, that little punk Hamsley's dropped us right in it."

"What are you talkin' about?" Mendetta sat on the edge of the small table, which rocked under his weight. "Dropped us where?"

"Hamsley's been digging Poison's wife. He's been playin' her for a sucker for weeks. She's spent a heap of jack on him."

"That's what he's at the Club for, ain't it?" Mendetta demanded impatiently. "Ain't he givin' you a cut?"

Grantham laughed bitterly. "It's not that. The old siren fell for him, and he couldn't take it. She took him out last night and tried to rape him. He ran away, the yellow punk."

Mendetta's fat face relaxed a little. "Well, what of it? You can't hold the boy up for that. Hell! I've seen that dame. She'd turn anyone's stomach."

"That so? Well, know what she's done? She's squawked to Poison. Said Hamsley's tried to rape her. How do you like that?"

"She's crazy. Poison ain't goin' to believe a yarn like that."

"No? Well, let me tell you he's hoppin' mad right at this moment. Maybe he doesn't believe it, but she's got herself in such a state, she does. That's enough for Poison. She's makin' him get mad. Listen, Tootsie, this is serious. Poison's goin' to try an' close us up."

Mendetta sneered. "Let him," he said. "What the hell do we care? They've got nothin' on us. He can't close us up."

Grantham cleared his throat. "You don't know Poison as well as I do. He'll attack us in that rag of his. He might turn somethin' up."

Mendetta considered this. "Not as long as I'm alive," he said at last. "I'll go round an' see that guy. We'll give him Hamsley, but he's got to lay off us."

"Will you do that?" Grantham sounded relieved. "Get round tomorrow early, Tootsie. This ain't the time to be down on it."

Mendetta stood up. "Leave it to me," he said. "I'll fix him," and he hung up.

Jean came out of the bathroom. She looked strikingly beautiful in her silk wrap. Perhaps her mouth was too large, but it gave her a generous look that was not in her nature. She was tall, with square shoulders, a narrow waist and thick hips.

"Who was it?" she said.

Mendetta went over to the table and gathered up the cards. He didn't feel like patience any more. "Grantham," he returned, putting the cards carefully in their container. He was a very tidy man. He took two little sips from the whisky.

She looked over at the clock. "What did he want? It's late."

Mendetta nodded his big head. "I know," he said. "Go to bed. I'll come in a little while."

She turned her head so that he couldn't see the sudden vicious look that came into her eyes. "Don't be so secretive," she said lightly. "Is he in trouble?"

He stubbed out his cigar. "He's always in trouble. That's why I'm here—to pull him out." He plodded over to her. His big heavy hand rested on her hip. "Go to bed. I shan't be long."

"Tootsie, I must know," she said. "Has something happened at the Club?"

He looked at her with a curious expression, half angry, half amused. He turned her towards the bedroom door. "It's nothing," he said. "Go to bed," and he smacked her across her buttocks very hard.

She went away from him, her knees weak and her insides coiled into a hard ball of hatred. She went across the bedroom to the window and pulled back the curtains. Leaning against the window-frame, she looked down into the street below. She remained like that for several minutes before she regained control of herself. If Mendetta had seen her expression as she stood by the window he would have been uneasy. As it was, his indifference to her feelings prepared the way for what eventually happened.

In the street, Raven crossed the road casually and walked towards the apartment block. When he neared the lighted entrance he stopped and knelt down to adjust his shoe-string. From under his slouch hat, he surveyed the doorway thoroughly. He was not satisfied with the empty doorway, so he crossed the street again and passed the block on the opposite side. His caution rewarded him.

A little guy, dressed in black, lounged against the wall in the shadows near the entrance. He kept so still that Raven wouldn't have noticed him at all if he'd come straight into the blinding light of the doorway.

The little guy had his hands deep in his coat pockets, and he watched

Raven pass on the other side of the street, indifferently.

Raven went on, crossed the road again and turned down a side street. He turned to his right after a few minutes' walking and approached the rear of the apartment block. This time he kept to the shadows. He hadn't gone far before he spotted another little guy, also dressed in black, lounging near the rear exit.

So it wasn't going to be the easy way. He might have known it. It was a cinch that if Mendetta had guards outside the block, there would be guards inside as well.

Raven went on, his head thrust forward, the line of his jaw fixed, and his thin lips compressed. He knew Mendetta couldn't escape from him. It was just a matter of time.

4

June 5th, 1:40 a.m.

Jay got round to the 22nd Club twenty minutes before it closed down for the night. There were a lot of people dancing and drinking, and he went immediately to the bar.

The bartender looked at him and rang a bell in Grantham's office by pressing his toe on a button on the floor. His well-disciplined face smiled at Jay, and he asked him what he'd like. Jay ordered a beer.

Benny Perminger came up at the moment, very hot and damp, and ordered a double Scotch. He seemed delighted to see Jay.

"What a stranger," he said; "and drinkin' beer too! Don't you know it's bad etiquette to drink beer in a joint like this?"

Jay shook hands with him. "I don't have to worry about such things," he said seriously. "No one expects a newspaper man to behave like a human being. How's the motor trade?"

Benny shook his head. "Lousy," he said. "There's too much competition. Seriously, Jay, I'm havin' a bad time just gettin' along."

Jay pursed his lips. There were always guys who had a bad time getting along, but they went to places like the 22nd Club and spent as much in a night as he earned in a week. Benny was one of these.

"I saw your chief, Poison, the other night. My God! Have you seen his car? It's just a ruin on four wheels. It's time he had a new one."

Jay shrugged. "Poison's old-fashioned. He likes that car. Maybe he's got sentimental memories."

"I don't believe it; he's just mean. Listen, Jay, could you put in a word for me? If I could get that old buzzard to take a trial run I'd hook him, but I can't get near him."

Jay promised to do what he could.

"There's another guy who I want to get in with. That's Mendetta. He could use a flock of my cars. I do trucks now, you know. Beggars can't be choosers. I guess that guy could use a lot of trucks. I've been trying to persuade Grantham to get me an introduction, but he doesn't seem keen. I suppose I'll have to offer him a split in my commission."

"Does Grantham know Mendetta?" Jay asked, suddenly interested.

"Know him? Why, of course he knows him. I thought everyone knew that. Mendetta put up the dough for this Club. He's got his finger in every pie."

Jay drank some beer. "Aaah," he said, putting the glass down. "Mendetta's a bad guy. I'd forget about him."

Benny shrugged. "What the hell. His dough's good, ain't it?" he said. "I don't care who buys my cars as long as he pays."

Jay finished his beer. "Maybe you're right," he said.

Just then a blonde came in, followed by a tall young man with heavy, horn-rimmed glasses. The blonde wore a red dress, very tight across her small breasts, and when she climbed up on the high stool at the bar she showed a lot of her legs.

Benny looked at her. He stared so hard that she giggled suddenly and adjusted her skirt. Benny sighed. "There're an awful lot of swell dames around tonight," he said to Jay. "She's nice, ain't she?"

Jay wasn't very interested. "Sure," he said; "they're all nice. Where's your wife? How is she, anyway?"

Benny still looked at the blonde. "Sadie? Oh, she's fine. She's out there with my party. I sort of wanted a drink. Did I? No, that's wrong. I came out for a doings. Seeing you put it out of my mind. I guess I'd better get on." He shook hands again and went off.

Jay ordered another beer. While he was waiting for it, he saw Grantham come in. Grantham was very tall and thin, with silver-white hair. His face was hard. Two lines ran from his nose to his mouth, and he looked very grey. Jay only knew him by sight, he'd never spoken to him. When he saw him, he turned back to the bar and paid the bartender.

Grantham came up and stood at his elbow. "What do you want?" he said. His voice was very hostile.

Jay looked at him by turning his head. "Should I know you?" he asked. "Are you someone I ought to know?"

Grantham introduced himself. "We don't have newspaper men in here, you know," he said; "we don't like them in here."

Jay raised his eyebrows. "That's interestin'," he said. "That's very interesting. No newspaper men, huh? And who else? Tell me your black list. I bet you don't like the cops in here either."

Grantham tapped a little tune on the counter. "Don't let's get sore about this," he said evenly. "I'm just telling you. Maybe you didn't know."

"Is this your idea, or did Mendetta suggest it?"

Grantham's face hardened. "That sort of talk won't get you anywhere," he said quietly. "I'm just telling you to keep out of here, that's all."

Jay shook his head. "You can't do that. This is a place for public entertainment. I should forget about it. A line or two in my paper could upset your business pretty badly."

Grantham nodded. "I see," he said; "I was just giving you a hint. You don't have to take it. You're quite right, of course. You have every right to come here. Only you're not welcomed."

"Leave me now, pal," Jay said, turning away, "I'm goin' to have a good cry."

Grantham looked at the barman and then at the clock. "You can shut down, Henry," he said, and walked away.

Jay finished his beer, nodded to the barman, who ignored him, and went out into the big lounge. People were beginning to move out. He saw Clem Rogers, who played the saxophone in the band, putting his instrument away. He knew Rogers quite well.

He went to the cloakroom and got his hat, and then he went outside. He had to wait ten minutes before Rogers came out, and then he followed him away from the Club. When they got to the main street he overtook him.

Rogers seemed surprised to see him. "You're late, ain't you?" he said, peering at his wrist-watch. It was just after two o'clock.

Jay fell in step beside him. "We newspaper guys never sleep," he said. "How about a little drink? There's a joint just down here that keeps open all night."

Rogers shook his head. "I guess not," he said. "I want to get home. I'm tired."

Jay put his hand on his arm and steered him down a side turning. "Just a short drink, buddy," he said, "then you can go home."

They went down some steps to an underground bar. The place was nearly empty. A short, thick-set Italian dozed across the bar. He raised his head sleepily as the two entered.

"Good evenin'," he said, rubbing the counter-top with a swab. "What will you have?"

"At this time of night, Scotch," Jay said. "Bring us the bottle over there." He indicated a table at the far end of the room.

Rogers followed him across and sat down. He yawned, rubbing his eyes with his hands. "God! I'm tired," he said. "I wish I could get some other job. This is killin' me."

Jay poured out a big shot of whisky in each glass. "I ain't goin' to keep you long, but there's just one little thing you might help me with."

"Sure, I'd be glad to. What is it?"

"You must see everything that goes on at the Club. I've got a feeling it ain't quite on the level. I want to find out."

Rogers sat back. His sleepy eyes suddenly woke up. "I don't know what you mean," he said.

"Just that. How does the place strike you?"

Rogers blinked. "You tryin' to get the place shut down?" he asked, a little coldly.

Jay hesitated, then he said, "That's about it. Now, look here, Rogers, you know me. I wouldn't make things difficult for you. I know you've got to think of your job, but if you helped me I'd see you all right."

"Yeah? How?"

"How would you like to work for Cliff Somers? I could get you an in with his outfit if you fancied it."

Rogers' face brightened. "Honest?"

Jay nodded.

"I'd like that. I've always wanted to work for Somers. He's got a swell crowd."

"I know, but I'd only get you in if you made it worth while. You've got to tell me things."

Rogers shook his head. "I guess that's too bad," he said. "There's nothin' to tell. The Club's like hundreds of other clubs. Maybe there's a fight now and then between two drunks, but that's nothin'."

Jay pulled a face. "I didn't think there was anything wrong with the joint," he admitted, "but I was hoping you'd know something."

Rogers shook his head. "No, I guess not." He finished his drink.

"Think back," Jay urged him. "Hasn't anythin' happened that made you curious? Anythin' that somebody did or said."

Rogers yawned. "No, I don't think so," he said, staring with sleepy eyes at the bottle of Scotch. "Mind you, there was one violent drunk that made a bad scene a couple of months ago, but that wasn't anythin' really."

Jay shifted impatiently. "Well, tell me."

"There was nothin' to it. Some guy wanted to see Grantham. He wasn't well dressed. Looked like a clerk in an office or somethin'. I thought it was odd that he should come to the Club. When Grantham didn't show up he started to shout. Some bull about where his sister was or somethin'. We didn't pay much attention to him. They gave him a bum's rush. Treated him pretty roughly. We haven't seen him again."

"What about his sister?"

Rogers shrugged. "Search me. He's lost her or somethin'. Seems to have thought that Grantham knew where she was. I guess he was drunk."

"Did he look drunk?"

"No, now you come to think of it, he didn't, but I guess he must have been. You don't start shouting around a joint like the 22nd unless you're drunk, do you?"

"Still it's rum, ain't it?" Jay turned it over in his mind. "Know who he is?"

Rogers frowned. "I did hear his name. I've forgotten. It wasn't important, you see."

"Think. I want to find that guy. Maybe he knows somethin'."

Rogers tried to concentrate. "It was quite an ordinary name. I tell you what. Gerald Foster, the shipping man, seemed to know him. He was having dinner at the time. When this guy started shouting, he looked round and seemed to recognize him. He got up and told him not to make a fool of himself. You might ask him."

Jay said he would. He stood up. "I ain't keepin' you out of your cot any longer," he said. "Keep your ears open, won't you?"

Rogers got up. "You really meant what you said about Somers?"

"I'll see him tomorrow," Jay promised.

They went out into the street.

"It's mighty dark, ain't it?" Rogers said, groping his way up the stone steps.

Jay followed him. "It's all right when you get used to it," he returned. "Come on, I'll go some of the way home with you."

They parted when they came to the trolley stop. Rogers went off to collect his car from a near-by garage, and Jay waited for a trolley. He was quite satisfied with his evening's enquiries. He didn't expect to find anything but at least he could tell Henry that he was following up an angle that might bring in something. If they could only keep Poison quiet for a week or so, he might simmer down.

He saw the lights of the trolley as it swung round the corner. He'd be glad to get home, he told himself.

5

June 5th, 2:15 a.m.

Raven couldn't sleep. He moved through the dark streets, his sour, bitter hatred refusing to let him rest. He walked automatically, not noticing where he was going. He wanted to vent his vicious hatred on someone who couldn't strike back. He wanted to sink his hands into flesh and rend.

The picture of Mendetta, comfortable in his luxury apartment, carefully guarded, made him sick with jealousy. Mendetta had got to go. Once he was out of the way, the organization would fold up. It was Raven's chance. He could step in then. They were all afraid of him. There might be a little trouble, but not for long. It was Mendetta who held them together. It was Mendetta who was keeping him away from power. Grantham would be easy. He was too fond of the things he already possessed to risk anything. Raven knew that he had only to walk into the 22nd Club to take over when Mendetta was out of the way.

He turned left into the darkness and plodded on, his mind busy with schemes. The muscles in his legs were fluttering, crying out for rest, but his brain was too active. He had been walking a long time, thinking, planning and scheming.

Out of the darkness, someone called to him. The sound of the voice startled him, and he stiffened as he turned his head.

A girl stepped away from the railings of a house and came close to him. He could see the pale blur of her face and the inviting, swaying movement of her body as she came towards him.

She said in a soft, husky voice, "Come home with me, darlin'."

Raven hated her viciously. His first conscious reaction was to smash his fist in her face. He found that he was too tired even to do that. Instead, he moved on, ignoring her.

She took two quick steps and was beside him again. "Come on," she said urgently, "it's just round the corner. Spend the night with me, honey. I'm good—honest, I wouldn't tell you if I wasn't."

He stopped walking and half turned. It suddenly dawned on him that she must be one of Mendetta's whores. She was in Mendetta's district. A murderous desire suddenly surged through him.

She came very close and put her thin white hand on his sleeve. He couldn't bear her to touch him, and he shook her off savagely.

"What's the matter, honey, ain't you well?" She began to draw back, suddenly uneasy.

He looked up and down the deserted street. No, not here. He'd have to go back to her place. His thin mouth curled into a smile. This would make Mendetta sit up all right. He said, "Well, come on, then. Where do we go?"

At once she became bright again. He felt against his face her little sigh of relief. She said, "Gee! You scared me. I thought you were a cop."

He began to move down the street with her, taking long, shambling, unsteady steps.

As he didn't say anything, she went on, "A girl's gotta look out for herself. It's a tough life, darlin'. You're goin' to give me a nice present?"

Still he didn't say anything. Her voice, her scent and her walk all infuriated him, but she was one of Mendetta's possessions. He mustn't say or do anything that would frighten her until he got her where she couldn't get away. As he didn't trust himself, he kept silent.

He was conscious that she was looking at him closely, and that her step lagged a little. He put his hand on her arm and hurried her along. "Where is it?" he said.

"Here," she said a little breathlessly. "Let me get my key."

He stood back while she searched in her cheap little bag. They were directly under the street light. He could see her brass-coloured hair, her wide rouged mouth, her short nose and her hard, professional eyes. She only came to his shoulder, and under her tight bottle-green dress he could see the outline of her small, firm breasts.

He said harshly, "For God's sake hurry."

She giggled nervously. "I'm hurrying."

He could have spat in her face. She turned and smiled at him. "There's a hole in the lining, I guess," she said.

At the corner of the street, a cop suddenly appeared. Raven saw him instantly. The inside of his mouth went very dry, and he said once again, "Hurry."

The tone of his voice startled her, and something of his urgency infused her with panic. She fumbled with her key, jabbing at the keyhole unsuccessfully.

With an obscene word on his lips, he snatched the key from her fingers and opened the door. He put his hand on her shoulders and shoved her inside, stepping in behind her and closing the door softly. He could feel the cold sweat under his arms.

She said a little angrily, "Why did you do that?"

"Put a light on."

He could hear her fumbling along the wall, and then the passage was swamped with a bright hard light. He said, "Well, go on. Don't stand there."

She hesitated. "I don't know about you. There's something I don't like about you."

He pushed his hat to the back of his head and looked her full in the face. They looked at each other for a long minute.

"Do you always yap like this?" he snarled at her. "Take me to your room."

They went upstairs. He followed her closely. As she went up before him he could see how her hips rolled as she lifted her feet. The professional skirt was so tight across her hips he could see where her suspender belt ended and where the little knobs of the suspenders caught her stockings.

They went up three flights in silence. Then she stopped and opened a door. He caught a glimpse of a little brass plate on the door as he entered a box-like hallway. He closed the door behind him. She took him into the bedroom.

He stood in the middle of the room, his ears intent, listening.

She said, "Come on, darlin'. Don't stand there."

"You alone up here?"

"Sure, we won't be disturbed."

Still he stayed listening. She said again impatiently, "What is it?"

He chewed his lower lip, looking at her thoughtfully, then he said, "Mind if I look?" and went out, throwing open the other doors without entering. He glanced in the other two rooms, satisfying himself that they were empty.

She followed him into the hall. Her face was hard and her eyes glittered angrily. "What the hell do you think you're doin'?" she snapped. "This is your room here. The rest of this joint is private—do you get it?"

Raven again felt like smashing his fist in her face, but he held himself in. "Okay, okay," he said, walking past her into the bedroom.

She shut the other two doors and then followed him in. Once more her lips broke into her professional smile, but her eyes were dark and suspicious. She said, "Come on, darlin'. Let's get it over."

Raven took off his hat and ran his fingers through his short, wiry black hair. He sank on to the bed, which gave under his weight.

The room was shabby and not over-clean. The strip of carpet that lay on the floor was threadbare, and from where he was sitting he could see a small stack of soiled underclothes behind an easy-chair.

While he sat there she took off her dress by just pulling a zipper and stepping out of it. Underneath she wore a pair of pink step-ins and a brassiere. She swayed a little before him, turning this way and that, so he could see her. Then she said, "My present?" Her hard face lighted up with a glittering smile.

Raven put his hand in his pocket and offered her a twenty-dollar bill. It was all the money he had in the world. The amount took her breath away. She clutched at the bill and stood staring at it. "Migod, you're cute!" she said. "Gee! I'll give you a good time for this."

The bill disappeared into the top of her stocking, and she hurriedly stripped down to her suspender-belt. She said, coming round the bed, "Come on, darlin', come on."

He said, "Don't be in such a hurry. Put on a wrap or somethin'. I want to talk to you."

He saw her go a little limp. "Aw, come on, darlin'. We can talk afterwards."

"No."

She hesitated, then, shrugging, crossed the room and took a dark red silk wrap off the door-peg.

Raven, sitting in the chair, looked at her indifferently. He noticed she had a little roll of fat above her hip bones, and he thought her buttocks looked ridiculous framed in the soiled suspender-girdle. A dame had got to be good just wearing a girdle, stockings and shoes. This whore wasn't so hot.

She put the wrap on and wandered over to the bed. "You've got to be quick, darlin'," she said. "I can't keep you here all night."

Raven shook his head. "I shan't stay all night," he said. "Who's underneath?"—pointing to the floor.

"No one. All offices," she said. "I keep telling you no one'll disturb you." Then a thought crossed her mind. "Say, the bulls aren't looking for you, are they?"

A thin smile came to Raven's lips. "Not yet, they ain't," he returned.

There was a long silence. His cold, wolfish face, his hooded eyes, made her very uneasy. She'd kicked around with plenty of toughs and hoods in her time, but this guy was different. She felt suddenly scared of him, and horribly alone. He just sat there, gripping the arms of the chair, watching her indifferently.

She felt a little sick. "Hell!" she thought. "What a dumb thing to have told him I'm alone!"

He said, "You belong to Mendetta s bunch, don't you?"

Her eyes opened very wide. She didn't expect anything like that. "Mendetta? I've never heard of him," she said hastily.

"No?" Raven crossed his leg. "You surprise me. Mendetta runs all this territory, including the whores."

"Don't call me that," she snapped. "If you're goin' to be funny, you better beat it."

"Mendetta's a big shot around here. He runs everything. He makes plenty of dough, but he ain't goin' to last. Do you hear, baby? He ain't goin' to last."

She looked over at the door. "Can't you lay off this crap? I don't know what you're talkin' about. I'm tired. I gotta get some sleep. Let's get this over, an' then you beat it."

Raven nodded. "Don't work yourself into a lather, sister. Get on the bed. We're goin' to get some sleep right now."

She dug up a false smile. "That's fine, darlin'. I don't know anythin' about this Mendetta guy." She went over to the door. Her heart was beating wildly, and she kept her eyes averted so that he shouldn't see her panic.

He said in a chilly voice: "I said get on the bed."

She put her hand on the door-knob. "I'll be right back," she said hurriedly. "I'll be right back."

Before she could open the door, he had left the chair, shoved her away from the door, slammed and locked it. He took the key out of the lock and dropped it into his pocket.

The look on his face terrified her, but she tried to bluff. "Get out of the way an' unlock the door," she said weakly.

He thrust out his hand and sent her sprawling over the bed. He leant against the door. "When I tell you to do a thing—you do it."

She struggled to a sitting position. "Unlock that door, you big bastard," she said. "Get out of here. Go on, take your dough and beat it." She flipped the twenty-dollar bill from the top of her stocking and threw it at him.

Raven bent slowly and picked it up. He walked over to the bed and sat down beside her. She saw the look in his face. She saw he was going to kill her. The blank, set look in his eyes paralysed her. She could only thrust out her arms. "No… don't!" she cried. "You're not to—do you hear?… No!… Keep away…."

He leant slowly towards her. As he came nearer, she crouched away until she lay flat on the bed, his face hovering just above her. She couldn't scream. Her tongue curled to the roof of her mouth and stayed there. She couldn't do anything. Even when his hands slid up to her throat she only clutched feebly at his wrists, shaking her head imploringly at him.

He said softly, "It won't hurt, if you don't struggle."

She shut her eyes, and as the blood began to drum in her ears she suddenly realized that this was death, and she began to fight him frantically.

She had left it too late. His knee, driving into the little hollow between her breasts, pinned her like a poor moth to the bed. The vice-like grip of his fingers cut the air from her lungs.

He said, "Mendetta will hear about this. He'll hate it. He'll know then someone is after him. Do you hear, you silly little fool? You couldn't earn enough to live decently. Look at this room. Look at the poverty of it. When I run this territory my broads won't live like this. Do you hear?"

She beat his face with her hands, but she had no strength. Her legs thrashed up and down, at first violently, then jerkily, and then not at all.

As her tongue filled her wide-open mouth, and her eyes tried to burst from their sockets, he turned his head slightly so he couldn't see her. He said in a whisper, "You ugly little bitch." Then blood ran on to his hands from her nose, and she went limp. He climbed off her and stood looking down at her.

He knew that he could go home and sleep now. For a time his hatred had gone out of him.

6

June 5th, 10:15 a.m.

The sun came through the windows of Mendetta's apartment and made patterns on the white carpet.

Remains of breakfast on a silver tray stood on a little table by the settee. An ash-tray gave out a thin grey smoke of a dying cigarette.

Jean, still in a bed-wrap, lay on the settee, her eyes closed and her thoughts far away. She was trying to imagine her life without Mendetta. It was difficult to imagine. It would be difficult also to replace this luxury. But she knew that she couldn't live with Mendetta much longer.

The telephone rang shrilly. It startled her. She reached out and took the receiver off. "Who is it?" she said. Her voice was deep, almost man-like.

Grantham said, "Where's Mendetta?" He sounded very excited.

Jean looked up at the ceiling. She hadn't much use for Grantham. "He's out," she said briefly. "What's wrong?"

"Where is he? I've gotta get in touch with him."

"He's gone round to fix Poison. You can't get him there. What is it? I'll tell him."

There was a pause. "No, I guess I'll wait." Grantham sounded worried.

"Listen, tell me. Maybe I can get hold of him."

"It's one of the girls. She was strangled last night."

Jean's eyes narrowed. "Well, what of it? Tootsie can't do anything about that."

"I know he can't; but he's gotta know."

"All right, I'll tell him. Who did it?"

"The cops don't know."

"I didn't ask that. I said who did it?"

Again there was a long pause. Then Grantham said, "You're not to tell Mendetta this, it'll only make him mad, but I think Raven did it."

Jean sat up. "Why do you say that?"

"One of the patrolmen thought he recognized him going into the girl's apartment. You know, O'Hara. He keeps an eye on that beat. I slipped him a hundred bucks to keep his mouth shut."

Jean thought for a moment. "Raven?" she repeated. "I wonder. Does that mean—?"

"I don't know, but he said he'd start something, didn't he?"

"He said he'd get Tootsie. Listen, what are you going to do if he gets Tootsie?"

"Don't talk like that," Grantham said sharply. "He won't get him. Tootsie's too big. He's too well protected."

"I know, but suppose he does. Raven's dangerous; he might, you know. What will you do?"

"What the hell can I do? I couldn't afford to fight him. He's got quite a big mob, and they're dangerous. At this time, we can't afford a gang battle."

Jean smiled. "You mean you'd let him walk in?"

"What else could I do? The boys only keep together because of Tootsie. If Tootsie went, they'd rat."

"I know."

There was a long silence.

"Listen, Jean, you don't think—?"

"I don't think anything, but you and me've got to look after ourselves, haven't we?"

"Well, yes, I guess that's so, but nothing's going to happen to Tootsie. I know nothing will happen to Tootsie."

Jean smiled again. "I'm glad to hear you say so," she said, and hung up. She lay thinking for a long time, then she picked up the telephone and called a number.

Someone asked roughly what she wanted.

"I want to speak to Raven," she said softly. "Yes, tell him it's Jean Mendetta. Yes, he'll speak to me all right," and she lay back, an amused smile on her mouth, waiting for Raven to come to the phone.

7

June 5th, 11:20 a.m.

Jay took a taxi to the east side of the town. He was feeling pleased with himself. As soon as he had reached the office he had got Gerald Fisher on the phone and asked him about the scene Rogers had told him about.

Fisher remembered it quite well. "What do you want to know about that for?" he asked suspiciously.

"I want to find the guy who made the scene," Jay said. "He might have an important bearing on a big case we're working on now. I don't say he has, but there is just the chance. I was hoping you might help me."

"As a matter of fact, I do know him. He used to be one of my clerks. That was why I was so surprised to see him at the 22nd Club. His name's Fletcher. Do you want his address? I could get it for you."

"Sure, that's just what I do want."

"Just a moment, then." Jay heard Fisher say something, then he came on the line again. "They're looking it up. We've got it on record, I know."

"He doesn't work with you any more?"

"Good God, no! I couldn't have a fellow in my office like that. He made a frightful fool of himself. He had to be tossed out. I gave him the sack next morning."

"What was the trouble, Mr. Fisher?" Jay asked.

"I don't know. He must have been drunk. He kept on yelling about his sister. I mean to say, that sort of thing isn't done at the 22nd. No, I had to get rid of him."

Jay grinned. "Sure," he said.

"Ah, here's the address."

Jay wrote it down, thanked Fisher, and hung up. He thought maybe he was going on a fool's errand, but it was worth trying, anyhow.

The taxi drew up outside a large tenement house. The driver said apologetically, "This is it, boss."

Jay got out and paid him off. He walked up the steps and rang on the bell. The place was dirty and horribly sordid. He felt people watching him behind ragged curtains all down the street.

An old woman, very dirty, with a sack for an apron, opened the door and looked at him suspiciously.

Jay raised his hat. "Mr. Fletcher in?" he asked.

"He's on the top floor. You can go up." She stood aside to let him in. "You tell that guy to pay his rent. I'm gettin' sick of askin' him myself."

Jay ignored her and went up the stairs. A big negro lounged against the wall on the first landing and looked at him insolently. As Jay passed he spat on the floor.

On the top floor a large fat woman sat just outside her door, peeling potatoes. Jay asked her where Fletcher's room was. She jerked her thumb to a door without saying anything.

Jay rapped on the door and pushed it open.

A man lay on a dirty mattress. He'd got a three days' growth of beard, and Jay saw he was blind in one eye. He sat up, a scared look on his face, as Jay entered.

"What do you want?" he said. He had quite a cultured voice.

Jay looked round the dirty room and grimaced. "I'm Ellinger of the *St. Louis Banner*. I want to talk to you, pal," he said.

Fletcher got off the bed. "I don't want to talk to anyone," he said.

Jay thought he looked horribly thin. He began to cough and he had to sit on the bed again.

Jay pulled up a rickety chair and sat down too. "Listen, Fletcher, don't fly off the handle. You're lookin' in a bad shape. I might be able to help you."

When he had stopped coughing, Fletcher said rather wildly, "Look what they did!"—pointing to his eye. "They did that. Threw me down a flight of stone steps. One of the heels hit me in my eye with his elbow."

Jay lit a cigarette. He didn't like the smell of dirt in the room. "That's what I've come to see you about," he said. "What's it all about? If I can help you I will."

Fletcher looked at him suspiciously. "Why?" he demanded. "Why should you want to help me?"

"Now don't get that way. Been out of a job some time, haven't you? Now come on, spill it."

"It's Janet," Fletcher began. Then suddenly his thin face crumpled and he began to cry.

Jay pushed his hat to the back of his head and blew out his cheeks. He was very embarrassed. "What you want is a drink," he said. "You wait. I'll get you one."

Fletcher controlled himself with an effort. "No, don't go away," he said. "I'm all right. I guess I'm sort of low. I haven't had much grub."

"Well, come on. I'll buy you a lunch." Jay got up.

Fletcher shook his head. "Not now. Later, perhaps, but I want to tell you."

Jay sat down again. "Go ahead," he said.

"It's my sister, Janet. She went away one morning to work and she didn't come back. I've hunted everywhere. I've told the police, but they can't find her."

Jay sighed. He knew there were a lot of girls in St. Louis who went out and didn't come back any more. "Maybe she went off and got married. Maybe she thought she'd like to go to Hollywood. There're a lot of girls who suddenly get a bug in their conks and beat it without telling anyone."

Fletcher looked up. His one eye burnt fiercely. "You don't believe that rubbish, do you?" he said. "That's what the police said."

Jay shifted. "Well, what else could have happened to her? You don't think she's dead, do you?"

"I wish to God she was!" He beat his fist on his knee. "The Slavers have got her!" he shouted. "Do you hear? The Slavers have got her."

"You don't know that. You only think they have. There ain't much of that stuff going on now. We've cleaned it up."

"You're wrong. It's going on every day of the year. Decent girls leaving their homes and being trapped. Decent girls forced into brothels. Any amount of them. And there's nothing done about it. The police know all about it, but they keep their mouths shut. Anyone who gets to know about it is given money to keep his mouth shut."

"You can't talk like that unless you've got some proof. Why did you kick up that row at the 22nd Club?"

"Can't you guess? Grantham's working the racket."

"You're crazy. Grantham? Don't talk bull."

Fletcher lay back on his elbow. "I've been watching him," he said. "One night, when the Club was closed, I saw a car draw up outside the Club. The street was empty. No one saw me. They took a girl out of the car. She had a rug over her head. Just as she got to the door she got the rug off and she screamed. They hit her on the head with something. They hit her very hard. I could hear the sound very distinctly from where I was standing. Then they carried her inside. You don't think anything of that? Well, I'll tell you some more." There was a crazy gleam in his eye. "Another night I got on the roof. You've never been on the top floor of the Club, have you? Nor have I. But I've been on the roof. I've listened, lying on the tiles with my ear close to the roof, listening. I've heard things. I've heard girls screaming. I've heard the crack of whips. I've heard a lot of horrible things."

Jay was interested now. "You're sure of all this?" he said.

Fletcher leant forward and grabbed his coat lapels. "Do you think I'd make it up? Don't you realize what all this means? My sister was one of those girls. She was taken into that place. They beat her until she was willing to do what they wanted. She's somewhere in this town, selling her body to anyone who'll pay for it. Do you hear? And everyone sits around, blast them, and tells me that it couldn't happen here. That this town's been cleaned up. And it's going on now… now… now!"

Jay pushed him back on to the bed gently. "Take it easy," he said. "I believe you, anyway. Listen, Fletcher, you've got to use your brains. It's no good getting in a state about this. You'll be wanted to give evidence. I'll see that you get some money and I'll fix a job for you. You'll have to leave everything to me. I'm going out after this business. We want to close the Club up, and you've given me the right lever to do it with. Leave it to me. I'll fix those heels."

Later, after he had made arrangements for Fletcher, he took a taxi back to the *Banner* office. The taxi couldn't drive him fast enough.

8

June 5th, 10:40 p.m.

Benny Perminger just wasn't interested in the fight any more. From the first gong he'd sat forward, his jaw set and thrust out, and his hands clenched on his knees. He'd given them three rounds to get warmed up. These big guys couldn't take chances in the first few rounds. They'd got to get set and take stock of each other, so Benny was patient.

All right, this was the fifth round coming up and nothing had happened. These two punks just seemed to love each other. They poked feebly, and then shuffled into a clinch, then they'd break away, look at each other like they were surprised to see they were still standing up, and then start poking and clinching all over again.

Benny sat back suddenly with a long-drawn-out sigh of disgust. That's when it happened. His ears slid along silk stockings. You don't go getting your head between a dame's knees every day. It shook him up. It took his mind right off the fight and kept it off.

The dame shifted back fast enough, but it didn't alter the fact. Benny had had his head between her knees. She had been sitting right behind him on the tier seat. Maybe she'd never seen a fight before, so she got excited. She came forward, with her knees hovering over Benny's head.

Benny was sitting forward too. There was nothing in it, both sitting forward trying to squeeze some excitement out of a punk fight. It was different when Benny sat back suddenly. It gave her quite a shock when Benny's head banged between her knees. The way that dame slid back on her seat was nobody's business.

Her boy friend was quick too. One of those guys who missed nothing. He said, "Go on, give it away. Put it on a plate an' hand it round. Don't mind me."

Benny heard him. He sounded tough, so Benny sat still, feeling a little sick. He kept his eyes on the two punks shuffling around on the resin. He stole a quick look at Sadie, sitting beside him, but she hadn't noticed anything. She was half asleep.

Fights bored her, anyway, but she'd got into the habit of going places with Benny. She liked best when they went to movies, because he didn't get excited, or look at other women, or curse.

It was a lucky break for Benny that one of the fighters suddenly thought it was time to go home. He began to hit more seriously and immediately got the other guy in trouble. All the crowd began to shout and get excited, so Benny felt a lot less scared.

All the same, he had lost interest in the fight. He wanted to have a look at this dame behind him. He knew that if he did he'd start something, so he just stared down at the brightly lit ring and made up pictures of what she might look like.

It wasn't long before he'd got such a picture that he could hardly sit still. There were two more fights on the programme, but they weren't going to keep Benny sitting in that hall. He wanted to get home with Sadie, just as fast as his car would take him. He said, "Come on, honey, let's get outta here."

Sadie woke up and blinked around, stared at the two little men way down in the ring, and then looked blankly at Benny. "Where's the fire?" she said.

Benny looked at her. She was good. She was just the right height, and her hair was curly, black and silky. She reminded Benny of the cuties who give you thoughts from the front cover of *College Life*. They'd been married now two years, and Benny liked her a lot. He had even kept off other girls. Sadie had been pretty good to him. The first six months had gone well for them both.

Then Benny got used to it, and he began to slip back.

At first he'd walk along with Sadie and compare her with other dames. Sadie was good, so she came out well in that game. When he began wondering what the other dames were like, then that wasn't so good. He knew what Sadie was like. Then, from just looking, he had to make remarks. He'd say to Sadie, "Did you see that dame, just then? Gee! What a figure! Did you see anythin' like that?"

Well, Sadie felt pretty safe, and she thought Benny was just kidding her, but Benny wouldn't leave it alone. He'd say, "I bet that dame's a hot one.

Yeah, look at the way she swings her can. Gee! I guess that dame gets pushed around plenty."

Nothing in it, but it hurt. It did more than that, it got on Sadie's nerves. She knew that one of these days he was going to cheat. Once he'd started cheating he'd go on cheating. It was no good. She'd done everything she could to hold him, but he'd got that sort of a mind. He couldn't help himself.

When he went and put his head between that floosie's knees, something snapped inside Sadie. That finished it. He didn't think she'd seen that. All right, it'd be a surprise for him.

Benny said again, "Come on, honey. Those punks'll drive me crazy."

They pushed their way past the other people and got to the gangway. Benny looked back. Sadie was waiting for him to do that. Benny's heart jumped when he saw the dame. Boy! She was good. It made him go limp inside just to think that he'd slid his ears along her stockings.

Sadie said it for him. "I know," she said; "don't tell me. She's cute. She's got everything. She's a menace to good men, and she's the world's biggest push-over."

Benny blinked at her. "Hey! Where do you get that stuff?"

Sadie walked down the gangway, not listening to him. She was conscious of some of the men drawing their eyes reluctantly from the fight to watch her go. She swung her hips. "Go on," she thought, "take a look at me. I'm not so bad myself."

Benny came running after her. "What was that stuff about the dame?" he said angrily. "I don't like that line."

Sadie looked at him over her shoulder. "Looked to me like you were having a good time," she said, without stopping.

Benny nearly fell over. She'd seen after all. Hell! He might have guessed that she couldn't have missed that.

He had almost to run to keep up with her. "You ain't mad about a little thing like that?" he said anxiously. "It was an accident—you know that."

She said bitterly, "Sure it was an accident. Pretty nice for you, wasn't it?"

They got to the car, and she beat him to opening the door. She climbed in and sat close up to the door, away from him. He started the engine and began to drive slowly down the winding exit.

"Forget it, baby," he said. "It was just one of those things. Anyway, she wasn't so hot."

Sadie knew he was lying, but she suddenly felt very tired, and she leant back, shutting her eyes.

As she didn't say anything, Benny hopefully assumed she wasn't mad any more. He drove along, his mind half on the traffic, thinking of the dame. She'd been a smasher. To think that had happened. If Sadie hadn't been there, and if that tough hadn't been there, maybe he could have dated her up. It would have been a pushover. It was a natural. He could hardly wait to get the car away.

Sadie leant limply against the wall of the little elevator as it droned up to the sixth floor. She didn't look at him. Benny stood close to her, watching her anxiously as he wiped his sweating hands with a handkerchief. She was looking tired and a little irritable, he thought. Anyway, if he went about it in the right way it'd be all right.

In the early days of marriage he would come in from work, sweep her off her feet into the bedroom, leaving the supper to burn. She'd always protested, but he knew she was pleased as he was when it was over.

The elevator stopped at the sixth floor, and Sadie walked out. On the opposite passage Tootsie Mendetta had his apartment.

It always made Benny mad to think that a rich guy like Mendetta should live just across his passage, and he'd never set eyes on him. He knew he was there, but he'd never seen him. Anyway, right at this minute, he didn't give Mendetta a thought.

He fumbled at the keyhole, making two attempts before he sank the key. His hands shook a little.

Inside the small apartment he let her take off her hat and coat, and then he sidled up behind her. He put his arms round her from behind. "I love you, honey," he said, his voice shaking.

"Put me down!" There was a snap in her voice that jolted him. He put her down and turned her. The cold, hostile look she gave him brought him up short, just like he'd rammed his face against a brick wall.

"Say, what's wrong? I got to thinkin' of you in the car. I thought—I thought maybe we could go back a couple of years."

She said, "Think again."

"What the hell is this?" he said, his disappointment making him suddenly mad with her.

She walked back into the sitting-room. He saw her put her hand to her eyes.

He wandered after her, feeling a suppressed rage welling up in him. He leant against the door-post. "What is it?" he asked.

She said, "You know what it is." Her voice sounded full of tears.

"Don't talk in riddles. If you've got anythin' to beef about, why not save it? Listen, honey," Benny said urgently, "this ain't the time to start fightin'. Come on with me. We'll have a good time together—how's that?

You'll feel fine—"

She said, interrupting him: "Wait a minute. You've got a one-track mind. That floosie's got you burnt up, and you think you can take it out of me. 'Pretty-daughter-sitting-on-father's-knee-makes-it-hard-for-mother' complex. Not this mother, it doesn't."

Benny took off his hat and threw it across the room. He was mad. "What the hell's come over you?" he demanded, his voice rising.

Sadie went over and sat on the sofa. "I'm sick of the way you look at women. I've stood as much of it as I'm going to stand. Every woman who walks past you, you must look at. You're not content with just looking. You must tell me. All right, if you want every dame in the street, go and have her, but I shan't be around."

Benny rubbed his nose. "So that's it, is it?" he said, suddenly very quiet. "You're jealous, that's what you are. Listen, I haven't put my hands on one single dame since I married you. Why shouldn't I look at 'em? What's the harm in it, anyway? I'm not doin' anythin' wrong, just looking, am I?"

"That's the way you look at it. I can't do a thing about it. So I've got to walk along the street with you and watch you gape at every girl for the rest of my life, have I?"

Benny sat in a chair opposite her. With a great effort he tried to control his patience. In a patronizing tone he said: "Now, don't be screwy, honey. This is just crazy talk. You're feeling low. Tomorrow, we'll laugh about this. Get all these ideas out of your head and you'll have everything."

"No, I won't."

"You'll have everything."

"No, I won't."

"Now, don't go on like that. I said you'll have everything, and I mean you'll have everything."

Sadie sat up stiffly. "Shall I tell you what? When I said I won't, I mean I shan't have what I want. I'll have what you give me."

Benny felt the blood mounting to his face. "Okay, if that's the way you feel. You'll have what I give you—so what?"

"Nothing. It's going on the same way as it's been going on for the last six months. Do you know what that is?"

"All right. You tell me."

"I'll be here cooking your food every damn day of the week. I'll be washing out your clothes when they want washing out, which is mighty often. We'll be living in this great apartment, without any servant, so that you can impress your friends. We'll be wondering every day how we are going to meet all the bills. I'll be getting into bed with you and waiting to see if you're too drunk, or if you're too tired. Then I'll be lying awake half the night wondering if anything's gone wrong while you're sleeping. Then I'll be so woke up that I shan't ever get to sleep until it's time to get your food again. That's what."

Benny said between his teeth, "Would you do something for me? Somethin' for me right now?"

Sadie looked at him. "Go on," she said.

"Will you shut up? Will you shut up before you say something that nothin' you'll ever say after can make any difference?"

She shook her head. "No," she said, "I guess not. I guess I'm finished with that stuff. I'm going on talking until I've said my piece. I've waited long enough."

Benny reached for a cigarette. He lit it, noting that his hands shook a little.

Sadie hugged her knees, looking over the top of them at him.

There was a long pause, then she went on: "I've kidded myself until I just can't kid myself any longer. I thought you were a great guy, Benny, honest I did. I thought the world of you. It's not your fault, it's just that I've been kidding myself. You're not a great guy. You'll never be a great guy. You've got something that's stopping you. You want things. You work hard for them, and then you throw them away. You haven't got any feeling for something you've won, only for something you're winning. You got me. I know you didn't have to work hard. I met you halfway. I wanted you too. But I wanted you in a way that you didn't understand. I wanted you to keep. I wanted you in the morning as well as at night. I wanted to go places with you. I wanted you to eat with, to talk with, and to laugh with; but not you, Benny. You didn't want that."

Benny said between his teeth, "I think you'd better stop."

But she went on, as if he hadn't spoken. "Do you think it's fun for me to hear all about the other dames? Don't I keep myself nice? At first, it hurt. Then I got thinking, wondering why I couldn't hold you. I looked at myself. I gave you everything I had. I even did things you wanted me to because I thought you'd be satisfied, but you weren't. When you wanted me, I got to wondering if you were using me and thinking of some other woman you'd seen in the street on the way home. All women are alike in the dark, aren't they, Benny? Well, I'm sick of it. I'm not doing it any more. Go out and have them, Benny, go out and have them."

Benny said, "Have you finished?"

She shrugged. "Don't get mad. It doesn't do any good. Let's face it. One day you'll want to make a move. One day when I'm not nice any more. Then you'll make a move. You won't just look and talk, you'll sneak off and do things. I'm not waiting for that, Benny. I want the break to come now, not when I can't fight it."

Benny got slowly to his feet. "Well, you've had your say, an' I hope you liked it. I'm through. From now on we'll follow our own set of rails. I hope you'll like it. Maybe, after you've done some work, you'll be glad to come back. Anyway, go and try. I'm spending the night somewhere else." He picked up his hat and without looking back, he went out, shutting the door violently behind him.

Sadie sat very still for some time, then she began to cry.

9

June 5th, midnight.
Mendetta nodded to the guard as he passed into the hallway. It gave him a sense of power and security to have guards patrolling the building all night. Not that he took Raven seriously. He didn't. He regarded Raven as a small-town gangster with a trigger itch. The idea that Raven even had the nerve to threaten him made him laugh. All the same, he took precautions, but it was seldom during the day he remembered that Raven had promised to get him.

He took the elevator to the sixth floor and walked heavily to his apartment. He let himself in and was surprised to find the place in darkness. For a moment he hesitated, and his hand groped for a gun he no longer carried. Then he swore softly and turned on the light.

The room was empty.

He walked over to the settee and took off his hat and light dust-coat. He felt annoyed with himself for being momentarily scared. It was a long time ago since he carried a gun. The time when he had been Legs Diamond's bodyguard. A lot of water had gone under the bridge since then. Now he paid other guys to carry guns for him.

He was also irritated that Jean wasn't in. He felt like amusing himself with Jean tonight. He wondered where the hell she had got to. Wandering into each empty room in turn and not finding her, he turned to the living-room, sulkily. He'd got to ring Grantham, anyway. By the time he was through she'd turn up.

He sat down by the telephone and dialled Grantham's number.

Grantham came on the line almost immediately.

"Well, I fixed it," Mendetta told him. "There ain't goin' to be any trouble.”

"No? Well, I'm mighty glad to hear it. Ellinger was in last night, snooping around. I got one of my boys to look after him. He went out with Rogers; then this morning he went round to that screwy little punk Fletcher. Do you remember him?”

Mendetta was faintly bored with all this. "No,” he said, "I don't, but it doesn't matter. I'm telling you—”

"Listen, Tootsie, it does matter,” Grantham broke in. "Fletcher was the guy who caused that spot of trouble at the Club a while back about his sister.”

Mendetta's hard eyes narrowed. "I thought you got rid of that guy,” he said angrily. "You say Ellinger's been to see him?”

"Yes.”

"Well, what about it?”

"Nothing. I thought I'd tell you.”

"You thought you'd tell me!” Mendetta sneered. "Don't you ever use your head? Must I tell you what to do?”

There was a pause, then Grantham said, "Okay, I'll see to it. Poison's fixed, is he?”

"You've got to get rid of Hamsley. Poison didn't know I was interested in the Club. I've got one or two things on Poison.” Mendetta smiled into the black mouthpiece.

"Suppose Fletcher told Ellinger something?”

"What if he did? Ellinger's working for Poison, ain't he? Poison will tell him to lay off. I've fixed that.”

"Are you sure it's all right?” Grantham insisted anxiously.

"Of course I'm sure. Now forget it, but see that Fletcher is looked after. That guy's been around too long now.”

"I'll fix him,” Grantham said viciously, and hung up.

Mendetta glanced over at the clock. It was twelve-fifteen. Where the hell was Jean? He got up and took off his coat, going into the bedroom for his silk dressing-gown. When he had fastened the cord about his thick middle he went back to the living-room and fixed himself a drink. He didn't know why, but he felt uneasy and restless.

Wandering over to the card-table, he picked up the deck of cards and shuffled them slowly. His mind wasn't on patience. He stood there, brooding, letting the cards slide through his fingers. He became aware that he was listening intently for any unusual sound. He could hear the faint whine of the elevator and the click of the grille as it moved between floors. The sharp sound of a car hooter and the steady beat of traffic outside suddenly became real to him instead of a background of unconscious noise.

"What the hell's the matter with me tonight?" he growled irritably, throwing down the pack of cards. He walked over to the window and threw it wide open.

The night was hot and still. The full moon, floating just above the distant roof-tops, flooded the street below with a silvery light. He stood watching the traffic for several minutes, letting the hot air fan his face. Then, just as he was about to return to the room, he paused. He leant far forward, looking into the street. His eyes tried to probe the shadows. Except for an occasional car the street was deserted. The guard, who should have been standing by the entrance, was no longer there. Mendetta couldn't believe his eyes. For three months now the guard had stood there, his hand on his gun, watching those who entered the block of apartments. No one could go in who roused his suspicions. For three months Mendetta could look down on him, and smile to himself, confident in his safety. This came as a great shock to him.

He turned back to the room hurriedly. His first thought was to ring Grantham and tell him to send one of the mob over fast to investigate, then he hesitated. It wouldn't do for Grantham to think that he was getting soft. He tried to remember if he had a gun in the place. It was such a long time since he had had a gun. Maybe Jean had one.

He crushed down the little panic that was beginning to form in his brain. This wouldn't do, he thought angrily; the guy down there maybe was standing inside the hall where he couldn't see him. The best thing would be to ring down to the hall porter and find out.

As he went over to the house phone he heard a key turn in the front-door lock. He stiffened, and stood waiting. He was furious with himself to find that his mouth had gone very dry.

The door opened and Jean came in. She was wearing a smartly cut black two-piece suit. She came in slowly, as if she were tired.

Her presence reassured Mendetta, who said angrily, "Where the devil have you been?"

Jean didn't say anything. She stood looking at him, her eyes very scared, and her face thin and bony.

Mendetta repeated, "Where have you been? Did you know the guard ain't on the door? Was he there when you came up?"

Jean shook her head. "No."

"Well, where is he? What's all this about? You look as if you were expecting someone to die."

She looked at him in horror. "Don't say that," she said fearfully.

He took a quick step towards her, but she got out of his way and half ran round the settee. He stood very still, staring at her. "Well, tell me," he said between his teeth, "where have you been?"

She said, "I—ran into an old pal of yours. He insisted on—seeing you." She waved her hand towards the door.

Mendetta turned his head slowly. A cold chill ran down his back. Raven stood in the doorway, his cold face expressionless. A limp cigarette dangled from the side of his mouth, and in his right hand he held a long-barrelled gun.

Mendetta shivered with the shock. His big white hands fluttered, imploring Raven to go away. "What do you want?" he whispered.

Raven jerked the gun. "Sit down, Tootsie," he said, "we got things to talk about."

Mendetta sat by the card-table. He folded his twitching hands on the green cloth. From where he sat he could see Jean, kneeling on the floor. She had covered her head with her arms. Her attitude reminded Mendetta of a woman who is witnessing an unavoidable head-on collision, and turns away in horror before the crash. He suddenly felt very sick.

Raven continued to lean against the doorway. "It's taken time to get around to you, Tootsie," he said, "but I've done it. I said I'd do it, didn't I?" He jerked his head to Jean. "She ratted on you, Tootsie. Don't trust women, they always let you down. She got the guard to go away. She let me up here, just because she was tired of sleeping with you."

Mendetta's face twitched, but he didn't say anything. Jean got suddenly to her feet and ran into the bedroom, shutting the door violently behind her.

Raven shrugged. "She thinks I'm goin' to look after her. You don't have to worry about that. I don't trust her, an' I wouldn't want anythin' you've had your hands on. No, I guess she'll be sorry for what she's done."

Mendetta said in a whisper, "You want this territory, don't you, Raven? Well, you can have it; I'm through."

Raven nodded. "Yeah, you're through all right."

"Listen, let me get out of town. I'll sign it all over to you. You wouldn't want to kill me if I gave it all over to you?"

Raven shook his head. "I don't want to kill anyone. Why should I?"

Mendetta searched the cold face to try to find some comfort for himself there. He could read nothing in the cold, blank eyes. "I'll sign anythin'," he said eagerly. "What do you want?"

Raven pointed to a pad of paper on the table. "Just write saying that you're giving me your share of the Club. That's all I'll need. Grantham won't make any trouble."

Mendetta hesitated. "I can go if I do that?" he said. "You'll let me leave the town?"

Raven looked at him. "Why should I want to stop you?" he asked.

The two men looked at each other. Mendetta, fat, well dressed, but terrified; and Raven, cold, thin and shabby.

Raven said, "I can't stay here all night."

Already Mendetta's brain was formulating a scheme. His signature on a bit of paper would mean nothing. He would give the signal as soon as Raven had left to have him killed. My God! He'd been a fool not to have got rid of him before. He reached out and pulled the pad towards him. With a hand that no longer trembled he wrote, handing his share of the 22nd Club over to Raven. He signed it with a flourish.

"Give me until tomorrow," he said, throwing the pad across the table. "I'll get out by tomorrow."

Raven stretched out his hand and took the pad; he glanced at the writing and then put the pad in his pocket.

"You don't have to go, Tootsie," he said quietly. "You'll be better off here."

Mendetta suddenly went cold. He got slowly to his feet. "Listen, Raven," he said feverishly, "this is on the level. I've done what you wanted—" He broke off as he saw the vicious gleam in Raven's eye. With a whimper of terror, Mendetta turned and ran blindly across the room and began to pound on Jean's door. "Don't let him kill me... Jean! Stop him! Stop him! Jean, you wouldn t let him kill—"

Moving softly, Raven stepped behind him and shot him through the head. The gun only made a little hissing sound.

Mendetta was opening the door as he fell. The door swung open violently and he sprawled into the room. Jean crouched against the wall and screamed.

Raven looked at her and raised his gun. She saw the little black hole of the barrel pointing at her, and she hid her face in her hands. The heavy .45 bullet smashed two of her fingers before it blew the top of her head off. She fell first on her knees with a thud that shook the room, and then straightened out, her head hitting the carpet with another muffled thud.

Across the passage, Sadie sat up in bed. She thought she had heard a scream in her sleep, but she knew that she had heard the sound of someone falling.

She listened intently, suddenly wishing Benny was by her side. She could hear nothing, but the scream was so real that she got out of bed and hurriedly put on a wrap. She went out of the bedroom into the little hallway. It was all very dark and silent. Putting on the hall light, she went to the front door and raised the letter-box flap. She could see Mendetta's front door, and the gleam of light coming from under it. Seeing the light warned her that she too was showing light, and she turned off the switch, then she resumed her watch on the opposite door.

She was conscious of her heart beating rapidly, and she felt frightened and alone. A presentiment told her that something was going on in Mendetta's apartment, and she stayed there watching for some time. Then, just when she had decided that she had made a mistake, she saw the door opposite opening silently.

Raven stepped out, a bundle of papers under his arm, and his long-barrelled gun in his hand. He looked up and down the passage and then, shutting the apartment door softly, walked swiftly away.

His ruthless look and his gun scared Sadie badly. She lowered the flap softly and ran into her bedroom. She dived into bed and hurriedly pulled up the sheet. She lay shivering, seeing Raven's cold, wolfish face, and wishing that Benny would come back to her.

10

June 5th, midnight.

Jay pushed open Henry's door and strode in. Henry was just going home. He was putting on his hat and admiring himself in the mirror. He looked over his shoulder and scowled at Jay.

"No more tonight," he said firmly. "Look at the time. I ought to have been home hours ago."

Jay sat down in the arm-chair and lit a cigarette. "I got something to tell you," he said; "you'll be interested."

"Yeah? Well, I've got something to tell you. You can forget about the 22nd Club. Poison's just been through."

Jay shook his head. "Oh no," he said. "I've got somethin' on that Club that's goin' to make headlines."

Henry looked at him keenly. "What is it?" he said.

"Grantham's mixed up in a Slave Ring. He uses the Club for immoral purposes."

"You're crazy. Where did you get that stuff?"

Jay grinned. "That's what I thought," he said. "But I've got a guy who's seen and heard things. I'm inclined to believe him. The place wants watching, and maybe we'll find somethin' out."

Henry sat down. "Poison told me to lay off the Club. He's seen Mendetta and they've had a little talk. Mendetta's got an interest in the

Club, so Poison doesn't want to do or say anything to upset him."

Jay sneered. "Maybe Poison doesn't know about this Slave angle. It'll make a grand story."

Henry hesitated and then he reached out for the phone. "Shall I see what he says?"

Jay hesitated, then he shook his head. "Will you come with me and meet this guy first? Once you've had a talk with him you'll understand why I'm interested."

"What, now?" Henry demanded. "I can't come now."

Jay got to his feet. "What's the matter with you, Chief? This is goin' to be a big story. We're right in it on the ground floor. I've been waiting a chance to pin somethin' on Mendetta for the last two years. Slavin' is a fine club to beat that heel with. Come on, let's go."

Henry followed him into the elevator. "You're goin' to get somewhere one of these days, Ellinger," he said. "I don't know where, but you'll get there all right."

Jay grinned. "I ain't sentimental, but that guy certainly made me think when he talked about his sister. You gotta daughter, ain't you? I've seen her; she's cute."

Henry looked at him from under the brim of his hat. "What's my daughter got to do with it?"

They walked out of the elevator and crossed the big lobby.

"That's just it, Chief. You guys with daughters don't think about the girls who disappear every year. Let me tell you, if I had a daughter I'd never take my eyes off her. I hope I don't have one."

They got in a taxi and Ellinger gave Fletcher's address.

"What are you talking about?" Henry demanded. "What girls disappearing?"

Jay looked at him. "You know as well as I do. We can't do anythin' about it so we just say they've gone off to get married, or gone to Hollywood or some other excuse. This guy Fletcher is pretty sure that his sister's been slaved. He thinks Grantham, and that means Mendetta too, is trading women. We know there's no proof of it, but, by heavens, think what a stink we could make if we got the proof."

Henry lit a cigar. "All right," he said, "let's see how this guy strikes me. If I think there's anything to it you can go ahead, but Poison will have to give his okay first."

"Poison will okay it if we can convince him. That's why I've got you to come down now. If you think it's all right we'll both go an' see Poison and give it to him with both barrels."

The taxi drove up outside the tenement block. There was a large crowd standing around the front door. An ambulance and two police cars were parked on the opposite side of the street.

Jay bundled out of the car. He looked quickly at Henry, and together they ran up the steps. A big cop stepped in their way. "Take it easy," he said, "you can't come in here."

Jay said, "We're goin' in, buddy. Meet the Editor-in-Chief of the *St. Louis Banner.* Big stuff, boy. Where's your red carpet?"

The cop didn't move. "Yeah?" he said. "If that old guy's the Chief of anythin', then I'm the mother of kittens."

Jay looked at Henry. "He's got you there, Chief," he said with a grin.

Henry said with cold dignity, "What's going on in here?"

Two plain-clothes men from the Homicide Bureau came down the stairs and made to pass them. Henry knew one of them. "Hey, Bradley, tell this flat-foot who I am. I want to go up!"

Bradley looked at him keenly. "For Pete's sake, it's Henry! What are you doin' here?"

Henry smiled easily. "I was passin', saw the ambulance, and thought I'd see my man work first hand."

Bradley shook his head. "It ain't much," he said regretfully; "just another shootin'. Still, you can go on up."

Jay said, "Who is it?"

"Guy named Fletcher. I guess someone owed him a grudge."

Jay shook his head. "I guess we won't bother," he said grimly. "Come on, Chief, that's small-town stuff."

They returned to the taxi, and Jay told the driver to go back to the *Banner* office.

"Does that interest you?" he said quietly. "Grantham must have found out he'd talked to me, so he shut his mouth. This looks like the real thing."

Henry said doubtfully, "Maybe it was a coincidence."

"Maybe it was nothing of the sort. It sticks out a mile. Who'd want to shoot a guy like Fletcher? Ask yourself. He was just an out-of-work clerk. No, guys don't risk killing a poor punk like that unless it's very important. I'd like you to speak to Poison."

Henry said, "What are you thinking of doing?"

"I'd like to take this up on the quiet. Keep an eye on the Club, find out what I can, and if I get anything worth while, go for it with two hands."

Henry relaxed. "Yeah," he said, "I'll speak to Poison."

"Let's go an' see him now," Jay said. "The old buzzard won't be in bed yet."

Henry groaned. "All right," he said. "It looks as if I'm not going to get any sleep tonight."

"You'll get all the sleep you want after you've seen Poison," Jay said, giving the new address to the taxi-driver.

They had to wait nearly half an hour before Poison would see them. Then he walked into the small reception-room, a heavy scowl on his face and his hands thrust deeply in his trouser pockets.

Poison looked what he was: a millionaire newspaper owner. Hard as nails, a terrific worker, and greedy for dollars. He stared at Henry as if he couldn't believe his eyes. "What do you want?" he snapped. "What is this?"

Henry said respectfully, "This is Ellinger, who's responsible for crime news. He's got a little story that I thought would interest you."

Poison didn't even bother to look at Jay. He tapped Henry on his chest with a long bony forefinger. "Listen, I pay you to listen to interesting stories, and to print them. I'm far too busy to bother with things like that. Go back to the office, hear his story; if it's any good, print it, if it isn't, tell him to go to hell."

"This story's about Mendetta and the 22nd Club," Henry said patiently. "In view of what you said to me this morning, I thought I'd ask you first."

Poison's eyes snapped. "I said leave the 22nd Club alone. Leave Mendetta alone. When I say a thing I mean what I say."

Henry stepped back. "Very well, Mr. Poison," he said.

Jay said, "Mendetta's running a vice ring. He's trading in women. Decent girls are being kidnapped from their homes. I've got proof that he is using the Club for this purpose. I want your permission to make an investigation."

Poison stiffened. His thin hatchet face went white with anger. Without looking at Ellinger, he said to Henry: "I will not discuss this further. I've told you our policy. Leave Mendetta alone, and leave the Club alone. If any of your staff disobey our policy, get rid of them. Good night." He turned on his heel and walked stiffly out of the room.

Henry looked at Jay. "You heard him," he said.

"I wonder how much Mendetta gave him, the dirty rat-faced heel," Jay said, picking up his hat. "If he thinks he can stop me he's made a big mistake."

Henry looked worried. "You've got to leave it alone, Jay," he said. "Poison's the big shot."

"Yeah? Well, I don't spell it that way," and Jay slammed out of the house.

I I

June 6th, 12:30 a.m.

Grantham sat behind his neat desk, writing. A cigarette burnt lazily in an ash-tray at his elbow, and the room was silent but for the faint scratch of his pen.

He heard his door open, and he glanced up irritably. Raven stood looking at him. Behind Raven, Grantham could see Lu Eller, white-faced and uncertain.

Grantham laid down his pen very slowly. The colour went out of his face and a muscle in his jaw began to jump.

Raven said, "Tell this monkey to go away."

Grantham knew that Mendetta was dead. Raven would never have come if Mendetta wasn't dead. He told Eller with his eyes to go away. He didn't trust his voice.

Lu Eller lifted his shoulders. He seemed relieved that Grantham didn't want him. Raven came in and shut the door. He put a slip of paper on Grantham's desk silently.

Without touching it, Grantham read it. It was in Mendetta's handwriting.

"Is he dead?" Grantham said. His voice was very low.

Raven sat down and looked round the office. "He had a little accident," he said. "Things'll be very different now."

"What are you going to do?" Grantham studied the shabby figure sitting before him.

Raven settled back in his chair. "Plenty," he said. "This town was too small for Mendetta and me. One of us had to go. Now I'm takin' it over."

Grantham licked his dry lips. "Mendetta had plenty of protection," he said. "You won't get far without that."

Raven inclined his head. "I've thought of that," he said softly. "That's where you come in. You're going to be my front, Grantham. I've got it all worked out. I'll tell you what to do an' you'll do it. You've done the same thing for Mendetta, so you can do it for me. The difference is that I'm goin' to make more money than Mendetta ever did, an' you're goin' to do a lot more work."

Grantham didn't say anything.

"Don't think you can get out of it. I haven't the time to play around with guys. If you don't like it you'll run into an accident too. Get it?"

"I'll do it," Grantham said quickly. "I've been waiting for you to take over. I knew Mendetta wouldn't last."

Raven inclined his head. "Yeah? You're a smart boy. Okay, tomorrow you an' me'll have a little talk. I want all the dope. I want the names of all the girls who worked for Mendetta. Listen, that guy didn't know how to organize vice. Well, I do. Ever been to Reno, Grantham? No? Well, I have. They make a lot of dough in that town. They understand vice. Well, I've got some ideas. We'll get together." He stood up. "Just so that you don't feel worried about all this, there's a ten per cent cut coming to you on everything if you play ball. If you don't, you'll get a bullet. Think about it."

He wandered to the door.

"I'll be down tomorrow at ten. Get all the stuff together," and he went out, shutting the door softly.

Grantham sat back, feeling slightly sick. So it had happened. Where was Jean? He picked up the phone and hastily dialled Mendetta's number. The operator told him after a short delay that no one was answering. He hung up.

Lu Eller came in. Ever since Mendetta could afford gunmen, Eller had been looking after them. He was a tall, powerfully built man, with a heavy jaw and ingrowing eyebrows.

"What's he want?" he said, standing just inside the doorway.

Grantham lit another cigarette. "That's your new boss," he said bitterly. "Mendetta's met with an accident."

Lu raised his eyebrows. "That's too bad. You standin' for Raven?"

Grantham put his elbows on the table. "Let's face it, Lu," he said. "Since Raven moved in, what's happened? Mendetta lost his grip. We know that. They both came from Chi. Mendetta used to carry a gun for Diamond. He thought he was too big for that, so he moved over here. Well, he got on. What Raven did in Chi, I don't know, but when he came here he certainly scared Mendetta. He offered to come in as a partner, but Mendetta turned him down. You've seen him, haven't you? Looks like he's down to rock bottom, till you look at his face. That guy's going to be big, and Mendetta knew it. When he turned Raven down he signed his death warrant. Raven promised him he'd fix him, and he has. I think Raven can make me more money than any guy in this town. I ain't interested in anything else but making a lot of dough. Raven's good enough for me."

Lu looked at him admiringly. "That's the swellest bit of lyin' I've ever heard. It nearly convinces me, but not quite. Shall I tell you why you're saying welcome to Raven? Because you're yellow. Because Raven's a killer, and you know it. Because Raven's got a little mob that is as tough as hell and could smash us up in half an hour. Yeah, that's why."

Grantham got to his feet. "What about you?" he said. "You goin' to tell Raven where he gets off?"

Lu shook his head. "Sure I'm not," he said, shrugging his shoulders. "What's good enough for you suits me. I'm yellow too."

"Instead of yapping like this, suppose you go over to Mendetta's apartment and find out what's happened. I'm worried about Jean."

Lu shook his head. "Be your age. Suppose the cops walk in when I'm there? Where should I be? You'll have to wait. The papers'll have it fast enough."

Grantham said uneasily, "Do you think he's killed her too?"

"Why should you worry? She ain't anybody. If you want to know so badly, go an' see for yourself."

Grantham paced up and down the room. "We've got to find out, Lu. This is serious. Suppose Jean talked?"

"She won't talk."

"She might about Raven. If Raven gets pinched, where should we be?"

Lu considered this. "Maybe you're right. Say, isn't O'Hara on that beat?"

"I don't know. Is he?"

Lu turned to the door. "I'll go down there and see. If he is I'll tip him to go up and investigate. What the hell are we payin' that guy two hundred bucks a month for if he can't do a little thing like that?"

Grantham looked relieved. "That's an idea. Get after him right away." Lu left the room at a run.

12

June 6th, 1:10 a.m.

Sadie had just fallen into a light doze when a sound outside her apartment made her sit up, wide awake again.

She listened, her heart beating wildly, the memory of Raven horribly clear-cut in her mind. She wondered if he had returned. For several minutes she lay listening, then, cautiously, she pulled back the bed-clothes and reached for her wrap.

Silently she went to the front door and looked once through the letter-box. The burly figure of a police officer relieved her of all her fears. He was just going into Mendetta's apartment. She opened the door and stood waiting.

The police officer came out of the apartment in a few minutes. His start of surprise when he saw Sadie puzzled her.

"Is—is anythin' wrong in there?" she asked.

He looked at her suspiciously. "Who are you?" he snapped.

"I'm Mrs. Perminger, I thought I heard someone cry out a little while back and I thought I heard someone fall." Sadie looked at him with big eyes.

O'Hara could have killed her. He'd gone up on Lu's instructions just to look around. He had no intention of reporting Mendetta's death. He had no reasonable excuse for being up there, and now this dame must come and put her oar in.

He said, "I'll come in your place for a moment, Miss. Don't want to be seen in the passage; might scare the folks."

Sadie coloured. "I don't think you'd better come in. I'm—I'm all alone."

O'Hara nodded. "That's all right," he said; "if you'll just let me stand in the hall." He was most anxious that nobody else should see him.

Reluctantly Sadie stepped back and let him in.

"Now then, Miss," he said, taking out his note-book. "You say you heard someone cry out?"

Sadie nodded. There was something about this cop that she didn't like. She wished he'd go away.

"What time was that?"

"It was just after twelve."

"Did you see anythin'?" O'Hara looked at her closely.

Sadie hesitated, then she said, "Yes, there was a man who came out of the apartment. He had some papers and a gun in his hand."

O'Hara felt the sweat break out under his arms. "Yeah?" he said. "You're sure of that?"

"Of course I'm sure."

"Would you know him again?"

"I'd know him anywhere," Sadie said firmly. "He was middle height, dark, dressed in a shabby black suit. His face was very thin, with thin lips and horrible cold eyes. I don't think I'll ever forget him."

O'Hara hadn't much time. He knew that Lu must hear about this. Grantham hadn't picked him for nothing. He had his head screwed on all right.

"Well, lady," he said, "there's been a little accident over there. I guess we'll be looking for that guy. Now will you get dressed? I'd like to take you down to the station house."

"What, now?" Sadie's eyes opened.

O'Hara nodded. "Sure," he said. "We'll get you to look through some of the photos we got down there. You might spot the guy right away."

Sadie wished Benny was there. She felt suddenly extremely helpless and alone. She didn't want to go, but she supposed she had to. "Will you wait here? I'll go and dress."

O'Hara touched his cap. "I'll meet you downstairs, lady," he said. "I don't want you bothered with newshawks. If they saw me leave with you we'd never shake them."

He went away, walking very rapidly.

Sadie dressed. She felt vaguely uneasy and wished now that she hadn't told O'Hara anything. Well, they couldn't do anything to her at the station house. She'd just tell them the truth and then they'd let her go. As she was about to leave the apartment she suddenly thought of something. She ran back to the sitting-room and scribbled a note to Benny. She put it on his pillow, hoping that if he came in he'd find it at once. Then she picked up her bag and went down to the hall.

In the meantime O'Hara met Lu, who was waiting in the street. "Listen, boss," the cop said quickly, "we're in a jam. Both Mendetta and the jane are dead, but there's a little dame up there who saw Raven leave. She can identify him. I thought you wouldn't like that. She's on her way down now. I told her I was taking her to the station."

Lu cursed under his breath. He stood thinking for a moment, then nodded. "Listen, tell her I'm a cop when she comes down. I'll take her to Grantham's apartment and he must decide what to do with her. When I've got her out of the way, continue your beat. You don't know anythin' about the killing, get it? The longer it remains under cover the better. It'll give Raven a chance to get set."

O'Hara nodded. "This'll cost me my job if it comes out," he said with a sly look.

"Don't worry your head about that," Lu said impatiently. "We'll look after you. I'll see you get somethin' extra for this."

"See that it's worth havin'," O'Hara said, and went back into the hall.

Sadie came down as he entered. He touched his cap respectfully. "An officer of the Homicide Squad is outside with a car, lady," he said. "You go with him. I gotta do some phoning."

He led her out to Lu, who was standing by his car. Lu raised his hat.

"This is Mrs. Perminger," O'Hara said with a broad grin. "She's the little lady who saw the guy I told you about."

Lu opened the car door. "I'm sorry to get you up at such an hour, Mrs. Perminger," he said, "but you're goin' to be a big help to us."

Sadie thought he wasn't at all her idea of a plain-clothes cop, but she got in the car, because she was scared that they'd think she had something to hide. Lu got in beside her.

O'Hara stood watching the car drive away. He spat into the street. "I wonder what they'll do with her?" he thought. "Nice little dame," and he turned and resumed his patrol with measured steps.

13

June 6th, 2:30 a.m.
Carrie O'Shea ran the only high-class brothel in East St. Louis. There were plenty of other such joints in the town, but none of them came anywhere near Carrie's for class.

For one thing, it stood opposite the District Attorney's office. That alone gave it class. Then Carrie, who ran the house, saw to it that she got a fresh batch of girls each month. That wanted some doing, but Carrie knew variety is the spice of life and her clients never knew from one visit to the next who they were going to find there.

She organized the change by shuffling the girls round from the various other houses, ruthlessly selecting only the young fresh ones and refusing anything that the bookers thought they could hoist on to her.

It was only when Mendetta began his Slaving racket that Carrie really ceased to worry. Now, through a careful system, she was getting new girls pretty steadily. Of course, a lot of them made trouble, but that didn't worry Carrie a great deal. She knew how to handle girls who refused to fall in line.

The system worked this way. Trained thugs carefully combed the town for suitable girls. The qualifications that they considered suitable chiefly consisted of having no relations, being down on their luck, or to have committed some petty crime that the bookers could use as a form of blackmail.

There wasn't a great deal of material to fit these qualifications, and after a while the supply dried up. The bookers got a little more daring. They'd go after girls who wanted jobs as models. They persuaded them to pose in the nude, take photos secretly, and then threaten to show the photos, which had mysteriously become exceedingly obscene by clever faking, to narrow-minded parents. This succeeded for a time.

Although Carrie had ceased to worry about the supply of girls, the bookers were continually having headaches. They got well paid for new material, but they were constantly having to think up new ideas to ensnare unsuspecting girls into the racket.

Finally they got so bold that they'd kidnap girls and hand them over to Carrie to break in. This meant a lot more work for Carrie to do, but she realized their difficulties and she entered into her new task with philosophical fortitude.

Some of the girls were so popular that she kept them in the house as permanent workers. They had been well broken in, they got good money, and they showed no inclination to leave. Such were Andree, Lulu, Julie and Fan.

They were sitting in the big reception-room waiting patiently for Carrie to tell them to go to bed. The last client had gone over half an hour ago. Carrie made a habit of having a word with her girls before turning in for the night: to hear any complaints and to hand out punishment to any of them who hadn't given satisfaction.

The girls were all dressed in flimsy knickers, black silk stockings and high-heel shoes, with big showy garters to keep their stockings in place. They had all thrown wraps round their bare shoulders as soon as the front door closed behind the last client. Carrie thought it was all very well to sit around half naked when the guys were in the house, but when they had gone she liked to see her girls look decent.

Lulu reached for a cigarette, yawning. "Gee!" she said. "Am I tired? I've gotta get my hair fixed tomorrow morning and I don't know how I'll make it."

Fan, a red-headed girl with a superb figure, but a hard, almost brutish face, gave a short metallic laugh. "You don't want to bother about that," she said. "Get a guy to fix it for you. Do it on the exchange system."

Lulu frowned at her. "You've got a dirty mind," she said. "If I had a mind like yours I know what I'd do with it."

Julie, a little silver blonde, broke in: "Save it, you two. Let's have a little peace once in a while."

Lulu shrugged. "I'm not startin' anythin'," she said. "I'm just tellin' her she's got a dirty mind—so she has."

Julie went on, "I had the nicest and queerest guy tonight. Gee! The dough he had! When he got upstairs he was terribly shy—"

Fan groaned, "We'll now listen to a leaf out of Julie's life story."

Lulu said, "Go on, Ju, don't mind about her. Maybe she's got the crabs."

Julie pouted. "Well, I guess I won't tell you if you don't want to hear," she said. "Only he was such a nice guy—"

Fan sneered. "I know those nice guys," she said. "I've had one or two. What did he tell you? The one about his wife being an invalid?"

"Can't you leave her alone?" Lulu demanded fiercely. "What's the matter with you tonight?"

Andree, a tall brunette with long tapering limbs, gave a little giggle. "My Gawd! I saw that guy Julie's talkin' about. He looked as if his Ma was waitin' outside for him."

Julie nodded. "That's the one. He gave me ten bucks as soon as he got in the room"—she put her hand over her mouth and spluttered with laughter—"in an envelope. Can you tie that? He was so genteel he gave it to me in an envelope."

Even Fan smiled.

"Well, go on," Lulu said. "What was he like?"

Julie shook her head. "He didn't do anythin'. When I started to undress he nearly had a fit. What he thought he'd come up there for I can't guess. He said, all embarrassed, that he just wanted to talk to me. And would I put on a wrap as he thought it was tough for a girl like me to sit around as I was. Believe me, you could have knocked me over with a mangle."

"Yeah?" Fan said bitterly. "I guess I'd sooner sleep with a guy than listen to him talk. A guy who likes talkin' about it can go on for ever."

"Oh, he talked about all kinds of things. He was ever so interestin'," Julie said stoutly. "I liked the guy. He didn't once ask me why I lived here, or if I liked it, or any of the other crap guys always ask."

Fan got bored. "Gee! I thought you were goin' to tell us somethin' worth listenin' to," she said.

"Didn't I tell you she'd got a dirty mind?" Lulu chimed in triumphantly.

Just then the door opened and Carrie came in. Carrie was a tall, thin, muscular mulatto. Her face was cut in hard, etched lines. Glittering black eyes, like glass beads, gave her a look of cold, calculated suspicion and cruelty. Her broad flat nose disfigured what would have been an otherwise strikingly handsome face.

"Time you girls were in bed," she said sharply. "Break it up. Go on, get off to bed."

Obediently, all of them except Fan got up and murmured respectful good nights and went out of the door. Fan continued to sprawl in the chair.

Carrie eyed her with reluctant admiration. She had never been able to tame Fan entirely. She was wise enough to realize that Fan with a broken spirit would be a poor proposition, and she took more from her than any of the other girls put together.

She knew that Fan liked the racket. She knew also that Fan would never have admitted it, but Carrie had long ago come to realize that Fan was physically built for the game.

Carrie said, "You smoke too much. It ain't going to help you when you get older."

Fan looked at her. "Listen, nigger, I like smokin'. To hell with that stuff about getting old."

"You'll see. I'm tellin' you when you start slippin' I'll turn you out. Make no mistake, sister, I've got no time for worn-outs."

Fan got up and gathered her wrap around her. "I'll be gone long before that time," she said. "One of these days I'm goin' to start out on my own."

Carrie had heard all this before. She knew Fan was too lazy to hunt up her own clients. "Sure," she said—"one of these days."

Fan stubbed her cigarette out and then crossed to the big mirror on the wall. She stood looking at herself carefully.

Carrie grinned. She knew that Fan was secretly worried about getting old and useless. She didn't want her to be discouraged. "You're all right," she said; "one of my best girls."

Fan looked at her and sneered. "You bet, nigger," she said; "you an' I ain't the only two who know it."

She went out of the room, leaving the door wide open.

Carrie went into the little office that led from the reception-room and sat down behind a small desk. With a neat hand she entered some figures in a ledger, and then locked the ledger in a wall safe. She was quite contented the way the business was paying. Tonight had been a good one.

She looked disapprovingly at the clock on the wall. Time was always her enemy. She was a tireless worker and begrudged herself the hours wasted in sleep. But she looked after herself very carefully. She wasn't taking any chances of falling ill. Mendetta was the kind of guy who liked you a lot when you were bringing in the dough, but cast you off once you lost ground. She always gave herself six hours' sleep.

As she was getting up from behind the desk the telephone rang shrilly. She picked up the receiver. "Who is it?"

Grantham's voice floated over the line. "Carrie? Listen, I've got a girl I want you to look after."

Carrie's mouth twisted. "That's fine," she said. "Must you ring up at an hour like this to tell me a little thing like findin' me a girl? I've got plenty."

"Lu's bringing her round right away," Grantham went on. "This is important. She's not to talk to anyone. Do you understand? Hell's been poppin' tonight and she knows all about it."

"What's happened?"

"Tootsie's been bumped. Raven's taken over. And this dame knows a hell of a lot more than she should do."

"Mendetta's dead?" Carrie repeated.

"Yeah. About a couple of hours ago. They haven't found his body yet. You're not to know anythin' about it. The news mightn't break for a couple of days."

"What's this about Raven?"

"He's moved in. You've got a new boss now, Carrie."

Carrie's fist tightened on the phone. "Why the hell did you let him move in? I tell you, Grantham, that guy's goin' to cause a lot of trouble."

"Never mind about him. You look after the girl."

Grantham hung up before she could reply.

Carrie put the phone down slowly. She stood looking at the opposite wall with blank eyes. So Raven had got there at last. She had watched him closely ever since Mendetta had turned him down. She knew that Raven would be a very different boss from Mendetta. Maybe he wouldn't be so mean, but he was going to be a lot more ruthless. Carrie suddenly found herself anxious for her girls. She didn't mind how she treated them herself, but it made her feel dismayed to think that Raven was going to control them all in the future.

She went back into the reception-room and sat down to wait for Lu.

14

June 6th, 9:30 a.m.

Jack Caston, under-manager for the local branch office of Preston Motors, walked into the Preston building with a light springy step.

The commissionaire saluted smartly and escorted him to the elevator.

Caston was the kind of guy who got up early in the morning and did breathing exercises in front of an open window. He was bouncing with good health and his big pink face was torture to anyone with a morning hang-over.

He walked into his office, rang the buzzer on his desk, and then hung up his hat. He walked over to the mirror and adjusted his tie and smoothed down his hair. He was very satisfied with what he saw in the mirror.

The door opened and his secretary walked in. She was a ritzy-looking dame, with corn-coloured hair, blue eyes, and a neat little figure.

Caston smiled at her and sat down at his desk. She thought he looked like a very nice good-humoured pig.

"Well, well," he said, stretching out his hand, "and very nice too!"

She kept her distance and inclined her head. She knew Caston.

"Now, Marie, don't be high hat. Come over here and let me look at you," he said, still keeping his hand out.

"You can see me just as well here, Mr. Caston," she said. "Did you want anything?"

Caston withdrew his hand and fiddled with a pencil. His pink face lost a little of its brightness. "Sit down," he said, "I want to talk to you."

Marie sat down, carefully adjusting her skirt as she did so. Caston leant a little forward and watched the operation with considerable interest. He considered any girl with a nice pair of legs should show them at every possible occasion.

"That's the beginning of a ladder you're getting there," he said. He leant forward, staring at her leg with fixed concentration.

Marie bent forward to investigate. She could see nothing wrong with the faultless silken hose.

"Look, just there, a little higher up. Too bad with socks as expensive as those."

Marie lifted her skirt a trifle and couldn't find anything. Caston got out of his chair and came round. "You're not lookin'," he said severely. "Look, here." He pulled her skirt well above her knees, and she promptly smacked his hand and hastily pulled it down.

"I might have known it," she said bitterly. "Just another of your tricks."

Caston beamed at her. "Well, maybe I was mistaken," he said, sitting on the edge of the desk and reaching for her hand. "But I might not have been, you know."

She allowed her hand to remain in his big pink fingers, and she waited, her neat shoe tapping impatiently on the polished boards. "When you're through with all this," she said, "suppose we get to work?"

Caston shook his head. "I'll never train you," he said sadly. "You know, baby, you and me might get somewhere if only you'd co-operate."

Marie sniffed. "The one place I'd get to if I did would be a maternity hospital," she said acidly, snatching her hand away. "Shall we get to work?"

Caston sighed. You never knew with women. Some mornings Marie was quite willing for a little fun and games. He got off the desk and sat down in his chair. He looked at her closely. She certainly looked tired and irritable. Being a man of the world, he didn't pursue the matter, and began to dictate the few letters that required his attention.

It was ten o'clock by the time he was through, and he dismissed her with a kind smile. "Listen, baby, if you don't feel well take the rest of the day off. I've got to go out in a while and I don't think I'll be back. Just please yourself, will you?"

She looked at him suspiciously and then went out. Caston sat back in his chair and frowned. This was not starting the day well. Why the hell couldn't people be a bit more lively?

The door opened and Benny Perminger wandered in. Caston gave him a quick look and groaned. This was certainly not going to be his day. Benny was looking like something the cat had dug up.

"And what's your trouble?" he asked shortly.

Benny sank into the arm-chair and sighed. "Nice bit that, ain't she?" he said, pursing up his mouth.

Caston frowned. "Who's a nice bit?" he demanded.

"Miss Mackelsfield," Benny explained. "Lucky guy havin' a secretary like that."

"Well, I don't know," Caston said. "What of it?"

Benny closed one eye and leered. "You bachelors," he said; "I bet you an' she have a grand time."

Caston sat up stiffly. "Now see here, Perminger, I don't like that kind of talk. This is a business place, and business only is conducted here."

"Nuts! What kind of business? All you guys do in these offices is to horse around with your secretaries. I know. It's guys like me out in the general office that don't get the chances."

Caston thought it wise to shift the ground. "Well, you didn't come in here to tell me that, did you?"

Benny's face fell, and he became depressed again. "No," he admitted, "I didn't. As a matter of fact, Caston, old boy, I came for a little advice."

Caston smiled. Things were looking up. He liked giving advice. He settled back in his chair and lit a cigarette. "Sure," he said. "What's the trouble?" For a moment he had a sudden qualm that Benny was going to touch him for some dough, but on second thoughts he knew that wasn't Benny's usual opening when he made a touch.

Benny hung his feet over the side of the chair. "Well, Sadie and I have had a quarrel," he said bitterly. "She properly shot her mouth off last night."

Caston made sympathetic noises. "Nice girl, Sadie," he said. He often wondered why a swell looker like Sadie had fallen for Perminger. He could have gone a long way to have made her himself.

"Sure, she's a nice girl, but she's got a damn odd way of looking at things. Would you believe it, she's accusing me of always lookin' at girls? She even had the neck to say that I'd be makin' a pass at one of them one day."

Caston shrugged. "Well, won't you?"

Benny looked vacant. "Well, yes, I suppose I will," he admitted. "But she won't know about it."

"Listen, Perminger, wasn't that a dame I saw you out with the other night?"

Benny scowled at him. "What else do you think it was?" he snapped. "A horse?"

"Steady, buddy," Caston said. "No need to go off the deep end. What I meant was, she wasn't Sadie?"

Benny shook his head. "No, she was a business client. She wanted to buy one of our models."

Caston blew his nose. "I suppose you were taking a fly out of her eye?" he said sarcastically.

"Will you leave it? I want your advice, not a goddamn sermon," Benny returned. "I've walked out and left Sadie high and dry. What the hell am I going to do?"

"You've left her?" Caston asked, his eyebrows raising. "You crazy or something?"

"I tell you we had a stand-up fight. I couldn't just go to bed after it."

"You left her all night?" Caston wished he'd known that. He might have called and done himself some good.

"What I want you to bend your brains on is how am I going back?"

Caston shrugged. "Easiest thing in the world. All you do is to walk in, kiss her, tell her you were tight and all will be well."

Benny stared at him. "Do you really think so?" he asked. "Gee! I wish it would work like that."

Caston was getting a little bored, anyway. "Sure," he said, getting up, "you try it. Don't forget, she might be pretty sick about it herself today. You go down there right away. You might find her in."

Benny got to his feet. "I'll do it. That's mighty white of you, Jack. If there's any little thing—"

Caston led him to the door. "On your way, pal," he said, "and if it works, give her one for me."

He watched Benny hurry down the corridor before turning back to his office.

I 5

June 6th, 9:45 a.m.
Raven sat on the edge of his bed and looked round at the three men who stood or leant against the wall opposite him.

There was Lefty, Little Joe and Maltz. For eighteen months these three men had elected to follow Raven, and they had for this period experienced a very thin time. Raven didn't excuse himself. He had just told them to be patient and they had believed him. He had never let them go hungry. Somehow, by dangerous raids, hold-ups and the like, they had managed to make a little money, but all the same they had all had a bad time. Such was their faith in Raven, however, that they had not grumbled. It was now that he could tell them that their faith in him was justified.

He knew these three men for what they were. There was no spark of human feeling in any of them. They wanted money: not just money, but big money. They didn't care how they got it, but they knew that none of them had the brains to make that money. They knew Raven could make it, so they had been contented to wait.

Raven looked round at them, and he gloried in his triumph. "Well," he said, "I've sent for you guys because somethin's happenin'. I told you it would, and it has."

The three shifted a little and regarded him with blank, stony eyes. Three jaws moved rhythmically as they turned the chewing-gum in their mouths.

"When I first came to this burg I wanted to play ball with Mendetta. But the dirty rat said no. He was in the position to say no. I had to take it. You guys thought I'd get a break. You've stuck around for a long time waiting for that break. You haven't bellyached. You've done what I've told you—well, by God, we've waited long enough. We're takin' over the burg."

Still the three stood silent. They waited for facts.

"Mendetta had protection," Raven said, stressing the past tense. "We couldn't start anythin' as long as he was alive. Now he's dead—so we move in."

The three fidgeted.

"I've seen Grantham. He won't be any trouble. In a day or so I'll have my hands on some dough. We're goin' to organize this burg. We're goin' to milk it dry. We've got everythin' just where we want it. I'm tellin' you what to do, an' you'll do it. That way we'll all be in the dough."

Maltz, a little wop, with a heavy sneering mouth and bloodshot black eyes, straightened away from the wall. "You said you'd do it, boss," he said, "and we knew you would. Why didn't you get one of us to rub Mendetta?"

Raven shook his head. "Who said I killed him?" he asked quietly.

The three exchanged glances and grinned. They thought that was a good joke.

Raven got to his feet. "Stick around, fellas," he said, "I gotta go an' talk with Grantham. By tonight I'll know how much dough's comin' to us."

He went away, leaving them still standing in his bedroom.

16

June 6th, 10:30 a.m.

Johnson, the desk sergeant, chewed the end of his pen and regarded Jay with an unfavourable eye. He never had much use for crime reporters. They were always bobbing up at the wrong time and always asking embarrassing questions. Jay was no exception to this. In fact, he showed a lot of talent for being a nuisance.

Jay, with his hands full of petty and uninteresting crimes, was feeling irritable. He wanted a free hand to work on the Mendetta affair. The fact that Poison had warned him to lay off did not deter him. He was as determined to go ahead and find out what had happened to Fletcher's sister as he had been before hearing Poison's threat of dismissal. He knew he was good as a reporter and he knew he wouldn't have far to look for another job. What did rile him was the number of small cases that had suddenly arisen during the night which he was bound to cover, and now he found himself chained by the leg to the station house, awaiting fresh evidence. It looked like he'd be there all the morning. Then he had to write up his two columns, so Fletcher's sister would have to wait until the evening.

Johnson sighed. "It's a pity your paper can't find you a job of work to do," he said sourly. "I'm gettin' tired of seein' you loafin' around this joint. Why don't you go out an' take a little exercise?"

Jay put his feet up on the wooden bench and closed his eyes. "Leave me alone," he said. "I'm sick of breathin' the same air as you, but this is what I'm bein' paid for, so leave out the cracks."

The sergeant grunted and began to write laboriously in the charge book. "Well, there ain't much about," he said, blotting his neat writing carefully. "You guys live pretty soft, I must say."

"It's when there's nothin' about that we work hard," Jay told him. "Look what we've got today. Petty thieving, an embezzlement, and a small-time forger. How would you like to make a column out of that little lot? What I want is a nice rape or a good murder. Somethin' that'll take my column on the front page."

Johnson scowled. "Horrible lot you newspaper guys," he said.

"Do you know how many girls have been reported missing this year?" Jay asked.

Johnson shook his head. "Not my department," he said promptly. "You want the Missing People's Bureau. You lost someone?"

Jay shook his head. "I was wonderin', Johnson, if there's anythin' in this White Slave rumour I've heard about."

Johnson laughed. "Not a word," he said. "You think about it for a moment and you'll see that there can't be anythin' in it."

"You tell me. It'll save my energies."

Johnson spread himself over his desk and folded his arms on his blotter. "It's like these rape cases we get," he explained. "It ain't possible to rape a woman against her will. In the same way, it ain't possible to keep a woman in prostitution against her will in a big city like this. Sooner or later we should hear complaints. Guys that go to these houses would report that a woman was being held against her will. But we never hear of them. Obviously, the women are in the game for what they get out of it, and the stories we hear about Slaving is so much junk."

Jay considered this. "Suppose these women were terrorized?" he said. "How about that?"

Johnson shook his head. "Too risky," he said. "We'd give them protection if they wanted to squawk. All they have to do is to walk in here, lodge a complaint, and we'd look after them until an investigation's been made."

"Suppose they can't get out?" Jay persisted.

Johnson frowned. "What you hintin' at?" he demanded. "Do you know anythin'?"

Jay shook his head. "Nope," he confessed; "but I'm interested. I believe that a woman could be terrorized into prostitution, and I'm lookin' into it from this angle. I may be wrong, but if I ain't, I'm going to keep you mighty busy bookin' the heels who run the racket."

"You're wasting your time," Johnson said. "What you want is an excuse to play around with undesirable floosies. I bet part of your investigation will be meetin' and talkin' to these dames."

Jay shook his head. "I'm serious, Johnson," he said. "You wait and see. If I do strike on anythin' you'd better get ready for some heavy work."

A police officer came in, followed by Benny Perminger. The officer went up to Johnson. "This guy thinks we've got his wife in gaol," he said. "Will you speak to him?"

Johnson looked at Benny doubtfully. "What's the trouble?" he demanded.

Benny was looking scared. "I'm Ben Perminger," he said. "I want to see my wife."

Johnson closed his mouth into a thin line. "I ain't stoppin' you," he said coldly. "She ain't here."

"Well, where have you taken her?"

"What is all this?"

Benny began to look bewildered. "Well, I don't know," he said. "I found this note when I got home." He gave Johnson a slip of paper.

Jay sat up on the bench and watched all this with interest. He smelt a news story.

Johnson read the note and handed it back. "There's no one of the name of Perminger booked last night. We didn't pull anyone in from that address. I guess she's havin' a game with you."

Benny stood staring at the note. "Maybe they didn't bring her here. Could they take her anywhere else?"

"There's the station on West 47th Street. I'll ask them." Johnson pulled the phone towards him and put the enquiry through. After a short wait he shook his head and hung up. "No, they don't know anythin' about it."

Benny began to sweat. "What am I goin' to do?" he asked.

Johnson was getting bored with him. "It's your wife, buddy," he said. "Most like she's havin' a little game with you. You go back home. You'll find her waitin' for you."

Benny turned away from the desk and moved slowly towards the door.

Johnson looked at Jay. "That guy's got a leak in his conk," he said under his breath.

Jay got up and followed Benny out of the station house, ignoring Johnson's yell for him to come back.

Benny walked down the street in a daze. He didn't know what to make of it. Surely Sadie wouldn't pull a stunt like this if it didn't mean anything? She had said that she was being taken down to the station house as a witness and would Benny come at once.

Jay overtook him at the corner. "Hey, Perminger," he said, "what's all this about your wife?"

Benny blinked at him. "Where the hell did you spring from?" he said, shaking hands.

"Come over an' have a drink," Jay said, taking him by his arm and steering him into a near-by bar. "I overheard what you were tellin' Johnson. What's happened to Mrs. P.?"

Seated at a small table away from the bar and assisted by a large iced beer, Benny unburdened. He told Jay how he had quarrelled with Sadie and how he'd left her during the night. "Well, I felt a bit of a heel this morning," he went on, "so I thought I'd get back and make it up. When I got in I found all the lights burning and a note on my pillow saying she'd been taken down to headquarters as a witness and would I please come." He paused to pull at his beer.

Jay puzzled. On the face of it, he thought, Sadie might be just teaching this guy a lesson, but his instinct for news was not satisfied. Why should she use such an odd way of scaring him? Why a witness? A witness of what? No, it didn't quite add up.

"I thought the police were supposed to help you," Benny grumbled. "The way that guy went on, you'd think I was crazy."

"You don't have to worry about him. He's gettin' all kinds of stories and complaints every hour, and he just doesn't take any interest. Where are you livin' now?"

Benny told him.

Jay suddenly sat up. "Surely, that's where Tootsie Mendetta hangs out?" he said.

Benny nodded. "That's right," he answered. "I've been wantin' an introduction to him for weeks. I want to sell him a flock of trucks. He lives just opposite my apartment, but I've never set eyes on him."

Jay got to his feet. There might be something in this story after all. It was a long shot, but he wasn't going to let it grow cold. "We'll go back to your apartment and have a look round," he said. "Come on, buddy, let's go."

Benny went with him and they took a taxi to the block.

Inside his apartment Jay couldn't find anything that excited him. It was just an ordinary joint of a man with a nice income. He wandered around, his hands deep in his trouser pockets, brooding.

Benny sat on the arm of a chair and watched him.

"Did she take a suit-case or anythin'?" Jay asked suddenly.

Benny looked bewildered. "I don't know," he said. "I hadn't thought of lookin'."

"Check that up, will you, pal?"

Benny went into the bedroom and after a while he came out again. He looked more bewildered still. He shook his head helplessly. "No," he said, "she hasn't taken anythin'. The only things that are missing are the clothes she wore yesterday and her handbag. Nothing else."

Jay didn't like the sound of this. No woman would run away from her husband without taking some of her belongings.

"Will you wait here?" he said. "I'll go across and have a word with Mendetta. Maybe he heard somethin'."

Benny suddenly went very pale. "You don't think anythin' bad's happened to her?" he asked.

Jay shook his head. "No," he said, "I don't think so, but we'll clear this up or find out somethin', so we can get the cops interested. You sit down for a moment."

He left the apartment and crossed the corridor. He rang Mendetta's bell. No one answered. He stood there waiting, and then he rang again. Still no one answered.

Benny came to his front door and stood watching him. "No one seems at home," he said.

Jay scratched his head. "Will you phone down to the porter and find out what time Mendetta went out?" he said.

While Benny was doing this Jay took a little instrument from his vest pocket and inserted it in the lock. He made no attempt to open the door, but by careful probing he knew that, if he wanted to, he could do so.

Benny came back, looking blank. "The porter guy says Mendetta hasn't left the building."

Jay put his thumb on the bell and kept it there. They stood listening to the angry whirr of the bell for several minutes. Then Jay made up his mind. "I'm goin' in," he said.

"You can't do that. Maybe he's asleep."

Jay looked at him. "I'm chancin' that," he said shortly. "Somehow, I feel there's somethin' wrong in there."

He once more probed with his instrument and a moment later the lock slid back with a little snick. Gently, he eased the door back and looked into the hall. Then he stepped in softly and entered the first room he came to.

He stood looking at Mendetta sprawled out on the floor. His big head rested in a pool of blood. Over the other side of the room Jean lay, one leg drawn up and her arms flung wide. Jean wasn't very nice to look at.

Jay caught his breath. Here was his front page murder. He spun on his heel and nearly collided with Benny, who had come in.

"My God!" Benny said, going suddenly very green.

Jay pushed him out into the corridor. "Keep your shirt on," he said roughly. "Go into your apartment and get some drinks lined up."

Benny went away hurriedly, and Jay carefully closed the apartment door. He followed Benny and grabbed the telephone. "Listen," he said, as he hastily dialled a number, "there's goin' to be a riot in a little while. Did your wife know Mendetta?"

Benny gave himself a long drink of Scotch. He shook his head. "You don't think she's mixed up in this, do you?"

Jay was already on to Henry. "Mendetta's been bumped," he said. "I've just been into his apartment. We've got the exclusive story. Even the cops don't know yet. Can you get this story on the street right away?"

Henry got very excited. "Let's have it," he said.

Jay sat down. In short, crisp sentences he fired off the discovery of finding Mendetta's and Jean's bodies.

"What the hell were you doin' up there?" Henry snapped.

"I'll fix that end," Jay told him. "You get that on the street in ten minutes and you'll beat the whole gang to it. I've got to tell the cops."

"When you're through come on back. I've got to see what Poison's got to say about this."

"To hell with Poison. This is the story of my life. If Poison's going to put a soft pedal on it I'm quittin'," and Jay hung up.

He turned to Benny. "Listen, pal, this is where you've got to be a big help. We're goin' down to get the porter to open Mendetta's door. It wouldn't look too good if they found out that I've broken in. Come on, we've gotta work fast."

Protesting feebly, Benny followed him downstairs.

17

June 6th, 11 a.m.

Sadie opened her eyes. The hard, naked light of the electric lamp blinded her and she rolled over on the bed, shielding her eyes with her arm. A stabbing pain shot through her head as she moved.

She couldn't think where she was or what had happened to her. Her mouth felt dry and her body ached. She lay for some time, only half conscious. Then, after a while, her mind began to function again. She remembered dimly leaving her home. She remembered Lu. Out of the mists Grantham's face appeared—Grantham, thin-lipped, standing over her with something in his hand that she couldn't see. She remembered her terror, and, as she started to scream, a hot hand coming from behind her, over her mouth. She remembered a sharp prick in her arm and her wild struggle, then she remembered nothing more.

Again she half opened her eyes. She was aware that she was lying on a mattress and the colour of the walls was a drab grey. Her heart began to thud wildly. It was no horrible nightmare, then. She turned over and looked round the room.

It was small. The thick carpet on the floor matched the walls. There was no other furniture in the room except the bed on which she was lying.

The door was opposite her. Slowly she sat up, holding her head between her hands. There was something the matter with the room. For a moment she couldn't make it out, then she realized that there was no window. The discovery did a lot to clear her brain. She knew that she was in acute danger. Of what she didn't know, but all the same it made her sick with terror.

Slowly she got off the bed and staggered across the room to the door. Her feet sank into the pile of the carpet, which deadened her footfalls. She tried the door, but it was locked. She stood pulling weakly at the handle, and then she slid down on to the floor and began to cry.

Her head hurt so. She was so frightened. Where could she be? she asked herself. She stayed like that for some time, and when she couldn't cry any more she again got control of her nerves. She knew she would get nowhere just crying, and, taking herself in hand, she stood up.

She tried the door, pulling at the handle without success, and then she hammered on the panels. That gave her a horrible shock. The panels were covered with a thick layer of rubber. Her small fists bounced back every time she struck, and she could make no sound as she hammered.

She turned and stumbled blindly to the opposite wall and put her hands on it. Rubber again. The room was sound-proof, lined with heavy rubber, even to the ceiling.

She knew then that something horrible was going to happen to her, and she began to scream wildly.

18

June 6th, 12 noon.
Raven came out of the 22nd Club and signalled to a taxi. His thin white face was expressionless, but there was a triumphant gleam in his eyes. He carried a leather document case, and he climbed into the taxi with a new dignity that off-set his shabby clothes. He gave the address of his hotel and sat back.

The taxi was a symbol of his success. He hadn't ridden in a taxi since he'd left Chi. Now things were going to be different. In the document case were papers that made him a rich man. Grantham hadn't raised any objection. He had turned Mendetta's shares over to him without a word. They were all bearer bonds. Nothing to connect Raven with him. But they meant money. He had been willing to have shared all this with Mendetta, but the rat had said no. Now he had it all.

The taxi swerved and pulled up outside the hotel. Raven paid him off and hurried upstairs. The three were waiting for him, still chewing, blank, stolid expressions on their faces.

Raven looked round at them and they in turn looked at him. He raised the case so that they could see it. He knew it was no use explaining anything about holdings or shares or bearer bonds to them. They hadn't the mentality to understand. All they could understand was money. Not in cheques or bonds, but in notes and coin.

He took from his pocket his small, fast-vanishing roll. He peeled off two notes and gave them to Little Joe. "Go and get some Scotch," he said. "Get glasses from downstairs. Make it snappy."

A little grin came to the faces of the three. This they could understand. A guy doesn't buy them one drink, he sends for a bottle. That must mean dough.

While Little Joe was away Raven took off his hat and combed his hair carefully. He adjusted his frayed tie and regarded himself for a long while in the fly-blown mirror.

The other two watched him with interest. Raven took no notice of them; he was waiting for Little Joe. They knew this and were content to wait. Little Joe had tagged along with them; he was entitled to hear what was to be said as much as the others.

Little Joe came back with the Scotch and glasses. At a sign from Raven he poured drinks out all round.

Raven took his glass. "Money and power," he said, and they all drank.

Sitting down, Raven lit a cigarette. "It's fixed," he said. "We're movin' to the St. Louis Hotel right away. When we're settled we can look around for somethin' better, but that'll do to get along with."

The St. Louis Hotel was the best hotel in town.

Maltz said, "Gee! That joint's too swell for us guys."

"You've got to change your ideas—all of you. This is no longer a small-town party. We're big shots," Raven said, sipping his whisky carefully. "I want to talk to you guys. We're startin' work right away. You've got to go round the bars and spread the rumour that all whores are to get off the streets or else…. Do you get it?"

Little Joe scratched his head. "Say, what's the idea?"

Raven knew he'd got to be patient with these guys. "We're goin' to clean up the whole town. It's goin' to be a hell of a job, but it's got to be done. You three have got to get so many hoods in each district of the town who are tough enough to run the whores off the streets and to deal with their bookers. That's your first job. I'll make myself plain. What happens to a guy who smokes a lot and suddenly finds out he can't get tobacco?"

Lefty knew that one. "He goes nuts," he said simply.

Raven nodded. "That's it, he goes nuts. Then supposing some guy comes along and offers him tobacco after a while at a greatly increased price? What happens?"

The three looked at each other. This was getting beyond them.

"He pays more because he can't get it elsewhere," Raven said patiently.

"So what?" Little Joe said.

"That's what we're goin' to do. Once we get organized, no whore on the streets will be safe. She's got to be treated rough, so she's too scared to work. We want them to leave town. It'll take a little while, but if you treat 'em rough enough they'll go. If they don't, then we've got to start shootin', but that'll be the last straw. We don't want trouble with the cops. If we knock 'em about, cut 'em a little, the cops won't do anythin', but if we kill 'em, then they'll have to get busy."

"It's goin' to be tough on the guys who like whores," Maltz said, thinking of himself.

"Now you're gettin' somewhere," Raven said. "We're goin' to set up houses. Not these fancy brothels that Mendetta ran. There's no big dough in those. He took a ten per cent cut on the house. The girls got fifty and the rest of the dough was put into expenses. That's a crazy way of workin' it. I'm doin' it differently." He edged forward. "Each girl will be paid a fixed salary. She'll never see the dough. It'll be put to her credit in a ledger. Out of this she'll have to pay rent for her room, her clothes, smokes, drinks and whatever else she wants. The balance, if there is a balance, will be used to buy shares in the house to give her a business interest." Raven smiled crookedly. "When she wants to go she can sell out at the market price—which will be fixed by me—and she can beat it."

Lefty understood a little of this. "She doesn't see any dough at all, then?"

"That's right. I'm using that dough as capital."

"These dames like to see money. They won't like this, boss."

Raven smiled. His thin lips just showed his teeth. It was more of a grimace than a smile. "They're not supposed to like it," he said. "They're goin' to do as they're told."

The three exchanged glances. "Rough stuff again, boss?" Little Joe asked.

"Ever been to Reno?" Raven said. "I have. Know what they do to a dame who won't play ball? They pour turpentine on her belly. They play ball all right after that."

There was a long silence. The three digested that piece of information. "I guess that hurts all right," Lefty said. "Gee! I'd hate that to happen to me."

"It wouldn't hurt you as it hurts them," Raven said. "You think about it." He got to his feet. "I'm goin' to the bank to get some dough. I'll stake you guys to a roll. You've got to get yourselves some new clothes. Don't forget you're livin' at the St. Louis from now on. When you're fixed you've got to start work." He broke off abruptly and stood listening.

The others sat very still.

Through the closed window they could hear a lot of shouting in the street. Raven took two quick steps to the window and threw it up. He looked down and then turned away.

"It's out," he said briefly. His eyes were very bright. "They're tellin' the world that Mendetta's dead."

The others made a move to the window, but he stopped them. "You've got to work fast now," he said. "The sooner we're organized the quicker we make dough."

He went out of the room hurriedly.

The three made a dash to the window. Across the road they could see a newsvendor standing busily handing out papers. When the crowd thinned a little they could read his placard:

MENDETTA AND MOLL SHOT TO DEATH

Lefty heaved a big sigh. "Didn't I tell you that guy was somethin'?" he said proudly.

19

June 6th, 12:50 p.m.
Grantham's office door burst open and Lu came in. He shut the door hurriedly and waved a newspaper. "It's out already," he said excitedly. "Look, boss, they're playin' it on the front page."

Grantham reached out and took the paper. He glanced at it and then tossed it on one side. "Quicker than I thought," he said, lighting a cigarette. "There's goin' to be a lot of guys yellin' at me very soon."

Lu sat on the edge of the desk. "That dame Perminger," he said. "Was it the right thing to turn her over to Carrie?"

Grantham looked at him coldly. "Why not?"

"Suppose she gets away an' talks?"

"What do you want me to do? Finish her?"

Lu nodded. "That would have been a lot safer."

"Listen, I'm the guy with brains. I want to keep that dame just where I can reach her in a hurry. You and I are under Raven now. As long as he brings in the dough, it's all right with us. Have you thought that, maybe, he won't succeed? Suppose we don't get anythin' better out of this change-over? Would you like the job of shifting Raven?"

Lu glanced away. "Where's this leadin' to?"

"As long as we've got a witness that Raven killed Mendetta we've got Raven where we want him. If he slips, then the Perminger dame goes to the cops with my love."

"Yeah? And she spills that you've been holding her in a knockin'-shop."

Grantham's thin mouth twisted into a smile. "She'll do what she's told, and she'll say what I want her to say."

Lu raised his eyebrows. "She may be tough," he said.

"Carrie likes 'em tough." Grantham reached forward and knocked the ash off his cigarette. "I've told her to start softenin' her as soon as she comes to the surface. Carrie knows her job."

"If Raven gets to hear about this it's goin' to be just too bad for you."

"Raven won't hear about it. Carrie knows me well enough not to open her mouth. You're the only other one. If you say anythin' to him you'll only do yourself dirt. You an' me get along all right, don't we?"

Lu nodded. "Sure," he said. "I was just thinkin' of Carrie."

The phone bell rang sharply. Grantham picked it up.

A girl said, "Judge Hennessey wants you."

"Put him on the line," Grantham said. "It's that old heel Hennessey," he whispered to Lu.

Hennessey's voice sounded agitated. "What's this about Mendetta?" he demanded. "Is it true?"

"Yes, Judge, I guess it's true all right. He was shot last night."

"Who did it?"

"We all want to know that." Grantham winked at Lu.

"Listen, Grantham, what are you doin' about it? I want to know where I stand. Who's goin' to take over?"

"It's all right, Judge, Tootsie fixed everything up with me months ago. He was expectin' trouble. Yeah, he left everythin' in my hands."

"In your hands?" Hennessey's voice sounded doubtful. "Can you carry on?"

"Sure I can carry on. Mendetta left everythin' straightforward. The thing runs itself now, Judge."

"I see." There was a long pause, then he went on, "You been through the books yet?"

"Just this minute startin' on them, Judge. You don't have to worry. We want guys like you around."

"Of course you do," the Judge snapped. "Your outfit would look mighty sick without me. Mendetta sent it to me on the first of the month. You'd better do the same."

"That's okay with me, Judge. First of the month? Sure, it'll be along."

"Well, I wish you luck, Grantham. Maybe it does run on its own power. You watch it, won't you?"

"I'll watch it." Grantham hung up. "Rat number one," he said, pursing his mouth. "Wanted to know if his rake-off was to continue. Didn't care a damn that Tootsie was dead. Just dough."

Lu grinned. "It ain't every organization who's got a Judge in its pocket," he said. "That guy may be expensive, but he's done some nice work for us."

Grantham unlocked a drawer in his desk and took out a little leather-bound note-book. He flicked through the pages and then, finding what he was looking for, he studied the page carefully. "Yeah," he said; "last year he had seventeen of our girls before him. Twelve dismissals, four warnings and one small fine. Yeah, I guess he's worth the dough all right."

Once more the phone rang. "Yeah?" Grantham said, again picking up the receiver. "Yeah, it's Grantham speaking. Is that you, Mr. Hackensfield?... How are you?... Mendetta? Sure we know he's dead.... Yeah, too bad.... No, you don't have to worry.... Sure we want you to work along with us. First of the month?... Yeah, we're lookin' into it right now.... Sure you're useful.... That's all right, Mr. Hackensfield. It'll be along." He hung up.

Lu said, "They like their dough, these guys."

Grantham nodded. "The District Attorney wanted to know if Mendetta's death was goin' to make any difference to his income," he said, leaning back in his chair. "This is goin' on all day, Lu. I may as well get used to it."

"Are you makin' any changes?"

Grantham shook his head. "Raven's seen the list. He wants it to go on for a time. When that guy's settled down he might start somethin'. He's wise. He's waitin' until he's strong enough to get tough."

Lu moved towards the door as the phone went again. "I'll leave you to it, boss," he said. "See you in church." He went out of the office.

Grantham grimaced and picked up the phone. "Mr. Poison wants you, Mr. Grantham," a girl said.

"Put him through." A cold, hard gleam came into Grantham's voice. "Grantham?"

"That's right. I wanted a little word with you, Mr. Poison.... Sure—about Mendetta. You're wonderin' about those shares?... So am I.... That's right, I said I was wonderin' too.... Sure I've taken over. Mendetta left everythin' in my hands.... Why? Well, I'm the only guy who knows how the business is run.... That's right."

Poison said furiously, "He's crazy to have left it to you. You don't understand this business, Grantham. I've got to safeguard my investment. You've got to find someone who can look after the outside organization. You stick around all day in the Club. You've got to have someone outside watching those women. They're lazy by nature. Mendetta understood them. He got the best out of them."

Grantham smiled unpleasantly. "Take it easy," he said. "I told you I'm runnin' this business, and I am. I don't care a damn about anythin' you say, so leave off throwin' your weight around."

"By God! You can't talk to me like this," Poison exploded. "Half my money's financing this business, and I've got a right to say how it should be run."

"You've got a right to receive dividends when they come due," Grantham said sharply, "but that's all. I'm the boss around here and don't you forget it."

"You be careful how you talk to me," Poison said, his voice thick with rage. "A word in the right direction would make things mighty unpleasant for you."

Grantham laughed. "Forget it, Poison," he jeered. "You can't scare me with that stuff. What about you? How would you look if it got around that half your money comes from brothel investments? I've got your signatures, don't forget."

There was a long pause, then Poison said more mildly: "Don't let us quarrel, Grantham."

Grantham nodded. "We won't quarrel. Don't you worry about the business. If it doesn't keep up its returns I promise you I'll have a talk with you in three months' time—how's that?"

"Very well. I'll see how you manage for three months."

"By the way, Poison, how come your paper was the first on the street with the news?"

"I'm not responsible for that," Poison said, his voice sinking to a very mild note. "I've got a crime reporter who's pretty good on his job."

"Yeah? He's too good, Poison. He's cut my working time down badly. I reckoned on another twenty-four hours to get organized. There might be a little trouble with the bookers now."

"He knows all about it," Poison said grimly. "I've told him to lay off the case."

"It's a bit late now," Grantham said. "I suppose it's Jay Ellinger?"

"Yes, do you know him?"

"I know him all right. He's been snoopin' around a little too much lately. Can't you send him out of town?"

"Well, I could."

"I'd like you to do that. He makes me nervous. Can't you send him somewhere out of the way for a little while? I want time to get organized, and I think he's gettin' a little too near the truth."

Poison thought a moment. "Yeah," he said, "I'll get him to cover the Tammany Hall trial. That'll keep him in New York for at least a month. Every paper is sending a reporter. He can't refuse to go. I could get him on the black list if he did."

Grantham sighed with relief. "Do that, Poison, and I'll guarantee you results."

"Consider it done," Poison said, and hung up.

Grantham replaced the receiver and relaxed. So far as he could see it was going all right. It depended a lot on Raven. If Raven's ideas were good the organization would hold together. After all, Mendetta had built it up on sound lines. He had over two hundred girls working for him. He had the Club, which paid very well, and his protection rackets were bringing in big dough. Yes, on the face of it it looked all right.

Grantham reached for another cigarette as the phone rang again.

20

June 6th, 2:45 p.m.

Benny made up his mind to get drunk. He couldn't take any more. From the time Jay called the Homicide Bureau he had been pushed around as if he'd been the one who had shot Mendetta.

Cold-eyed cops had come into his apartment and looked him over. They had asked him questions about Sadie. They wanted to know where she was. When he showed them the letter she'd written they didn't believe a word of it.

Carter, the officer-in-charge, had taken him into a corner. "See here, Perminger, your tale stinks. Why was Mrs. Perminger alone in this apartment all night?"

Benny clutched his head. "I keep tellin' you," he groaned, "she an' I had a tiff. So I walked out on her."

"What was the quarrel about?"

Benny tried to explain, but Carter sneered at him. "You mean to tell me that you walked out of this joint because your wife objected to you lookin' at dames? Now, think about it. Isn't that the lousiest story you've ever heard?"

"Well, it wasn't only that. She an' I were at the fights, an' by accident I got my head between some dame's knees—"

Carter's eyes bulged. "You did what?" he said.

Benny wrenched at his collar. "Yeah, that's right. You see, she was sittin' right behind me…."

Carter turned away. "Hi, Murphy, this guy's got a hot one here. He goes around sticking his head between dames' knees."

Murphy raised his eyebrows. "Well, tell him to stop doin' it. Tell him one thing leads to another."

Carter scowled at Benny. "You gotta be careful what you do, guy," he said. "We can't take you in for that, but mind it's your head next time."

And so it went on. The cops were far too excited looking at the dead bodies of Jean and Mendetta, hunting through the desk and drawers, to be really interested in Benny. When he tried to bring up about Sadie they told him to go down to the Missing People's Bureau.

Finally he gave up and sat down to wait for them to go. When they were through photographing the bodies, testing for finger-prints and ransacking the apartment, Carter found a little time to speak to him again.

He said, "We'll want you, buddy, so stick around. There's goin' to be a big stink over this, an' you're goin' to be right in the middle of it. When we want you we'll send for you."

They all went off after that and left Benny alone. So he decided to get good and drunk.

A little while later Jay found him, sitting in his armchair, a bottle of Scotch by his side and a glass clutched firmly in his hand.

Jay looked at him. "Hey, soak," he said, "anythin' left for me?"

Benny got hastily to his feet. "Am I glad to see you?" he said, shaking hands vigorously. "Sure, have a drink. I'll get you a glass."

Jay pushed him back into the chair. "I'll get it," he said. "You take it easy."

When he came back from the kitchen, holding a glass, Benny had just given himself a long shot.

"Wait a minute," Jay said hastily, taking the bottle away. "You've got to keep sober for a while." He poured himself out two fingers and sat down on the edge of the table. "Listen, buddy, I want to talk to you."

Benny shook his head. "I can't stand any more of it," he said. "Those cops have been making my conk buzz."

"Never mind about the cops. You an' me've got a job of work to do. You want to find your wife, don't you?"

"Why, goddamn it, of course I do."

"All right, then. Now listen. You don't know anythin' about how a murder is investigated. Well, I do. I've been watchin' these guys. They're puttin' on a front. They don't want to find out who killed Mendetta. They don't want to find out where your wife is. So they fool around, ask a lot of bull questions and then leave it at that. Maybe they'll forget all about you."

Benny sobered. "That's cock-eyed," he said. "It's their job to find out things like that."

Jay smiled grimly. "That's what you think, but you don't know anythin'. This is serious, Perminger. If you're not ready to do somethin' your wife'll never be found."

"What have I got to do?"

"I'll explain things so you can understand. Do you know what Mendetta did for a livin'?"

Benny shook his head. "I know he'd got plenty of dough," he said. "And I've heard he was mixed up with some rackets. What they are I don't know."

Jay nodded. "Well, I'll tell you. He was runnin' brothels."

Benny blinked. "You sure of that?" he said.

"I'm sure."

"Mind you, I wouldn't like to earn my dough that way, but brothels are necessary, ain't they?"

"Not Mendetta's brothels. I've heard he fills them by Slave methods. I don't want to scare you, buddy, but I think your wife's in one of his houses right now."

Benny stared at him. "What!" he said.

Jay nodded. "I think so, Perminger."

"You're crazy!" Benny said, his voice rising. He got to his feet. "That's a goddamn dirty lie, and you know it. Take it back, you heel, or I'll kick the nuts off you."

Jay reached out and shoved him in his chest. Benny flopped over into the chair again. "Quiet," Jay said. "You've got to listen to this. You don't know how deep it goes."

Benny said between his teeth, "You're goin' to be sorry for this, you heel!”

“Aw, shut up; let me tell you. Mendetta’s dead. Who killed him? Some guy who thinks he can make more dough out of the racket. There’s Grantham at 22nd Club. It might be he, but I don’t think so. He hasn’t the guts. Never mind who it is just yet. Mendetta’s girls never had a conviction. Time after time I’ve been in court when one of them was brought in for soliciting, and every time they got off. Every time one of his girls came up Judge Hennessey was the guy who found them not guilty. Why? Ever heard of corrupt judges? All right. Mendetta must have had a lot of protection. That means he paid out a lot of dough. When he was killed, I’m bettin’ those guys who got regular dough started gettin’ scared. If they find the guy who killed Mendetta they won’t get any more easy dough. They’re givin’ him a run. If he keeps up payment, as Mendetta did, then he’s safe. That’s the way the racket is worked in this town.”

Benny said, “What the hell has it to do with Sadie?”

Jay leant forward. “Suppose Sadie saw the killer? Suppose she reported it to the cops? Suppose they got excited and saw that she was goin’ to bust up their racket? What would they do? Give her a cake and a bronx cheer? Like hell!”

Benny sat very still. “What could they do with her?”

“They could either knock her on the head or else give her over to Grantham. You’ve got to face it, Perminger. If her body ain’t found in a week or so, then she’s in one of his houses.”

“They can’t do a thing like that!” Benny said wildly. “By God! I won’t let them do it!” He got to his feet.

Jay said, “You don’t understand. You’ve got to take it. There’s nothing we can do. Now listen; they know I’m on to their racket, so what do they do? I’ve got to go to New York to cover the Tammany Hall trial. That’s just getting me out of the way. I’ve got no come-back. I gotta do it. If I turn it down I’m on the black list, and I can’t afford to be on that.”

Benny said thickly, “And what am I supposed to do? Sit around and let them get away with it?”

“If I hadn’t told you, you wouldn’t have done anything. I’ve got no proof of all this. No, you’ve got to wait. Go and see Grantham and try and sell him some trucks. Try and find out who’s taken over the organization. Maybe it is Grantham, but somehow I can’t see him holding a job of work down as big as that. Anyway, snoop around. Don’t start anything. Just snoop. When I get back I’m goin’ to go after this business with both hands.”

Benny said, “If you think I’m going to sit around while Sadie’s in those bastards' hands you're crazy. I'm going right over and split Grantham open."

"You sucker," Jay said. "How far will that get you? If you make it too hot you'll run into a belly-load of slugs. Will that help Sadie? No, there's only one way of handling this, and that's by taking it slow. We can't help her now. Whatever's happened to her or is going to happen to her we can't stop. The cops won't listen to you. You can't force your way in twenty brothels and search for her. You've got to consider she's dead. Do you understand? You're not looking for her, you're avenging her."

He got to his feet and went to the door. "I've got to catch my train. Stick around, Perminger, and take it."

Benny sat in the chair and watched him go. His hands gripped the chair-arms until his knuckles showed white. He began to swear slowly and obscenely, using words that he never spoke aloud. Then quite suddenly he put his hands over his face and began to cry.

21

June 6th, 3 p.m.
Sadie opened her eyes as the door swung open. She had fallen into an exhausted sleep and her dreams had been terrifying. She sat up on the bed, her hand going to her mouth and her eyes dark with fear.

Fan came in and shut the door behind her. The silk wrap that she wore outlined her full figure. There was no mistaking what she was.

Sadie caught her breath when she saw her. Her mouth was so dry that she couldn't say anything.

"Take it easy," Fan said, leaning against the door; "I've been told to have a little talk with you."

Still Sadie couldn't say anything. She continued to stare at her with growing horror.

Fan said crossly, "Don't look at me like that. You're givin' me the hee-bies. Relax, sister."

"Who are you?" Sadie managed to get out.

"What does it matter?" Fan asked, giving a hard little smile. "You worry about yourself. You're in a spot."

"Where am I? What does all this mean?"

Fan came over to the bed and sat down. "I've got to talk to you," she said. "Don't think I want to, but when I'm told to do anythin' in this joint it's easier to do it than to kick. The old cow downstairs has sent me up to scare you. Well, I ain't goin' to. I'm goin' to tell you what'll be good for you, and what you ought to do."

Sadie said, "But tell me where I am."

"Can't you guess?" Fan said bitterly. "Take a look at me? What do you think I am—a nun?"

Sadie felt herself go suddenly very cold. She flinched away from Fan.

"Skip it, sister," Fan said roughly. "You don't have to take it that way. You're in the same boat as me. I don't know why they've picked on you, but they're goin' to put you through it. If you take my advice you'll do as you're told and get off lightly."

Sadie looked at her in horror.

"There's a nigger who runs this house. She's tough. Make no mistake about it. She's had dozens of girls like you through her hands. Some of them stuck it for a hell of a long time. They wouldn't do what she wanted. But they did in the end. You'll do it too. Maybe you don't think you will, but you will."

Sadie said, "Get me out of here. I'll give you anything if you'll get me out of here."

"Skip it. No amount of that talk will help. I can't do anythin' for you. All I can tell you is what'll come to you if you buck."

Sadie controlled her nerves with a great effort. "They won't make me do that," she said fiercely. "They'll have to kill me first. I won't!"

Fan took a packet of cigarettes from her pocket. "Have one?" she said, shaking two out on the sheet.

Sadie didn't even look at them. "If you won't help me, then I want to see someone else," she said. "You can't do this sort of thing in this country and get away with it."

Fan lit a cigarette and put the odd one back in the packet. "Don't be a sap," she said. "A kid like you don't know anythin'. Listen, sister, have you ever been whipped?"

Sadie flushed hotly. "What's that got to do with it?"

"You tell me. Have you?"

"Of course I haven't. Why should I be?"

"Well, I have." Fan said grimly. "And believe me it ain't pleasant. When Carrie comes up she'll explain what she wants done. You'll say yes or no. If it's yes, then you'll be okay; if it's no—Gawd help you. She'll tie you to that bed and she'll whip you. She'll whip you until you say yes. Don't think she'll get tired of it—she won't. She'll whip you every hour of the day until you can't take any more of it. And when she's broken you you'll be doin' what you said no to in the first place."

Sadie said quietly, "She can do anythin' she likes to me—but I'll never agree."

Fan sighed. "It's always the same," she said. "My God, I'm sick of all this! She sends me up to talk you kids into being sensible, but you all say the same. You all think you've got enough guts to take it and in the end you give way. Why don't you be sensible? What the hell's the use of being bashed about, losing your nice skin, just because you ain't got the brains to know when you're sunk?"

Sadie shook her head. "Nothin' you can say will make any difference," she said.

"Carrie distrusts a dame she has had to beat into submission. She makes sure that she'll stick when she finally gives in. There won't be much kick-back coming from you. Can't you see this is the one time you can't beat the rap? You can't get away. Carrie's got everything the way she wants it. She won't have any mercy on you. I'm tellin' you. Use your nut and give in right away. It'll be tough, but it ain't goin' to be the hell you'll make for yourself if you try and stick it. I've said my little bit. It's up to you. She'll be up in a while. Think it over." She got off the bed.

Sadie beat her to it. She darted across the room, wrenched open the door and ran into the passage. Fan grimaced. She made no attempt to intercept her.

Sadie could see a flight of stairs at the end of the passage. Blindly she ran towards them. Halfway down the stairs she became aware that someone was waiting for her at the bottom. She brought herself up with a jerk.

Carrie, her flat face expressionless, looked up at her. "Go back to your room," she said harshly.

Sadie didn't move. Her heart pounded against her side. She felt as if she had suddenly become involved in a horrible nightmare.

"Go back to your room," Carrie repeated.

Sadie retreated one step up. Then, realizing that this would be her one chance of escape, she said, "You've got to let me go—do you hear? You can't do this to me."

Carrie began to climb the stairs slowly. Her big mouth gaped in a grin. "Go on back," she said. "I'm comin' to talk to you. Look what I've got for you."

Sadie saw she was holding a thin length of whalebone in her hand. She caught her breath and turned to run up the stairs. A powerfully built negro was standing at the head of the stairs, blocking her escape. He grinned at her; his thick lips seemed to split his face in half.

Paralysed with terror, Sadie turned again. Carrie was right on her. She said, "Go to your room."

Sadie suddenly clutched her head between her hands and began to scream. Her screams resounded against the walls.

The negro ran down the few stairs and grabbed her. She nearly went mad with terror as his great damp hands closed on her.

"Get her upstairs—quick!" Carrie said angrily. "She'll disturb my people."

The negro, grinning broadly, carried Sadie up the stairs. Her arms and legs banged against the sides of the wall as he carried her. She twisted and struggled frantically, but the grip round her arms and thighs was immovable. She continued to scream until she heard the door shut with a thud, and then she went limp.

Carrie said, "She doesn't know anythin' yet. Put her on the bed, Joe."

The negro lowered her on to the bed and stood away. His face beamed. Sadie half lay, half crouched, looking at Carrie.

The mulatto stood, her big hands hanging loosely at her sides and her big eyes blazing with a curious animal expression. "My girls know how to behave themselves in this house," she said. "You better learn."

Sadie had lost her fear. She was nearly suffocating with rage. Her Southern blood had revolted at the touch of the negro. She said furiously, "You'll pay for this! How dare you touch me!… How dare you touch me!"

Carrie glanced at the negro. "All right, Joe. Fix her up for me."

The negro shuffled across the room. Sadie could see little red tints in his eyes as he came towards her. She said wildly, shrinking back on the bed, "Don't touch me!" And then he was on her. The horrible rancid nigger smell of him sickened her, and she struck at him twice before he pinned her hands. He muttered, "She'll sure take the hide off you for this, baby," and twisting her arms, he turned her over on her face. His knee rammed down between her shoulders and she felt her hands being fixed to the bedposts.

Sobbing with rage, she kicked and twisted, moving the bed half across the room. One of her ankles was seized and fastened to the lower bedpost. She kicked wildly with her free leg and she felt a jar as she caught the negro in his chest. He grunted, grabbed the flaying leg and fastened that too. Then he got off the bed and looked at Carrie with a little smirk.

Sadie pulled and strained on the cords that held her, but they only bit further into her flesh. She was securely tied, face down on the bed.

Then she gave herself up for lost. No one would come at the last moment and save her from this horror. She knew that she would not wake up to find that it had only been some strange and horrible nightmare. It was real and it was happening to her. And when the negro began to rip the clothes off her back she screamed like a terrified child.

PART TWO

I

August 16th, 10:15 p.m.
Little Joe walked into the pool-room at the corner of 29th Street. He was pleasantly conscious of the sudden hush that greeted his entrance. Even the guys at the tables paused in their game and looked at him with interest.

He was something to look at now. His suit was heavily padded at the shoulders and its colour compelled a second glance. When Little Joe first saw it hanging in a window of a Jewish tailor his mouth watered. He'd never seen a suit quite like it. He knew there couldn't be another on the streets that came anywhere near it, so he went inside and bought it. Also he was persuaded to buy a pair of yellow shoes, a bowler hat that only just fitted him and a necktie that, to say the least, was completely surrealist. The barman wiped down the counter and smiled at him. "Why, Joe," he said, "you're lookin' pretty good tonight."

Little Joe adjusted his bowler. "Like it?" he said. "I bet you ain't seen anythin' quite like this, huh?"

The barman said truthfully he hadn't. His tone was so dubious that Little Joe scowled. "Ain't nothin' the matter with it, is there?" he said. "I gave a heap of jack for this outfit."

The barman told him hastily that it was swell.

Little Joe relaxed a trifle. "Gimme some Scotch," he said. "Not every guy could wear a suit like this," he went on, pouring out a liberal shot; "you gotta have somethin' to get away with it."

A big fat guy, who had been playing snooker over the other side of the room, suddenly laid down his cue and came over. He owned a bunch of taxi-cabs that beat up a good business in the lower East side of the town. His name was Spade. Little Joe knew him well enough to nod to.

Spade was looking worried. When he got close to Little Joe he said, "I've been wantin' to talk to you, buddy. Come over to the table, will you?"

Little Joe followed him to a corner of the room and sat down.

"Well, what is it?" he asked, taking off his hat and brushing it carefully with his sleeve. "What do you want to see me about?"

Spade rubbed his hand over his fat features and shook his head. He certainly looked as if he was in a lot of trouble. "What's come over the town, Joe?" he said.

Little Joe stared at him. "What the hell are you talkin' about?"

Spade fingered his glass. "Where've the girls got to?"

Little Joe was non-committal. "What girls?" he asked.

Spade shook his head again. "You know. There ain't a floosie poundin' a beat this side of 27th Street. A couple of months ago you couldn't take a step without fallin' over them. Well, where've they gone?"

Little Joe grinned. "Can't you find any comfort?"

"It ain't that," Spade said. "It's ruinin' my business. I've gotta find out what's wrong."

"What do you mean—ruinin' your business?"

"What I say. When one of those floosie's found a sucker she took one of my cabs. My cabs were kept mighty busy doin' that business—now it's all gone."

Little Joe looked perplexed. He hadn't thought of it in that light. Spade was a member of the Hack Drivers Union and he'd got a certain amount of political influence.

"What makes you think I know anythin' about it?" he said cautiously.

"I use my eyes and my ears. They said Raven's at the back of the vice ring now. I know you've done a lot for Raven. You're in the dough now. Anyone can see that by the fancy uniform you're wearin'—"

"Let me tell you," Little Joe said heatedly, "this suit cost me—"

"Skip it," Spade said roughly. "What's goin' on?"

Little Joe hesitated. "Maybe the girls've got scared," he said at last.

"If they've got scared, someone's scarin' them. You'd better lay off, Joe, an' you can tell Raven to lay off too. No one's goin' to bust up my business without hearin' from me."

"Take it easy," Little Joe said hastily. "I don't know a thing about it— honest. I'll have a word with Raven. I can't promise anythin'. He's a hard guy."

Spade got to his feet. "So am I," he said shortly. "Tell him that, too."

Little Joe watched him walk across the room and resume his game. He took a little splinter of wood from his pocket and began to explore his teeth thoughtfully. Then he got up and walked out into the dark night again.

He knew Spade was a dangerous guy to cross. He'd got a lot of pull and he might make things difficult for them. Well, anyway, that was Raven's look-out. He wasn't paid to strain his brains.

He made his way in the direction of St. Louis Hotel. The fact that he had now plenty of dough did not allow him to take a taxi. He had been so long used to being short that he could not bring himself to throw money away on unnecessary luxuries.

It was a hot night, dark and moonless, and Little Joe moved slowly, his eyes searching the shadows. At the head of the street he noticed a woman step out of the darkness and stop a guy who was hurrying towards the main street. The guy paused, then waved his hand impatiently and went on.

Little Joe grinned. Some dame was ignoring the warning he had circulated through the bookers. He put his hand in his pocket and his fingers touched the little bottle he always carried around with him. He took the bottle out and carefully removed the glass stopper. He put the glass stopper in a small metal box. Then, holding the bottle between two fingers, he sauntered slowly towards the woman.

As he drew near he could see she was scared. She was watching him as he came on. He slowed down and looked at her, his free hand adjusting his tie.

She must have thought he was all right, because she smiled at him. He could see her now. She was only quite a kid. She looked a little shabby, but she wasn't a bad looker. Her professional smile wasn't very gay.

He said, "I bet you're a naughty girl."

She came close to him. "Do you want a naughty girl?" she said, smiling with her mouth only. "I've got a little place just round the corner."

"What's the big idea?" Little Joe asked. "I've walked two blocks an' you're the first girl I've met."

He saw the little twitch of panic at her mouth. "I—I don't know," she said. "Anyway, you've found me—"

"Yeah, I've found you all right. Maybe the other girls think it healthier to stay at home," Little Joe said, tossing the vitriol into her face. He heard the little hiss as the acid travelled through the air. Then she began to scream horribly.

Little Joe broke into a run. He knew the district very well, and by doubling down an alley and then a side street he reached the St. Louis very quickly.

Raven would never let any of his mob come in through the front entrance. They all came in by the staff door. He knew that there'd be a lot of trouble from the hotel if Little Joe kept coming in and out in that suit of his.

Little Joe rode up in the small elevator, very pleased with himself. How he dealt with that floosie would get around. The girls would think twice before coming out. He rapped on Raven's door, and Maltz let him in.

"Boss in?"

Maltz nodded. "Yeah," he said in a bored voice; "he's playin' with his toys."

Little Joe grinned. "I'll get his mind on to somethin' else," he said, moving towards the big double doors at the end of the passage.

"Not a chance. That guy's very busy right now."

Little Joe opened the doors and stepped quietly into the big room.

Raven had spread himself. The suite at the St. Louis was costing him plenty, but it did him a lot of good. It had increased his own confidence.

He lay on the floor in a red silk dressing-gown. All around him was a complicated network of railway lines. Miniature stations, signals, buffers, engine-sheds and the like surrounded him. Trains, dragging long lines of carriages, flashed over points and rattled over the gleaming metal track. They disappeared beneath furniture, only to reappear again, running in an endless circle.

He lay there, his hands on a master switch, controlling the current that sent the trains forward. A limp cigarette hung from his thin lips, and his eyes were cloudy and intent on the fast-moving little trains.

"What is it?" he said suddenly. "One of these days you're goin' to collect a handful of slugs if you sneak up on me like this."

Little Joe grinned nervously. "Sure, boss," he said.

Reluctantly Raven closed the switch, bringing the trains to a standstill. He rolled over a little on his side so that he could look at Joe. "Nice outfit, ain't it?" he said with a proud smile.

"Yeah." Joe wasn't very interested. "It's all right."

Raven turned back again and set the trains in motion. "Well, what is it?"

"A floosie on 7th Street was peddling. I gave her a little tonic."

Raven grunted. "You gotta watch those dames," he said. "Another month an' we'll have it where we want it."

"Before that, boss," Little Joe said, sitting on the arm of a big overstuffed chair. "The guys are yappin' like hell now."

Raven directed a train to a station and threw the switch. He leant forward to uncouple it. "Always wanted an outfit like this when I was a lad," he said. "I never got anythin' when I was a kid." His voice was suddenly very bitter.

Joe didn't say anything.

Raven started a complicated move of shunting the train to the engine-house. Little Joe couldn't understand why he didn't just lift the train off the track and put it in the shed. He thought it would save a lot of time.

"Well, what is it?" Raven repeated for the third time.

"Spade's bellyachin'."

"So what?"

"He says we're ruinin' his taxi business."

Raven at last got the engine in the shed. "That's too bad," he said, stubbing out his cigarette in an ash-tray by his side. Then, as an afterthought, he said, "Are we?"

"His taxis take the floosies to their joints," Little Joe explained.

Raven paused and thought. "I don't want trouble with Spade," he said at last. "He's a tough egg, ain't he?"

"You bet he is," Little Joe said.

Raven began to unload some tiny milk churns on to the platform. "I'll get Lefty to take care of him," he said. "We ain't had any shootin' in the town yet, have we?"

Little Joe looked worried. "Gee!" he said. "We don't want to shoot Spade."

"Nice to hear your views," Raven said, recoupling the line of trucks; "I'll make a note of that."

Little Joe shifted uneasily. "You're the boss," he said hastily.

"Sure." Raven turned the switch and the trains began to move slowly along the track.

Little Joe waited for a little while, and as Raven continued to ignore him he went out, closing the door softly behind him.

Raven turned his head and looked at the closed door. A cold, far-away look came into his eyes. "So we don't want to shoot Spade?" he said softly. "These guys are gettin' soft."

2

August 17th, 11:25 a.m.

When Grantham rang the bell the negro doorman let him in.

Grantham was looking old and tired. He asked for Carrie in a voice tight with nerves.

Joe showed him into a little reception-room. "She'll be right down, boss," he said. His big eyes searched Grantham's face questioningly, but Grantham turned away and felt for his cigarette-case.

When Carrie came in she found him pacing up and down the room, smoking furiously. She shut the door. "What's the matter?" she asked abruptly. She always liked to get straight to the point.

Grantham motioned her to a chair. "Things ain't goin' right," he said shortly. "I don't know what the hell Raven's playin' at."

Carrie rested her big hands on her knees. "He's a bad man," she said. "It was wrong to let him take over."

Grantham threw away his cigarette impatiently. "Don't go over that again!" he snapped. "I couldn't stop him. He's playin' some deep game, and I don't know what's at the back of it."

Carrie shook her head. "One of his hoods threw vitriol over a hustler yesterday. All the girls are too scared to work. It's crazy, Grantham. Most of the business is done on the streets. It's only a certain class that come to the houses."

Grantham nodded. "We're losin' money," he said. "I'm goin' along right now to have it out with him. Before I see him I wanted to know about the Perminger girl. She all right?"

Carrie smiled. "Sure she's all right."

Grantham stroked his jaw with a hand that shook a little. "That dame may be very useful to us if Raven doesn't behave," he said. "You understand that, don't you?"

Carrie nodded.

"Where is she?"

"Upstairs. Do you want to see her?"

Grantham hesitated, then he stood up. "No. It's better not for me to see her yet. I'm relyin' on you, Carrie. You've got to keep her the way we want her—don't forget that."

"It's all right."

"He hasn't been here, has he?"

"I haven't seen him. Lefty's been in. He looked the girls over and took all their names."

Grantham's eyes snapped. "Did he see the Perminger dame?"

Carrie nodded. "Sure. He went all over the house. He came in unexpected. I couldn't get her out of the way."

"Did he speak to her?"

"He spoke to them all."

"Did she behave all right?"

"I was right behind her." Carrie gave a cruel little smile. "He just thought she was one of the girls."

"You're sure? She didn't do or say anythin' that'd give a guy like Lefty ideas?"

"It was all right, I tell you," Carrie said a little shortly. Grantham sighed. "I'm tippin' you, Carrie. If Raven knew about this, he'd finish both of us."

Carrie shrugged a little. "Maybe it'd be better to get rid of her," she said. "It's a pity. She's a nice bit of meat."

Grantham suddenly stiffened. "You ain't usin' her?"

"Why not? She uses food, don't she? I don't have dead heads around here."

"You mean you've hired her out?"

"Only to the guys who I can trust. She doesn't know who's a stranger or not. If she opens her mouth she'll get another lickin'. You'd be surprised how she hates a lickin'." Carrie laughed.

Grantham shook his head. "I don't like it," he said.

"I know what's right," Carrie returned. "She's lost all her starch now—that was the only way to make her lose it."

"All right, I'll leave it to you," Grantham said, opening the door. "I'll go and see Raven."

When he had gone Carrie went upstairs. She went into the big reception-room, where the girls were getting ready for the evening's work.

Lulu was painting her nails. Julie and Andree were doing some limbering-up exercises. Fan, her face screwed up with concentration and the tip of her tongue protruding, was writing a letter. In the far corner of the room Sadie sat in a yellow wrap, reading the newspaper.

They all looked up when Carrie came in. Fan sneered and returned to her letter. Carrie was aware of the long look of hatred that she got from Sadie. That didn't worry her any.

She said, "You—I want you."

Sadie put down the newspaper and got to her feet. Her face was now a hard, cold mask. "What is it?"

"Come on out here. I want to talk to you."

They went out together. Sadie followed Carrie into her own little room.

"You hate me, don't you?" Carrie said with a little grin. "Well, that's all right. But you'd hate the guy who got you here a damn sight more, wouldn't you?"

Sadie stood by the door. She didn't say anything.

Carrie said, "Do you know why you're here?"

Still Sadie didn't say anything. Her eyes smouldered with bitter hatred for the mulatto.

"You've seen too much," Carrie told her. "You saw the guy who killed Mendetta."

Sadie flinched.

"Yeah," Carrie went on, "he's a bad guy. He runs this house. One of these days, baby, you're goin' to get a chance of puttin' that guy where you want him. That'll make you happy, won't it?"

Sadie clenched her fists. "One of these days," she said, "I'm goin' to even the score out all round. You don't think you can get away with this for ever. You've turned me into one of these women because I haven't got the guts to fight you, but I'm not forgetting. Make no mistake about that."

Carrie laughed. "Go back to your room. You've got to work tonight."

Sadie went out silently.

3

August 17th, 10:30 p.m.

Lefty walked softly down the dark alley, his hands in his coat pockets, his hat drawn well over his eyes, and a cigarette glowed in the darkness, moving up and down as he shifted it in his mouth.

Spade's big garage ran half the block, and Lefty was walking down the alley that ran immediately behind it. As he came to a lighted window he threw his cigarette away. Stretching up, he took one quick look into the room, saw Spade sitting there checking a ledger, and grinned.

He went on until he came to the back door and let himself in. He moved quietly down the dark passage. Faintly he could hear the crews in the garage washing the cabs down. He could hear the murmur of voices and an occasional laugh.

He knocked gently on Spade's office door and went in. Spade looked up sharply. His face cleared when he saw Lefty. "Come in," he said. "Raven sent you?"

Lefty shut the door softly. "Yeah," he said. "You got a little trouble, ain't you?"

"Sit down. I'm glad you've come. It's time we had a talk. Why didn't Raven come himself?"

"He's busy," Lefty said, still standing. "You know a lot, don't you?"

Spade shrugged. "You mean about Raven? Why, sure. It's my job to know things. Raven's been behind Grantham since Mendetta was bumped. I know that too."

Lefty nodded. "Bright boy," he said. "What else do you know?"

Spade reached for a pipe and began to load it. "I know, for some reason or other, Raven's driven the girls off the streets. It ain't that he wants a clean town. Raven ain't that sort of a guy. He's done it for something that'll fill his pockets, but I don't like it."

"Too bad," Lefty said, and smiled mirthlessly.

Spade struck a match and for a moment his big face was hidden behind blue smoke. "I want to know why," he said.

"You know a lot. Why don't you find out?"

"If you're goin' to take that angle, I will," Spade snapped, his face darkening. "Listen, Lefty, this isn't the way to take it. I'm willin' to work with you boys, but I can't let you ruin my trade. What the hell is all this about? Can't you see you ain't doin' yourselves any good clearin' the streets like this?"

"Raven thinks it's a grand idea."

"Well, I don't. I'm tellin' you it's gotta stop." Spade thumped his fist on the desk. "I thought you'd come along to talk business."

Lefty shook his head. "Nope, we can't help you, buddy. The girls stay off the streets."

Spade nodded. "Okay," he said. "Then you can't blame me if it gets tough for you boys. I ain't givin' way on it. I can't afford to. I'll give you till next week. If the girls ain't workin' then I'll have to start somethin'."

Lefty took a blunt-nose automatic from his pocket. "You'll just be a big smell in the ground, buddy," he said evenly. "Raven sends this with his love."

The automatic cracked once. Spade half rose from his chair. A big blot of blood suddenly appeared between his eyes. He spread out his hands and then fell forward over the desk.

Lefty ran over to the window, threw it up and climbed into the dark alley. He ran very quickly to the car parked at the end of the alley. Maltz swung the door open for him and Little Joe started the car rolling. Long before Spade had been found the car was out of sight.

Maltz said, "Did you get him?"

"Sure. He went out like a light. Raven was right. He knew too much," Lefty said.

Little Joe said uneasily, "There'll be a hell of a row about this."

"Aw, shut up!" Lefty snarled. "It's time we got tough in this burg. I've been fed up just hangin' around chasin' dames off the street."

"Where the hell's it goin' to get us?" Little Joe said, heading towards the St. Louis Hotel. "Ain't we got enough dough?"

Maltz said very softly, "Turnin' yellow, Joe?"

Little Joe said hastily, "No. I was just wonderin'."

"Well, don't wonder, then."

They drove the rest of the way in silence.

Raven was waiting for them. His thin, wolfish face was hard and set as they came in. "Well?" he said.

Lefty nodded. "It's okay," he said. "Nobody saw me."

Raven took a turn up and down the room. "We're goin' to get goin' now," he said. "Grantham's been in. He's yellin' about bad business. I want you and Maltz to come with me. We're goin' to look Mendetta's houses over."

Lefty nodded. "I've got the list of dames in each house," he said. "Shall I bring it along?"

"Of course." Raven went to the door. "Let's go."

In the car Lefty said, "Carrie's house is the best one." Raven nodded. "We'll go there."

When they ran up the steps the negro Joe thought they were the cops. He rang the alarm bell. Carrie appeared on the scene, her eyes snapping with fury. When she saw Lefty she ran towards him. "What the hell's this?" she said angrily. "Do you want to ruin my business?"

Lefty pushed her on one side. "Keep your chest in place," he said. "The big shot's come to look the joint over."

Carrie turned quickly. She had never seen Raven, although she had heard a lot about him. She said, "You can't come in here. I've got my customers to think of. The girls are busy."

Raven looked her up and down. "Clear all your customers out," he said shortly; "I want to look the girls over. Come on, jump to it."

Carrie said, "Like hell I will. You come in the morning."

Raven looked at Maltz, who swung his fist, hitting Carrie very hard on the side of her jaw. She went down in a heap on the floor.

"You heard me the first time, nigger," Raven said.

Carrie got slowly to her feet. A livid mark showed on her yellow skin. She turned and went away slowly.

Raven said, "The girls I select will be taken to Franky's place. The other girls can pack up and get out. Do you understand that?"

Maltz nodded. He went to the front door and signalled.

A large van drew up to the curb and four men got out. They stood waiting.

It was early. There were only three clients in the house. They came downstairs, looking scared.

Raven opened the door for them. "It's all right," he said with his crooked grin. "Just checkin' up. You boys can get off home."

They looked at him furtively and left quickly. Carrie stood at the bottom of the stairs, waiting.

Raven nodded at her. "Bring all your girls down here fast," he said.

Carrie went upstairs again. A few minutes later she came down, followed by seven lightly clad girls.

Raven went into the reception-room. "Come in here," he said.

The girls all looked at Carrie, who was nearly speechless with rage. "Go on in. Didn't you hear him?" she snarled.

The girls went into the room and stood staring at Raven. Lulu fluffed up her hair. "Take me, darlin'," she said. "I'll show you some tricks."

The other girls giggled.

Raven said, "Shut up!" Then he turned to Maltz. "Are they all here?"

Maltz took out his list and checked the numbers. "One ain't," he said briefly.

Raven looked over at Carrie. "I said all of them."

Carrie hesitated a moment, then went upstairs again. After a few minutes Sadie followed her down.

Raven's eyes lit up a little when he saw her. This one was good, he told himself. When he looked at her he saw her go suddenly very white and her step falter. Carrie took her arm and shoved her forward. She muttered something that Raven didn't hear. He made a mental note to look into this. Sadie stood beside the other girls, her dark eyes big with fear, gazing steadily at Raven. It made him a little uncomfortable.

He looked away from her. "I've got somethin' to say to you girls," he said abruptly. "I'm Raven. I run this racket. There's goin' to be some changes. Get into a line, you girls. Snap to it!"

A little buzz filled the room as the girls stared at him. Maltz stepped forward. "Quiet," he said loudly. "Get into a line. Go on, damn you, get into a line!"

They slowly formed into a line and stood giggling and nudging each other.

Raven lit a cigarette. "Take your things off. All of 'em. Your stockings as well."

"I ain't takin' orders from a bum like that. What's the game, Carrie?" Lulu shrilled.

Raven made a little sign to Maltz. Maltz stepped forward and dragged Lulu out of the line. He slapped her twice across her face with his open palm, before she could dodge, and then he shoved her back into the line again.

She was so dazed by the heavy blows she could only rock on her heels, blinking away the tears that had started to her eyes.

Raven said, "The next dame who cracks wise will get a boot. Get undressed."

Muttering angrily, the girls took off their things. Raven stood by watching them. "Now stand still and let me look at you."

Sadie was the only one who didn't undress. Maltz took a step towards her, but Raven stopped him. He looked the girls over as if he were inspecting cattle. Then he grunted: "They're all right. Take the lot."

Little Joe, who was standing by the doorway with a large embarrassed grin on his face, clapped his hands. "Break it up, girls," he said. "Get dressed quick. We're goin' for a ride."

Raven beckoned to Maltz. "What's that dame's name?" he asked, pointing to Sadie.

Maltz consulted his list and then told him.

Raven nodded. "Take her to the St. Louis. I want to talk to her. Lock her up. See she doesn't start anythin', an' keep your hands off her."

Maltz looked hurt. "Gee!" he said. "I could use a honey like that."

"If you touch her, I'll fix you," Raven snarled. "Get on with it." He turned to Carrie. "Get all these girls upstairs. Get 'em dressed to go out. Tell 'em to bring stuff for a night and you come yourself. Hurry."

Carrie opened her mouth to say something, but thought better of it. She shepherded the girls out of the room.

Upstairs, she turned on Sadie. "You're not to tell that guy you know him," she said. "Do you understand? When the time's right, then you can fix him… not before."

Sadie didn't say anything.

Carrie went on: "If you blow the gaff I'll come after you. I'll find you okay. Then I'll do things to you until you wish you were dead. I mean that."

Sadie flinched away from her and continued to dress. The other girls were puzzled and angry. All their questions were met with a stony stare from Carrie. All she would say was, "He's the boss—ask him."

Downstairs, Raven jerked his head to Lefty. "Come on, we've got a lotta houses to look at before we sleep. These guys will look after the girls. Watch that pippin, Maltz."

Maltz nodded. "You bet," he said sourly. "I'll watch her."

Raven and Lefty went out and drove away.

Little Joe came up to Maltz. "This racket's gettin' interestin', ain't it?" he said. "That's the best bit of striptease I've seen for a long time."

Maltz ignored him.

4

August 18th, 2:10 a.m.

Raven walked into the lobby of the St. Louis Hotel, followed by Little Joe and Lefty. He went immediately to the elevator which took him up to his suite.

Little Joe leant against the wall of the cage, his eyes half closed and a look of tired satisfaction softening the lines of his face. "I ain't seen so many floosies all at one time in my life," he said. "Gee! Some of them were hot numbers."

Lefty shrugged. "So much meat to me," he said. "I've got no use for it when it's tossed at me like that."

"Shut up, you two!" Raven said savagely. He had had a trying evening, but the first step of his scheme was successfully launched.

They went into the suite. Maltz was sitting in a large chair, dozing. He started up as they came in.

Raven looked at him hard. "She all right?"

Maltz rubbed his eyes. "Yeah," he said; "she's sleepin' in there."

Raven nodded and sat down. He tossed his hat on to the table. "Get me a drink, one of you," he said, lighting a cigarette.

Little Joe went over to the wall cupboard and began to fix drinks.

Raven stretched. "Right now," he said, "there ain't a girl hustling in this town." He said it with great satisfaction. "Over at Franky's we've got a hundred and forty picked hustlers. The rest of the stuff is finished. Tomorrow we're calling a meeting of bookers. I'm goin' to explain what they've got to do. In another week we'll reopen the houses. Then we'll make money."

Maltz took a whisky from Little Joe. "What are the bookers supposed to do?"

"They're goin' to work for a change," Raven said grimly. "We've got twenty houses. Each house can take thirty hustlers. We've got a hundred and forty already. They got to get me four hundred and sixty new girls. They've got to get them fast. I've been working this out. We can get girls from Kansas City, Jefferson City, Denver, Springfield, and Cleveland. Once I get these houses started we'll organize houses in these towns as well. In every case we're goin' to secure a monopoly. Hustlers are not to work on the streets. We can't check on their earnings if they do. This'll take time. It's goin' to be big. The bookers will have to organize themselves and have a clearing-post. This can be at Sedalia. I don't care how they get the stuff. That's their look-out. The girls will only stay at one house for a week, then they'll be moved on to another house. Grantham's got to do some work. I'm takin' him out of the 22nd. Any guy can run that joint. Grantham's got brains, but he's lazy. You three guys have got to get busy too. Give me two months and you'll all be makin' more dough than you'll know what to do with."

Little Joe's face fell. Actually he was already getting more money than he knew how to spend.

Raven finished his drink and stood up. "Tomorrow you guys beat up the bookers and take them along to Franky's. We'll have a general meeting and then I'll explain to the girls what's comin' to them. Get some of the boys. I want the tough ones. Tell 'em to bring clubs. We might have a little trouble with some of those dames."

The three nodded and left him.

Raven wandered up and down the room, thinking. He knew he would have to play his game very carefully. It was worth the risks. If he slipped up on the Mann Act he was sunk.

He tossed his cigarette away and went into the bathroom to wash his hands. He didn't feel like sleep. His brain was too active. Quietly he crossed the room and opened the door of the spare bedroom. His hand reached out and groped for the light switch.

Sadie said out of the darkness, "Who is it?" Her voice sounded husky with fear.

Raven turned on the light.

She sat up, holding the sheet close to her chin. Her eyes looked very dark and big and her face was the colour of chalk.

Raven came and leant over the bedrail. "I want to talk to you," he said quietly.

There was a long pause, then he went on, "How long have you been hustlin'?"

She didn't say anything.

He came round and sat on the bed. "If you don't answer my questions I'll hurt you," he said. "How long?"

She looked at the thin face, the cold, merciless eyes and the paper-thin lips. She said, "I was forced into this two months ago."

"Why?"

"I don't know."

"Why didn't Carrie want me to see you?"

"I don't know."

Raven said, "Get out of bed and take that thing off."

Sadie shook her head wildly. "No..." she said, clinging to the sheet. "Leave me alone."

"Do it," Raven said.

"No. You're not touchin' me. I'll scream—I'll scream...."

Raven hit her on the side of her jaw very hard. Her head snapped back and she went limp, falling against the top of the bed with a little thud.

He got off the bed, went into the other room and found some cord. He came back again, stripped off the sheet, turned her over on her face and tied her hands behind her. He turned her again and gagged her with her stockings that hung over the bedrail. Then he fastened her ankles securely to each of the bedposts. By the time he had finished she had recovered from the blow. Her eyes pleaded, but he didn't look at her.

He went out and came back after a few minutes with a small bottle containing some colourless fluid. He sat down beside her on the bed. "After tonight you'll do anything that I tell you without hesitation. I ain't got time to persuade you. I like a dame to obey. You'll obey after this."

He took the cork out of the bottle and, bending over her shrinking body, poured the fluid on to her nightdress, low down.

She jerked as the cold fluid ran down her body. A strong smell of turpentine filled the room. Raven got up and replaced the cork. "It'll take a couple of weeks to get over this," he said with a little grin. "But I can wait. I shan't have to do it again."

She lay very still, a puzzled look in her eyes. She couldn't understand why he had done this. She felt nothing, only the cold wetness on her skin. She could understand pain, she could understand beating, but this defeated her.

He made sure that her bonds were tight, testing the knots carefully. He adjusted the gag and then he straightened.

The puzzled look in her eyes suddenly gave way to fear. The fluid began to penetrate. She twisted this way and that as the horrible burning sensation began to grow.

Raven nodded. "I'll see you in the morning," he said, turning out the light, and went away, leaving her writhing in the heavy darkness.

5

September 7th, 2:20 p.m.
When Special Prosecutor Dewey said, "Don't you remember any testimony about Hines and the poultry racket there by him?" Jay Ellinger dropped his pencil and sat back with a gasp.

Hines's defender, Stryker, was already on his feet, shouting, "I demand a mistrial. Your Honour! Your Honour! I demand a mistrial!"

Ellinger whispered to the *Tribune* reporter, "It's over. They've been waitin' for a loophole like this."

The *Tribune* reporter shook his head. "Naw," he said, "they'll go on. This goddamn' trial will last for years."

But Ellinger knew in his bones that Dewey had made just that one little slip that would give the Judge the chance of getting Hines freed. Although the trial dragged on over the weekend, by Monday everyone knew that Dewey's tremendous work of bringing Hines to trial had to be started all over again.

Ellinger got his copy off and then immediately caught a train back to East St. Louis. He was determined to resign before he could be sent on some other job that would keep him from the work he had been impatiently waiting to tackle.

Since he had been away he hadn't heard one word from Benny. He had been so busy attending the Hines trial that he had not been able to check up with the home town news. Now, as he stepped out of the train, he could hardly contain his patience to get started.

He took a taxi to the *Banner* offices and went immediately to see Henry.

He burst into the office. Henry gaped at him. "What the hell are you doin' here?" he snapped. "I want—"

"Save it," Jay said quickly; "I'm through. I quit. I resign.... Get it?"

Henry relaxed in his chair. "Wait a minute," he said. "You gone crazy?"

Jay sat down. "No," he said, "I'm just through. I thought I'd get that in before you gave me another little job out of town. Poison ain't keeping me muzzled any more, Henry. I'm working on my own for a while."

Henry sighed. "Okay," he said, "I'll tell him."

"Now listen, Chief, tell me what's been goin' on. Anythin' new on the Mendetta angle?"

Henry lit a cigar. "Plenty," he said briefly. "Vice's been organized on a big scale here. From reports that I hear, whoever it is who's running the game is doing it on a real money-making scheme. He's got the monopoly here. The girls have been driven off the streets. You've never seen anything like it. You won't find one single girl poundin' a beat. Even the cops couldn't clean up a town as this guy's done. But he's got houses everywhere. At his own prices. The rake-off must be colossal."

"Who is it?"

Henry shrugged. "They say it's Grantham. He's payin' all the bills. The cops are so well oiled that they leave him alone. Poison won't let a word in his papers. The other rags follow his lead. Everyone is making money, as far as I can see, except the girls themselves."

"Any girls missing?"

Henry nodded. "The Missing People's Bureau has been taken over by a guy named Goldburg. He's in Grantham's pocket. No one does anything about the girls. They just write up particulars and that's all. The increase in missing girls is up forty per cent. They're gettin' girls in from outside too. The guys I've met who've been to the houses tell me that every week there's a new set of girls. They're drilled in every form of vice imaginable."

Jay rubbed his hands. "I'm goin' after this racket, Chief," he said. "I'll smash it or bust."

Henry looked worried. "It's too big for you," he said. "These guys are makin' dough now. They're dangerous."

"If I can find out anythin' to prove it I'll turn the whole thing over to the F.B.I.," Jay said. "I ain't tacklin' them single-handed."

"What the hell do you think the F.B.I. are doin' now?" Henry snapped. "They're just waitin' to pounce. This guy is so smart they can't move yet. If they catch him in the Mann Act they can move. But no one knows how he gets his girls across the State line."

Jay got up. "Well, I'm free. I've got nothin' to do. So I may as well look this over. If I can tie Poison up to this I'll do it."

Henry reached out his hand. "Good luck," he said. "If I'd the guts I'd get out of this game myself. I'm too old now to look for anything else."

Jay shook hands with him. "Leave it to me," he said. "If I want any help I'll come and see you."

Henry smiled crookedly. "After today, Jay," he said, "you and I've got to take different roads. Poison will make me go after you."

Jay went to the door. "Okay," he said, "I'll remember that," and he went out fast.

6

September 7th, 10:45 p.m.

The smart little dance-hall was crowded. Soft lights, heady swing, and laughter. It drew the girls and their partners like moths to a naked flame.

A tall, good-looking Jew, well dressed, a small diamond glittering in his tie, glanced carefully round the room as he sat at a quiet table. Particularly, his eyes dwelt on the line of unattended girls who sat chattering to each other, laughing and giggling, but hoping for a male to take them on to the floor.

The Jew examined each girl swiftly as his eye swept down the line. He selected one. She was pretty, young, with a nice figure. She looked a lot more lively than the others, and in a mild way was trying to catch the eyes of the guys who every now and then walked along to find a new partner.

The Jew knew that this particular dance-hall always had a lot more girls than partners. It was a happy-hunting-ground for him. He got languidly to his feet and walked over to the line. He made straight for the girl he had selected.

He said in a soft voice, "I'd like a dance if you'll give me one."

She got up at once. "Sure," she said. She knew he was a Jew, but he was tall and handsome. She didn't mind. They danced in silence. He knew his stuff and she thought he was a swell dancer. When the band cut out he took her back to her seat. He was satisfied she was the right type.

"That was grand," he said. "I'd like another later."

He went out almost immediately and signalled to a car, parked across the road. Then he went back to the hall. The band had started playing again, and he saw she was dancing with a little guy who kept tripping over her feet.

He sat down at the table. He was used to waiting. At last the dance finished and she went back to her seat.

When the short interval was over he got up and went across to her quickly. She saw him coming and got up with a smile. That was what he wanted. She was already getting used to him.

As he swung her through the crowd he hummed the melody the band was playing. He could sing.

She said, "Nice voice."

"Nice girl," he returned, smiling.

She laughed a little. "You don't mean that, do you?"

"Sure. You're so nice I can't believe you're here on your own."

She pouted a little. "I haven't got a regular boy."

"Then I'm lucky," he said.

"Don't be smart."

"When this dance's over, will you have somethin' to drink?"

She shook her head. "I don't."

"Well, come and watch me."

She didn't say anything, and the Jew grinned to himself. He was pretty experienced. This was going to be a push-over.

The band ceased abruptly, and he led her back to his table. They sat down together.

"I bet your Pa doesn't know you're out," he said, offering her a ciga-rette.

She giggled. "How did you know? Pa hates me dancing. I sneak out once a week. Even Ma thinks I'm in bed."

The Jew smiled. "You're a bad girl. I ought to take you home."

They both laughed. A waiter came and hovered near them. "Come on, have a beer," the Jew said. "It's from the ice here, and it's swell."

She said, "Just one, then, but I don't usually drink with strangers."

The Jew gave the order to the waiter. "You're quite right," he said. "A nice-lookin' girl like you can't be too careful." He put his fingers into his vest pocket and took out a little white pill. He kept the pill between his first and second fingers. The girl didn't notice anything.

When the waiter brought the drinks the Jew pointed suddenly behind the girl. "Who's that guy?" he asked.

His hand hovered over her glass as she turned her head, and the pill slid into the liquid.

She shook her head. "I don't know. Why?"

"I've seen him about a lot. Wondered who he was. Quite a guy, ain't he?"

She turned back to the beer. It looked very inviting. He raised his glass. "Hey, beautiful," he said with a flourish.

They both drank deeply. She shuddered when she put the glass down. "It's horrid stuff," she said.

He laughed. "Beer's an acquired taste, baby; you'll grow to love it." He pushed back his chair. "Come on, let's dance."

Halfway across the room she lost time. He changed step and steered her towards the exit. She suddenly grew very heavy and her hands clutched at his arms.

"I'm goin' to faint," she said in a far-away voice. "Get me out of here."

He was already leading her to the door. One of his arms was round her waist and he had to support her. No one noticed anything wrong. When they got out into the open she collapsed and sank down on her knees.

The closed car swung across the road and one of the doors opened.

The Jew picked her up and shoved her hastily into the car. The door slammed and the car drove away very fast.

The Jew watched the tail-light disappear and then he went back to the dance-hall. It was easy. He sat down at the table again and took out a little note-book. He made an entry. Then he put the note-book away and sat back, his eyes once more searching the line of girls waiting for partners.

7

September 8th, 9 a.m.
Raven opened his eyes. He had a knack of being instantly awake after a heavy sleep. He never struggled back into consciousness. One moment he was asleep, then next he was fully awake. He stared up at the ornate ceiling, feeling the soft comfort of the bed under him.

Three months ago he had been a bum. Now he was powerful, rich and feared, but he was smart enough to know it couldn't last. Some time someone would squeal, and he'd have to go into hiding. It would be different now. He had money banked in several banks under different names. He had a lot of money in the apartment. He could skip to Europe if necessary. That sent his thoughts in another direction. Why not skip out while the going was good? Grantham could run this racket now he'd got it started. He could go to France or to the Argentine. There was a lot of scope there for a guy with his brains.

He turned and looked at Sadie, who was sleeping by his side. He was pleased with her. She'd got class, she was a looker, and she didn't make trouble. He'd tamed her all right.

He leant upon his elbow and studied her thoughtfully. She had little dark smudges under her eyes and her mouth was a little slack. Still, she was a looker for all that. She'd last for another couple of months, then he'd send her back to one of his houses and find someone else. His hand groped for the bell, and he rang it. Then he climbed out of the bed and went into the bathroom. By the time he'd shaved breakfast had been brought in.

Sadie woke up. She yawned and stretched her long white arms. Raven poured himself out a cup of coffee. "Do you want some?" he said.

"Might as well," she said listlessly, climbing out of bed. She struggled into a wrap and went off to the bathroom.

Raven glanced through the paper and then chucked it on one side. He found a pile of letters on the tray and began to glance through them. Most of them were for bills. They were all addressed to J. J. Cruise, the name he had adopted when he moved into the St. Louis Hotel. The last envelope was bulky and it contained a catalogue of trains. He was reading this carefully when Sadie came back.

She poured out some coffee and sat watching him indifferently. A great change had taken place since she had gone away with O'Hara. She knew it herself. She could no longer struggle against this man. He had proved himself so utterly ruthless and hateful that her resistance had been completely shattered. She no longer lived. She sat about waiting to obey his commands. Her terror for him had long burnt itself out. It was just a matter of automatically complying with his wishes. She found that if she did what she was told he was bearable. They went out together, lived together and slept together. She had no animation, but he seemed satisfied with being seen about with her. She didn't care what people thought or who saw her. Her will had ceased to exist.

The catalogue revived his interest in the trains. He looked up. "Get that train outfit," he said. "Put it up in the other room. I'll amuse myself with it, I think."

She put down her cup and went out of the room immediately. Raven scowled and stared after her. Sometimes her obedience bored him. He wished she'd refuse so that he could vent his spite on her. He shrugged and, still frowning, continued to turn the pages of the catalogue.

The house phone buzzed and he shouted for her to answer it. She came out of the other room and, after listening at the receiver, said, "A Mr. Grantham wants to see you."

Raven nodded. "Send him up," he said.

She spoke again to the clerk and then went back into the other room. Raven could hear her setting out the tracks.

A knock sounded on the door and Grantham walked in.

Raven nodded. "Come on in," he said. "Nice little place this, hey?"

Grantham hadn't been up before. He glanced around. "Very," he said shortly, taking off his light dust-coat. He selected a chair and sat down.

Raven watched him narrowly. "Well, what's wrong?"

Grantham came to the point at once. "Ellinger's in town," he said.

Raven shook his head. "I don't know him."

"Ellinger is a reporter on the *St. Louis Banner*. He covers the crime angle. We've had trouble with him before. Now it looks as if he means to stick his neck out. He's left the *Banner* and has been makin' a lot of enquiries about me. I don't like it."

Raven sneered. "You guys are helpless," he said. "Scare him. Turn some of the boys on to him. He'll quit."

"He's not that type of guy," he said. "The harder we try an' scare him, the harder he'll stick."

"Then arrange a little accident. Don't bother me with these trifles." Raven finished his coffee. "How's the business goin'?"

Grantham nodded. "It's goin' all right." He sounded doubtful.

"Well, what is it? Ain't you satisfied?"

"Of course I am, but don't you think we're takin' a hell of a risk? Some of these girls will squeal. They're bound to. I think we ought to stick to the professional. Seventy-five per cent of the girls you send me are kidnapped into the game. It's getting tough keeping them in order. There's a big yap coming from Denver and Cleveland about the number of girls that are missing."

Raven laughed. "You're just a small-time hick," he said. "Guys don't want the professional type of hustler. They want fresh innocent stuff, and you know it. The guys that pay big dough don't give a damn where they come from or what song they sing as long as they have them. So you can't keep them in order. I've got a little jane who was traded. I'll show you how I've made her toe the line."

He called, "Come here."

Sadie came in. "Yes?" she said.

Grantham stared at her and then went pale. He recognized her at once. He'd been wondering where the hell she had got to. Carrie had been sent to Kansas City, and he had lost track of her. He had made efforts to trace her as he knew Sadie would be with her, and he'd failed.

Sadie looked at him, recognized him as the man who got her into this trouble, and flinched away from him. Raven noticed the changes in their expressions.

He said to her roughly, "Get out!" And when she had gone he turned on Grantham. "You know her?"

Grantham wondered if this was a trap. He eased his collar with a limp finger. "Yeah," he said, "she was one of the first girls I shanghaied."

Raven nodded. "That's right," he said; "I found her at the nigger's house. She's got reason to hate you, hasn't she?" and he laughed.

Grantham was very uneasy. He wasn't sure how much Raven knew. If Raven had an inkling that Sadie could name him as Mendetta's killer, surely he wouldn't have her around? He was so bewildered that he wanted to get away and think about it. He moved to the door. "So you think Ellinger can be taken care of?" he said.

Raven studied his nails. "Why not?" he said, pulling his dressing-gown cord tighter round his waist. "Make an accident of it... you know."

Grantham nodded. "I'll get it done," he said, and went away.

Raven sat brooding. There was something he couldn't understand about Sadie. First Carrie and now Grantham. They both showed uneasiness when they were in his presence and Sadie's. He went into the other room.

Sadie was kneeling amid the tracks and the big outfit. She looked up quickly.

"Old pal of yours, huh?" Raven said.

She looked at him searchingly and then went on adjusting the line.

Raven felt a sudden vicious spurt of rage run through him as he stood behind her. He knelt down at her side and pushed her over. She fell off balance across the tracks and her shoulders flattened a miniature station. She gave a little cry as the tin of the station dug into her flesh.

Grinning at her, Raven pushed her flat and then, amid the railway, flattened by their bodies, he had her.

8

September 8th, 10:30 a.m.

Jay Ellinger parked his car in the big courtyard of the Preston Building and asked the commissionaire for Benny Perminger.

The commissionaire shook his head. "He left here a couple of weeks ago," he said. "Mr. Caston would tell you where he went."

Jay followed him into the reception hall. After a delay of phoning the commissionaire jerked his head to the elevator. "Third floor. Sixth door on the right," he said.

Jay found Caston looking worried. He shook hands with him and accepted a chair.

"You a friend of Perminger's?" Caston asked.

Jay nodded. "I've been out of town for some time," he explained. "I wanted to get in touch with him. It's important."

Caston played with his penholder. "Well, I'm glad someone wants to find him," he said. "I've been worried about that guy."

"He's left here?"

Gaston pulled a face. "Between you an' me, he was hoofed out. I liked that guy, you know. He was a good salesman. Then his wife ran away from him. That put him on the skids. I've never seen a man go to pieces so quickly."

"What happened then?"

"He began hittin' the bottle. It got so bad that we couldn't keep him any longer. We all tried to hide it up, but the management got on to it in the end. He didn't get any business. We had complaints. It was a bad show."

Jay grunted. "Well, where is he? What's he doin' now?"

Gaston shook his head. "I don't know," he said. "The last time I heard from him he was working for an addressing agency. Not much in that, you know." He opened one of his desk drawers and searched, then he produced a little note-book. "He's staying at an apartment house on 26th Street. If you can do anything for that guy I'll be mighty pleased. He wants looking after."

Jay scribbled the address down and got up. "Thanks, Mr. Caston," he said, "I'll go an' see him."

The apartment house reminded Jay of Fletcher. He thought, as he went up the steps, that this Slave racket was not only ruining the lives of hundreds of girls, but its repercussions were affecting the lives of their menfolk. It made him all the more determined to burst it open.

On the top floor he found Benny seated at a table scribbling away at a furious pace. A large stack of addressed envelopes lay on the table and bundles of other envelopes lay around the room. Benny looked a complete wreck. He hadn't shaved for several days, and his eyes were heavy and glazed. A strong smell of stale whisky came from him as he lurched to his feet, nearly overturning the table.

He said, "For God's sake," and shook hands eagerly. "I've given you up. Sit down, buddy, an' have a drink."

Jay looked round the grimy room. One glance was enough to tell him that Perminger was up against it. He refused the drink, but lit a cigarette. Benny poured himself a long shot of neat spirit. He held the unlabelled bottle to the light and scowled. "Hell! Someone's been stealing this stuff." He said angrily, "There was half a bottle here last night."

Jay said, "Forget it. I want to talk to you. What's all this business?" He waved his hand around the room.

Benny shrugged. "I gotta live," he said. "It's a lousy job, but it pays for this." He tapped the bottle and winked.

Jay got up and wandered to the window. "You didn't turn up anything when I was away?" he said over his shoulder.

"Listen, I ain't interested any more." Benny's voice was sullen.

"Lost your guts?" Jay said.

"Yeah, so would you."

"Well, come on, let's have it. Have you found out anything about your wife?"

Benny poured himself out another drink. "I haven't got a wife," he said.

Jay lost patience with him. He came back to the table. "Listen. Don't be a heel. Your wife disappeared, didn't she? She's probably working for this Slave racket right now. I'm going to find her, and you're going to help me."

Benny's face was white and his eyes looked wild. "No, you're not," he said, speaking through clenched teeth. "She wasn't slaved. I've seen her. It was a trick. She's livin' with some guy at the St. Louis Hotel. I even spoke to her, but she cut me dead. Wouldn't even look at me."

Jay stiffened to attention. "You're sure of this?" he demanded.

"Think I'd make a thing like that up?" Benny said, looking at him with hurt, angry eyes. "Of course I'm sure. She's livin' with that guy in luxury. That's what she's always wanted. She was always bellyachin' about doin' the washin' and lookin' after the apartment. Now she's got what she wants. The dirty little chippy."

"You may be misjudging her, Perminger," Jay reminded him. "She might have to be there."

Benny sneered. "Don't talk bull. I tell you I spoke to her. She just looked through me. She could have got away if she wanted to. She was by herself. I followed her to the hotel. I found out from the porter all about them. The guy's name's Cruise. She's posin' as his wife."

Jay sat down limply. He felt the ground had been cut from under him. "Who is this guy Cruise?" he asked.

Benny shrugged. "I don't know, an' I don't care. I ain't goin' to start anythin' with him. If that's the life she likes, she can have it. I'm through with her."

Jay got slowly to his feet. He felt that it was only wasting time. He said, "Well, I'm sorry, Perminger. It's tough," and shook hands.

Out in the street he paused before getting into his car. On the face of it it looked as if the whole of the business had fallen to pieces. The only thing he had to go on was Fletcher's testimony, and Fletcher was dead. He got in the car and engaged the gears.

Who was this Cruise? Had he anything to do with Grantham? Could it be possible that Perminger's wife had really gone off with him and had made up the note about going to police headquarters? It didn't seem likely. There was something wrong there. He made up his mind abruptly to take a look at Cruise. If he looked all right, then he'd try some other angle, but if he didn't, then he'd keep a watch on him.

He drove over to the St. Louis Hotel and parked. He knew the house dick and went straight to his little office.

The house dick was resting his feet and reading the newspaper. He glanced up as Jay came in.

"Hyah, Harris," Jay said, shaking hands. "How you makin' out?"

Harris was a little plump guy, who lived in a bowler hat. He shook hands suspiciously. "Well, what is it this time?" he said. "I haven't been bothered by you for months."

Jay grinned at him. "I've been covering the Tammany Hall trial. Too bad that guy got off."

Harris grunted. "They'll get him the next time, you see," he said. "Now what do you want? I'm busy."

"All right, all right, keep your shirt on." Jay grinned at him. "Can you give me a line on a guy named Cruise who hangs out here?"

Harris's little eyes opened. "Aaah!" he said. "Now, I was wonderin' when you boys were goin' to get on to him. What makes you ask?"

Jay shrugged. "Curiosity. I've never seen the guy, but I've heard about him."

Harris wasn't to be drawn. "What have you heard?" he asked, looking cunning.

Jay knew there was only one short cut to getting anything out of Harris. Reluctantly he took out his roll and thumbed off ten bucks. He dangled the notes in front of Harris's nose. "No questions," he said.

Harris grinned and grabbed the notes. He tucked them in his vest pocket. "Well," he said, "I don't like him. I don't like the mob he has up in his suite. I don't like the dame who lives with him."

Jay waited patiently.

"For one thing," Harris went on, "no respectable guy associates with the kind of hoods that go up there. I've had my eye on him ever since he moved in. He's a mean-lookin' guy himself. I'll swear the dame ain't his wife. She acts sortta strange. She's scared of him. Three punks see him every day. They drive up in the staff elevator. You ought to see the way one of them dresses. Still, they pay all right and we've got nothing against them, but I'm watching 'em."

This sounded promising to Jay. He said, "Can I get a room on their floor, Harris?"

"Like that, is it?" Harris looked interested. "Yeah, I guess that could be arranged. Shall I fix it?"

Jay nodded. "Another thing. Maybe this guy's got a record. Suppose you get his prints?"

Harris sneered. "Talk sense. I can't do a thing like that."

Jay took out his silver cigarette-case. "Take this up to him. Push it into his hands. Tell him you found it outside his apartment and you think it's his. Then bring it back and let me have it. I'll take it to the F.B.I. for a test."

Harris gaped at him. "Jeeze," he exclaimed, "that's smart!" He took the case from Jay and got up. "I'll see him right away. You wait here."

He came back again after some time, his fat face beaming. "That's a laugh," he declared. "You've lost your case. He took it all right, said it was his, gave me a buck for my trouble and shut the door in my face."

Jay sat back limply. "Goddam it," he said with a weak grin, "that shows he's a crook."

Harris nodded. "I've fixed a room for you," he said, "you can move up whenever you like."

Jay got to his feet. "I'm on my way," he said, and left Harris still grinning.

9

September 8th, 4:30 p.m.

Lu Eller walked casually down the corridor leading to Raven's suite. He knew Raven was out. He had seen him leave not five minutes ago. He'd been waiting for him to go for a long time. Even now he'd got to be careful. Someone else beside Sadie might be in the suite.

He listened outside the door for several minutes, but couldn't hear anything. Then he knocked softly.

Sadie came to the door. When she saw him she started back, trying to close the door, but Lu'd got his foot in the way. "Raven in?" he asked pleasantly, tipping his hat.

She shook her head. "No—go away. No one's in."

That's what Lu wanted to hear. He smiled. "He said I was to wait. He won't be long."

Sadie was terrified of him. "You can't come in," she said; "wait downstairs."

Lu had heard tales about Raven and Sadie. "He said I was to wait here," he told her firmly. "You don't want him to get mad with you?"

She dropped her hand from the door and stepped back. Lu looked hastily up and down the corridor and then came in. He shut the door.

Sadie backed away from him, and then almost ran into her bedroom.

Grantham had been very plain. "She's got to go, Lu," he had said. "We can't use her against Raven any more. He's doin' well, an' any time she might spill it. Raven would tumble it at once. No, she's got to go."

Lu eased his fingers a little. He'd got to work fast. Raven might change his mind and come back any moment. Lu was a little nervous. She wasn't small and she might be stronger than he could manage. There was no question of shooting. His hand groped round to his hip pocket and he drew a short heavy-bladed knife from its sheath. He slipped the blade up his cuff, holding the handle hidden in his palm.

He went over to the bedroom door and rapped.

She said with a little catch in her voice, "What do you want?"

Softly he turned the handle and looked in. "Can you fix me a drink, lady?"

"Get out of here!" Sadie was frightened of him.

"Aw, come on, lady, Raven said for you to make me at home." Lu smiled at her. He edged his way further into the room.

"Get out, or I'll scream," Sadie said, retreating to the other side of the room.

"What's bitin' you, lady?" Lu asked, moving forward very slowly. "I just want a drink. Ain't anythin' in that."

He was halfway across the room by now. Sadie saw the cold, merciless gleam in his eyes and she screamed. Lu swore softly and jumped forward. The blade gleamed as it swung towards her. She dodged desperately, thudded against the wall and fell.

Lu grunted and stabbed down at her. She rolled away, the knife cutting through her sleeve and making a long scratch on her arm. She screamed again.

Lunging again, Lu nearly had her this time, but with unsuspected speed she again dodged him, and ran past him into the outer room.

Lu was getting into a panic. She'd have all the hotel up in a minute. He went after her. She was just opening the front door to get into the corridor. He didn't hesitate. His arm flashed up and the knife hissed through the air. Sadie heard the sound and flung herself sideways. The knife buried itself in the fleshy part of her arm. She fell on her knees with a faint cry of pain.

As Lu ran towards her a thunder-bolt struck him. Jay, hearing the uproar, had come to investigate. He saw Sadie lying on the floor and Lu coming at her, his face livid with fury and panic, and Jay launched himself full tilt at him.

The two men went down in a heap. Lu brought his knees up and tossed Jay away. Both of them scrambled to their feet. Lu's hand flew to his gun, but Jay was already on him again and they went down in a mass of flaying arms and legs. Jay brought over his right and hit Lu hard on his cheek-bone. Lu's hands got a grip on Jay's throat and they rolled over and over across the corridor.

Jay got hold of Lu's wrists and tried to break his hold, but Lu was too strong for him. Already the pressure on his windpipe was beginning to tell. His head seemed to be expanding like an inflated toy balloon. He drove his fist into Lu's face. The grip loosened as Lu grunted with the unexpected pain. Jay hit him again and wriggled clear. Lu recognized him then. In that split second of recognition Lu realized that this guy must not escape. Grantham had given instructions to shoot at sight. Now he was here, right in the middle of everything.

He groped for his gun, swearing because it had caught in the lining of his pocket. He jerked feverishly on the handle.

Jay came at him again, his fists hit Lu on the side of his head and face, smashing him to the floor. The gun came away from his pocket.

"No, you don't," Jay panted, stamping on Lu's wrist. The gun dropped on the thick carpet, and Jay kicked it away.

Lu dived after the gun, stooped to grab it, and got a paralysing kick that sent him hurtling down the corridor. He picked himself up and ran. Jay chased him to the end of the corridor, but Lu beat him to it. He fell down the first flight of stairs, and then, picking himself up, he beat it as if hell were at his heels.

Jay dusted himself down and went back to Sadie, who was half sitting up watching with fascinated eyes the steady flow of blood from her arm.

Jay picked her up. "Take it easy, sister," he said, "I'll get you out of here."

He carried her into his room and kicked the door closed. When he put her on the bed he ran back and turned the key in the lock. Then he went into the bathroom, grabbed a couple of small hand-towels, and stopped the bleeding.

She went very white when he took the knife out, but she didn't faint.

He said, "That's fine. I'll get you a drink. Just lie quiet."

He rang down to Harris. "Listen, bud, I've had a little trouble on up my floor," he said, when Harris came on to the line. "Will you come on up and keep an eye on me?"

Harris said, "What sort of trouble?"

"Now don't start askin' questions, come up an' bring a rod." He hung up with a grim little smile.

He fixed Sadie a drink from the small flask he always carried around with him, and then went out into the corridor to meet Harris.

Harris came up at a run. His big face was alight with excitement. "What is it?" he asked.

"If this guy Cruise shows up I want you to tell him that some hood tried to stab his wife. Tell him the cops took both of them down to the station. For God's sake don't let him know I've got her in this room."

"I can't do that," Harris exploded; "it'll cost me my job."

"Do it," Jay said shortly; "this guy won't go near the cops, I'm sure of that. If he gets an idea that I've got her here he's goin' to get very tough. If you do this I'll give you twenty bucks."

Harris's eyes brightened. "Let's have it," he said quickly.

Jay gave him the money. "Look, go into his apartment and get that cigarette-case of mine. Snap into it."

Harris returned in a few minutes, holding the case. "Here it is. Now what?"

"Just hang around the corridor until he comes back. You'd better make a good show or else that guy will do things to you." Jay left him and went back to Sadie. She was lying on the bed. Although she was still very white, she looked stronger.

Jay locked the door and came over to her. "I'm Jay Ellinger, late of the *St. Louis Banner*," he said. "You're Mrs. Perminger, ain't you?"

Sadie sat up, once more terrified. "No—no! You've made a mistake. I'm Mrs. Cruise," she said.

Jay sat down on the bed. He took out a packet of cigarettes and offered her one. "Go on," he said, when she refused. "It'll steady you."

She took it nervously, looking at him all the time. Sitting close to her, he could see the ravishes of time and horror stamped on her face. He could see the hard lines, the frightened eyes, and he knew that she'd been through some terrible experiences.

When he had lighted the cigarettes he said, "This is your chance to get out of this mess. I know you're Mrs. Perminger. I was talkin' to your husband a while ago."

Sadie looked at him, and then her face crumpled. She hastily put up her hands and began to cry.

Jay said, "Take it easy. You're safe now. Tell me. It's true, isn't it?"

She nodded without speaking.

"Now listen, Mrs. Perminger. It's goin' to be all right. You've got to take me into your confidence. I can guess something of what happened to you but I want the full story. You saw the guy who killed Mendetta, didn't you?"

She sat up, terrified. "Who told you?" she gasped.

"I guessed that's how they tricked you to leave your apartment, wasn't it? That would explain the note you left."

Sadie nodded. "I saw him coming out of the room. Then a policeman came and made me go away with that man you were fighting with. They took me to a house and kept me there. There was a negress who beat me. I tried and tried to stick it out, but I couldn't. She beat me every hour of the day. I had to give in." She sat up and beat her knees with her fists. Her face was twisted with fear and rage. "Do you understand? I wouldn't do what she wanted me to do. So she kept on and on and on. Every day they tied me to the bed. There was a nigger who stripped me.... Do you understand that? She let him put his filthy hands on me. He stood and laughed at me when she beat me. I tried… but I couldn't stand it any more." She sobbed again. "What was I to do? There are other girls, decent girls like me. They were brought to the house and men were sent into their rooms. I can still hear their screams. Beasts of men used to pay money—lots of money—to assault them. They liked them to fight and scream—they paid more and more money if they really fought. It was horrible."

Jay tapped off the ash from his cigarette. This made him feel bad.

"Then this man Cruise came one day. He inspected all the girls. He took them all away. I don't know what happened to them. He treated them as if they were cattle. He took me. He brought me here. I was to be his slave. Well, I was crazy. I refused. I told him to get out. So what do you think he did?" Her sobbing was so violent he could hardly hear what she was saying. "He tied me to the bed and he—he poured turpentine over me. Do you know what that means? He left me lying there all night. I was gagged. I couldn't move, and it burnt…. Oh, God! How it burnt!"

Jay thought: "Here it is. Right with the lid off. This is the stuff that I want. I can start somethin' now." He said to her, "Grantham? Does he come into this?"

She nodded miserably. "He works for Cruise," she gasped. "He comes here and they talk. I've heard things. They got houses all over the town. They get girls from Denver, from Springfield—everywhere. Don't you understand? They're good girls. They take them from their homes and they make them do this work. Oh, you must stop it! You must stop it!"

Jay patted her hand. "I'll stop it," he said grimly. He got up and reached for the phone. "Give me the Federal Bureau of Investigation," he said.

10

September 8th, 5 p.m.

Grantham looked round the large room, his face cold and sneering. There were some thirty girls standing around the room. Some of them had on wraps, others just wore knickers and black stockings. They were all looking sullen and were only suppressing their fury because Madam, a big, hard-featured woman, stood behind Grantham.

Grantham said, "You girls've got to shake up your ideas. We've done badly here this week. I'm going to try a little experiment. Next week you'll all go on a commission basis. See how you get on with that." There was a low murmur from the girls. Madam said, "Shut up, you!"

Grantham's lips twisted into a sneering smile. He turned to Madam. "You've been too soft with these bitches," he said. "Get hold of the ringleaders and turn them over to my men. They'll knock the starch out of them. What the hell do they think they're here for—fun?"

Out of the crowd of girls Fan suddenly pressed forward. "Hey, bastard," she said, "let me tell you something. Since you've taken over, we girls ain't had any breaks. We don't get money. We don't know how much we've earned. Now you say you're just giving us commission."

Grantham looked her over. "Who do you think you're talkin' to?" he said.

"Heel number one," Fan returned. "I for one ain't goin' to take any more from you—see?"

Grantham turned to Madam. "What you waitin' for? That's one of 'em who wants handlin'."

Madam walked over to Fan, who stood her ground, her eyes flashing dangerously. She said, "Lay off, or you'll get hurt."

There was a long pause, then the door jerked open and Lu came in with a rush. His face was covered with livid bruises and his collar and tie were missing.

Grantham stared at him. "What the hell—?"

"Come on, boss," Lu panted, "I've got a car outside. The lid's blown off. Let's go."

"You mad?" Grantham said, forgetting that the girls were listening curiously.

"I tell you we've got to beat it. That swine Ellinger's got the Perminger dame. She'll spill everything."

Grantham went white with rage. "I told you to get her," he snarled.

"I know—I know. Don't stand arguing. I tried. He got there first. Come on, boss."

Grantham turned to the door. Fan got in his way and he shoved her to one side. "Get out of my way, you cow!" he shouted.

Fan seemed to go mad. She sprang at him, shrieking for the other girls to join in. Grantham flung her away, and then went down under a heap of furious harpies.

Lu hesitated, then turned and bolted for the door. Julie threw herself in his way and they went down on the floor together. Three other girls piled on top of him.

Fan was shrieking like a madwoman. "Give it to the swines! Tear 'em apart!" she yelled, making a dive at Madam, who ran screaming out of the room.

Grantham fought his way to his feet, hitting out right and left with his fists. He was badly frightened. It was only by swinging his arms violently that he kept off the claw-like fingers that quested for his face. He took a couple of steps back as the shrieking girls bore down on him, and then his heel was seized by one of the fallen ones and he went over with a thud that shook the room.

Lu was bawling for help as he twisted and squirmed under the mass of girls. Grantham had his hands too full to do anything. He beat them off a second time and got to the door.

"Don't let him get out!" Fan screamed. "Bring the bastard down!" She rushed across the room and flung herself on Grantham, biting and tearing at him with her teeth and nails.

Grantham swung his fist and hit her in her throat, sending her reeling backwards. He pulled open the door and got out into the hall.

Andree and Julie pulled him down as he reached the front door. Andree traced three livid marks on his face with her nails. Grantham began to sob for breath. He kicked them away and bolted upstairs.

Lu was helpless in the hands of the girls who had seized him. There was a girl hanging on to each of his limbs, pinning him to the floor. His clothes were in ribbons and his face was a mask of blood where they had clawed him. He screamed on a high note with terror as they dragged the rest of his clothes off him.

Fan fought her way to him, pulling off the girls and throwing them on one side. "Let me get at the heel!" she shrilled. "I'll teach him somethin'. Get out of the way!"

The girls drew back, their faces savage and lustful. They crowded round again, as Fan knelt over the sobbing man.

"Get a knife, someone," she shouted. "I'm goin' to fix this guy so he doesn't play around any more."

A knife materialized from somewhere and was handed over the heads of the girls. Fan seized it.

Lu gave a horrible strangled scream when he saw the flash of steel, and when she laid hands on him he nearly went mad. "Don't do it—don't do it!" he screamed. "No—no—no—aaah! Aaaaah!"

The girls suddenly drew away, leaving him lying there. A long ribbon of blood ran towards them so that they drew further back, shuddering.

Fan, her eyes gleaming madly, shrilled, "What are you waitin' for? Where's the other one?"

In a body they stampeded for the door. Andree and Julie had already gone upstairs. They could hear them thumping on a door.

Fan, her hands covered in blood, ran up the stairs, with the others behind her. They brushed the two girls away from the door and threw themselves forward. The door creaked and bulged, but held.

Grantham backed against the wall, terrified. He rushed to the window and threw it up. Far below him he could see cars passing and people moving about in the streets. He leant far out of the window and began to yell at the top of his voice.

Faces turned towards him. People stopped and pointed. Cars came to a standstill, and people got out to look at him. He saw a policeman move towards the house with a slow measured tread. Behind him he heard the door creak, and he yelled again, his voice going off pitch with terror.

Then with a crash the door flew open, and he spun round, his back to the window.

Fan stood there, her hair wild and her eyes savage. He saw the blood-stained knife gripped in her hand and he turned back to the window. He heard his own voice screaming in panic as he tried to climb out.

They all came across the room in a wave. Hands seized him and dragged him back. He went down under them with a thin wail of terror.

I I

September 8th, 5:30 p.m.

Raven glanced at the clock and stood up. It was time he got back to his hotel. He nodded to Maltz. "It's goin' all right," he said. "We'll have to open some more houses. The girls are comin' in now faster than we can handle them."

Maltz grunted. "The cops at Denver are workin' on this, boss," he said. "There's been a hell of a lot of squawks from that town. Maybe we ought to ease up on the girls there."

Raven nodded. "Sure," he said; "put a little more pressure on Cleveland. When things start getting hot, try somewhere else."

He went to the door. "I'm goin' back now," he said. "You might go over to the 22nd tonight. I'm expecting a batch of girls to come in. Grantham's gettin' too busy to handle that sort of thing now."

Maltz said he would, and Raven went out. He walked down the stairs, his face thoughtful. All the afternoon he had been worrying. He knew someone wanted to get his finger-prints. When the St. Louis house dick had brought him the cigarette-case his suspicions had been aroused. It couldn't be the authorities. They would never have used a broken-down flatfoot like Harris.

The last three months of easy living had not blunted his finely developed sense of self-preservation. He had got on too well to risk anything now.

Out in the street he hesitated before calling a taxi. Something told him that he shouldn't return to the hotel. Yet, he told himself savagely, he'd got to. All his dough was there.

As he neared the hotel he leant forward and told the driver to go straight on past. He crouched back in the cab and examined the hotel carefully as they went by. He saw nothing there to alarm him. Still he wasn't satisfied. He stopped the taxi at the next block and paid him off. Then he went into a phone booth and rang his apartment. The clerk said apologetically that he could get no answer. He asked sharply if his wife was out. The clerk told him he hadn't seen her go. Raven hung up.

By now he was a little alarmed. He wondered if Grantham knew anything. When he rang Grantham's office he was told that he was out, but was expected any minute.

"Where's he gone?" he asked.

The girl said, "To Madam Lacey's house."

Raven hung up and immediately rang Madam Lacey's. A hard voice answered him. It was a man's voice he couldn't place. He asked for Grantham.

"Who are you?" the voice snapped.

Raven sensed that it was a cop. He felt cold sweat suddenly break out under his arms. "Tell him it's Fleming," he said; "I want to talk to him."

"He's busy right now," the voice said. "Suppose you come down."

"I'll be right along," Raven said, and hung up. There was something wrong. He rang up Maltz.

"Go over to the hotel and sniff around," he said, after explaining what had happened. "Don't give yourself away. Just poke around quietly and meet me at Franky's in an hour's time."

Maltz said he would.

Raven came out of the phone-box and lit a cigarette. He hailed a taxi and gave Madam Lacey's address. "I want you to cruise past the joint slowly, but you're not to stop."

The taxi-driver said he'd do that and set the cab rolling. They reached the house in a few minutes, and Raven could see something was wrong. There were two police cars and an ambulance standing outside. A policeman stood at the door frowning at the large collection of people standing staring.

At the end of the road Raven paid off the taxi and walked slowly back towards the house. He kept on the opposite side of the road, his hand touching the handle of his hidden gun. He mingled with the crowd and stood watching.

Three patrol wagons came racing down the street, their sirens wailing, and drew up outside the house. The crowd surged forward, carrying Raven with them.

"What the hell's going on here?" he asked a guy who stood near him.

"They're raidin' a brothel," the guy said with evident relish. "Seems a riot broke out inside. They say the dames in there set about two fellas and killed them."

Raven started. "What do you mean—killed them?"

"That's right," a sheep-faced man broke in. "Two punks who ran the house. The girls got tough an' gave them the works—serve the lousy punks right."

Just then the front door opened and the police began to bundle the girls out into the street. The crowd raised an ironic cheer. The girls were herded into the wagons, cops applying their night-sticks to their backsides as they fought and protested. It was a real outing for the crowd. The sheep-faced man yelled, "I bet those cops'll have a treat tonight." The crowd raised a loud laugh. "Can we help you, copper," another man bawled, "or can you manage that little lot yourself?"

Raven recognized Fan, Julie and Andree. He noticed they were handcuffed. Fan was being very troublesome, and the cops were treating her rough.

Raven was livid with suppressed rage. Each one of those girls brought him in a large income. What the hell did the cops mean by breaking into one of his houses? Then he remembered what the sheep-faced man had said. Uneasily, he waited. The wagons moved off, and then two white-coated attendants came out, carrying a stretcher. The crowd gave a groan of satisfaction and shoved forward some more. By stretching his neck Raven caught a glimpse of a figure covered with a white sheet being slid into the ambulance. Almost immediately two more attendants came out carrying another stretcher.

"What did I tell you?" the sheep-faced man demanded triumphantly. "Killed two guys those girls did. An' serve 'em right, I say."

Raven had seen quite enough. It was dangerous to stay here any longer. He broke away from the crowd and walked hurriedly away. His brain was on fire with worry. Maybe Maltz would find out something. It was obviously very unsafe to return to his hotel. He passed a telephone booth, hesitated, and then went in. He rang up the D.A.'s office.

"Hackensfield?" he asked, when a man answered the phone. "This is a friend of Grantham. What's happened? What the hell are you raiding one of our houses for?"

"Who are you? What's your name?" Hackensfield demanded. He sounded tough.

"Never mind who I am. If you want to stay on our payroll you'd better get those girls off at once," Raven snarled.

"You're crazy. I can't do it," Hackensfield said, throwing caution to the wind. "Don't you know what they've done?"

"What have they done?"

"They set about Grantham and Eller. My God! You ought to see those guys. The things they did to them. I tell you we've got to prosecute. The authorities will demand an enquiry. We can't get out of this."

Raven felt a little sick. "You've got to!" he shouted violently. "If you get those girls to testify the balloon goes up. Once they start openin' their mouths they'll never shut them again. The racket'll go sky-high, an' you'll go with it. Listen, Hackensfield, you've got to stop them testifying. I don't care how you do it, but you've got to stop them. Do you understand?"

Hackensfield's voice cracked in his panic. "I tell you we can't do it. Two murders have been committed. The newspapers have got all the details. They'll splash it in every newspaper. The public will demand a trial. This is the most horrible and sensational crime that's ever been committed in this town. You'll have to get the hell out of here and leave it to me to handle. Can't you see that?"

"If you think I'm goin' to pass up nearly a million dollars of investments just because you're too damned milky to stop it, you're crazy. I'll stop it if I have to break into the gaol and shoot every one of those whores. Now do you understand that I mean business?"

There was a pause, then Hackensfield said, "It won't work. Think about it. Statements will be taken from the girls as soon as they get to the station. They'll find out that some of the girls have come from other States. The F.B.I. have already gone down to the station to see if they can horn in on the investigation. We can't keep them out. As soon as they know there are girls from other States they can take charge through the Mann Act. No, it's all up. Every one of us'll have to save his own hide."

Raven hung up and stepped out of the phone booth, trembling with suppressed rage. Hackensfield was right. The thing had come too fast for him to act. The F.B.I. would take over and he'd be on the run again. There wasn't a moment to delay.

He climbed into the taxi and gave Franky's address. He had to pick Maltz up, although by now Franky's wouldn't be safe. During the drive he took out his wallet and counted the amount of money he had on him. He'd got just over two hundred dollars. When he thought that he could put his hands on nearly a million dollars if he could only get back to the hotel, he shivered with rage and frustration. He'd got to get that money, even if he raided the hotel and took it at the point of a gun.

He paid off the taxi at Franky's and, holding the butt of his gun, walked in.

Maltz, Little Joe and Lefty came across the lobby as soon as they saw him.

"You got a car?" he snapped.

Lefty nodded. "At the back."

"Then let's get out of here," Raven said.

They went through Franky's place and got in the car. "Where to, boss?" Lefty asked.

"Drive around. I want to talk," Raven returned, lighting a cigarette. "Just keep moving."

The car swung away from the curb.

"Well, what did you find out?" Raven asked Maltz.

Maltz seemed bewildered. "The cops are in your apartment," he said. "They took Sadie away. What the hell's happenin'?"

Raven's face twisted. "It's that rat Grantham," he snarled. "I was crazy to have trusted him. I told him to get rid of Ellinger and he didn't do it. Now Ellinger's finished us."

Little Joe scratched his head. "What do we do now?" he asked. "Shall we beat it out of town?"

Raven shook his head. "Before we go we've got to have some dough. We're goin' to the St. Louis Hotel an' collect the dough I've got in my apartment."

Maltz said patiently, "I told you the cops are in there. They'll have found it by now."

Raven shook his head. "No guy's goin' to open my safe in a few hours. We've got to get that dough, Maltz."

Lefty said, "The G-men will be up there too."

Raven showed his teeth. "Yeah? What of it? We'll go up the back way with Thompsons. They won't have a chance."

The others looked at each other uneasily. "Those guys can shoot," Little Joe said nervously.

Raven nodded. "So can we. St. Louis Hotel, Lefty."

I2

September 8th, 6:50 p.m.

Campbell, special agent of the Federal Bureau of Investigation, smiled at Sadie reassuringly. He sat behind a large desk in a severely furnished office.

"Before you give me your evidence," he said, "I'll tell you something about this guy Cruise. For one thing, that's not his name. Fortunately, Mr. Ellinger obtained a perfect set of prints for us. We've had these checked. They belong to a man whom we know as Raven and who we've been looking for for some time. This Raven had a bad criminal record in Chicago. He made things too hot for himself and pulled out. He pulled out in a stolen car and crossed a State line. That gave us a chance of getting after him. We lost sight of him here, although he was reported to have been seen further south. Never mind that. As far as you're concerned, you're safe from him. We shall give you special protection, and until he's rounded up you'll stay out of town with a special guard. You're very important to us. Not only can you prove that he was the guy who killed Mendetta, but your testimony on his Slave racket will get him on the other counts we are bringing against him."

Sadie moved restlessly. "Will it take long?" she asked.

Campbell shrugged. "I don't think so. We mustn't underrate this man. He's clever, and he may still give us the slip, but with your help I think we'll get him quickly. Can you tell me anything about his habits? Did he like movies, for instance? You see, what we have to do in a case like this is to find out everything we can about a wanted man. They have their own little peculiarities. Some of them are crazy about racing. Sooner or later they'll appear on a race-track, and we catch them there. You see what I'm getting at?"

Sadie drew a deep breath. "He was crazy about toy trains," she said.

Campbell lifted his eyebrows. "Now, that's something." He made a note on a pad. "I was goin' to ask about that. We found a big outfit in his rooms."

Sadie nodded. "When he wasn't working he used to make me set out the tracks and he'd spend hours playing with the trains."

"Anything else?"

Sadie shook her head. "No. Just the trains."

"Did he smoke or drink heavily?"

Again Sadie shook her head. "Just average, I think."

"You've been through a pretty tough time, Mrs. Perminger," Campbell said quietly. "I hate to remind you of some things, but every little help you can give us will make our task less difficult."

Sadie said tonelessly, "I understand."

Taking from his desk drawer a thick portfolio, Campbell selected a large batch of pictures. "Here are photos of girls who have been reported missing during the last three months. I want to see if you can identify any of them. You were in one of the houses for some time and there is a chance that you saw some of them."

Sadie took the batch and went through them slowly. Campbell watched her thoughtfully. It seemed incredible to him that she should be so cold and calm after what she had been through.

She handed him back about thirty photos. "All these girls were one time or another in my house," she said.

"Can you explain how this business was worked?" Campbell asked. "Some of these girls came from Springfield, Cleveland, Denver, and such places. Did they come willingly, or how did he get hold of them?"

Sadie shook her head. "It was all horribly simple. He had special men who were always on the look-out for lonely girls—girls who weren't happy at home; girls who wanted a good time. They had to be pretty and young. When these men found them they either drugged them and took them by car to Sedalia, which was their clearing-post, or else they invented some story about an accident and got them to come that way. The method differed each time, but it was always a quick, simple plan that was unlikely to arouse suspicions."

"Sedalia?" Campbell repeated.

Sadie nodded. "Every girl I spoke to had been taken there."

Campbell reached for his phone and gave some rapid orders. "I'll get that place looked over immediately," he said to Sadie. "When they got them to Sedalia, what happened then?"

Sadie flinched. "Must I talk about that?"

"I know just how you feel, but if we're to save other girls from this business we must know all about it."

"From what I heard, the girls were put in separate rooms and left to sleep off the drugs. When they recovered they found themselves in bed with a coloured man. It was always a coloured man. Sometimes it was a Chink, or a nigger, or even a Philippine. They relied on the psychological shock to lower the girl's resistance, and in most cases it was successful. Some of the girls refused, of course, and then they would beat them into submission." Sadie shuddered. "No one knows what that means unless you've actually experienced it. To be beaten every hour of the day until your body is swollen and so tender that the weight of a sheet makes you scream in agony. No one can stand that, Mr. Campbell. I don't care who it is."

Campbell nodded. "I understand," he said.

"When Raven took over he had other methods of subduing girls. He poured turpentine over them. That was worse than the beatings." Sadie put her hand to her eyes. "Mr. Campbell, this man mustn't get away."

"He won't. I promise you that." Campbell got to his feet. "I think that'll do for the moment," he went on. "I'm sending you out of town to a quiet little place where you can rest. I want to congratulate you on your courage. After the things you've told me, it is remarkable that you've stood up to it so well."

Sadie stood looking at him, her face cold and hard. "Do you think I can ever forget?" she said. "My life's ruined. I can't go back to my husband. I can't settle to anything. I want revenge, Mr. Campbell. It may be wicked to say that, but I want to see this Raven suffer as I was made to suffer. Thank God those girls killed Grantham and Eller. If I could do the same to Raven I should die happy."

Under her glance of cold, malicious hatred Campbell turned uneasily away.

13

September 8th, 6:10 p.m.

Lefty parked the car just outside the back entrance of the hotel. There was no one about.

Raven got out of the car. His face was very white. "Get the Thompsons out," he snapped, looking up and down the deserted alley.

Maltz pulled up the back seat and took out three Thompsons. Raven took one and Lefty another.

Little Joe said uneasily, "Shall I stick with the heap?"

Raven shook his head. "We'll want everyone up there," he said grimly. "Don't forget, boys, there's nearly a million bucks in my safe. We split."

"As long as there ain't a million G-men, that'll be fine," Lefty said with a tight smile.

Raven walked quickly into the hotel. The porter, sitting in his little office, gave them a startled look. When he saw the Thompsons his hand went out to the telephone. Raven lifted the long muzzle of the machine-gun.

The porter gave a sickly smile and took his hand away.

Raven said to Lefty, "Fix that bird."

Lefty took two quick steps and the butt of his gun crashed down on the porter's head. The porter slumped down on the floor of his office.

"Fast, now," Raven said, stepping into the elevator.

The others crowded in after him. They were all very nervous. The elevator whined up between the floors.

Raven said, as the cage slid to a standstill, "Gettin' out's goin' to be a picnic. Shoot first an' talk after."

He stepped out of the elevator and began a stiff-legged walk down the corridor.

His suite was round the first bend.

Little Joe took off his hat and wiped his face with his sleeve. This was scaring hell out of him. He clutched his blunt-nose automatic, ready to flop at the first burst of fire.

Raven crept to the bend in the corridor. Every sound was muffled by the heavy carpet. He knew this was sheer madness, but he wasn't going to part with all that dough without a fight. If he got his hands on it he was all right. The thought of once more being on the run, without money, frightened him far more than a hail of lead.

He looked round the bend. Two cops stood in the passage looking towards him. They saw him at the same time as he saw them. He swung up his Thompson and gave them a short burst. The sudden clatter of the gun as it spat lead crashed down the corridor. One of the cops fell forward on his face, but the other darted into Raven's room.

Swearing softly, Raven ran forward, the others following him. The door was open, and Raven paused as he reached it. He had no intention of rushing in. Kneeling down, he swung the muzzle of the gun round the door, spraying lead.

A revolver cracked twice in reply and bullets thudded into the opposite wall. Raven glanced at the wall, saw the angle, which told him the cop was lying down, and lowered the muzzle; firing at the same time.

He heard the cop give a gasp, and he took a chance. He burst into the room, firing wildly. The cop was lying in a pool of blood, the top of his head blown off.

Maltz crowded in and, holding his gun at his hip, ran into the other rooms. There was no one else there.

Raven grinned at him as he came back. "Stand by the door," he said, "while I get the safe open."

He laid his gun down and ran over to the small wall safe. Feverishly he spun the little knob, muttering the combination out loud as he did so.

The others stood in the corridor, tense and expectant.

It took several minutes to open the safe. As he pulled the door open he heard the wailing of sirens in the street. He grabbed two large packets of notes that he knew he'd find there. "I've got 'em," he shouted, picking up his gun. "Come on, let's scram."

Just as he stepped into the corridor the main elevator door opened and several cops spilled out.

Maltz fired on them, falling flat. The cops opened up with a withering fire and Raven only just darted back into the room in time. Stuffing the packets of money inside his coat, he ran into the bathroom and threw up the window. Down below he could see police-cars drawing up outside the hotel and cops crowding out. There were a lot of them. He turned back once more and ran into his bedroom, which looked out on the back alley. He knew there was a fire-escape there.

All the time he could hear the gun-battle raging outside in the corridor. He couldn't think of the others now. They'd have to look after themselves. As he threw up his bedroom window he heard a crash of something exploding and then faintly the smell of pear drops came to him. Tear gas! He swung out on to the fire-escape. It wouldn't be more than minutes before they'd get after him. He raced up the iron stairs. Below him he heard a shout, and then someone started firing at him. Bullets zipped past him, unpleasantly close. As he threw himself blindly over the parapet of the roof one of the packets fell from inside his coat and landed with a little thud on the iron staircase. He knew he couldn't get it. It would mean exposing himself to the fire below. Cursing, he took the other packet and put it inside his shirt, then he ran across the roof top, lowered himself over another parapet, took a stiff drop on to another roof, and ran on again.

Any moment he expected to hear shots behind him. Now that he was on the rim he felt once more the bitter calculating thing of destruction he was before he made money. Every instinct was razor sharp, and even as he climbed across the roofs of the buildings he was already making plans well in advance.

He must get out of town. Stations and roads would be watched. He knew he couldn't get out of town without aid. He thought of the various people whom he had known, and bitterly he was forced to reject each one. There was no one he could turn to. Grantham, Eller, Lefty, Little Joe, Maltz and the rest of them were finished. He knew that. He was on his own now. He didn't mind that. He'd got money. That would always be his best friend.

By now he'd reached the end of the block. Peering round a chimney-stack, he could see the police climbing on to the hotel roof some distance away. They began to move very cautiously towards him. Well, they'd take a little while to catch up at that rate.

By his feet was a trap-door. He lifted it carefully and lowered himself into an attic room, drawing the trap-door in place after him. He knew the block was by now surrounded. He took the bundle of money out of his shirt and split it into four small packets. These he distributed carefully in each pocket of his suit. It was no use carrying the Thompson any longer. He put it in the corner of the room and then opened the door and walked into a corridor.

As he walked towards the head of the stairs he loosened his automatic in its shoulder-holster. The place seemed to be a block of offices. When he reached the second landing, rows of frosted-panelled doors confirmed this. At the end of the corridor he saw a gentleman's toilet. He hesitated a moment and then went in.

The only occupant was a window-cleaner, who was leaning out of the window. Raven eyed his uniform and realized his chance.

The window-cleaner, hearing him come in, looked over his shoulder. "Seems like there's a lotta excitement poppin' at the St. Louis," he said with a grin. "The place is lousy with cops."

Raven came to the window and looked down. A heavy cordon had been thrown round the block and the street was packed with interested sight-seers.

"What's it all about?" he asked, stepping back.

"Search me," the window-cleaner returned, still looking down into the street. "Some excitement."

Raven drew his automatic and let the barrel slide into his hand, then he dealt the window-cleaner a crushing blow at the back of his head.

14

September 9th, 10:25 a.m.

Jay Ellinger walked into the F.B.I. offices and asked for Campbell. He was shown up immediately.

Campbell got up from behind his desk and shook hands. "Sit down, Ellinger," he said, pushing over a box of cigars. "Make yourself at home."

Jay shook his head at the cigars. "Too early for me, thanks," he said, taking out his cigarette-case. "I just looked in to hear how things were going."

Campbell smiled. "You're free, ain't you?" he said. "I mean, you're lookin' for some sort of job?"

Jay looked surprised. "Why, sure," he said, "I guess I am."

"Ever thought anythin' about this racket?"

"What? A Federal Agent?"

Campbell nodded. "I've been on to Mr. Hoover's chief of staff. We think you'd make a good agent, Ellinger."

"Why, sure," Jay said eagerly, "I'd jump at it."

"Seeing that it was through your efforts this big Slave Ring's been exposed, we thought it only fair to let you in at the death. What do you say?"

"It's mighty nice of you."

"Okay, then I'll fix it. A Federal Agent has to sit for all sorts of examinations and has to go through all kinds of tests and training before he can join up. I'm goin' to let you off these for the time being. You'll work with one of my operators and you'll just be his assistant. When we've cleaned all this business up you'll be posted to one of our trainin' centres. Right now there isn't the time for it."

Jay nodded. "That's fine. You can rely on me to do as I'm told. I'd like to see the end of this guy Raven."

"So you shall." Campbell pressed a bell. "I'll get Hogarty to come in."

A moment later a tall, thick-set man entered. "Mornin", Chief," he said, tipping his hat.

"Hogarty, meet Jay Ellinger. You've heard about him. I'm sending Ellinger along with you. He might be able to help. When all this is over he's being sworn in."

Hogarty shook hands with Jay. He seemed pleased to know him. "You've done a smart bit of work already," he observed.

"Okay. Now what've you to report?" Campbell asked, signing Hogarty to another chair.

Hogarty sat down. "Well, Chief, he's got away. I'm sorry about it, but somehow or other he slipped through the cordon."

Campbell shrugged. "I didn't expect it to be that easy," he said. "He can't leave town, can he?"

"He'll be damn clever if he does," Hogarty said grimly. "The place is sewed up tight enough."

"What about the other guys?"

"Two of them are dead, and Little Joe's ready to squawk."

Campbell nodded. "You better see he's put somewhere where they can't get at him," he said. "What about Mrs. Perminger... she all right?"

"Yeah. We've got her out in the country. I've put three operators on to her and she's got a woman to keep her company. She'll be right on the spot when the guy comes to trial. Jeeze! Does she hate that fella?"

Campbell's face hardened. "She's got a lot of reasons for hatin' him," he said. "It beats me how she came through at all."

Hogarty climbed to his feet. "Women are tough," he said. "And when a dame hates like that Mrs. P., I'd sooner be a long way away from her."

"What are you goin' to do now?"

"Stick around. It takes time, Chief. If he's run to ground we'll have to wait for him. Sooner or later he'll make a slip an' then we'll get him."

"You're sure the town's sewed up?"

"It's tight. Every road's bein' watched. The stations are looking out for him and the airport too. No, I guess he'll have to stay out. It's a pity he got away with all that dough. It makes things much easier when they're broke."

"All right, take Ellinger along with you. Get after him, Hogarty; we want quick results."

Hogarty jerked his head to Ellinger. "Sure," he said, and as they went out he winked at Jay. "Maybe he does want quick results, but he ain't goin' to get them," he told Jay as they walked down the passage. "Sometimes it takes months before a guy breaks from cover. We just have to wait."

Jay followed him out into the crowded street.

15

September 9th, 10:45 a.m.

On the third floor of a shabby little hotel Raven slept behind the locked door of the grimy bedroom he had rented. He slept uneasily. A gun lay beside him on the soiled sheet. He hadn't taken off his clothes. Newspapers covered the floor so that anyone approaching his bed would, by the rustle of the papers, wake him.

He wore a smart black suit that the hotel owner had obtained for him. The hotel owner was a guy called Goshawk. Raven had paid him well and he hadn't asked questions. Already he knew who Raven was. Everywhere pictures of Raven proclaimed him as a wanted man. As long as he continued to pay Goshawk he knew he was safe, but he knew that if he was to make his get-away and have enough to start some other racket he couldn't stay long. Goshawk knew how to charge.

Raven stirred uneasily and then sat up quickly. His hand closed round the gun as he listened. He heard nothing, and relaxed.

The four grimy walls of the room oppressed him. He wanted to get up and go out, but he knew he daren't do that. Even from his bedroom window he could see a poster on a hoarding carrying his photograph. The F.B.I. weren't taking any chances with him.

He swung his legs over the side of the bed and got up. He glanced at the clock. It didn't matter to him what time it was, he'd got no place to go.

Moving across to the wash-basin, he bathed his face and decided to shave. While taking his collar and tie off he happened to look across the road at an opposite house. He stood still staring.

A girl, dressed in a white flimsy step-in, was wandering backwards and forwards in front of the window. She seemed to be doing a dance routine. By listening carefully he could hear the faint strains of a gramophone.

Keeping carefully out of sight, he stood watching her. His first reaction was that she'd be a good type for one of his houses, then his second reaction was a sudden forgotten lust that made him want her as he had never wanted a woman before.

She was medium height, with a mass of corn-coloured curls. Even from where he was standing he could see she had an exceptionally good figure. She drifted round the room smoothly, and then, as the record came to an end, she disappeared from view.

Thoughtfully Raven picked up his shaving-brush and began to lather his face. He kept his eyes fixed on the window. It was only when he'd finished shaving that she reappeared. This time she was dressed in a red-and-white-spotted dress, and she came out on the little iron balcony and looked down into the street.

Raven could see a lot more of her. Again he felt a pang go through him. A tap at the door startled him and he growled, "Who is it?" laying his hand on the gun.

"Goshawk."

He crossed the room and unlocked the door.

Goshawk came in with a tray. He was a little scraggy man with hard gimlet eyes and a heavily dyed moustache. He set the tray down on the bed.

Raven took him by his arm and pulled him to the window. "Who's that dame?" he asked.

Goshawk stared and shook his head. "Search me," he said indifferently. "Why?"

"Never mind why," Raven snarled. "Find out at once. Send someone over to that house and find out who she is. I don't care how you do it, and don't make anyone suspicious, but find out." He gave him a twenty-dollar bill. "Ten more if you get what I want."

Goshawk shook his head. "Make it another twenty," he said.

Raven, his face going white with fury, seized him by his scraggy neck. "You down-at-heel louse," he said furiously; "you try an' twist me an' see what comes to you."

Goshawk backed away hurriedly. He felt his throat tenderly with his grimy hand. "All right, Mr. Raven," he said, touching his forehead with a long bony finger.

Raven said through his teeth, "Don't call me that!"

Goshawk backed away and went out of the room. Raven locked the door after him and then went to the window. The girl had gone.

He turned back to his breakfast. A newspaper lay on the top of the tray, folded in such a way that his photo stared up at him. He picked up the paper savagely and tossed it across the room.

He had no appetite for his breakfast, and after a few mouthfuls he pushed the tray away and lit a cigarette. How was he to get out of this place? Everywhere his picture reminded the crowded streets to look for him. He went over to the mirror and stared at himself. If he grew a moustache and dyed his hair he might get some place. He could wear tinted glasses too. Yes, that was it. He found himself quivering with excitement. Goshawk would have to help him, but then Goshawk would know of his disguise. A cruel smile came to the thin lips. Maybe Goshawk would have a little accident.

16

September 9th, 11:45 a.m.
Goshawk said, "I found out about the dame over the way. Her name's Marie Leroy. She's flat broke an' wants to go to Hollywood. Thinks she's a dancer. She's an orphan, and can't get a job. At the end of the week she'll be told to dust."

Raven lit a cigarette. His fireplace was littered with stubs. "What's she goin' to do?"

Goshawk shrugged. "I'll tell you what she won't do," he said with a sly smile. "She won't decorate no guy's bed. That kind of a dame is a so-far-and-no-mother dame."

Raven sneered. "That's what you think," he said. "Given the opportunity, the time, and if you kid 'em enough, it's a cinch with any dame."

"Yeah?" Goshawk shook his head. "You ain't thinkin' of havin' a try, are you? I shouldn't have thought your mind was on dames. You've got your hands full, ain't you?"

Raven ignored him. He got up from the rickety armchair. "I want you to get me a pair of tinted eye-glasses," he said, "an' some bleachin' stuff for my hair."

Goshawk's eyes narrowed. "Thinkin' of pullin' outta here?"

"Nope. Just makin' myself look different."

"Okay, I'll get 'em," and he went out.

When he had gone, Raven turned away savagely. He knew that as soon as he stopped paying the rat dough he'd squeal. That type always did. All right, when he was ready to pull out he'd fix him.

He went and sat by his window, keeping just behind the dirty white curtain, and looked across at Marie Leroy's room. The empty window made him more lonely than he'd ever felt, and he just sat there smoking, waiting for her to come back.

When Goshawk brought him his lunch he was still sitting there. A pair of tinted glasses and a bottle of peroxide was also on the tray.

Raven ate his meal moodily, every now and then glancing at the window. His active mind was already making plans. After lunch he sat down and wrote a letter. He spent some time in composing it, and when he had finished he sat back and read it through.

Dear Miss Leroy,

I understand you are interested in a chance to get to Hollywood. I'm going there myself. Shall we go together? I've got a car and the expense of the trip is in my hands. This is entirely a business proposition and I'm asking you to accompany me on the trip as it is essential for me to travel with someone like yourself. I'll explain more fully when I meet you, which I propose to do in a few days' time.

> *Yours sincerely,*
> *James Young.*

He put the letter in an envelope and put it on the tray. When Goshawk came to take the tray away he told him to mail it.

"Whorin' by mail now, huh?" Goshawk said.

"Do what you're told, an' shut your trap," Raven snarled at him.

When Goshawk had gone he set about bleaching his hair. It took time, but when he'd finished the result in the mirror startled him. It certainly altered his appearance. He tried on his glasses. It still wasn't good enough. With a moustache it would be better. All right, he'd raise a moustache. It wouldn't take him long. He felt the little bristles already growing on his top lip.

He sat on the edge of his bed and thought. Today was Tuesday. Tomorrow she'd get the letter. At the end of the week she'd have to leave her room. It ought to work. She was up against it. This was a chance right in her lap. Thursday night he'd go across and see her. Friday night they'd go. In the meantime he'd got to get a better suit and he'd got to get a car. How the hell was he going to do that? If Goshawk knew he was pulling out, would he keep his trap shut until he was gone, or would he yap at once? If Raven promised to pay him a lump sum if he got away safely he'd have to keep silent. Yes, that was what he'd have to do.

Tomorrow he'd get Goshawk to arrange about the car. He'd have to steal some spare plates. He sat there making his plans until the room grew dim in the evening light, then, remembering, he wandered over to the window. Across the way she had come in and had put on the light. He sat down and watched her behind the curtain. She didn't dance that night, but sat limply in a chair, staring at the opposite wall, as lonely and as dejected as Raven himself.

I 7

September 10th, 10:15 a.m.

Raven regarded himself in the mirror. He saw reflected there a thin, well-dressed man, whose eyes were hidden behind dark glasses. His hair and slight moustache were almost white. It wasn't the Raven he knew. He was confident that no one could possibly recognize him.

He drew a deep breath.

"You look pretty good," Goshawk said, looking at him. "I guess you could walk past any cop an' get away with it."

Raven nodded. "I'll be tryin' in a few days," he said.

Goshawk gave a little snigger. "I'd like to be there to see it," he said. "Yeah, I certainly would like to be there to see it."

Both men smiled. Both men had their own secret thoughts, only Raven knew what was in Goshawk's mind. It was only by exerting tremendous self-control that he didn't smash his fist into Goshawk's face there and then.

When Goshawk had gone he went to the window. He felt strangely excited. Marie Leroy was getting ready to go out. She was adjusting a little hat in front of her mirror.

He hesitated no longer. Crossing the room, he opened the door and went downstairs. In the street he took several deep breaths. It meant a lot to him after being cooped up in that one little room. Then he hurriedly walked to the end of the street.

A policeman came sauntering past him, and Raven felt a little tightness round his chest as he passed. The policeman took no notice of him and at the corner of the street Raven stopped and turned.

Marie Leroy had just come out of her house and was walking towards him. He liked the way she walked. She took long, graceful steps and her body swung in harmony. He could see her breasts under the thin covering of her dress jerk a little as she moved. There was no doubt she was a honey all right.

He advanced towards her and as she drew level he raised his hat. The sun reflected on his pale silvery hair. "Miss Leroy?" he said. "My name's Young—James Young."

She stared at him. He could see she had very blue eyes. Then she said,

"Oh yes," and stood looking at him.

His thin lips smiled. "I guess you think I'm a little crazy, but I ain't. You got my letter, didn't you?"

"Yes. I don't know what to make of it."

"We can't talk in the street. There's a coffee-shop further along here. May we go there?"

He turned and began to move along the street. She fell into step beside him. He nearly laughed. It was a push-over.

"My letter may have been a bit mysterious," he said. "But when I explain, you can see how absurdly simple it is. Before we go any further, I'd like you to know that I'm a director of Lazard Film Company. I've just been back here to look up my old folks. I'm returning to Hollywood on Friday."

He saw her eyes sparkle. "Gee!" she said. "You really mean you direct films?"

He nodded. "Yeah, an' believe me it's a lousy job."

They entered the cafe and sat down. He ordered coffee and crackers.

"Now let me explain. I've got myself hooked up to an absurd bet, and I'm wantin' you to help me out. It's like this. One of the guys back in Hollywood was saying that every girl in the States wanted to be an actress. I told him he was crazy. So we got into an argument and one thing led to another until somehow or other I betted him that I could stop the first girl I met and could bring her back to Hollywood, and she wouldn't want to be an actress. Do you follow me?"

Marie Leroy nodded, her blue eyes puzzled.

"Well, sister, believe it or not, every girl I've asked so far wants to be an actress. Well, I've quit tryin'. I've gotta go back on Friday an' I'll have to say I was licked. Well, it sticks, sister. I don't like admittin' I'm licked. So I'm thinkin' I'll cheat a little. I heard from a guy that you want to go out there and you want to be a dancer. Okay, I'll take you there if you want to go, if you'll first of all come to see my boy friend and tell him you want to dance and not act. And if you do this I'll see you get in one of the dancin' troupes down there."

She said, "You wouldn't be kiddin', because if you are you're playin' an awful mean game."

Raven shook his head. "I'm not kiddin'. Why so serious, sister? Are things goin' badly for you?"

She nodded. "I guess they are," she said, looking out of the window at the crowded street beyond. "I'm broke flat and nowhere to go."

"Looks like your lucky day," Raven said, feeling the blood surging through his veins. "Is it a bet?"

"It's business, isn't it?" she said.

Raven nearly laughed in her face. What the hell did she think? If she thought he was going to drive her half across America and not give her a tumble she was crazy.

"You don't have to worry about that angle," he assured her. "You won't have any complaints."

She played with the handle of her spoon. "You don't mind if I'm straight with you, do you, Mr. Young?"

Raven shook his head. "I'd like it."

"I want to go. In fact, it is the chance I've been dreaming about, but it's too good to be true. I feel there's a catch in it somewhere."

"There isn't, but if you feel nervous about it, I won't press you."

She looked at him as if trying to read his mind. She didn't like the cold eyes or the thin mouth, but she knew she'd go. She couldn't afford to do anything else. She had to get to Hollywood.

She said, "Well, thanks, I'll go, anyway. Don't think I'm ungrateful, but a girl's got to be careful."

Raven nodded. "It does me a lotta good to see you hesitate," he said. "Some of the dames I've spoken to would have thrown in a lot of things to come with me. I don't like that type of dame." He finished his coffee and stood up. "Friday night about nine-thirty. I'll pick you up. Don't bring too much baggage, will you?"

He didn't offer to shake hands. Out in the street he raised his hat. "Thanks a lot for helping me out, Miss Leroy."

He watched her walk away and then he returned to his room. With a dame like that at his side, and a good car, his changed appearance, he'd get out of town. He wouldn't even bother to sneak out. He was confident that he could go by the main streets and even wave to the Feds as he passed them.

18

September 13th, 9 p.m.

The night was very hot and the moon rode high in tattered clouds.

Raven paced slowly backwards and forwards in his room. He had carefully drawn the blinds, and now he waited for the first step in his escape. In a few minutes Goshawk would come up. Around at the back was a two-seater car that had cost Raven plenty, waiting to take him to liberty. No one knew about his changed appearance except Goshawk. Raven's thin face twisted a little.

He heard steps coming down the passage, and from force of habit his hand slid inside his coat, gripping his gun.

Goshawk knocked and Raven let him in. The two men looked at each other.

"So you're off?" Goshawk said. "Takin' the little dame with you?"

Raven controlled his face. This guy knew all the answers. He shook his head. "Car outside?"

"Sure!"

"Is she full?"

"Yeah. Take you a couple of hundred miles, if you ain't stopped before then." Goshawk sniggered.

Raven sat down on the bed. "Well, I guess I'll settle up with you," he said. He took out a small roll from his side pocket that he had specially prepared for Goshawk. "Let's see, I've paid for the car and for a month's rent. I'll make you a present of that. Then I guess you'll want a little consideration for keepin' your trap shut, won't you?"

Goshawk rubbed his hands. "They're offering five grand for information that'll lead to your arrest."

Raven stiffened. "Five grand?" he repeated, staring at Goshawk.

"That's right. A nice slice of change, ain't it?"

Raven almost laughed. The fool had signed his own death warrant. No matter how much Raven gave him now, he'd squeal as soon as he could get to the cops. Five grand was too much money to pass up.

Raven got off the bed. "If I give you the same, you'll be happy, won't you?"

Goshawk's little eyes glittered. "Sure," he said. "That's fair enough."

Raven took another roll out of his pocket. "You'll find five grand here, I think. Count it." He put the roll into Goshawk's trembling hands and wandered away to the window. He lifted the blind a trifle and glanced over at Marie's room. He could see her moving about the room hurriedly. He guessed she was packing. Time was getting on. He glanced over at Goshawk, who sat on the bed counting the notes.

Drawing his gun and holding it by the barrel, he approached Goshawk. "You've got enough dough there to make you rich," he said casually, coming closer step by step.

Goshawk nodded, muttering figures as he laid the bills down on the bed. Raven was right behind him, and he swung his arm. Goshawk suddenly cringed and he gave a thin little cry of terror as he saw Raven's shadow on the soiled sheet, the upraised arm coming down and the gun, looking three times its size, in the big distorted hand.

The gun-butt cracked his skull and he fell across the bed, blood and brains oozing out of a hole that appeared suddenly in his head.

Raven stepped back hastily. He knew he didn't have to strike again. The blow had jarred his hand and arm badly. He stood looking down at Goshawk, a feeling of relief surging through him. The one man who knew enough to have him burnt was silenced for ever. Now he was free. All he had to do was to walk out, get in the car, pick up the Leroy dame and beat it.

He dragged Goshawk further on to the bed and covered him with a blanket. Anyone looking in the room would think that Raven was there, sleeping. He covered the head with a pillow and then he paused to light a cigarette. He glanced at the clock. It was twenty past nine. All was working satisfactorily. As he turned to the door his eye alighted on the wall calendar.

FRIDAY, 13th SEPTEMBER

It made him pause.

"My lucky day," he said with a forced laugh, and went out, locking the door and removing the key.

He met no one as he went downstairs. He let himself out the back way and at the end of the alley he found the big Chrysler waiting for him. He climbed in and started the engine. He could hardly believe that he was off, that he had a fast car under him, and that in a few hours St. Louis would be a long way behind.

He drove round the block once, and as the hands of a street clock moved to the half-hour, he drew up outside Marie Leroy's apartment house.

She was standing in the hallway waiting, and as he drew up she picked up two handbags and ran down the steps. He made no effort to get out. From where he sat he could see people peering round curtains all down the street. He wasn't going to let them give his description to the cops if anyone got suspicious.

"Can you manage?" he called. "The bags can go in the boot behind. It's quite easy to open. My engine's cold. I've got to nurse her along for a minute."

"That's all right," she said, and he felt two thuds as the bags were dumped in the back. Leaning over, he opened the off-door and she got in. She wore the same red-and-white-spotted dress, and as she sat down the skirt rode up. Her long tapering legs sent a little shiver through him. She pulled her skirt down and laughed nervously. "Some car," she said.

"Like it?" He engaged the gears. "We've got a mighty long way to go. I've been sleepin' all the afternoon an' I want to get as far as I can tonight."

She relaxed back against the upholstered seat. "I like driving at night. When you get tired may I drive?"

He looked at her. "Can you?"

"Of course."

This was something he hadn't thought of. If they took it in turns to sleep and drive they'd halve the time.

"That's fine," he said, and meant it.

He drove steadily, keeping to an even forty miles an hour. He had no wish to get an excited speed cop on his trail. Goshawk had given him forged license papers, but even with those he wasn't going to take chances.

As they neared the outskirts of the town Marie said, "Look, there's a barricade ahead. How exciting! You'll have to stop."

Raven eased the gun loose in its shoulder-holster and stopped the car a few feet from the swinging red light.

Three State troopers came up to the car. Two of them carried Thompsons.

Raven felt his mouth go dry, but he kept his head. Marie leant out of the window. "What is it?" she asked. They played a powerful light on her and then turned it on.

Raven, who had quickly removed his hat. "What's the trouble, officer?" he asked. "I wasn't goin' too fast, was I?"

"Let's have a look at your papers, buddy," the State trooper said, resting his foot on the running-board. Raven noticed that the other two troopers had relaxed and were no longer pointing their guns at him.

He produced his papers. "Here you are," he said.

Marie seemed to be getting on well with the other two troopers. Raven couldn't hear what she was saying as she was leaning out of the window, but one of the troopers laughed suddenly and he heard her laugh too.

Hardly glancing at the license papers, the trooper returned them. "Your wife, I guess?" he asked.

Raven nodded.

"Okay, bud, on your way."

Raven engaged his gears and the car slid past the barricade. A sudden thought had struck him. He'd got to be damn careful with this girl. What a fool he'd been not to have remembered!

She said excitedly, "They're looking for Public Enemy No. 1. A man called Raven. He's supposed to be hiding in the town. Isn't it exciting?"

"Yeah," he said, with a little grin, "but I've got some news for you that'll startle you. I was crazy to have brought you, sister."

Her eyes opened. "Why?"

He continued to drive. "Ever heard of the Mann Act?"

"Why, yes? What's that got to do with it?"

"Plenty. It's an offence to take any dame but your wife over a State line. There's a twenty-years rap hanging to it."

Marie's eyes opened. "But—but they let us through."

Raven's mouth twitched. "Yeah—I told 'em you were my wife. The car, the clothes and the general set-up passed us."

There was a long pause. Then Raven said, "Unless you agree to bein' my wife on this trip, we'd better turn round."

Marie stared straight in front of her. Then she said bitterly, "I might have guessed I'd have to pay one way or another for a trip like this."

Raven put his foot on the brake and the car came to a standstill. "Say the word, sister, and back we go."

She looked at him and shook her head. "It's okay. I dare say it won't kill me," she said, and settled once more comfortably.

Raven sent the car shooting forward. He knew it was in the bag now.

Neither of them spoke for some time. The Chrysler tore through the night, ripping miles off the State Highway. As the hands of the dashboard clock crept on the night grew colder. Both of them began to feel stiff and chilly.

Raven said, "Just ahead is Williamsburg. I guess we'll stop there for a drink."

Marie rubbed her bare arms. "I'll get a coat out when we get there," she said.

In ten minutes they reached the town and Raven stopped the car outside a small all-wood hotel. He went round to the boot and helped her get out a light dust-coat. He also took out a rug.

They went into the hotel together. The clock was just striking a quarter to twelve. They went into a deserted lobby and ordered coffee and rum from a startled negro waiter.

"Tired?" Raven asked, as they sipped the steaming coffee.

She shook her head. "We'll go on." She was very decided about it. Raven grinned to himself.

They got up to go when they had finished. She said, "Shall I drive?"

He nodded. "Sure, if you want to. We'll go on to Columbia, then maybe we'll get some sleep."

She bit her lip. "Couldn't you sleep now? Then we could drive all the time."

"So we could," he said. "You're sure in a hurry to get there, ain't you?"

And he followed her out to the car.

19

September 14th, 11:10 a.m.

Hogarty said, "Think it's Raven?"

Jay and he stared down at the battered Goshawk. Two cops who stood in the room watched them with bored eyes. They never had much use for Federal Agents.

Jay shrugged. "It might be."

"Let's go over the ground again," Hogarty said, turning from the bed. "The girl downstairs says that the guy who had this room never went out. Goshawk always took up his meals. No one else in the hotel ever saw him. That points to Raven, don't it?"

Again Jay shrugged. "Maybe," he said.

"Then the girl over the way. How does she fit in?"

"Suppose we talk to the kid again?"

They went downstairs, where a round-eyed maid stood waiting. Hogarty jerked his head. "Come inside here, sister, an' let's go through with it again. Your name's Alice Cohen, ain't it?"

The girl nodded.

"Your boss sent you across to the apartment house opposite to ask after a certain Marie Leroy—right?"

Again she nodded.

"Well, go on."

"He wanted to find out who she was. The landlady told me. She was a dancer who wanted to go to Hollywood."

"Why should this guy Goshawk want to know that?"

"I don't know. He didn't say."

"You never saw the guy who had that room?"

"No, but Mr. Goshawk sent me out for some tinted spectacles and a bottle of hair bleach. He didn't use them himself. I got to thinking they were for this fella who had the room."

Hogarty and Jay exchanged glances.

"I see," Hogarty said. "Anythin' else?"

"I heard Mr. Goshawk arrange about buying a Chrysler car. I was surprised, because Mr. Goshawk was always tight with his dough. I thought he was steppin' out a bit."

"All right, baby, you're doin' fine." Hogarty was excited. "I'll talk to you again in a while. Just stick around."

When she had gone he turned to Jay excitedly. "It looks like it. The troopers at the west barricade report that a blond guy with his wife passed through in a two-seater Chrysler." He checked himself from a note-book. "They say the girl was wearing a red dress with pinhead white spots. Let's go over an' find out if that's the dress this Leroy dame was wearing. If it is, we'll get after them. They're heading for Hollywood by the U.S. Highway 40."

Jay followed him out of the hotel.

20

September 14th, 11:50 p.m.
Raven said, "We'll stop at Odessa for the night."

Marie clenched her fists, but said nothing. The continuous driving had unnerved both of them, and Raven had lost patience. He wasn't going to drive like this day and night, with her sitting at his side. What the hell did she think? She wasn't just goin' to sit around all day and all night, letting him take her free of expense all the way to Hollywood. It was time she paid for her trip.

"It's a tough little town," he said, "but it'll do for the night. We'll stop again at Kansas City. You'll like that."

She said, "It'll take us weeks to get to Hollywood."

"Not after tonight it won't," he said with a little grin. "Time'll go fast enough after tonight."

She looked at him uneasily, but said nothing. A few minutes later they drove into Odessa.

Raven stopped at a petrol station and had his tank filled. He asked where a hotel was, and then drove in the direction indicated.

As they got out of the car he said, "Mr. and Mrs. Young, baby, an' don't forget it."

She walked into the lobby without answering. A negro came out at a run and took their bags. Raven went over and signed the register. The clerk blotted the ink, looked at the name, gave a little start, and glanced up at Raven searchingly.

"Anythin' wrong?" Raven asked, his eyes suddenly going hard.

The clerk shook his head. "Quite okay, sir," he said. "You've omitted to say where you've come from."

Raven took up the pen and scribbled "Jefferson City," then he turned away.

"A double room?" the clerk asked.

Marie stiffened.

"Sure," Raven said, smiling at her. "An' a double bed." There was no elevator, and they followed the negro up two flights of stairs.

"These hick hotels give me a pain," Raven said.

Marie found she couldn't answer him. Her heart was beating wildly, and she felt a little sick.

They went into a large, shabbily furnished room. The big iron double bed took up a lot of room. When the negro got his tip he left them with a broad grin.

Raven took off his hat and dust-coat and yawned. "How do you like it?" he asked, looking round.

"I think it's horribly sordid," Marie said with a little shudder. "Mr. Young, must we go through with this? You could have given me a single room, couldn't you?"

Raven grinned at her. "Sure I could."

"You said it was business. You said I didn't have anything to worry about. Can't you see this is all horribly sordid?"

Raven sat on the bed. "I've brought you so far," he said, "and I guess I'm entitled to a little consideration from you. But I won't force myself on you. I'll put it like this. If you want to go on with me you'll stay here tonight and be nice. If you want either to stay in this burg an' rot or walk back to St. Louis, then I'll go off now an' take the car an' leave you to it. What's it to be?"

She said, "Oh, all right. You've got me where you want me, haven't you? I trade my body for the ride. That's what you mean, isn't it?"

Raven's face twitched. "I thought of lettin' you down easy," he said between his teeth, "but if you're goin' to swap smart cracks you'll go the whole way."

She sat on the other side of the bed away from him and began to cry. "My God!" she said. "I've been a fool."

He suddenly lost patience with her and pushed her on to the bed. She saw the sudden lust that had come into his eyes and for a moment a scream hovered in her throat.

Raven said, "Don't yell." He pinched her jaw between two fingers. "Do you want to go through with this or shall I beat it?"

She lay flat on her back and looked up at him. She saw the blank lustful look that made him almost animal.

She could see the little beads of sweat standing out on his toad-coloured skin. She could see his body trembling and she could feel the vibrations shaking the bed. She wanted to say no, but she knew he'd have no mercy on her. He'd leave her here. She had one dollar and forty cents in her purse. What could she do with that?

So she shut her eyes, blotting out the strange inhuman face so close to hers, and through dry lips she told him to go ahead.

He put his hand on the front of her dress and ripped it. The thin material tore easily. She half sat up, but he shoved her down again. "Stay still," he said, his eyes blazing savagely. "I'll buy you everything you want. Stay still."

"No, not like this," she said, taking his wrist in both hands as he gripped her slip. "Please—it's horrible. Not like this."

"Let go. Do you hear? Let go."

Her hands dropped away as he ripped the silk from her and the hot night air slid over her frightened nakedness. She put both her hands over her eyes and began to cry.

Her long white body and her tight drawn-up breasts inflamed him. He reached out two shaking hands towards her, when a heavy rap sounded on the door.

For a second Raven stood paralysed. Then his instinct overrode his lust and he jerked up, his hand pulling his gun from its holster.

"What is it?" he said. His voice sounded cracked and hoarse to him.

Marie half turned on her side, hiding her head in her arms. Her white shoulders heaved with her crying.

"Come on out, Raven, with your hands in the air," someone called.

Raven turned very cold. His mind sprang to the clerk and the start he'd given when he had signed the book. He was trapped. He hadn't even the Thompson, which, like the crazy fool he was, he'd left in the boot of the car. He fired one shot that crashed through the door and he heard footsteps move hastily away.

Marie sat up on the bed with a scream. "What is it?" she said, staring at his gun. "Why are you—shooting? What—"

Raven turned on her savagely. "Shut up!" he snarled.

"Hi, Raven," someone called again, "you can't get away. The place's surrounded. Better give up. You've got no chance in the world."

"Come an' get me!" he shouted back savagely, sending another shot through the door.

"Raven?" Marie gasped. "Are you Raven?"

He turned on her. "Yeah. Now you know, you stupid little bitch. You got me outta town, do you understand? Now, by God, you'll get me out of here too!"

Shoving his gun into his side pocket, he grabbed her by her arm and pulled her to her feet. He wrenched off the ripped clothes that hung on her.

She was too terrified to feel her shame. "What are you going to do with me?" she said.

"You're goin' out there," Raven told her, pulling his gun out again. "You're goin' to walk in front of me. If they shoot at me it's goin' to be too bad for you."

"You can't do that. It's not my fight. You wouldn't force me into this… please… not like this!"

Twisting her arms behind her, he gripped her two wrists in one of his hands, then, crouching close behind her, he shoved her to the door.

"I'm comin' out!" he yelled. "Don't shoot. I'm comin' out."

In a low, savage voice, he said to her, "If you faint, or try any tricks I'll spread your goddamn' guts all over the town." He rammed the cold gun into her backbone, making her cry out with the pain, then he unlocked the door and pushed her out.

The two Federal Agents were so startled when Marie suddenly appeared that for a moment they hesitated. It was that moment that Raven had gambled on. He fired twice almost as one shot. The flash of the gun burnt Marie's arm and she screamed wildly.

The two Agents slowly folded up, one of them shot through the head and the other in the middle of his chest.

Raven said, "Keep moving."

He ran her along the passage, but there was no one about. They went downstairs. At the bottom of the stairs the night clerk lurked, staring up with terrified eyes.

The sight of Marie's naked body seemed to mesmerize him. Raven shot him between the eyes.

He shoved Marie down the stairs fast and they crossed the deserted lobby. Through the open door he could see the Chrysler still parked outside. Another car stood near it, but it was empty.

His brain worked swiftly. The clerk would have reported to the Federal Field Office that he'd come to the hotel. The Feds would send out the alarm and then come on over. In a town like Odessa it was nearly a safe bet that there were only two Feds. The talk of surrounding the place was bluff.

Cautiously he pushed Marie out into the street. No one fired at him. Taking a deep breath, he ran her across to the car. "Get inside," he snarled. "Quick."

She pulled open the door and climbed in. Raven looked over his shoulder, saw something move in the shadows, fired once and then scrambled under the wheel. Desperately he trod on the starter, and as the engine sprang into life he set the car bounding forward.

Marie sat crouched away from him, covering her breasts with her arms and shivering as the cold wind bit into her body.

"Sit still and hold your trap," Raven said, "or I'll finish you."

He knew it was too risky to go on to Kansas and he turned off on to the dirt road that led to Fayetteville. The needle of the speedometer climbed until it stood at 65. On a dirt road that was fast enough. As he drove his mind crawled with schemes. His hair no longer afforded him a disguise. They must be on to that. God! These Federal dicks were smart. If he could only put enough miles between them before they reached Odessa he might stand a chance of beating them. Otherwise it would mean a show-down.

Marie said in a low voice, "Can't you stop a moment? I'm freezin'."

"I'd rather you freeze than me burn," he said with a savage laugh. "Sit on the floor, it's warmer down there. I ain't stoppin' for no one."

She slid off her seat and crouched down on the floorboards. "Can't you let me go?" she pleaded. "I'm no use to you now."

He considered this, then decided to take her a little further. "You shut up," he said. "I don't want another yap outta you."

The road improved as the car ate up the miles, and he was able to increase his speed. He swung through Fayetteville at a terrific speed, and headed south again.

He knew he'd got a tank full of petrol, and with luck he ought to shake them. After a few miles he slowed down and got out.

He said to Marie, "If you move I'll shoot you."

He ran round to the boot and opened it, pulling the Thompson out. He hesitated about taking out one of her bags, then slammed the boot to. To hell with it, he wasn't going to waste time on her.

He stood looking back into the darkness. Far away he could make out two pin-points of light. He knew what they were at once. A car was coming at a great speed. It might not be the Feds, but it was too risky to take chances.

He ran back to the car and climbed in, putting the Thompson behind his head along the top of the seat.

He started the car again and drove off at a furious pace. He glanced at the clock on the dashboard. It showed 2:30. Somehow or other he'd got to get under cover before daylight. He'd got to ditch the car and he'd got to get another. He looked down at Marie, who seemed to have fallen into a doze. He'd got to get rid of her.

His mouth tightened. It was tough on her, but she'd have to go for good. The pin-points of light were no nearer. He could see them dancing in his rear mirror. They must be three or four miles away. Maybe they could see his own headlights. He hesitated, then reached forward and turned them out. The road, down which he was roaring, suddenly disappeared and he automatically eased up on the accelerator. He sat forward to peer into the darkness. This wasn't going to help his speed, but at the same time he wasn't showing himself to the Feds.

Ahead of him he could just make out a turning; he swung the car, braking as he did so. It was quite a narrow road, bordered by tall trees. He forced the car forward again, gaining speed. There was a good chance that the pursuing car would go on past. They might think he was heading for the State Highway again, which he knew linked up the road he'd been on previously.

He glanced back and then he felt the car run off the road. Instinctively he jammed on his brakes, but he was too late. The car crashed against some trees with such violence that he was nearly shot through the wind-screen.

Marie woke with a start and gave a little scream. Raven climbed out of the wrecked car, cursing. He was badly shaken, and lurched when he walked.

Through the trees, on a crest of a hill, he could see the lights of the following car coming towards them rapidly. He turned and dragged Marie out of the car.

"Not a sound," he said, his gun digging into her side.

She stood close to him, her body shivering with shock and cold, and they both watched the lights come nearer. Faintly the wail of a siren split the air.

Raven showed his teeth. It was a Federal car, then. He waited, holding his breath as the lights grew larger. Then with a snarl and a roar the car swept past the turning he had taken and roared on into the night.

Raven relaxed limply. He wiped the cold sweat off his face. "Come on, you," he said to Marie, "we've got a little walk on."

Then, as she moved slowly towards the car, he suddenly realized that he couldn't take her any further. Now was the time to finish her, not later.

In the misty moonlight he could see her tall white body with its graceful lines, and again he wanted her. Throwing caution aside, he took two quick steps towards her and pulled her round. She gave a gasp of terror when she realized what he was going to do. She began to struggle and he was startled at her strength. They swayed together on the uneven ground and then she began to scream.

Raven broke away and swung his fist. It landed on her cheek-bone, high up. She staggered and, still screaming, fell to the ground. Raven knelt at her side, pinning her flat. "Shut up!" he said, gripping her arms viciously. "Make another sound an' I'll finish you."

She stopped screaming, but she still fought, twisting and pulling, trying to get free.

He said, "Lie still. Do you hear—damn you? Lie still."

She went limp suddenly, throwing her arms wide. One of her hands touched a heavy stone and her fingers closed round it. She tried to get the stone out of the ground.

Something was happening to her. She said: "No—no—no—" But one of his hands gripped her throat, and then, with a tremendous effort, she swung the stone wildly and hit him violently on the side of his head.

2 1

January 3rd, 11:45 p.m.

Snow fell heavily, but there was quite a crowd outside the State Prison gates.

Hogarty and Jay pushed their way through and showed their passes to the guard. They were glad to get inside for warmth.

Jay said, "It gets me why the hell those guys come to stand outside."

Hogarty took off his coat. "They're hopin' to catch a glimpse of the executioner. They don't know, but they haven't got a chance. He comes in a side entrance."

Jay looked round the bare room nervously. "I'll be mighty glad when this is over," he said. "I never liked executions."

Hogarty shrugged. "It'll be a pleasure to see a rat like that burn," he said. "I wouldn't miss it for anything."

"It's a long time ago, isn't it?" Jay said. "At least, it seems like it to me."

Hogarty nodded. "Come on and meet Davies. I know him quite well."

Jay hesitated. "Davies? You mean the executioner?"

"Yeah. Quite a guy. Come on an' meet him."

Jay followed him out of the room. One of the guards nodded to Hogarty. "What do you want, pal?" he said.

"Goin' along to see Davies," Hogarty said.

The guard told him where to go.

The execution-shed was across the courtyard, but they went round to it by a long passage and came in through a back door.

As they entered the little room Jay felt a slight sinking feeling. The chair stood opposite several wooden pews. A tall, thin man was standing by the chair, watching an electrician working. He glanced up when Hogarty crossed the room. His worn face lit up a trifle when he saw Hogarty. He shook hands. "This is your case, ain't it?" he said.

Hogarty nodded. "I want you to meet Ellinger," he said. "Ellinger, this is Davies."

Jay shook hands.

"Ellinger was the guy who first got on to Raven. He's one of us now," Hogarty explained.

"Some case," Davies remarked, chewing his long moustache. "I got a kick out of readin' about it in the tabloids. You know, I'm glad I'm going to be the guy who sends him over. I've never felt more convinced that a man deserves this as this guy does. Some of those dames he handled had a mighty bad time of it."

"Well, they avenged themselves all right. That Leroy dame caught him. We'd lost him all right when we heard shots, and when we got to them there she was half crazy, stark naked, running round in circles and he lying there knocked silly. Believe me, if she hadn't popped with the gun, we'd have gone past."

Davies grunted. He turned back to the chair. "I've just got to test this, if you boys'll excuse me."

The electrician handed him a board on which were a number of electric light bulbs. He put the board across the arms of the chair and then went over to the switch.

"Know anythin' about this, mister?" he asked.

Jay shook his head.

"Take the switch. It opens in oil. See? That prevents it sparking. We use 2,000 volts. Now watch." He turned the switch away from him. The bulbs across the chair-arms flashed up. "That means the juice is goin' through all right. It's the only way to test the current. Okay, Joe," he said to the electrician. "You can disconnect."

He picked up a small suit-case and opened it. "I always bring my own electrodes." He took out a baseball helmet. "This is for the head. I've got an electrode in here, and, as you can see, the helmet is lined with sponge. The sponge is moistened with a saline solution. It stops burning. You gotta watch all that. You gotta watch sparks as well. Wouldn't do to have burning an' sparks; upsets the witnesses."

He went over to the bucket and moistened the sponge.

Hogarty said in a low voice, "I guess we'd better sit down. The witnesses will be in in a minute."

They took up their positions in the last pew. Jay said, "This is giving me a guts-ache."

Before Hogarty could answer the door opened and a number of solemn-faced people filed in. There was a little confusion as they selected their seats.

Jay said suddenly, "For God's sake," and pointed with his eyes.

Sadie Perminger had just come in. She stood in the doorway, hesitating for a moment, and then she walked quickly to the front pew and sat down.

Jay had only a brief flash of her face, which was cold and bitter. She was dressed in black with a little black-and-white hat.

"How the hell did she get here?" Jay whispered.

"Raven asked her. You know the condemned can ask one person to see him go. Well, he asked her."

Jay stared at him.

"Maybe he thought it would amuse her," Hogarty said dryly.

Jay half looked over his shoulder. "They're coming," he said.

Down the corridor they could hear the steady tramp of feet. The door swung open and two guards came in. Raven walked after them. The minister and the Warden came last.

Raven looked round the small room and walked to the chair. His face was the colour of a fish's belly, but otherwise he seemed quite calm.

"That the guy?" he said, looking at Davies.

Davies came over to him and offered his hand. Raven looked at it, then shook hands.

"I'll get it over quick, son," Davies said in a low voice.

"Don't rush yourself," Raven said with a little sneer. "It's all the time I've got."

Two guards led him to the chair and he sat down.

The Warden came close to him and whispered. Raven said in a hard voice, "Sure, I'll say somethin'."

He looked slowly at each face in front of him, until his eyes met Sadie's. She looked at him with cold, implacable hatred, and he grinned.

"Well, boys," he said, still keeping his eyes on Sadie, "this is my last little speech. I've had a nice run for my money an' I ain't scared of goin'. You all know what my racket was. If you guys didn't want women, my racket wouldn't have lasted long. Don't forget that. All you smuglookin' heels who've come to see me burn are as much to blame as I am. You get tired of your wives an' you want to have a fresh girl. So you come to me. That's all it is. The supply can't meet the demand. As long as you guys have the itch for a fresh girl, so will this racket go on. Nothin' can stop it. Cops certainly can't stop it. You can, but no one else. When you've all made up your minds to spend the rest of your nights with your wives, then girls won't have to trade their bodies. But you'll never do that. When I'm gone, someone else will take my place. There's always a demand and someone's gotta supply that demand."

He looked round the room again and then his eyes met Davies. "Come on, pal," he said, "get me outta here quick. These punks make me sick."

The guards, while he had been speaking, had already strapped him to the chair. Davies fixed the electrode to his leg and then swiftly the baseball helmet was fitted on his head.

Raven drew a long deep breath. "It's a pity I've got to leave my trains," he said. "Let her rip."

Davies had already stepped to the switch. He glanced at the Warden, who nodded. The switch went over and the lights dimmed. There came a sharp crackling sound and a whining cry of the current. Raven pitched forward, straining against the straps. A few sparks shot off the electrode on his leg, and a wisp of grey smoke appeared, coming from the top of the helmet.

Davies pulled the switch back so that Raven slumped limply in the chair, then, after a pause, the switch was thrown forward again. Raven once more plunged against the straps, only to sink back as the current was cut off.

Jay found he was trembling. He glanced over at Hogarty, who continued to chew, unmoved.

The doctor stepped forward and gingerly opened Raven's shirt. Jay could see the flesh bright red and sweating. With a towel the doctor wiped the sweat away, then with his stethoscope he listened for heartbeats.

He stood up. "I pronounce this man dead," he said.

The guards made signs for the witnesses to leave. As they were filing out Sadie suddenly turned back. Her face was still contorted with hatred, and now she looked a little mad. Before anyone could stop her she darted forward and spat in Raven's face.

The End

JAMES HADLEY CHASE
BIBLIOGRAPHY
(1906-1985)

No Orchids for Miss Blandish
    (1939; reprinted as The Villain
    and the Virgin, 1948)
The Dead Stay Dumb (1940;
    reprinted as Kiss My Fist!, 1952)
Twelve Chinks and a Woman
    (1940; reprinted as 12 Chinamen
    and a Woman, 1950, and as The
    Doll's Bad News, 1974)
Miss Callaghan Comes to Grief
    (1941)
Get a Load of This (1941; stories)
Miss Shumway Waves a Wand
    (1944)
Eve (1945)
I'll Get You for This (1947)
Last Page (1947; play, filmed as
    Man Bait)
The Flesh of the Orchid (1948)
You Never Know With Women
    (1948)
You're Lonely When You're Dead
    (1949)
Lay Her Among the Lilies (1950;
    reprinted as Too Dangerous to be
    Free, 1951)
Figure It Out for Yourself (1950;
    reprinted as The Marijuana Mob,
    1952)
Strictly for Cash (1951)
The Double Shuffle (1952)
The Fast Buck (1952)
I'll Bury My Dead (1953)
This Way for a Shroud (1953)
Tiger by the Tail (1954)
Safer Dead (1954; reprinted as
    Dead Ringer, 1955)
You've Got it Coming (1955)

There's Always a Price Tag (1956)
The Guilty are Afraid (1957)
Not Safe to be Free (1958;
    reprinted as The Case of the
    Strangled Starlet, 1958)
Shock Treatment (1959)
The World in My Pocket (1959)
What's Better Than Money (1960)
Come Easy Go Easy (1960)
A Lotus for Miss Quon (1961)
Just Another Sucker (1961)
I Would Rather Stay Poor (1962)
A Coffin from Hong Kong (1952)
Tell it to the Birds (1963)
One Bright Summer Morning
    (1963)
The Soft Centre (1964)
This is for Real (1965)
The Way the Cookie Crumbles
    (1965)
You Have Yourself a Deal (1966)
Cade (1966)
Have This One on Me (1967)
Well Now, My Pretty (1967)
An Ear to the Ground (1968)
Believed Violent (1968)
The Whiff of Money (1969)
The Vulture is a Patient Bird
    (1969)
There's a Hippie on the Highway
    (1970)
Like a Hole in the Head (1970)
An Ace Up My Sleeve (1971)
Want to Say Alive? (1971)
You're Dead Without Money
    (1972)
Just a Matter of Time (1972)
Knock, Knock! Who's There?
    (1973)
Have a Change of Scene (1973)
So What Happens to Me? (1974)
Goldfish Have No Hiding Place
    (1974)

Believe This, You'll Believe
  Anything (1975)
The Joker in the Pack (1975)
Do Me a Favour Drop Dead
  (1976)
My Laugh Comes Last (1977)
I Hold the Four Aces (1977)
Consider Yourself Dead (1978)
Can of Worms (1979)
You Must be Kidding (1979)
Try This One for Size (1980)
You Can Say That Again (1980)
Hand Me a Fig Leaf (1981)
Have a Nice Night (1982)
We'll Share a Double Funeral
  (1982)
Not My Thing (1983)
Hit Them Where it Hurts (1984)

Omnibus Editions

Three of Spades (1974; includes
  The Double Shuffle, Shock
  Treatment and Tell It to the
  Birds)
Meet Mark Girland (1977;
  includes This is for Real, You
  Have Yourself a Deal and Have
  This One on Me)
Meet Helga Rolfe (1984; includes
  An Ace Up My Sleeve, A Joker in
  the Pack and I Hold Four Aces)

As Raymond Marshall
(reprinted as by Chase except *)

Lady Here's Your Wreath (1940)
Just the Way It Is (1944)
Blonde's Requiem (1945)*
Make the Corpse Walk (1946)
No Business of Mine (1947)*
Trusted Like a Fox (1948;
  reprinted as Ruthless, 1955)

The Paw in the Bottle (1949)
Mallory (1950)
In a Vain Shadow (1951; reprinted
  as by Marshall as Never Trust a
  Woman, 1957)
But a Short Time to Live (1951;
  reprinted as The Pick-Up, 1955)
Why Pick on Me? (1951)
The Wary Transgressor (1952)
The Things Men Do (1953)
The Sucker Punch (1954)
Mission to Venice (1954)
Mission to Siena (1955)
You Find Him—I'll Fix Him
  (1956)
Hit and Run (1958)

As James L. Docherty
(reprinted as by Chase)

He Won't Need it Now (1939)

As Ambrose Grant
(reprinted as by Chase)

More Deadly Than the Male
  (1946)

As René Raymond
(reprinted as by Chase)

The Mirror in Room 22 (1946;
story, appeared in Slipstream: A
Royal Airforce Anthology edited
by René Raymond and David
Langdon)

For further info on the works of
James Hadley Chase, visit
www.hadleychase.co.nr, compiled
by Dr. P. C. Sarkar. This is the
definitive Chase website.

Crime classics from the master of hard-boiled fiction...

Peter Rabe

The Box / Journey Into Terror $19.95
978-0-9667848-8-6
"Few writers are Rabe's equal in the field of the hardboiled gangster story."
—Bill Crider, *Twentieth Century Crime & Mystery Writers*

**Murder Me for Nickels /
Benny Muscles In $19.95**
978-0-9749438-4-8
"When he was rolling, crime fiction just didn't get any better."
—Ed Gorman, *Mystery Scene*

**Blood on the Desert /
A House in Naples $19.95**
978-1-933586-00-7
"He had few peers among noir writers of the 50s and 60s; he has few peers today."
–Bill Pronzini

**My Lovely Executioner /
Agreement to Kill $19.95**
978-1-933586-11-3
"Rabe can pack more into 10 words than most writers can do with a page."
—Keir Graff, *Booklist*

**Anatomy of a Killer /
A Shroud for Jesso $14.95**
978-1-933586-22-9

"*Anatomy of a Killer*...as cold and clean as a knife...a terrific book."
—Donald E. Westlake

**The Silent Wall /
The Return of Marvin Palaver $19.95**
978-1-933586-32-8
"A very worthy addition to Rabe's diverse and fascinating corpus." —*Booklist*

**Kill the Boss Good-by /
Mission for Vengeance $19.95**
978-1-933586-42-7
"*Kill the Boss Goodbye* is certainly one of my favorites." —Peter Rabe in an interview with George Tuttle

**Dig My Grave Deep / The Out is Death
/ It's My Funeral $21.95**
978-1-933586-65-6
"It's Rabe's feel for the characters, even the minor ones, that lifts this out of the ordinary." —Dan Stumpf, *Mystery*File*

**The Cut of the Whip / Bring Me Another
Corpse / Time Enough to Die $23.95**
978-1-933586-66-3
"These books offer realistic psychology, sharp turns of phrase, and delightfully deadpan humor that make them cry out for rediscovery."—Keir Graff, *Booklist*

In trade paperback from:

Stark House Press
1315 H Street, Eureka, CA 95501
griffinskye3@sbcglobal.net
www.StarkHousePress.com

Available from your local bookstore, or order direct with a check or via our website.

www.ingramcontent.com/pod-product-compliance
Lightning Source LLC
Chambersburg PA
CBHW071736190726
48292CB00003B/772